CROSS INTENTS

THE BATTLE

CROSS INTENTS

THE BATTLE

S.R. WELLS

ILLUMIFY
MEDIA.COM

Published by
Illumify Media Global
www.IllumifyMedia.com
"Write. Publish. Market. *SELL!*"

Library of Congress Control Number: 2023904836
Hardcover ISBN: 978-1-959099-24-6
Paperback ISBN: 978-1-959099-23-9

Typeset by Art Innovations (http://artinnovations.in/)
Cover design by Debbie Lewis

Sword and shield art by Phil Elsner
Author photo by Kimby Family Photography
www.facebook.com/kimbyfamilyphotography

Printed in the United States of America

To the King and to His glory

1

TEMPTATIONS

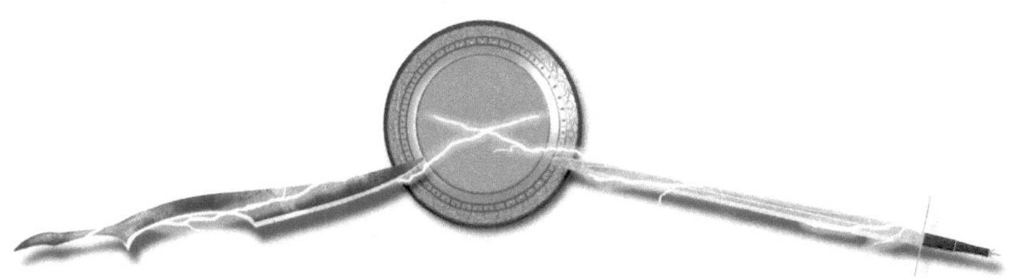

Battle minus 3 years

The cool night darkness owned the desert wilderness of Judea. The barren rocks lay silent under the shroud of shadow. Sleep covered the landscape. The long, long stretch of night had set its hooks deep and had no intention of letting go.

But a new day approached.

Like a silent thief, morning crept from beyond the horizon. Imperceptible at first. Then a glow quietly pushed its way in. The darkness clung to the shadows, but the predawn light melted away the waning stars and filled the air with warming hope.

Elric stood with his face toward the east—arms crossed, jaw set, eyes piercing through the darkness across the terrain. Jesus lay sleeping two sword-lengths away. Another day alone in the wilderness.

What's this?

In the Middle Realm, a thin, black mist rolled across Elric's feet from behind. He scanned the perimeter. A wispy carpet of black mist encircled him from all around. Inching inward, it closed in toward Jesus. Elric raised his chin and took a deep breath. He let it out slowly. Several minutes passed, and the ankle-high mist reached Jesus. The brilliant, pulsing light of the Spirit within Jesus radiated outward, even as He slept, and the mist that touched it evaporated, leaving a ring of undisturbed light around Him.

Motion from the left! Elric palmed his sword handle and turned his head. *Timrok.* He released the grip on his sword.

Timrok stepped close. "Good morning, Captain."

"Good morning."

"Day forty. It is a long time to fast. His flesh must surely be weak." Timrok swished his foot through the mist. "And it appears the enemy will be here today."

"Mm. It is necessary."

"My team is deployed and ready."

"Pull them in. We'll form a tight circle around the King. But we will not do battle today."

"Captain?"

"We have our orders."

"In His service."

* * *

The great demon commander Asherah stood with his back to the east and gazed out over the throng of beaelzur warriors assembled on the Judean wilderness. Ten thousand leathery beasts clanged their swords against the rocks, snorted yellow sulfurous smoke from their nostrils, and grunted with tense anticipation.

"It is almost dawn," Asherah growled to the group of twenty captains crowded around him. "On my signal, we will make our march. The rest of our forces, under the command of Molech, Yarikh, and Marr, will approach from the north, south, and east."

One of the captains grunted, "My troops are ready to decimate the flesh of the Son of Man."

Asherah laughed. "Then none of your troops have seen Him since His revelation at the river Jordan. His appearance is as the One who sits on the Throne, veiled only slightly by the body of flesh. There is none who can stand against Him."

The group of captains shuffled about, glancing at each other and down at their feet.

Nervous exasperation dripped from the voice of one of the captains. "Then what is the purpose of this muster? We thought we were going to destroy the Son of Man today."

An evil smile cut across Asherah's face, and a guttural chuckle escaped between his teeth. "We are here to *witness* the downfall of the Son of Man today and to glory in the dawn of a new kingdom. Our lord Satan himself will speak to Him, tempting Him in the ways of the flesh."

"Is it possible for Him to fall?" one of the captains called out.

"He is fully man. He has been fasting now for forty days. His flesh is weak. He will surely fall."

The captains shuffled again and nodded with smug sneers.

One captain asked, "What will happen when He falls?"

Asherah stuck his sword into the ground and leaned against it. "We do not know, exactly. Will it sever the triune Godhead? Possibly weaken Him to the point of ruin?" He cocked his head and paused. "It will certainly disqualify Him from the right to take authority on earth. Since man relinquished his authority to rule the earth to Satan, this authority must be won back by a man. When the Son of Man falls today, He forfeits His rights, and our lord, Satan, will forever seal his dominion. For *this* we gather to witness and to glory."

The captains beat their swords against the ground and grunted together in unison.

A small demon crossed overhead, making an erratic bat-like path across the sky. He blew a horn—low, hollow, and sinister.

"We march," Asherah announced. "Keep your forces moving forward, even when we make sight of the Son of Man. I don't want Marr or Satan to see weakness in our ranks."

* * *

Elric and Timrok stood with Timrok's team—Prestus, Chase, Nalyd, Micah, and Kylek—in a tight circle around Jesus just inside the ring of light that held back the black mist carpet all around them. They all faced outward—no weapons drawn, but vigilant eyes covering every direction. Jesus still slept.

The sun broke just above the horizon, and a deep horn blast echoed across the sky in the Middle Realm.

"Here it comes," Elric said.

"Are you sure we can't fight?" Timrok asked, kicking the mist away from his feet.

Elric clenched his jaw tight and lifted his chin.

A faint rumbling shook beneath his feet. The heavy steps of a marching army. Clearly in the Middle Realm. *Can Jesus sense it?* Elric turned his head to check. Jesus' face was tucked low behind a large boulder, and the sun had not yet driven back the shadow where He lay. *No, still sleeping.*

The black mist thickened. The rumbling became more distinct.

Timrok glanced over to Elric. "That is the sound of a very large company."

"Indeed. I was not expecting a full army. Surely they know direct conflict is futile."

The black mist reached the height of Elric's knees. The rumbling from the ground became thumping in his ears. Implements of steel clanked just over the horizon.

"Captain!" Micah called out, eyes facing north.

"Captain! Captain!" Prestus and Chase called out, one from east and one from the west.

"There they are," Timrok whispered, looking south.

Elric spun all the way around. Masses of dark creatures approached from every side. Loose ranks, out of step, swords clanking on the ground, thousands upon thousands of beaelzurim lumbered forward.

"Still want to fight?" Elric asked Timrok with a playful jab.

Timrok looked down at Jesus and smiled. "Of course. We have them outnumbered."

Elric let out a slight chuckle and nodded. "What does Satan hope to do with so large an army? What does he think . . . "

High-pitched shrieks split the air in the Middle Realm. Timrok and every one of his team gripped the handles of their swords. The screeches expanded like a shock wave, starting from the front ranks of the advancing horde and shooting back thirty rows. The front rows of demons fell into complete disarray—some collapsing backward, some stumbling without aim, some unfurling their wings—all squealing with eerie terror.

"Those are not war shouts," Timrok said. His hands released his two sword handles.

Elric nodded. "They just spotted the King."

Large demon captains rose from behind the faltering ranks—shouting, beating the retreating forces, and pushing them onward. They scuffled for several march beats, but the strong officers regained control, and the tentative advance inched forward.

"Captain," Kylek said, "I see Marr."

"I can see Molech," Nalyd said.

"Yarikh," Chase said.

"There's Asherah," Prestus said.

Elric nodded and crossed his arms. "The great prince and his three commanders. But still no sign of—"

Timrok said, "Captain, the King awakes."

The rising sun now shone full in Jesus' face. He wiped the sleep from His eyes and squinted. He stood, stretched, yawned, and sat down on a large boulder.

Elric said, "And now . . . He prays."

Shafts of light shot straight up into the heavens from Jesus' spirit. A deluge of light rained back down.

Renewed shrieks of terror broke out across the ranks of the advancing horde. Hundreds of leathery wings rose from the ranks and bolted away. The demon captains shouted and wrangled some back to the ground, but many escaped and disappeared over the horizon. Onward the remaining masses marched, now with captains in front. Closer. Closer. With an upraised arm from Marr, the advance stopped.

Hemmed in on every side, Elric and his team stood like stone statues, surrounded by a wall of restless malevolence, heaving noxious sulfur through stained, jagged teeth. Elric pulled his sword from its sheath in one slow, continuous motion and stuck the point into the ground in front of him. He leaned against it with both hands.

Jesus continued to pray.

Does He even know of the army surrounding Him? Can He see them? He shows no sign of—

A massive ball of fire exploded in front of Elric. A thick cloud of black smoke, four times his height, enveloped the flames. Red lightning shot outward from within.

Elric remained unmoved.

Jesus continued to pray.

The smoke sank to the ground, revealing an enormous figure. A cherub. The fallen cherub. Satan. Four wings—full of eyes. Twisted frame. Dark, cracked, leathery. He looked past Elric as though he wasn't there and fixated on Jesus.

Small and insignificant against this mountain of power, Elric stood his ground. He didn't blink. He didn't move. Satan would have to make the next move.

The dark cherub remained motionless—only his broad chest rising and falling with each measured breath. Every demon warrior froze and stared with bulging red eyes.

What is he going to do? What is he waiting for?

Jesus continued to pray.

Satan shot two wings upward to their fullest extent. Without taking his eyes off Jesus, he cupped his other two wings downward until their tips just touched the ground. He spun in place—an instant tornado. He became an indistinguishable blur with flames, black smoke, and red lightning blasting outward through the howling wind in the Middle Realm.

Before Elric could blink, the tornado tore inward and enveloped Jesus, flinging Elric and his team outward like leaves in a gale. Elric careened through the air and landed in the arms of the front row of beaelzur captains. His feet found the ground, but two demon captains grasped his arms while another wrapped his arm around his neck from behind.

His sword lay unattended on the ground.

The rest of the team fell into the clutches of the front row of captains.

The tornado stopped, the smoke subsided, and Satan reemerged in the form of a serpent. He circled around Jesus, his black forked tongue darting in and out.

Jesus continued to pray.

Timrok somehow broke free and brandished both his swords in a single motion. He spun around toward the row of demon captains, ready to do battle.

"Timrok!" Elric shouted.

Timrok's head drooped down. He let his swords drop to the ground, and the demon captains took him back under control. The snake glanced over toward Timrok, then toward Elric, and shot out his tongue.

Satan slithered up near Jesus' ear. With a voice smooth and sympathetic, he cooed, "You must be very hungry. If You *are* the Son of God, command that these stones become bread."

His words entered the Middle Realm like glowing orange plasma. The cloud of energy wrapped all around Jesus' spirit and squeezed inward. It reached His spirit but crackled and sparked at the surface.

Elric held his breath. *Can He see the tempter? Can He hear the words?*

The entire demon army hung in suspense. No one moved. No one breathed.

Jesus reached down and picked up a biscuit-sized stone. He held it up.

His spirit perceived, and His mind received the thought. He is being tempted as a normal man.

Marr whispered, "Do it."

Molech, Asherah, and Yarikh echoed, "Do it."

The captains and then the whole demon army chanted, "Do it! Do it! Do it!" Their words shot inward like fiery darts, but every one dissolved with a crackle at the surface of Jesus' spirit.

Jesus tossed the stone to the ground and said aloud, "It is written, 'Man shall not live on bread alone, but on every word that proceeds out of the mouth of God.'"

The army fell silent.

Satan snapped into a coiled-up mass and raised his head up like a cobra ready to strike. In an explosion of fire, he appeared again in the form of a cherub. Wrapping two of his wings around Jesus, he spun up like a tornado. Another explosion. Black smoke and silence.

The smoke dropped downward like a curtain. Satan—and Jesus—were gone.

"No!" shouted Elric.

"No!" wailed the rest of his team.

"You have no authority to take Him!" Elric shouted. "You can't do this!" He thrashed against his captors, but their grip only tightened.

The captain from behind tightened his chokehold, lifted Elric up off the ground, and whispered in his ear, "We meet again, Captain."

Captain Khilaf. Elric's left eye twitched twice.

Elric kicked and strained, shouting, "You can't . . . you can't . . . "

His left eye twitched twice.

The memory of an old wound rushed from his innermost being and flooded his mind. He became lost to the present and captive to an ancient time of unthinkable defeat.

2

FALL AT APHEK

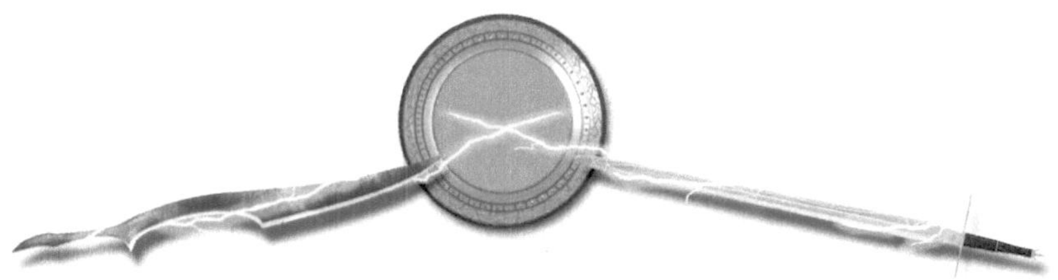

An ancient time: Day 1

On a hill overlooking the Hebrew army camp at Ebenezer, Elric awaited his lieutenants for the post-battle report. It was in the early days of the prophet Samuel, when the elderly prophet Eli still judged the land and Israel had no king. The sun drooped low near the horizon over the Philistine camp at Aphek. Between Aphek and Ebenezer—the battlefield, littered with the slain. Philistine warriors picked through the bodies and gathered the spoils—implements of war, clothing, anything of value. The wounded of Israel still hobbled into camp, and carts stacked with many fallen rolled away toward distant home villages. The groans of pain wafted upward with the smoke of the campfires throughout the tent settlement. Elric crossed his arms and breathed a heavy sigh.

The last of Elric's ten lieutenants arrived. The lieutenant's wings tucked away; he shook his head; and he looked down at the ground.

"How many?" Elric asked.

"Almost 4,000 men," the lieutenant answered.

Elric rubbed his forehead and grimaced. "Losses among the elzurim?"

A lieutenant stepped forward and answered, "Captain, 186 were overcome and bound during the combat. All have been loosed and recovered. We are at full strength."

Elric shook his head. "Almost twenty percent . . . "

A lieutenant spoke up, "Sir, the beaelzurim outnumber us almost two to one."

Another added, "And there are so many within our own camp. The men give place to them, and we have no authority to drive them out."

Elric quieted them with an upraised hand. "Our challenge is not the numbers of beaelzurim—it is the men themselves. They are hard of heart and dull of hearing. Their spirits wear layers of darkness, and our words produce little effect. We will need to concentrate our efforts on—"

A sudden roar of many voices rose from the camp near the tents of the elders.

Elric pointed toward one of the lieutenants. "Vann, see what this is about."

Vann unfolded his wings and shot downward into the camp. Elric crossed his arms, and the other lieutenants watched and waited.

Moments later, Vann returned. "Captain, the beaelzurim are stirring up the elders, telling them the *Lord* has defeated them before the Philistines. The elders are speaking these words to the men."

Elric scowled. "Standard tactic of the enemy."

"There is more, Captain. They are calling for the ark of the covenant to be brought from Shiloh."

The other lieutenants glanced at each other with wide eyes, fidgeting with their sword handles.

Elric squeezed his eyes shut and took two deep breaths. "The enemy seeks to capture the ark." He paused for two more breaths. He opened his eyes and said to Vann, "Make haste to Shiloh. Take a small team of your warriors and speak to Eli. He must not allow the ark to come here."

"Sir, you know Eli is not only blind in the flesh, but also in the spirit. His sons Hophni and Phinehas rule in his place—evil men, puppets of the enemy. The enemy owns these men, and there is little hope that we can reach them."

"We must try. Make every effort. The ark must stay in Shiloh."

"In His service."

* * *

An ancient time: Day 2

The next day, early in the afternoon, Elric strode up to the front of a tent filled with wounded soldiers.

A small demon with a gravelly voice stepped in front of him and said, "You have no authority here."

Elric pushed his shield against the side of the demon's face, muscled him aside, and stepped through the front wall. "Try to stop me."

Inside, Elric walked over to the wounded men lying on bed mats along the side wall. He eyed the three demons working the room. They all stopped and huddled close to the back wall. Elric knelt beside the closest man. Touching the man's shoulder, he said, "Strength." His hand glowed with blue energy which melted into the man's spirit. The man on the next bed mat moaned and tossed from side to side in a fitful state of sleeplessness. Elric cupped his hand over the man's forehead and spoke, "Sleep." Blue light transferred from Elric's hand to the man. Making his way down the line of wounded, Elric ministered to each.

He stood tall at the end of the line and squared up against the three demons. One held his sword up, prepared to strike. Elric glared at them without a word. He turned. He stepped out through the side wall. Behind him came the scurrying of beaelzurim feet and the muffled words, "Infection," "You are surely going to die," "God did this to you."

Elric gritted his teeth and moved on.

Every man he passed in the tent city, he touched and spoke a word. "Courage." "Strength." "Endurance." "Courage."

He turned up another aisle between the tents, and the lieutenant, Vann, alighted in front of him. His wings folded away.

"Captain, I regret to report that my mission was not a success. The men's hearts are too hard, and the enemy prevailed. The ark of the Lord will be here tomorrow."

Elric shook his head. "This is an unfortunate turn. And clearly part of the enemy's plan from the beginning. This battle is not to settle a dispute over land, as the men think. It is a battle to take the ark as a prize."

"Hophni and Phinehas—they are coming with the ark."

"They are not men of war. This is no place for them."

"They insisted. Pressed by the words of the beaelzurim who control them. I sense the enemy seeks to destroy these two sons of Eli."

"Of course. Oppose the King. Extract as much pain as possible in the process." Elric looked up and down the aisles at the disheartened men milling about. "Gather your forces. We have much work to do in the camp tonight and tomorrow. We must strengthen these men for battle. They must be ready to fight. We will, by no means, allow the enemy to seize the ark."

"In His service."

*　*　*

An ancient time: Day 3

The next day, just before sunset, shouts of men arose near the edge of camp. The commotion grew. Elric ducked out of the tent where he was ministering and winged toward the noise. Below him, the men in the camp bustled in the same direction.

It's the ark of the Lord. It must have just arrived. Elric landed on the nearby hillside and shook his head at the hysteria building below.

Every man from every part of the camp raced toward the ark, which proceeded inward with a grand parade. Even the wounded—those who were able—limped out of their tents and watched for a glimpse of the ark. Like a mound of frenzied ants, thousands and thousands thronged inward, shouting, clanging their shields, and blowing trumpets. The ground shook from the deafening roar.

The elzur lieutenants joined Elric on the hillside one by one. For hours the shouting, dancing, and celebration lit up the camp while

Elric and the lieutenants watched in silence. The energy finally died down, and most of the men trickled off to their tents. Night settled in.

Elric stepped forward and gazed over the full length of the camp. Thousands of dots of flickering lights from campfires spread across the valley. *Somewhere in the middle of all that, the ark of the Lord now sits under the cover of a tent.* He crossed his arms and turned around toward the lieutenants.

"How many times over the centuries have we seen this?" Elric said. "Men placing their trust in some object instead of the King Himself." He shook his head. "Nevertheless, the ark carries the anointing of the King and is still a symbol of the King's presence among men—even if His glory no longer rests upon it. We *will* defend it for the sake of His honor. The enemy wants to desecrate it, but we will not let that happen."

Elric took a deep breath. "We will do battle tomorrow. But *our* fight takes place tonight. Speak to these men. Tell them to turn to the Lord. Tell them there is no power in the ark itself. Convince them to call upon *Him.* If they do, the King will cause the enemy to scatter. He will strengthen our hands for battle. He will open their ears to hear our leading. He will bring about a great victory by our hands for His name's sake."

He paused and looked back over the camp. "If they don't . . ." His chest expanded. He held the breath. A long, slow stream of tension released through gritted teeth. "We must reach them tonight. Go. Pass this word to all your warriors. Time is short and these men's hearts are hard."

* * *

An ancient time: Day 4

Daybreak. The battle began.

A hundred thousand men bent on destroying each other smashed together in the plain between Aphek and Ebenezer. The clanking steel, the rising cloud of dust, the shouts of attack, the shouts of agony, the whizzing of arrows—the deafening cacophony of war shook the Physical Realm. As far across the plain as Elric could see, men fell. Israelites. Philistines. All with frail flesh and bright red blood.

Elric grimaced. *So much death and pain. And with every one that falls, the enemy wins another victory. Every one—a creation of the King. And so many cut down before they could make an eternal decision. How many Israelites might have turned their hearts to the King given another day? How many Philistines might have turned to the Lord given other circumstances?*

In the Middle Realm he had a job to do. Elric pressed forward with the regiment of men charged with the safekeeping of the ark of the covenant. He leapt forward, blocked a beaelzur fireball with his shield, hacked through an incoming demon with his sword, landed his feet on another demon's back, ran him through, and bound him in one fluid motion.

To the man beside him, he shouted. "Look left! Look left! Duck!" Too late.

He blocked another fireball.

To another man, he shouted, "Swing! Thrust! Step back!" Too late.

An incoming arrow headed straight toward another Israelite warrior. Elric commanded, "Fall!" His word became an explosion of wind in the Middle Realm, bending the space in the Physical Realm and deflecting the arrow trajectory just short of its mark.

He touched the back of another man and shouted, "Strength! Take him! Now!" Good.

A beaelzur warrior roared in from the left. Elric shot straight up, did a tight flip, and sliced through the demon's head on the way by. A cloud of yellow smoke spewed from the gash, and the demon crumpled to the ground. Landing beside a man, Elric yelled, "Avert!" His word formed a sloping hedge of energy, and a Philistine sword grazed just to the side of the Israelite fighter. "Swing your sword now!" Elric cried to the fighter. "Swing before—" Too late. Elric sprang back to the demon he had just downed. His wound was sealing quickly, and his dazed eyes blinked. Elric bound him, put his foot on the demon's back, and launched forward toward another attacker.

An hour of blood passed. Another hour.

One of Elric's lieutenants landed nearby, cutting down and binding a demon on his way in. "Captain," he called out. "These men . . . their hearts are too hard! They can't receive—" He deflected a fireball away from a man's head with his shield. Glancing to the right, he shouted, "No!" His word formed a small wall of light in the Middle Realm, and a Philistine arrow fell short.

"I know," Elric yelled over the din. "How are our forces holding up?" He pierced a beaelzurim through the chest, raised a foot up against his chest, and gave a powerful shove, launching the demon backward. Elric's sword pulled from the demon's chest, and sulfurous smoke billowed from the gaping wound.

"Many elzur warriors have fallen, bound. We are greatly outnumbered."

Elric scanned around at his team surrounding the ark. "Our forces here grow thin. Go gather a squad to reinforce—" He blocked an incoming beaelzur blade, parried twice, then carved through the attacker's arm. A crackling sizzle of a fireball approached from behind. Elric spun and deflected it with his shield inches from his face. "Gather two squads! We must protect the ark!"

Moments later, twenty elzur warriors flew in from all directions and joined the fight around the ark.

Another hour of blood passed.

"Courage!" Elric shouted to the men. "Stay in the fight!" His words shot like arrows of light toward the Israelite men protecting the ark. Little penetrated through the layers of darkness surrounding their spirits.

A logirhi alighted in front of Elric. "A word of the Lord."

Elric blocked a fireball. Spun. Blocked another. He turned his attention to the messenger.

"Remove the hedge of protection from around Hophni and Phinehas," the logirhi said. "Today, the sons of Eli receive the recompense of their ways."

"In His service."

"By His word."

"Wait! Before you go—the battle goes badly. Is the King sending reinforcements?"

The messenger shook his head. "The battle is yours, Captain."

A shock wave of pain surged through his left shoulder. The tip of a beaelzur blade emerged through the front, along with shafts of light from within.

"Aaughh!" Elric pulled forward away from the blade, spun, and sliced the demon attacker in two. Dazed and weakened, Elric blinked and fumbled to bind the fallen warrior.

The shoulder wound sealed and, with his strength returning, Elric blocked a fireball with his shield and bounded backward toward Hophni and Phinehas. Pretending to be great defenders of the ark, the two sons of Eli kept a safe distance away. But even there, the fighting was fierce.

Elric called to the six elzur warriors surrounding Hophni and Phinehas, "Leave these two to themselves. Come. I need your swords around the ark."

With a single flap of their wings, the six warriors repositioned and helped drive back the advancing horde. Within two heartbeats of their departure, an arrow whirred in over the mayhem and lodged into Hophni's neck. He opened his blood-filled mouth, but no sound came out. Eyes wide and filled with terror—he dropped cold. A demon stepped forward, stomped his foot on the back of Hophni, and bound his spirit with black cords.

Phinehas turned toward his fallen brother and screamed. In mid-breath, a Philistine spear rammed through his back. Phinehas crumpled forward and lay twitching in the dirt.

The demons all around shouted, "Ha ha!" "The sons of the high priest are dead!" "Victory!" "Take the ark!"

Elric fought back two demons at once. A third joined the fight. Elric shot upward in a spiral, taking out one, and landed near the ark. "Courage!" he shouted to the men. "Protect the ark!" All around, the Israelite soldiers fell in bloody heaps. More and more elzur warriors lay bound and out of the fight.

A lieutenant blasted in from the front. "Captain, the battle is lost. Nearly 30,000 men. And over half of the elzur warriors. We must retreat with the ark!"

"It's too late," Elric shouted. "We are surrounded."

To the angelic warriors around the ark, Elric called out, "Double your efforts! Drive these traitors back! They can *not* take the ark!"

From somewhere over the tumult came, "There are too many! We can't . . . aughh!"

A tidal wave of beaelzurim crashed inward over the mounds of bodies. The Philistines followed.

"Captain," the lieutenant exclaimed. "At least pull our team back. We can regroup and re-take the ark later."

"Never!" Elric spun, hacked, dodged, and flipped. His speed and intensity increased with the growing number of attackers. Clashing metal and war shouts filled the spiritual air. Elric shouted, "We . . ." swing, "will . . . " kick, thrust, "not . . . " spin, "surrender . . . " thrust, "the ark!"

He spun again, and there before him stood a hulking demon captain—at least twice his size. Elric's eyes stared straight ahead, just above the captain's waist, and skimmed upward. Below the demon's bulbous forehead were sunken red eyes, a square jutting jaw, and a stone-cold evil countenance.

"Koorleier? Is that you? My old—"

"It is Khilaf now. Koorleier was naive and weak. Now I am wise and powerful. I used to lead insignificant choir directors like you. Now . . . " he gestured with his hand over the plain, "now, I command legions."

Khilaf looked down at Elric and laughed. "And you . . . a captain. It is laughable. You don't possibly think you can keep me from my prize? The King has underestimated our strength. Today, I will—"

Elric took a swing. Khilaf batted his sword aside with his shield as though a mere toy.

Khilaf grunted once and thrust his sword toward Elric's head. Elric dodged hard to the right.

Too late!

The demon blade pierced through Elric's left eye.

"Aaugghh!"

Pain. Searing hot. Blinding white. Fading. Falling backward.

Elric squinted through his right eye, clinging to consciousness. Khilaf's foot . . . on . . . chest. Incoming blade!

Khilaf's sword ran through Elric's left eye again and pinned him to the ground.

Then, darkness.

3

VICTOR'S BREAD

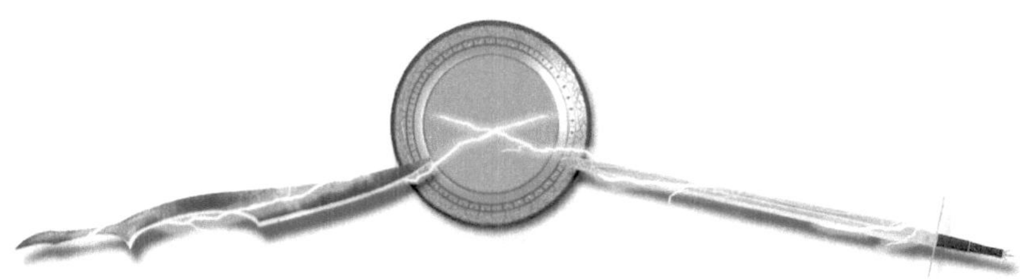

Battle minus 3 years

Elric opened his eyes. He squinted.

Captain Khilaf's arm from behind pulled tight against his neck. Two beaelzur captains clenched his arms.

He was back in the wilderness of Judea—where Satan had just disappeared with the King. Where Marr and his commanders held him and Timrok's team in helpless captivity. The awful sting of defeat. Yes, he knew it all too well. His left eye twitched twice.

"Oh, but we *do* have the authority," Marr graveled. "The King sent the Son of Man out here into this wilderness for this very purpose. And you know this." Marr paced in front of Elric with a pompous swagger. "Any moment now, the Son of Man will succumb to the weakness of His flesh, and our lord Satan will strip away all His legal rights to the Throne."

"Never!" Elric clenched his teeth. "He is the King of Glory and creator of all. He knows no sin, nor can He be tempted by it."

"He is the Son of *Man*," snapped Marr, spinning on his heels. His snarling face pressed close, and the noxious sulfur of his breath engulfed Elric's face.

Elric coughed without blinking.

Marr smiled. "He laid aside His glory when He entered the realm of man. Here, *we* have authority. Here, the flesh of man is weak. Here, He *can* be tempted. He *can* fall. He *will* fall. You will see—any moment now—"

A fiery explosion followed by thick black smoke rocked the Middle Realm. The demon armies all around erupted in victorious cheers. The smoke receded, revealing Jesus sitting on the boulder and the dark cherub standing ten paces in front of Him.

Satan took two steps back, his chest heaving in and out.

The armies fell silent.

Satan lifted his four wings upward and roared. The shock waves pounded against Elric's chest and smashed the inner ring of the armies backward. Flames spewed from Satan's mouth toward Jesus. Fireballs blasted from his hands. Thousands. Thousands. A continuous barrage of plasma pulses streamed from his hands. Elric couldn't see Jesus through the dazzling blaze.

Satan stopped. His wings drooped to the ground.

A deathly silence fell over all. Tufts of residual smoke wafted upward.

Jesus sat on the boulder, seemingly unaware and undisturbed.

"I will be back," Satan hissed. "At the opportune time . . . you will yield to me. Or I will destroy this body of flesh." He lifted his wings and, with a mighty flap, rose into the air. Like the sound of a passing hurricane, he disappeared over the horizon.

The remaining demon armies, their captains, the commanders, Marr—looked at each other in silence. Frozen with bewilderment, their arms fell slack and their jaws dropped.

Jesus began to pray. Shafts of light shot upward, and a deluge of light rained downward.

High-pitched demonic shrieks and squeals filled the air of the Middle Realm. Elric winced and put a finger in one ear. Thousands of terrified demons clawed over each other getting away. The restraints at Elric's arms and neck released. In less than forty heartbeats, every beaelzurim warrior disappeared.

Silence.

Elric readjusted his tunic, stepped forward, and picked up his sword.

Timrok grabbed one of his swords off the ground near his feet. "I still would have preferred to fight."

Elric picked up Timrok's other sword, smiled, and tossed it handle-first to Timrok's waiting hand. Timrok's team snapped into a tight line behind Jesus on the boulder.

"Where do you suppose Satan took Him?" Timrok asked, sliding his swords into their sheaths.

"It is hard to know. Someplace where he could tempt Him in other ways."

Timrok looked around, shrugged, and said, "Now what?"

A streak of light shot down from above. Fast as a meteor, quiet as a whisper. Grigor.

"A word of the Lord," Grigor said.

Elric nodded.

"The Son has completed His test. The Father is well pleased. You may minister to His flesh. His next task is to travel through the region by the Sea of Galilee and call disciples."

"In His service."

"By His word." Grigor unfurled his wings and disappeared as quickly as he came.

In the same instant, glowing bundles of energy drifted downward through the air of the Middle Realm all around them. Floating like gentle snowflakes, they hovered and bounced about on an unseen breeze before coming to rest on the ground.

"Look at this!" Timrok shouted.

Elric let one land on the back of his hand. "Amazing. We haven't seen this for over a thousand years."

Timrok's team lost all decorum—giggling and pointing and bouncing on their toes. Chase opened his mouth and caught a snowflake on his tongue.

Elric laughed. "Don't just stand there! You know what to do. Let's make manna!"

Like excited children at play, the team darted all around, snatching snowflakes from the air, scooping them up off the ground, and laughing. Even the mighty warrior Timrok bounded to life like a child. He spun and danced, plucking bundles of energy from the air between his fingers. One by one, he collected them in his palm until he had a good-sized mass of energy. Then he pressed it all together between his hands. He opened his hands and held up a solid white wafer to Elric.

Elric laughed.

Timrok and the team laid the wafers on the ground all around Jesus in a single layer in the Middle Realm. Elric formed a few wafers, mostly for the sake of nostalgia, but spent most of the time watching the others with a sparkle in his eyes and a smile on his lips.

The flurry dwindled. The flakes of energy stopped. A day's worth of wafers lay ready. Timrok's warriors snapped back into a line.

Elric smiled and said, "Ready?"

Timrok and his team gave enthusiastic nods.

"Bread of the King," Elric spoke in a clear, loud tone.

His words fluttered to the ground in the Middle Realm and spread outward like a carpet of white energy. In the Physical Realm, a thick mist formed ankle deep above the ground. It hung there for a full minute. Then, it faded away—revealing on the ground a pristine layer of fresh white wafers.

Jesus laughed aloud and said, "Manna! Thank you, Father." He hopped down and collected them up, nibbling them as He went. He returned to His seat on the boulder and, with a lap full of manna, ate for the first time in forty days.

Elric stepped up behind Him and spoke the word *strength* into his hands. A ball of white-blue energy formed in his palms. He started toward Jesus but stopped short.

"It seems so strange for *me* to touch *Him*," Elric said.

Timrok chuckled. "You heard Grigor. Minister to His flesh."

Elric took a deep breath and pressed the energy into Jesus. He left his hands on Jesus' shoulders and repeated, "Strength."

With his glowing hands still on Jesus' shoulders, he looked to Timrok. "Send word to Lacidar, Zaben, and Jenli. We will meet tonight after sunset at the regional war room in Capernaum."

4

CAPERNAUM BY THE SEA

Battle minus 3 years

Standing at the window casement of the house, Elric raised his nose and drew in deep breath. The cool, gentle breeze off the Sea of Galilee carried the freshness of the water, roasted fish, and a medley of wildflowers. *I do love the smell of a lake town.* Along the sloping coastline of Capernaum, lights from shoreline houses reflected off the water of the lake. The chattering gulls had gone quiet, and although he couldn't hear the lapping of the waves on the wooden hulls of the larger fishing boats from here, he could see their shadows bobbing lazily by the shore.

Turning to the inside of the house, Elric smiled at Zaben, Timrok, and Jenli, who talked in hushed tones in a huddle by the far wall. A good-sized house, for Capernaum, with multiple rooms surrounding a large center courtyard. Exposed wooden beams supported the low second-story sleeping areas under the flat wattle and daub roof. The plaster walls were white, except where stained by the smoke of wall-hung lamps. In the main living area where he stood, a long table stretched along one side wall, cluttered with all the things of life: pitchers of water, cooking pots, bowls, baskets of fruit and bread, jars of olive oil and vinegar and wine. Dried herbs and spices hung in lines near the ceiling from strings stretched across the room. Through the open door to the courtyard, a fire still smoldered in the clay lined cooking oven and—

Lacidar stepped through the side wall.

Zaben, Timrok, and Jenli looked over, and each spoke a word into their hand: "Wisdom," "Devotion," "Peace." Their words became plasma balls of energy in their palms.

Lacidar created his own plasma ball with the word "Joy."

The four met in the center of the room and pressed the energy together in an explosion of light. Tiny shards of wisdom, devotion, peace, and joy filled the room and drifted down like a shower of floating embers.

Elric laughed. "Very good, very good. Welcome to the regional command center for Galilee. A little different from John's cave by the Jordan."

Timrok, Zaben, and Lacidar looked around the room and nodded. Jenli rubbed the back of his stubbled head.

"This will be the center of our operations for the next phase of our mission," Elric continued. "Jenli—since you are the most familiar with the region, please update the others."

Jenli motioned with his hand. "This is the house of Simon, son of Jonah. He lives here with his wife, Joanna, and their daughter.

Simon's younger brother, Andrew, also lives here, as does Joanna's mother."

Zaben said, "Simon . . . and Andrew? The same Simon and Andrew who are on our list of—"

"We shall get to that," Elric said. "But yes."

Jenli continued, "You will notice that this place is not the stronghold we knew with the widow Hannah or with the prophet John. Yet. But it soon will be. The King plans to use this place as a home base when He launches out into the surrounding regions."

Timrok bounced on his toes. "To build support for His army!"

"And finally start—" Zaben began.

Elric held up his hands and restrained the growing excitement. "I know this is foremost on everyone's mind, but we must continue with patience. I have received more details for our next phase. And we still have a season of preparation."

He motioned for everyone to step back. He waved his hand over the ground in a long sweeping arc, and the multi-dimensional war map appeared. Layers of glowing colors pulsated and swirled with veins of scintillating energy stretching in all directions. Thousands of tiny lights blinked. Thousands of tiny black dots winked. Rolling waves of black smoke. Sparks and flashes of light. An endless, swirling mass of surging energy. The lieutenants stepped up and studied it.

"The King is leaving Judea and the Jordan and is coming here to Galilee," Elric said, pointing to their northern location on the map. "His primary purpose initially is to gather men for His inner circle."

"The twelve generals for His army," Timrok said.

Elric nodded. "Yes. And then He will travel to Jerusalem for the Passover festival."

"To begin His campaign?" Zaben asked.

"Not yet. He will still be gathering followers and building support. Then, back to Galilee. Using Capernaum as a home base, He will go out and proclaim the Kingdom. Our role—keep Him safe, as usual. The enemy can't touch Him. They are terrified of Him. They will do all they can to keep their distance. But that won't stop them from trying to reach Him through men. His exposure will be high, and we will have to be at our best."

"We have waited a long time for this day," Lacidar said. "I am always honored to bear up a load for extended seasons for the sake of the Kingdom. But I have to admit that I grow more excited every moment at the nearness of the day."

Elric smiled. "We all do."

Timrok, Zaben, and Jenli nodded.

"Now," Elric said. "An update on our twelve generals. Where are they? Are they prepared? How do we connect them with the King?"

"Simon and Andrew are ready," Jenli said. "Simon is my charge. Andrew is Brondor's. Simon is the oldest of all the twelve. A strong leader. Head strong. Enthusiastic and bold. He will be a capable general. Andrew is sincere with strong expectations of the coming Messiah. Not bound by traditional views, a man of action."

"Where are they now?" Elric asked.

"Here. In Capernaum. In fact, they are out fishing right now. They have already met the King by the Jordan with the prophet John. After Jesus withdrew to the wilderness, they returned home."

"James and John, the sons of Zebedee, are here also," Zaben said. "Also fishermen. They often partner with Simon and Andrew. They are cousins of Jesus—sons of Salome, Mary's sister. Salome is the only one of Mary's family who believed her story. And her sons are ready to follow Him. Christov and Carothim are assigned to these two."

"Very good," Elric said. "Jesus is coming here. Arranging their meetings will not be difficult."

Jenli added, "Levi, also called Matthew, is here in Capernaum, too. He is a publican, a tax collector. A man of some means, with his own house not far from here."

"Interesting," Elric said, rubbing his chin. "A Jewish agent of Rome—part of the inner circle. Hated by his kinsmen, and—I would assume—not anxious to see the Messiah overthrow Roman rule."

"You might be surprised," Jenli said. "He has a heart for God. He is well educated in Jewish tradition and is looking for the King. Kaylar has been preparing him. He will be ready."

Zaben continued, "Philip is from Bethsaida, but he has been at the Jordan with the prophet John now for months. After the King was revealed at the Jordan, Philip was one of the first of John's disciples to believe. He is already committed to follow Him. Jennidab has been watching over him."

"Where is Philip now?"

"Still at the Jordan with John."

"Good. We will pick him up when the King comes back from the wilderness on His way to Galilee."

"Philip is energetic and outspoken for the Kingdom. He introduced Nathaniel to the King at the Jordan."

"Nathaniel, another one of the twelve." Elric said.

"Yes," Zaben said. "Also a disciple of John. He also goes by Bartholomew. Jerem has been preparing him. The Lord described him as a 'man without guile.'"

"Is he still at the Jordan?"

"No. He is a farmer in Cana of Galilee. When the King went into the wilderness, Nathaniel returned home."

Elric nodded. "We need to make sure the King passes through Cana."

"Look," Jenli said, pointing to something in the map. "I think . . ." He pulled out his ledger and flipped through it. "Yes. There is a wedding in Cana for some friends of Mary. She plans to travel down from Nazareth to attend."

"Excellent," Elric said. "See that Jesus receives an invitation."

"Yes, sir."

"Who's next?"

"Thomas Didymus," Jenli answered.

"Didymus? A twin?"

"Yes, well . . . this is an interesting one," Jenli said. "Despite Jessik's best efforts, the enemy struck this family with a deadly infectious lung disease. His brother just died this week. It has been difficult. And now, Thomas is failing. He is a strong young man—courageous, analytical, and pragmatic. But without a healing touch from the King, he has less than two weeks."

"Where is he?"

"A small village in Galilee. Along the route to Capernaum."

"The Father will surely send the Son through there and heal him. Jessik needs to continue ministering strength to Thomas's flesh."

"Yes, sir."

"Next."

"I have been watching over another man named Simon," Zaben said. "This one is a Zealot. A fiery, ambitious man who is ready to topple Rome."

"A Zealot? That rebellion was crushed by Rome years ago."

"As a political organization. But there are many who still identify with their ideals. Simon is one."

"I anticipate interesting dynamics between the publican and the Zealot," Elric said.

Zaben nodded. "He will be in Jerusalem for Passover. We need only to make sure paths cross while the King is there."

"Good."

"Judas, from Kerioth in southern Judea, is Lorr's charge," Zaben said. "I saved him from the hand of Herod at the time of the King's escape to Egypt. He is another one strongly aligned with the ideals of the Zealots, though not as fervently as Simon. He will surely follow the Lord when he sees the hope of the Messiah. He also plans to travel to Jerusalem for the festival."

"Good."

"I have another set of brothers, James and Joses, sons of Alphaeus," Zaben continued. "Their mother's name is Mary. She is widowed of Alpheus, but he left them with a good inheritance. This whole family has true servant's hearts. I believe Mary will also follow the King—and probably help support the mission financially. Xarjim has watching over them."

"Joses is not named among the twelve?" Elric asked.

"No. He is even younger than James. But he will certainly join the campaign."

"Where are they?"

"Judea. But they, too, will be in Jerusalem for Passover."

"That's eleven," Elric said. "Who is the twelfth?"

Zaben answered, "Jude Thaddaeus, son of James, from Edessa. He came to down at the prompting of Emms to see the prophet John.

He was baptized by John and continues under his teaching now. We will try to connect him with the King when He collects Philip."

Elric crossed his arms and gazed into the war map. "The days of silent hiding are over," he said with a pondering tone. "Once the King begins asserting His kingdom in the enemy's realm, we are sure to encounter severe resistance." He motioned with his hand all over the map. "You can see the pressure building. Timrok, you and your team will continue to provide a close perimeter around the King."

"Yes, sir."

Elric pointed to the area around the prophet John. "There appears to be new activity of the enemy against John at the highest levels. Lacidar, what is happening down there?"

"On the surface, everything is progressing well. John's message remains the same, and many people are turning to the Lord. There are typical skirmishes over individuals, but the Spirit of the King is moving powerfully, and it is very exciting. However, Molech's minions are stirring up Herod Antipas against John."

"Over what offense?"

"John is not afraid to stand against sin, corruption, injustice. He speaks against all that is contrary to holiness, regardless of who is doing it. Herod has married Herodias, his brother Philip's wife. And John has condemned this as unlawful. Normally, a crazy man in the wilderness a hundred miles away at the edge of political jurisdiction would not be worthy of Herod's notice, but the enemy seeks to silence John."

"Mmm." Elric pursed his lips and studied the map. "You and your team stay close to John. You may have a difficult battle ahead."

"Yes, sir."

"And be quick to call for reinforcements. We will *all* be prepared to come and help protect John."

Lacidar nodded.

Zaben, Jenli, and Timrok nodded.

"Captain," Zaben said. "What of Mary? Is she to remain in Nazareth?"

"For now. After Jesus returns from the Passover, He will begin traveling throughout Galilee. At some point, He will visit Nazareth, and Mary will join the troop then."

Elric folded his hands behind his back and stepped away from the map. "Everyone is clear about their assignments?"

"Yes, sir," the four replied in unison.

"Go in the power of His might. Stay ahead of the enemy. Let's establish the Lord's kingdom here on earth."

"In His service." The four lieutenants expanded to their full size, extended their wings, and shot through the ceiling.

Elric stood alone in the war room, staring at the map. So much motion. So much turmoil. Staying ahead of the enemy—this was going to be the greatest challenge.

* * *

Daniel ducked away behind a utility shed, seeking shadows and seclusion while two of the other crewmen from the fishing boat stowed the tackle and nets in the shed with annoying knocks and clatter. Sinking to the ground, Daniel sat in a tight ball, covered his ears, and rocked back and forth.

These long, tortured days in the fishing town of Ein Gev after a night of working the lake were the hardest. The night's catch had been unloaded and the crew dismissed. Finally, no need for the pretense of getting along with people, of being responsible, of caring about anything. But now . . . now . . . he tightened his hands over his ears and rocked faster.

I just want to be alone.

Alone. Only—he never could be.

"I hate them," the demon Vorsogh grumbled in Daniel's deaf right ear.

Still rocking, his right hand made motions through the air—as though carving up the carcass of a dead swine. His left hand jerked with sporadic spasms while his fingers alternately tapped against his thumb.

"Alone," he muttered. "Alone . . . alone . . . alone . . . "

Stammering, rocking, carving, twitching—he drifted off into the fog.

Daniel stopped rocking, lifted his face, and grimaced. *How long have I been sitting here?* He squinted toward the sun. Well after midday. *Ugh. A long time.*

He sighed and resumed rocking.

What a pointless life. What's the use of all this? I hate my life. I hate all these people around me. I hate my stupid father. I hate this constant pain inside.

"It's your own fault, you know," the voice whispered in his ear. "You're the reason I was killed."

Daniel rocked faster. The vision of that Roman sword slicing across his brother Levi's belly filled his pounding brain. Daniel clenched his eyes shut and covered his ears, but the vision wouldn't stop. Even after thirty years and thousands of replays, every detail of that day remained razor sharp—the blood, Levi's horrifying scream, the warmth of Levi's intestines in his hands, so much blood, Levi's final gasps for life.

Daniel shook his head in a wild frenzy and screamed. His long, matted hair flailed all around and slapped against his face. He stopped and looked down at his forearms, panting shallow sighs. The diagonal scar on his left arm was pink and raised, but mostly healed. The similar wound on the right arm looked red, angry, and partially scabbed over.

He pulled a small dagger from the belt around his tunic and turned it slowly by the handle in his palm. With each turn, the sun glinted off the silver blade. He spun it faster, faster. Then, he stopped and placed the edge of the blade against his left forearm, just inches below the pink scar.

"Do it," the voice said. "Feel my pain. You deserve it. It's the only way to release your guilt."

Without hesitation, Daniel pulled the blade across his skin. The line of skin separated, and blood surged from the wound. A heartbeat later, the blood covered his whole forearm and dripped onto the ground. Expressionless, he watched it with cold detachment. The pain didn't even make him flinch. Instead, it filled him with a strange, evil satisfaction. He remembered all the times he'd awoke with blood all over his hands and arms.

At least I know whose blood this is. This pain is mine. All mine.

He closed his eyes, resumed rocking, and drifted back into the fog.

* * *

Elric and Zaben stood on the flat roof of Simon's house in Capernaum. The predawn sun filled the sky with a soft glow, but the day had not yet awakened.

"The town is quiet," Zaben said. "The enemy is gripped by fear. All the beaelzurim not attending specific assignments have left the area."

Elric's gaze stayed fixed on a secluded hill north of town. There, in the obscurity of the early morning, Jesus prayed alone. From this distance, He looked no larger than a jackrabbit amongst the stony backdrop. But the massive frame of Timrok, a stone's throw away, loomed large—conspicuous, powerful, ready.

"Mm. Through no work of our own," Elric replied. "They know who the King is. They may strive to obstruct His will, but they know they can never stand against Him."

"But, still, we stand guard?"

"These are our orders. We are in His service."

"But He is the everlasting one. Self-existent. Threatened by none."

Elric took in a deep breath and sighed. "In the King's Realm. But as the Son of Man, here in the Physical Realm . . . "

"He is still the King."

"Bound by His own word. He cannot violate any law He has established." Elric sighed again. "He must accomplish His work as man. Here. With all the vulnerabilities that implies."

They both stared off toward the distant hill. Jesus cast a long shadow from the rising sun. Timrok had no shadow.

Zaben shook his head. "Not the manner I expected for His coming."

"Nor I." Elric smiled. "I always pictured Him coming as a mighty warrior on a white horse, destroying His enemies with the word of His mouth. Us behind Him, marching to glorious victory. And then—"

"Peace. No more strife. Only order. Like it was before."

"And music." Elric closed his eyes and smiled. "Beautiful, pure, never-ending." He opened his eyes and sighed. "We are so close. The depths of this mysterious mission are beyond knowing. But this we do know . . . we are very close."

A commotion rattled below. Simon and Andrew emerged from the front door, followed by James, John, and Philip. The whole group searched the immediate area. Philip checked around the corner of the house.

"I don't see Him anywhere," Peter said.

"Why would a rabbi call followers and then leave them a day later?" James said.

"We will find Him," Peter replied. "James, you and John check the shoreline. Philip, you search the streets. Andrew and I will check the synagogue. Meet back here in an hour."

The group of men scattered. Five warriors in white bolted outward with a flurry of wings—Jenli, Brondor, Christov, Carothim, and Jennidab. Philip turned up one path and almost bumped into a pair of Roman soldiers on patrol. With his eyes to the ground, Philip shuffled around them. The soldiers stopped and watched him hurry off. Jennidab spoke words to the soldiers, and they continued their patrol.

Zaben said, "These men do not know His ways. He is always in prayer this time of day."

Elric nodded. "They will learn. He prays like no man I have ever seen. He is in constant communication with the Father."

"Well, we have collected five of the twelve generals. Next, Nathaniel and Thomas."

"Yes. Tomorrow is the Sabbath. Jesus will attend services at the synagogue. We will travel to Cana the day following. Then back here for a few days before we proceed to Jerusalem."

Elric looked back toward the hillside. Jesus remained undisturbed, unmoved, while waves of light flowed downward on Him in a continuous roll. Elric nodded and smiled.

5

SIGNS OF LIFE

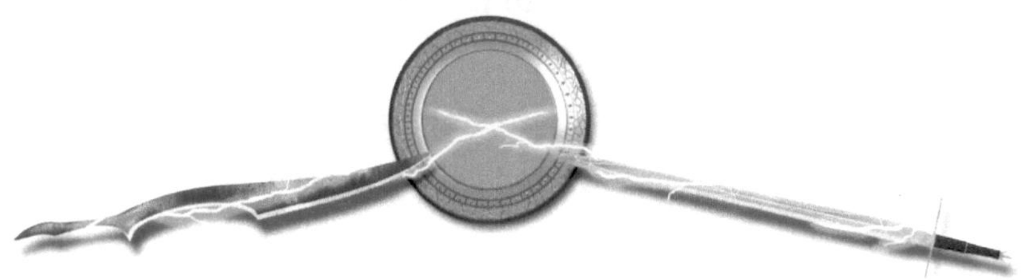

Battle minus 3 years

It had been only four months since Jesus' youngest sister Rachael's wedding, but Elric always enjoyed a good wedding. And this one in Cana of Galilee was a good one. Hundreds of wedding guests danced and laughed. Elric clapped his hands and stomped his feet with the beat of the music. Timrok, the oversized artist with no dignity at all, danced in the middle of the crowd. Plowing through all the other dancers in the Physical Realm, he skipped, pranced, hopped, and twirled—punctuating his wild exuberance with high aerial flips and pirouettes. Jenli danced with the people, joining the lines of men and doing high kicks and fancy moves with his hands and feet. Zaben clapped his hands and tried to remain vigilant for potential enemy movements, but Timrok kept grabbing him, spinning him, and launching him into the air. Elric laughed.

Lacidar claimed his place in the middle of the band. Four lute players plucked and strummed with enough energy to electrify the whole crowd. The largest lute, with its cavernous wooden pear-shaped body, thumped a driving bass line that Elric's foot couldn't ignore. The lyre player sat with his instrument on his lap and filled in countermelodies with its high, harp-like tones. Elric couldn't take his eyes off the pipe player, whose dancing, animated antics, and energic melodies brought life to the whole production. To top it all, a dozen women beat and shook timbrels, dancing through the crowd and pushing the beat forward. Lacidar's resonar soared above everything, and even though the human ears couldn't hear it, it sent waves of life and celebration pulsing into the Physical Realm. The music had no resemblance to the reverential songs in the temple, but the purity of the joy was sacred and brought down a sparkling rain of pleasure in the Middle Realm from the Throne.

I am so glad I insisted all the lieutenants attend this gathering. They needed it. I think I needed it. Elric couldn't help but direct the band with his hand. He laughed at himself, knowing no one was following his direction.

Right in the middle of all of it, Jesus danced and sweated like the rest of the men. His brothers, James, Joseph, Simon, and Jude all took turns dancing with Mary and their sisters Elizabeth and Rachael. The disciples, Simon and Andrew, James and John, and Philip started off at the fringes, but the music wouldn't allow them to remain outsiders.

Elric laughed at Simon. *His dancing reminds me of Timrok.*

Nathaniel had shown up, as arranged by Jerem. *He's a good dancer, too. But we still need to get him alone with Jesus. Perhaps tonight after . . . what's this?*

Mary and the father of the groom gathered by the house and spoke with the head servant, who seemed unsettled over something. They moved inside the house. Elric's foot stopped tapping. His eye caught Zaben's. With a single head nod from Elric, Zaben disappeared into the house. Elric waited.

Zaben emerged and flew to Elric with one flap of his wings. "They have run out of wine," Zaben said.

Elric chuckled. "It is a big party. I'm not surprised." He paused. "Is this a move of the enemy or just poor planning on the part of the groom?"

"I can't tell. In the worst case, the groom will lose face with his guests. But they are already merry and fed. I see no inroad for the enemy here."

Mary stepped back outside and strode over to Jesus with a purposeful gait. Elric watched with Zaben standing by. Mary drew up near to Jesus' ear and spoke something over the noise. He turned and walked toward the house with her.

Like bolts of lightning, Timrok and Jenli shot to positions on each side of the door to the house—swords drawn and eyes flashing. Lacidar appeared on the roof. Elric and Zaben followed close behind Mary and Jesus. Zaben drew his weapon.

The party in the Physical Realm continued without a hint of disturbance.

Inside, the door closed and the noise from the party became muffled. A dozen servants stood by with the head servant wringing his hands.

Mary stepped in front of them and turned to Jesus. "They have no wine," she said with a leading tone.

Jesus replied, "Woman, what does that have to do with us? My hour has not yet come."

The door opened and Philip, Simon, Andrew, James, John, and Nathaniel filed in.

"Is there a problem, Master?" Simon asked. The door closed again.

Mary placed her hands on her hips and looked at Jesus the way only a mother can. She waited with tight lips and an uplifted chin. Jesus' eyes softened.

Mary said to the servants, "Whatever He says to you, do it." She spun around and left.

Nearby stood six stone water jars, the kind used by the Jews for ceremonial washing, each holding thirty gallons.

Jesus said to the servants, "Fill the waterpots with water."

The servants scurried away with smaller pots.

Jesus turned to His disciples and said, "It is written in the law, 'It shall come about, if you listen obediently to my commandments which I am commanding you today, to love the Lord your God and to serve Him with all your heart and all your soul, that He will give the rain for your land in its season, the early and late rain, that you may gather in your grain . . . '" He paused a moment but continued with special emphasis, "'*and your new wine* and your oil. He will give grass in your fields for your cattle, and you will eat and be satisfied.'"

In the Middle Realm, small tornadoes of reddish-purple energy swirled above the rims of the large waterpots.

Elric whispered to Zaben, "Go get the others. They need to see this."

A moment later, Timrok, Jenli, and Lacidar popped through the front wall with Zaben. With wide eyes they spotted the development in the Middle Realm.

Jesus continued. "And elsewhere it is written that your 'barns will be filled with plenty, and your vats will overflow with new wine.'"

The tornadoes of energy grew and descended into the waterpots with their tops still whizzing above the top rim.

A line of servants burst through a side door and emptied their smaller pots of water one by one into the large containers. They each retreated with their empty pots for another load.

Jesus paid no attention to the workers but continued teaching the disciples. "This is the kingdom of God—blessing, abundance, life. The kingdom of God is at hand. The just will receive it by faith."

More servants appeared, emptied containers of water, and left.

Elric's gaze stayed fixed on the growing whirlwinds of energy in the Middle Realm.

"You know," Timrok said with an even tone, "it is nothing remarkable to see His word come to life in the Middle Realm."

"Yes," Jenli said, "but how often do we see a *man* with the faith to pull it into the Physical Realm?"

"He's going to do it," Elric said.

Another round of servants emptied their water containers into the large pots. Another round. Finally, each of the six waterpots reached capacity.

The tornadoes continued to swirl in the Middle Realm.

Jesus stepped forward, placed a hand on one of the pots and said, "Father, I thank you for the promises of your word."

Like giant sponges, the water in each of the pots absorbed the spiritual energy, and in a blink, the tornadoes vanished from the Middle Realm.

Jesus said to the servants, "Draw some out now and take it to the headwaiter."

One of the servants took a big bronze ladle and dipped it into one of the vessels. He poured it into a large cup and gasped at the sparkling red fluid that flowed from the ladle. He dipped another portion. He and two other servants rushed out the door with the cup of wine.

Elric stepped outside to watch the headwaiter's reaction. The headwaiter tasted it and contorted his face with a baffled look of amazement. He called the bridegroom over and said to him, "Every man serves the good wine first, and when the people have drunk freely, then he serves the poorer wine; but you have kept the good wine until now."

"I . . . do not know what you mean," the groom said.

"Taste this."

Elric stepped back inside.

The disciples stood around the large vats, tasting the wine and looking overwhelmed. Nathaniel kept shaking his head and staring at Jesus with eyes as wide as the coming full moon.

"Do you marvel at this?" Jesus said. "Truly, you will see greater works than this. Come, let us rejoice with the bride and bridegroom with grateful hearts."

"And so it begins," Zaben said.

Timrok gave a little hop. "I can't wait to see what happens when we get to Jerusalem!"

* * *

Inside a tiny synagogue in a tiny Galilean village, Jenli joined Jessik, stationed near the rear of the sanctuary. The room, square and austere, rested in the quiet dim glow of four oil lamps. The room was empty—except for a middle-aged woman, who sat weeping behind the half-wall barrier of the women's section. Jessik's glowing hands rested on her shoulders.

"Oh God," the woman moaned between sobs, "can you not see the bitterness of my soul? Already you have cut short the vitality of one my sons. Would you now take his twin brother, too? I am weary with grief, to the point of death. Is there no mercy? Is there no end to my sorrow? Do you not hear?"

Jenli shook his head. "I feel her pain. But always I wonder why they ascribe sickness and loss to the King. Do they not recognize the enemy's intent to kill, steal, and destroy?"

"It has been a hard morning for her," Jessik said. "Thomas's condition worsens. Without a touch from the King, his flesh will surely not survive the day."

"Today her mourning will be turned to gladness, and we will have another general for the King's army," Jenli said. "The King is already here in town. The time is now for her to leave the synagogue and make her appointed meeting."

"Yes, sir."

Without moving his hands off her shoulders, Jessik said, "Eliana, it is time to go."

His words rolled up in the Middle Realm like a tiny sparkling star and shot inward toward Eliana's chest. The light crashed against a layer of darkness surrounding her spirit and dissipated into the air.

"Eliana, you should leave here and go out to the street marketplace."

Again, Jessik's words did not penetrate her shell.

Jessik shook his head and said to Jenli, "I have been ministering to her all morning, and she has been unable to receive."

"Keep trying. Time is short."

"Eliana—"

A loud commotion from the street outside broke the silence in the room. Eliana raised her head and glanced at the door with red, puffy, tear-filled eyes. Shouting, clapping, and the roar of a crowd energized the air. A woman's voice, shrill and uncontrolled, cut through the clamor.

"Sara?" Eliana muttered to herself. "That sounds like Sara." Eliana jumped up and scrambled to the door. She opened it, and the sounds from the street burst in crisp and loud. "That is Sara!" She shouted, "Sara, what happened?" She ran out toward the crowd, leaving the door open.

Jenli smiled. "I had hoped she could have witnessed it firsthand, but this will be sufficient for a meeting with the King."

Jenli and Jessik sprang out of the synagogue with a single clap of their wings and landed at the outer fringes of a gathering of very excited people.

"This must be every resident in town," Jessik said.

Eliana pressed her way to the center of the crowd where Sara's hysterics had captured everyone's attention.

"He can see! He can see!" Sara screamed with a tone so high and broken that her words were almost unintelligible. "It's a miracle! Can you believe it? Look at this! Look at this!"

Eliana reached Sara from behind, grabbed her shoulders, and spun her around. "Sara! What happened? What's wrong?"

"He can see!" Tears streamed down Sara's face, and her whole body shook.

Eliana clutched Sara's quaking hand and steadied her.

Sara put her other hand on the top of a young boy's head, no taller than her waist and breathed with a lower tone, "He can see . . . "

Eliana's jaw fell open. She dropped down to her knees—eye level with the boy. "Jared, Jared can you see me?"

He pressed in tight against Sara's leg and buried his face into her tunic.

"Jared, it's me, Eliana. Look at me. Right here, honey. Can you see me?"

His sparkling brown eyes met hers and then darted all around. He nodded.

Eliana gasped. "Your Ima? Can you see your Ima?"

Jared looked up at Sara and nodded. Sara burst into hysterics again.

"And all these people? Can you see all these people all around us?"

He nodded.

Eliana fumbled back to her feet. "How? How did this happen?"

Sara pointed and said, "That man. He healed him!"

Jenli followed Eliana's eyes over toward Jesus. Jesus and His disciples—James, John, Simon, Andrew, Philip, and Nathaniel—huddled together away from the crowd. While the crowd strained inward toward Sara and Jared, Jesus spoke privately with the disciples.

Eliana turned back to Sara. "How? What did he do?"

"He . . . just . . . commanded his eyes to be open."

"How is that possible? Who is he?"

"I don't know. All I know is that when he spoke with me and told me God wanted to give Jared his sight, my heart burned within me and I . . . I believed him. I think he must be some kind of prophet. Since Jared was little, I have prayed for help—anything. But I never expected a miracle like this. I just can't believe it. How does a man simply speak a word . . . "

Elric stood at his post a sword's length away from the King—arms crossed, full-sized, and alert. Timrok and his team held a conspicuous perimeter around the group of disciples. The radiance of Jesus' spirit blazed in the Middle Realm like solar flares erupting and penetrating deep into the spirits of the astonished disciples.

"Look at that," Jenli said to Jessik. "His very presence breaks down barriers and fills them with faith and expectation."

"It's like nothing I have ever seen," Jessik replied.

The shafts of light radiated throughout the entire gathering, and many of the people's spirits pulsed with flickers of faith. Including Eliana.

"Now is our opportunity," Jenli said. "Speak to Eliana."

Jessik stepped three paces forward, wrapped one wing around Eliana, bent down low near her ear, and said, "The Lord hears your prayers. He wants to heal Thomas. Go—ask Him. Quickly, while He is near."

With glassy eyes and mouth wide open, Eliana stared at Jesus. "Uh huh," she muttered to Sara while patting her arm. "That's amazing . . . I'm so happy for . . . excuse me, I have to talk with him." Oblivious to everything else, she elbowed her way through the crowd to the ring of the disciples and squeezed in past them until she stood face to face with Jesus. He stopped talking. Their eyes met.

Jenli glanced at Elric, who gave him a smile and a nod.

Eliana averted her eyes downward and said, "Master, if you can give sight to the blind, truly you must be a prophet of God. Are you able to heal other kinds of afflictions?"

Jesus answered, "It is written, 'Bless the Lord, O my soul, and forget none of His benefits; who pardons all your iniquities, who heals *all* your diseases.'"

"I have a son at home who is very sick. His twin brother died of the same illness just last week. His fever is high, and the physicians cannot help him. I fear he will not survive the night. I have prayed and prayed, but he only gets worse. And he is very weak. I have no means to bring him to you. If there is anything you can do . . ."

"Do not fear. Only believe. Take me to him."

* * *

Elric's giant frame filled the corner of Thomas's small bedroom, dark, gloomy, and stale. Jessik stood beside him. In the Physical Realm, James, John, and Simon crowded around the bed, with Simon on the side near the head and James and John at the foot. Simon placed his hand on Thomas's forehead and gave a hopeless head shake to James and John. Thomas's feeble eyelids opened for a moment, blinked, and fell closed. Jesus entered and stood beside the bed.

"He has a burning fever," Simon said. "He is barely breathing. I'm afraid we're too late."

Jesus shook His head. "Do not look at the outward appearance. Only believe."

"Believe what, Master?" James said, "Can a man be drawn back from the edge of Sheol?"

"Believe in the Father's love. Believe His word. Believe in me." Jesus touched Thomas's arm. "Thomas. Thomas, wake up."

Thomas opened his eyes.

The gleaming light of Jesus' spirit filled the room in the Middle Realm. Elric smiled and crossed his arms.

Jesus laid His hand on Thomas's chest and said, "Thomas, Jehovah Rophe heals you. Rise up and follow me."

A bright blue aura of energy formed around Thomas's body, pulsing, humming, sparkling.

With squinted eyes, Jessik said, "How do these men not see this?"

Thomas raised his shoulders up, stopping to rest on his elbows. His eyes met Jesus' eyes and brightened with a tiny flicker of hope. He forced himself to a sitting position, and as he did, his spirit took hold of the entire layer of energy surrounding him and pulled it in.

"There you have it," Elric said. "All it takes is a word from the King, met with the obedience of faith."

Thomas coughed. A wet, raspy, shallow cough. He coughed again. He launched into an uncontrolled string of coughs, each wetter and deeper than the one before. He swung his legs over the side of the bed and leaned forward, coughing and retching.

"Master!" Simon stammered. "He grows worse!"

Jesus looked toward John. "A bowl. Bring me a bowl."

John darted out of the room and returned a moment later with a large clay bowl.

Jesus held it in front of Thomas with one hand and placed His other hand on Thomas's back. "Healing springs forth from within. And that which is unclean must come out."

Thomas coughed and heaved into the bowl—while Peter stood with his mouth wide open. James turned away and only half-watched over his shoulder, and John dropped to his knees with his hand covering his mouth. Jesus held the bowl and waited.

Several violent minutes passed, but Thomas's coughing became dryer and slower. Finally, he stopped. He sat up and looked at Jesus. Jesus handed him a towel, which he used to wipe his mouth and face.

"I feel . . . " Thomas cleared his raspy throat. "I feel better. I can breathe."

Simon reached over and felt his forehead. "His fever is completely gone!"

"Bring him some water," Jesus said. "And prepare food. He is still weak and needs the strength."

Thomas took drink of water and stood up. With small, measured steps, he led the way out of the bedroom.

Elric stayed behind with Jessik and chuckled at the squeals of joy and astonishment erupting from the next room. "The Kingdom advances. One life at a time."

Jenli emerged into the room through the side wall.

Jessik announced to Jenli, "Thomas is healed. He will surely follow the Lord. We have our seventh general for the King's army."

"We have more than that," Jenli said. "There are six others from town who plan to follow Him."

Elric smiled and put one hand on Jenli's shoulder and the other on Jessik's. "We'll spend the night here tonight. In the morning, we continue on to Jerusalem."

6

ZEAL FOR THE HOUSE

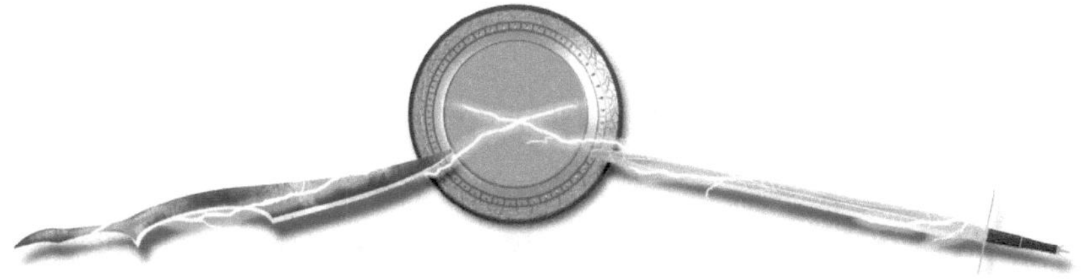

Battle minus 3 years

A dove alighted on the chest-high crenelated parapet atop the outer court wall of the temple in Jerusalem. It walked across the thick square stone, its head bobbing with each step until it reached the outer edge. It cocked its head to the side, paused, and flew off over the city below.

Zaben, with his arm resting on the stone balustrade facing inward on the outer court wall, grinned at the dove flittering away. "Enjoy your freedom, little one," he said under his breath. He glanced down toward the courtyard. "Your brothers down there will never know it again."

In the outer court, several dozen wooden cages housed hundreds of doves waiting to be purchased and taken to the inner court for sacrifice. The cages, stacked two and three high, formed neat lines along one row of vendors. The row of vendors off to the left had makeshift stalls filled with sheep. Much larger pens to the right contained a small herd of cattle and oxen. Near the center, in the main line of traffic, the money changers exchanged secular coinage for temple currency. Hundreds of people bustled around the court like a mound of ants. Buying, selling, merchandizing religion.

Zaben sighed. *The day before Passover. So much to do.*

He looked up toward the sun, shining full strength and warming the beautiful cloudless spring day—not unlike the autumn day he stood in the same spot on the old temple wall over a thousand years ago—the day Solomon initiated the dedication of the temple and the altar. The memories rolled through his mind—thousands of animals passing through this court toward the inner court, along with thousands of men and women in motion. But on that day, they were praying, singing, and rejoicing amongst the rich aroma of roasting sacrifices. And . . . the glory of the King was so strong in the temple that it saturated even the atmosphere of the Physical Realm. Zaben smiled, nodded, paused, glanced at the activities in the court below, and shook his head.

These are different times.

A commotion from behind rose from the street below. Zaben turned his head just in time to see the mighty senturim in front of the temple walls kneel with their faces to the ground and lay their massive broadswords flat before them. From the streets of Jerusalem, Jesus and a group of about twenty followers approached the steps to the temple gate.

Good. The King arrives. He raised one corner of his lips with a satisfied grin. *And finally, the senturim are allowed to acknowledge Him.*

He turned back to the inside of the court and located his charge, Simon the Zealot, standing with a small group of fiery-eyed men discussing the evils of the Roman empire.

My man is in place. I wonder if Lorr has been able to get—

Lorr appeared from out of the portico, two paces ahead of Judas Iscariot, who stopped at the outer perimeter of the group of Zealots. One man in the group spoke with exaggerated gestures. Judas nodded and stepped inward toward the group as though he had found men of kindred mind.

Good. Now we just need to arrange the meeting of Simon and Judas with Jesus.

Jesus and the small entourage entered the outer court flanked by Elric, Timrok, and Timrok's warriors. Jesus reached the main flow of the court and stopped, bunching up His human followers behind Him in an awkward mass. Timrok's team fanned out and formed a conspicuous perimeter with typical precision. Jesus remained motionless except for the slow turn of His head from one end of the court to the other.

Zaben bit his lower lip and furrowed his eyebrows. *What is He doing?*

In an instant, thick, dark clouds appeared and boiled over the temple complex. Zaben peered past them toward the sun, still shining in the Physical Realm.

These are spiritual clouds! Holy zeal from the Throne? I wonder what the King is—

Crack! A bolt of spiritual lightning flashed. The low roar of thunder shook the Middle Realm. The ominous clouds thickened and boiled like lava. *Crack! Crack!* More lightning struck the ground in the outer court.

The men in the court continued their merchandizing in the sunshine.

Demons in the Middle Realm scattered. Some dared to stay close to their men, but with lightning zapping close at their heels, most scrambled for cover. Unstoppable flashes of power. Reverberating thunder. Oblivious men. Frantic beaelzurim. An incoming lightning bolt sizzled downward. Zaben ducked. It whizzed past him into the courtyard. Just before it hit the ground, Timrok leapt forward, leveled one of his swords, and redirected the bolt at a retreating demon. The dark warrior squealed and flew away with smoke billowing from behind.

Zaben laughed aloud. "Ha, ha! Yes!" *But . . . what is the King doing?*

In the Physical Realm, Jesus emerged from the portico with long, thick cords. He raised them above His head and cracked them like a whip. He kicked over a pen fence, cracked His whip, and shouted, "Out!"

The sheep in the pen jolted outward, bouncing off each other and into the crowd of men.

*Crack—crack—*thundered the lightning in the Middle Realm

*Crack—crack—*echoed the whip in the Physical Realm.

Two more fences crashed under Jesus' foot, and the whole flock of sheep bounded from their pens.

All the people in the outer court froze and reeled around toward the disturbance.

Pushing the sheep toward the outer gate, Jesus reached the money changers and flipped a table over. Coins flew into the air and scattered with a metallic jingle. Two, three, four tables toppled. The money changers dropped to their hands and knees, clambering across the ground and scooping up their strewn coins. Skittish sheep stampeded through, bumping into bodies, stepping on hands, and bounding over backs.

The whip cracked again, and Jesus marched toward the bird merchants. With panic in their eyes, some of the merchants snatched cages in each hand and backed away, holding their cages above the surge of sheep. Too late. Jesus pulled a cage down from a stack of three, smashing it to the ground and sending all its captives flapping to freedom. Another cage crashed, and another small flock of doves took flight. They flew one direction, turned hard to another direction, and bolted up over the outer court wall just above Zaben.

Just as the doves passed overhead, a dark blur from below screamed upward. Zaben unsheathed his sword, stepped left, and intercepted the escaping demon's trajectory with the tip of his blade. Zaben's steel carved a valley through the demon, head to toe, sending it flailing to the ground outside the temple in a cloud of yellow smoke.

Jesus' voice rose above the mayhem. "Get these out of here! Stop turning my Father's house into a market!"

The King is setting His house in order! Yes! The campaign has truly begun!

"Yes!" Zaben shouted. "Yes! Yes!"

Simon—what is the Zealot doing? How is Judas?

The small group of men, so wrapped up in their political fervor just a moment ago, stood pinned and speechless against the wall.

A mass of wool, feathers, and confusion streamed in front of them toward the exit. Simon and Judas pushed their backs to the wall with the rest of the group and watched with wide, stunned eyes.

A crack of thunder—a crack of the whip. Jesus swung the cattle pen gate open. With cracks of His whip and slaps on the cattle's haunches, he drove the cattle out and herded them toward the exit.

"Out! Out! This is supposed to be a house of prayer!"

Jenli alighted on the wall beside Zaben. He looked up at the boiling storm clouds and ducked at a flash of lightning. He gaped at the spectacle in the outer court and said, "What is all this? What did I miss?"

Zaben smiled and raised his eyebrows. "The King . . . is cleaning house."

"But He can't start His military campaign yet. We have no army prepared. His generals aren't in place."

Zaben motioned to the storm in the Middle Realm. "The Son of Man only does what He sees the Father do. Today, the zeal for His Father's house has consumed Him. Tomorrow, I believe we will find our timetable unchanged."

"I don't know. This sure looks like . . . hey, look . . . temple officials are coming out to challenge Him."

"Can you hear them?"

"No. Can you?"

Zaben shook his head. "Too much noise. We shall see if He makes a move to take His rightful place in the temple."

The mass mayhem of livestock and vendors streaming out of the temple court continued. Zaben glanced at the clouds in the Middle Realm. The lightning strikes had stopped. Spiderwebs of lightning crackled within the clouds. The ground-shaking thunder reduced to a low rumble.

"Look," Jenli said. "The temple officials are backing away. I wonder what He told them."

Out of the shadows from under the portico, a man with wild, unkempt hair peered from around a column. With uncontrolled twitching and spasms, he screamed at Jesus over the crowd, "What have we to do with you, Jesus of Nazareth?" He lunged forward and stopped ten paces away from Jesus.

Prestus positioned himself between the man and Jesus and raised his sword. Timrok took a position just behind the man.

"Have you come to torment us?" the man screeched. "I know who you are. You are—"

"Be quiet!" Jesus shouted.

"I heard *that*," Jenli said to Zaben.

"Come out of him! Now!" Jesus commanded. His words shot like flaming arrows in the Middle Realm and found their mark.

The man fell to the ground, writhing. With a shriek, a demon emerged from the man's body, stood up, and stretched his wings—his glowing red eyes glaring at Jesus. Timrok grabbed the demon's half-unfurled left wing with his left hand and a fist full of wiry hair with his right hand. Lifting him as high a man's chest, Timrok hauled the demon to the edge of the courtyard and heaved him through the side wall like a sack of refuse. Jesus helped the man to his feet and spoke into his ear with his arm around the man's shoulders. Patting him on the back, Jesus turned back toward the crowd, now mostly patrons and pilgrims.

A few stray livestock still weaved toward the exit. Only half a dozen bird cages remained. Money changers still gathered their lost coins. The remaining people stood motionless, gaping at Jesus and whispering to each other.

The clouds in the Middle Realm stopped churning. They became flat, calm, and heavy. Zaben turned his eyes upward. No more lightning and thunder. "And next, I expect we shall see . . . "

Rain. A good, solid, cleansing shower. All the stench of worldliness and all the lingering clouds of yellow sulfur washed from the atmosphere in the Middle Realm. The ground soaked up every drop, leaving a fresh air of renewal. Zaben took in a deep breath and smiled.

In the Physical Realm, the sun still shone, but a palpable sense of peace settled over the court. Near the center of the court, amid toppled tables, a man lay moaning and clutching his leg. A small crowd gathered around.

John, the disciple, called out to Jesus, "Master, one of the money changers is hurt. Come quickly."

The court became silent. All the people stood still. Temple officials and priests clumped in small groups around the periphery and stroked their beards. Jesus' followers moved in close around the injured man. The group of Zealots, with Simon and Judas, moved inward. Zaben held his breath. Jenli leaned forward against the stone balustrade.

Stepping up to the man, Jesus said, "What happened?"

The money changer answered through clenched teeth, "A bull. I was trampled. I think my leg is broken. I cannot stand on it. I can hardly move it."

Jesus spoke loud enough for the crowd. "David declared, 'Lord my God, I called to you for help, and you healed me.'" His words formed a small cloud over the man in the Middle Realm. Like a powerful magnet, the cloud pulled light from around Jesus' spirit and descended on the man, enveloping him in a pulsing blue glow of energy. To the man, Jesus said, "Do you believe this word? For yourself?"

The man grimaced at first, but then nodded his head. "Yes. Yes, I believe."

Jesus took hold of the man, locking His hand around the man's wrist, and said, "Stand and walk. Be made whole." He pulled the man up, the cloud of blue energy entered the man's body, and the man stood up straight.

He put weight on the injured leg. He took a few steps. He hopped up and down. "It's healed!" he shouted. "It's completely healed. There is no pain! Look! Look at me!" He ran circles around the gathering, shouting, "I'm healed! I'm healed!"

People from all over the outer court pressed in, and within a few moments he became the center of a tight throng, all straining inward with curious eyes and tilted ears. He rambled on about some disturbance and all the confusion and his toppled table and the livestock and the bull that plowed him over and crushed his leg and broke it so badly that he couldn't move and all the people were stampeding and . . .

Jesus withdrew and sat down under the shade of the portico. The same spot where the rabbis would always sit and teach. The same spot where He used to sit and listen to the sages and challenge them with deep spiritual questions. This time, though, He sat down as the teacher. Without a word or explanation, He simply sat, closed His eyes, and waited. The small group of followers who came in with Him pulled away from the crowd and joined Him in the shade behind the majestic columns. Their mouths hung open; their eyes stretched wide; their faces shone with wonder, excitement, and anticipation. With their gaze gripped by the Master, one by one they drew in close and sat down.

Zaben rested his hand on Jenli's shoulder and said, "Exciting afternoon. I now have work to do." He unfurled his wings, leapt over the balustrade, glided into the court, and made a graceful landing near the group of Zealots.

Lorr met him with a nervous smile and a shrug.

"I know," Zaben said. "I did not expect any of that. Although, now that I think about it, it's not that surprising. How did Simon and Judas react?"

"Intrigued. A little shocked—but intrigued."

"We need them to be more than intrigued," Zaben said with a smile. "It looks like they need a nudge."

Speaking to the whole group of Zealots, Zaben announced, "Finally, a man with authority! A man who is not afraid to stand up against the establishment. This is the kind of man who could finally bring deliverance to Israel." His words formed a blazing wildfire, floating in the air of the Middle Realm. They swept across the group of Zealots and crackled on the boundaries of their spirits.

Zaben bit his lower lip and waited.

Judas leaned near Simon's ear and said, "Who was that man?"

Simon answered, "I don't know. I thought I heard someone say his name is Jesus."

"Is he a prophet?"

"I don't know. He is certainly a man of action. And he acts as one with authority."

"You don't think he could be the Coming One?" Judas asked.

Simon said, "I don't know. Perhaps. Have you ever seen someone healed like that?"

"No. Have you ever seen a demon cast out of a man?"

"No. Where did Jesus go?" Simon said. "I lost him in the crowd."

Zaben interjected, "Look, He is over there now, under the portico with His disciples. You should go listen to Him."

"There," Judas said, pointing. "There, behind those columns. Seated in the place of the rabbis."

"Do you want to go listen to Him?"

"I do. It's hard to explain, but something is burning in my heart."

Simon nodded. "Something that says—finally a man we can get behind who will lead us to victory over Rome?"

"Exactly. Let's go."

Walking toward Jesus, Simon said to Judas, "My name is Simon."

"I am Judas. I would give anything to see the deliverance of Israel."

"Me too. I am anxious to hear what this man has to say. Maybe we are seeing the beginning of our prayers fulfilled."

The two walked away with a brisk and purposeful pace, their voices fading below the noise of the crowd.

Zaben said to Lorr, "Our appointments are met. The King will certainly speak to them. We will have two more of our generals in place before the day is finished."

"And, after this demonstration, the numbers of our army are sure to grow."

"Hmm," Zaben said. "Look at those temple officials watching Jesus."

Four officials in priestly robes stood off to the side, examining Jesus and the small crowd seated in front of Him. Two demons leaned over from behind and whispered noxious words into the air. Clouds of yellow smoke in the Middle Realm enveloped the officials, blinding their spiritual eyes and clouding their minds. The men stroked their beards and glared with judging eyebrows.

"Shall I run the enemy off?" Lorr asked.

Zaben bit his lip and paused. "No. Net yet. It is early. However, I foresee this being a challenge for us. We will need the support of the Jewish leaders eventually. Let's see how this week of Passover progresses."

Lorr said, "It has been exciting so far."

"Exciting. Yes. The Day of the Lord is so close I feel as though I can grasp it with my hand."

7

BORN AGAIN

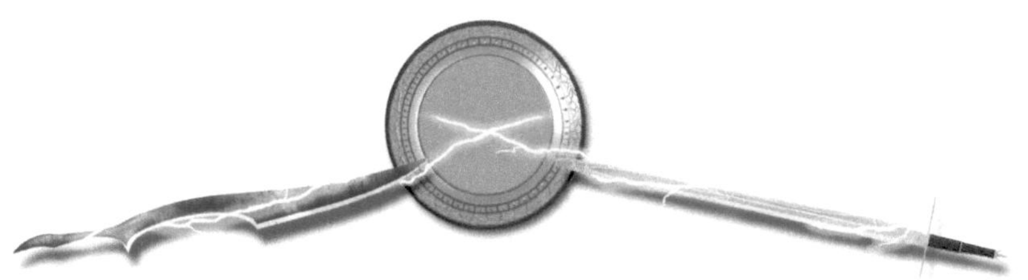

Battle minus 3 years

Elric and Jenli stood near the entrance of a weathered tent in the midst of the makeshift tent city on the outskirts of Jerusalem. The busyness of the day had slipped into the calm of night, but muffled conversations within the tents and around small campfires still vibrated throughout the encampment. Jesus' tent, large enough for eight men to gather, veiled the voices of the men whose shadows adorned the walls from within.

"Day five of the Passover festival," Elric said. He crossed his arms. "Eventful and unprecedented."

Jenli stroked the stubble on the back of his head. "Are you sure our timetable is correct? The campaign is progressing much faster than I expected. We came here with no more than twenty followers. Now, there are hundreds who are ready to join the ranks."

"Desperate hearts cling to a glimmer of hope," Elric said. "The people seek a deliverer."

"If we continue here, we will surely have numbers sufficient to challenge the enemy in a short time. It will be difficult to constrain them."

Elric shook his head. "I have word from Grigor, directly from the Throne—we still have a period of preparation. The generals are not all in place. And there is other work the Son of Man must accomplish."

"Then we cannot stay here in Jerusalem. The people will be ready to make Him king before the next moon."

"We'll finish the festival week. Then we are to return to Galilee after a brief time at the river Jordan. From there . . . " Elric turned his gaze down an aisle between the tents and raised his eyebrows. "Here comes Zaben. Who is that with him?"

An older man, gray bearded and dressed in priests' robes, stopped by a campfire and spoke to the men sitting around it. One of the men pointed toward Jesus' tent. Zaben stood by and then continued forward with the man.

"It looks like a rabbi—a priest from the temple," Elric said.

"I do not recognize him," Jenli said. "A Pharisee. Perhaps a member of the Sanhedrin. They have not been as receptive as the people. Were he not being led by Zaben, I would suspect malice in his approach."

Zaben reached Elric and Jenli ten paces ahead of the man. He wore a designing grin and a sparkle in his golden eyes.

"What is this?" Elric asked. "Where is your charge, Simon the Zealot?"

"Simon is asleep in his tent. I have ventured out on a side mission."

Elric raised his eyebrows.

The man reached Jesus' tent and inquired at the entrance.

"This is Nicodemus," Zaben said. "I have brought him to see the King, away from the influence of the other men and the enemy."

"Is he a threat?" Jenli asked, palming his sword. "Most of these leaders have not been—"

Zaben shook his head. "No. No. This is exactly why I have brought him. I have been watching these leaders all week. We need to win them back from the enemy. Nicodemus is one with an open heart. He could be our first inroad into their ranks."

Nicodemus disappeared into the tent. The shadows on the walls all stood up, shuffled around, and sat back down.

Elric smiled. "Once again, your keen eye for strategy leads us. This is wisdom and a worthy course."

"Can we go in and hear what the King has to say to him?" Zaben asked.

Elric motioned with his hand and followed Zaben and Jenli through the front wall of the tent. Elric shrank his frame as he entered but still ducked his head beneath the low ceiling. Inside, by the warm light of a single oil lamp, sat Jesus, James and John, Peter and Andrew . . . and Nicodemus. The pristine garb of the elder sage looked out of place among the simple, coarse linens of the other men. But his manner, his eyes, his voice carried no pretense.

"This is a man looking for truth," Elric said.

"Yes," Zaben replied. "As I said, I've been watching him all week. Unlike the others, he is ready to hear—"

"Shhh," Jenli whispered.

Elric picked up Nicodemus's sentence in mid-breath: " . . . that You have come from God as a teacher; for no one can do these signs that You do unless God is with him."

Jesus answered and said to him, "Truly, truly, I say to you, unless one is born again, he cannot see the kingdom of God."

Elric cocked his head.

Nicodemus sat up straight, glanced at the disciples, then back at Jesus. Nicodemus said to Him, "How can a man be born when he is old? He cannot enter a second time into his mother's womb and be born, can he?"

Jesus answered, "Truly, truly, I say to you, unless one is born of water and the Spirit, he cannot enter into the kingdom of God. That which is born of the flesh is flesh, and that which is born of the Spirit is spirit. Do not be amazed that I said to you, 'You must be born again.' The wind blows where it wishes and you hear the sound of it, but do not know where it comes from and where it is going; so is everyone who is born of the Spirit."

The four disciples looked at each other with puzzled eyes. Nicodemus stroked his beard.

Elric glanced at Zaben, who bit his lower lip, and Jenli, whose eyes darted back and forth between Jesus and Elric.

Nicodemus said to Him, "How can these things be?"

Jesus answered and said to him, "Are you the teacher of Israel and do not understand these things?"

Elric motioned with a head nod and stepped outside with Jenli and Zaben.

With a scrunched up face, Zaben whispered, "Born again. Here is a new saying."

Jenli looked to Elric. "Do *you* understand these things?"

Elric lifted his chin and set his gaze on the distant stars, searching for some ancient wisdom. "Body, soul, spirit. The nature of man is clearly understood. The body—mortal and corrupt. The soul—the venal bridge between the body and spirit, and arbiter of the will. And the spirit—dead, since the fall of Adam. These things we have understood and observed throughout the ages. But the King's words to Nicodemus speak of a rebirth of the spirit. This is a mystery. How is a man to bring about the resurrection of his own spirit?"

"Never has there been a living man with a reborn spirit," Zaben said. "Not even Moses or one of the prophets."

"Perhaps He speaks of the final resurrection," Jenli said. "The righteous dead are living spirits now."

"Still confined to Sheol," Elric said. "And they still await a glorified body. Jesus seems to be speaking of a reborn spirit—here, now, within these mortal bodies."

Zaben shook his head. "How can a man . . . "

Elric poked his head back into the tent, hoping to learn more.

Jesus' words entered the Middle Realm as flashing whirlwinds of energy. They filled the tent and radiated outward, forming an aura of light permeating every unseen recess of the Middle Realm: " . . . so loved the world, that He gave His only begotten Son, that whoever believes in Him shall not perish, but have eternal life. For God did not send the Son into the world to judge the world, but that the world might be saved through Him. He who believes in Him is not judged; he who does not believe has been judged already, because he has not believed in the name of the only begotten Son of God."

Elric pulled his head back from the tent and turned to Zaben and Jenli.

"Faith," Elric said. "Faith in Him."

"This is nothing new," Zaben said. "The King has always reckoned righteousness by faith. But that has never resulted in a reborn spirit."

"These are His words," Elric said. "It must be truth. Are we then to expect His followers' spirits to come back to life? Mortal bodies with living spirits? Can you imagine the power of an army alive to God? Led by the King Himself? They will crush the enemy and take back the dominion of earth. We are, indeed, at the threshold of the most astounding time in all history."

Zaben scrunched his face again. "But these disciples—they believe. They do not have reborn spirits, do they?"

"No," Jenli said with a flat tone. "Surely, we would see it."

"Then when shall this rebirth occur?" Zaben said. "What brings it to pass? There must be something missing. What are we missing?"

Elric nodded and crossed his arms. "There is something more. Something yet to be revealed. Always a shroud of mystery, this assignment."

* * *

The next morning, with the waning moon ready to set and the sun not nearly ready to rise, Jesus slipped out of His tent, pulled His cloak over His head, and headed out into the still darkness. Elric—with Timrok and his team—deployed. Alone, like a shadow hidden amongst the shadows, Jesus weaved through the tent encampment and toward the eastern side of Jerusalem.

Elric leapt to the top of the eastern wall and drew his sword half a handbreadth from its sheath. The blade flashed once. From down below, by the brook Kidron, a single flash of light returned.

Good. Xarjim is in place and has his man prepared.

Jesus passed out the Valley Gate and followed the trail down to the Kidron. Just before He reached the brook, a timid voice called out from just downstream.

"Rabbi? Master Jesus?"

Jesus stopped and turned.

Elric stepped up to Xarjim, his eyes scanning the entire area.

"Captain," Xarjim said.

"Good work," Elric said, still scanning.

"Yes?" Jesus answered.

"I . . . " the voice started. "I was hoping to see you . . . without all the crowds. And I noticed you always come out here early."

Jesus lowered His hood and stepped toward the shadowed voice. "What is it you desire?"

The shadow lowered his hood, revealing a young man. Even in the darkness, his smooth, hairless face made it clear he could be no more than seventeen. "I am James, the son of Alphaeus. I have been . . . I mean we . . . my brother Joses and I . . . we have seen you every day in the temple during the festival. We have heard your teachings and seen some amazing things. And we were wondering—"

Jesus said, "Joses, come out from behind the bush. Do not fear."

A boy even younger than James emerged from behind a bush and shuffled up just behind James's shoulder, never raising his eyes from the ground.

Jesus smiled at him and looked back to James.

With forced determination, James blurted out, "We want to follow you."

Jesus took a breath and cocked His head to the side. "I'm sorry, but I go to a solitary place in the garden to pray. You can see me in the temple later." He reached for his hood and started to turn.

"No, Master," James said. "We want to follow you after the festival. Become your disciples."

Jesus let his hood down and turned back.

"I know we are young," James continued. "But we are old enough to know true life when we see it, and we are ready to—"

Jesus held up His hand. "Let not any man despise you for your youth. The simple faith of the young pleases the Father. Of course, you may follow me." He paused. "But what of your mother, Mary? Who is to care for her?"

"You see?" James exclaimed to Joses while shaking his arm. "Who else but a prophet would know all about us? He knows Abba is gone. He knows Ima's name. He has to be . . . " He stopped short and turned back to Jesus with a sheepish grin. "I'm sorry, Master. Our mother knows we are here and wants to follow you, also."

Jesus smiled, pulled His hood up over His head, placed His hand on James's shoulder, and said, "And so you shall."

Elric waited until Jesus crossed over the brook. He put his hand on Xarjim's shoulder and gave a complimentary nod.

Xarjim returned a slight head bow and said, "Always in His service."

8

WATER WAYS

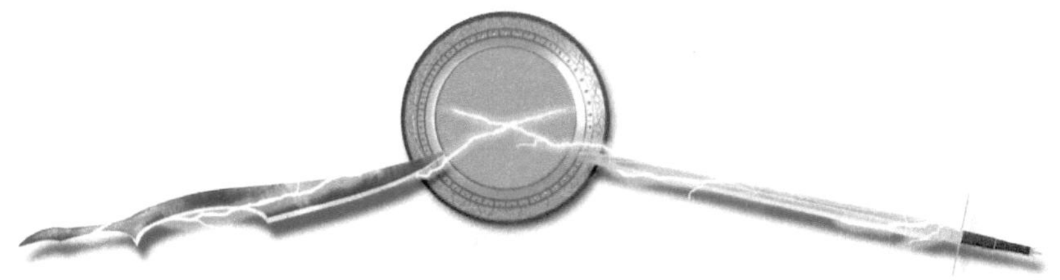

Battle minus 3 years

"This is a good location for the prophet, John, to work," Elric said to Lacidar, gazing out over the wide Jordan River valley.

From the north, the thick shrubs, trees, and undergrowth along the banks of the Jordan opened up into a flat grassy basin where the river spread out into calm, lazy currents on its way to the Dead Sea. Coves formed from river eddies with sandy beach approaches made for easy access to the water.

On the west side of the river, a sizable tent village covered the basin. Hundreds of men and women milled about the encampment, with wisps of campfires meandering upward, young children darting in and out of the aisles and main lanes, and beasts of burden tied to trees and clumped in makeshift pens.

A well-worn path led southwest to the nearby town of Aenon, and dozens of travelers greeted each other in passing before disappearing behind the trees just past a gentle bend of the trail to the right. Some coming, some going—all drawn to the prophet in the wilderness by an unexplainable stirring in their innermost being.

The prophet—hairy, unkempt, and wrapped with power and passion—stood at the riverside, gesturing with his hands, pointing here and there, and preaching to a crowd of several hundred men. Even from a distance, his booming voice rose over the burble of the river and drone of the tent village.

"Yes," Lacidar replied. "The move from Bethany beyond the Jordan a month ago was a good one. Being a full two days' journey from Jerusalem has reduced the amount of entanglement from the religious leaders. Most of the people who come out here seek truth and reconciliation."

Elric crossed his arms. "I see the entanglement with the enemy remains persistent."

Throughout the tent encampment, unknown to the men in the Physical Realm, skirmishes between elzurim and beaelzurim in close quarters filled the Middle Realm with non-stop turmoil. Sparks, clanging steel, flashes of light, tufts of sulfur clouds, and war shouts dotted the entire camp. At the river's edge, the battle raged with fierce heat. Every word John spoke shot outward like arrows of flaming light toward the men gathered around. The demons darted about like angry flies, blocking words, deflecting shafts of light, and clouding men's eyes with jets of smoke.

Elric focused on the front-line fight. The bolts of light firing from John's mouth in rapid succession carried seeds of life enough to reach every man. To the man near the front on the left, a demon slashed past an angelic contender and deflected the seed away in a splintered cloud of sparkling residue, floating down to the ground. Other seeds of light reached the man just behind and absorbed into his spirit. A demon lunged toward the man to the right with his sword outstretched. An angel snagged the dark warrior's wing and slung him back over the crowd of men. The seed of light reached its mark but only half-penetrated the man's outer shell. Another demon slinked in from behind and carved the seed away with a single slice of his curved dagger. A small group of men near the back dressed in priestly robes had thick layers of dark armor covering their spirits. A single beaelzurim stood by them, smirking with sword sheathed. The seeds of lights reached the men, but they deflected off the men's strongholds, and the demon blew them away with a simple puff of yellow smoke.

"Yes," Lacidar said. "They are relentless. But they can't stop *every* word from John. And this prophet is equally relentless. The Kingdom advances every day at his hand."

Elric nodded and smiled.

"The nights are the hardest," Lacidar said. "During the day, the enemy is too busy contending with John's words. At night, though, when the people are alone with their own thoughts . . . "

Elric nodded and grimaced. "It is the same in our camp. Jesus reached the Jordan last week. He is teaching His disciples and the followers who joined Him from Jerusalem. His disciples are baptizing many. The enemy is fighting hard to steal the word, but they are too afraid to get too close to the King. Nighttime, away from His presence, is when they are most active."

John finished his discourse, and the crowd dispersed—some individuals returning to the tents, some gathering into smaller groups, some approaching John. Elric spotted Emms standing near one of the side groups.

"Is that Emms with Jude Thaddaeus, one of our future generals?" Elric asked.

"Yes," Lacidar replied. "Jude has been a devoted disciple of John. He was not ready to leave John and follow Jesus when we collected Philip, but Emms has been preparing him."

"Let's check on his status," Elric said.

Elric and Lacidar unfurled their wings and glided down to the riverside. Tucking their wings away, they joined Emms at the outer perimeter of a group of six of John's disciples, including Jude, deep in discussion with another man.

"Why would he say that?" one of John's disciples said to the man. "Ceremonial washing of bowls and implements is one of the sacred traditions that distinguishes us from the unclean nations."

The man shrugged. "I was there, in the temple. I heard it. I sat and listened to his teachings all week. He claims it is not what enters a man's body that makes him unclean, but the unrighteous things that proceed from his heart that defile him."

"These sound like the words of a man who seeks to bring down our whole system, not the one who will lead us to victory over our pagan oppressors."

"He speaks with great authority. And He performs miraculous signs. Many are turning to Him."

"It's true," Jude said to the others. "He and His followers have come also to the Jordan. They are about half a day's journey south of here. Everyone is going out to Him and being baptized."

The other disciples of John quizzed each other with their eyes, but none had any answers.

The man from Jerusalem said, "Your own master, John, seems to believe He is the Coming One."

"We should talk to him."

The seven men marched over to John.

Elric, Lacidar, and Emms strode behind, each wearing a knowing grin.

One of John's disciples approached John. "Rabbi, that man who was with you on the other side of the Jordan—the one you testified about—look, he is baptizing, and everyone is going to him."

John replied, "A person can receive only what is given them from heaven. You yourselves can testify that I said, 'I am not the Messiah but am sent ahead of him.' The bride belongs to the bridegroom. The friend who attends the bridegroom waits and listens for him, and is full of joy when he hears the bridegroom's voice. That joy is mine, and it is now complete. He must become greater; I must become less."

Other nearby pockets of John's disciples stopped talking and turned toward John. The air became quiet, with only the rippling of the water to disturb the moment.

John spoke up louder for the whole area. "The one who comes from above is above all; the one who is from the earth belongs to the earth, and speaks as one from the earth. The one who comes from heaven is above all. He testifies to what he has seen and heard, but no one accepts his testimony. Whoever has accepted it has certified that God is truthful. For the one whom God has sent speaks the words of God, for God gives the Spirit without limit. The Father loves the Son and has placed everything in his hands. Whoever believes in the Son has eternal life, but whoever rejects the Son will not see life, for God's wrath remains on them."

Jude stepped up closer and spoke in a low voice. "Master, if this is so, are you going to give up your ministry and go follow Him?"

John smiled. "I have received only one word—prepare the way for Him. Until I hear another, I must continue on my current path."

"But what about us?" Jude pressed. "Are we to leave you and follow Him? You carry the very words of God, and our hearts know it."

John locked arms with Jude and pulled him in close. "When you speak with a friend, do you talk to him face to face, or do you talk to his shadow?" John turned and waded into the river. Lifting his arm high, he called out, "Come! Those who are ready . . . come and be baptized. Prepare your hearts for the coming King."

Jude backed away and joined a dozen other stunned-looking disciples.

Emms placed his hands on Jude's shoulders, spread his wings around half of the circle of men, bent down to ear level, and spoke. "Now is the time. John has released you. Go and find Jesus. Devote yourselves to Him as you have to John." His words spread outward like a calming blanket of light, full of peace and determination. They sank deep into the spirits of the whole group.

Jude closed his eyes and took a deep breath. He lifted his chin and nodded to himself.

Elric stepped up beside Emms and said, "Good work here today. This general will be in the Lord's camp before the week is done." He turned to Lacidar. "Continue your watch over John. His part in the Kingdom is not yet complete. The King will return to Galilee shortly, but John is to remain here for now. I have not received word, but I suspect there will come a time when . . . " Elric's eyes fixed on something beyond Lacidar. Something on the other side of the river.

Lacidar glanced over his shoulder, then back at Elric. "What, Captain? What is it?"

"There . . . on the eastern side of the river. Up on that knoll. That looks like four beaelzur captains."

Without looking that direction, Lacidar answered, "Yes, sir. Officers from Molech's court. Their presence has been growing more evident every day. They bring spies from Herod Antipas to catch John in a chargeable offense."

Elric crossed his arms and scowled. "We will do battle over John before this is finished."

Lacidar released a deep breath. "It appears to be unavoidable."

* * *

Out on the Sea of Galilee, the gentle lapping of the waves against the wooden hull and the rustle of the mild breeze in the sails should have been soothing balm to the soul, but to Daniel they chafed his raw brain like the endless, irksome grating of the sand on his skin when he was a boy working his father's sheep—but worse. The pleasant calmness that brought peace and satisfaction to everyone else on the boat only mocked Daniel's pain.

The warm glow of the lantern hanging from the mast should have shone like a beacon of life and vitality in the midst of the night waters, but to Daniel it provided a glaring spotlight on the superficial shallowness of life. True reality lay beneath the surface of the deep.

The darkness. The cold. The despair that had no bottom, no matter how deep you sank. In the flickering light, dozens of straight raised scars on his forearms stood out for the world to see. He pulled his sleeves down over his wrists.

The flopping of the knee-deep layer of fish in the open hold of the boat should have sounded like the fulfilling reward of a good night's work, but to Daniel it sounded like the slap of utter futility. You live. You die. Your brother beside you dies. What's the point?

Some of the other crewmen talked and laughed in the predawn darkness. Daniel sat alone near the bow. The sky was clear, but Daniel's mind floated along in a thick fog.

Ahead, the lights of a shore town became recognizable.

Capernaum. Good. We don't come here enough.

For the first time all night, something to look forward to. Get the fish unloaded. Get a large flask of wine. Go sit by the synagogue where the voice of Levi tended to be quietest. Maybe get some real sleep.

* * *

Late afternoon. From the top of Mount Gerizim in Samaria, Elric stared north at Mount Ebal and drifted back to the days of Joshua. He could still smell the smoke rising from the conquered city of Ai. And right over there, on Mount Ebal, Joshua built the altar of uncut stones. And just below, on the slopes of Gerizim, half of the Israelites faced the other half on the slopes of Ebal to confirm their covenant with the Lord. Thousands and thousands of voices thundered "amen" as the list of blessings and curses were called out. Blessings from Gerizim. Curses from Ebal. For the people, it seemed like such a day of commitment and solidarity. With the miracle at the

Jordan and the victories at Jericho and Ai, the people's hearts soared with every shout of "amen."

But for Elric, each affirmation tied his insides in knots. Even now, the remembrance made him grimace. These people would never keep all the requirements of the law. They couldn't. Their spirits had no life in them. With every "amen," they confirmed the curses that would consume them to this day. And though it brought the King no joy, He was bound by the words of the covenant, all of them. And the enemy—Elric gritted his teeth—the enemy had all the legal rights to exploit every failing.

All the pain, all the suffering, heartache, and despair; all the blood and violence; all the sickness, poverty, and strife of the generations echoed out between the two hills. Mount Ebal became blurry through the tears welling up in Elric's eyes. He dabbed his eyes with the palm of his hand. It wasn't supposed to be this way. Man was supposed to enjoy fellowship with the King. He was supposed to live under the King's blessings and walk in the fullness of His joy.

"One day," Elric whispered to himself. "One day the King will set all things aright."

Born again. Jesus' words to Nicodemus rumbled through Elric's brain. *Is it possible? What would it take for a person's spirit to come back to life—in this life? How do you get past the curses of the law? The King can bestow mercy on any He chooses, but how can He still satisfy the letter of the law? And how can any of this happen with the enemy still in authority? Perhaps after Jesus marshals His army and defeats the enemy, He will—*

Timrok alighted beside Elric. His wings tucked away. "Captain," he said, looking at Elric's eyes for just a moment and turning toward Mount Ebal.

Elric wiped his eyes again with a casual swipe and raised his chin. "Timrok." He glanced down toward the eastern part of the valley where Jacob's well stood as a central hub. "I see much of the town of Sychar has come out to see Jesus."

"Yes, sir. The woman who met Him at the well earlier ran back to town and compelled them."

"The woman . . . a Samaritan?"

"Yes, sir."

"What did they talk about? Did you hear?"

"Religious tradition—where to worship, Jerusalem or here at Gerizim. He told her things about her life that convinced her that He is a prophet."

"Mmm hmm."

"Oh, and He offered her water to drink. Water that would become a spring of water welling up from within to eternal life."

"What?" Elric's distance gaze turned to Timrok with a sharp focus. "Water springing up from within?"

"That's what He said."

"Water . . . water . . . obviously a picture of the Holy Spirit."

"Yes."

"But . . . springing up from within. This is something new. Never before has the Spirit been able to reside within a man. All the great men of old—Moses, David, the prophets, the judges—they were anointed for works of power or to deliver His word. But that was the Spirit resting *upon* them. Not living *in* them."

"Because He can't. Not in their fallen state."

"The King is working something new. Something we do not yet know."

Timrok ruffed his thick beard with his burly hand. "I do long to look into these things."

"We shall know them. Line upon line." Elric gazed back out over the valley and took a deep breath.

Timrok pointed toward the crowd of people around Jacob's well and said, "Strange, isn't it?"

"Strange?"

"Strange that so many from a Samaritan town should come out to see Him. If it had been up to His disciples, they would have traveled the extra days to reach the highway by the sea and avoid Samaria altogether. But He insisted on passing directly through. And now, He is turning the hearts of an entire town."

"He is not bound by the traditions and biases of men," Elric replied. He looked past Mount Ebal toward Galilee farther north. "The strange thing is this terrible divide between Israel and Samaria. It is the work of the enemy. This ground—it is at the center of the Promised Land. But the enemy has filled hearts with pride, religion, and hatred—so much so that the land is divided. And these two peoples with the same father Abraham are now enemies."

"It is a sound strategic move to gain a foothold in Samaria," Timrok said. "When it comes time for battle, it will be good to have allies."

Elric shook his head. "No. The King has never needed alliances. He is not after their swords. He seeks to win their hearts."

"Truly, He is doing that. They are urging Him to stay with them. It appears He intends to stay, at least for the night."

"Good," Elric said. He spotted the tents of Jesus' followers from Jerusalem and around the Jordan going up in a makeshift camp. "I suspect we may be here for a couple of days before we continue on to Galilee. We will travel west of Mount Gilboa and pass through Nain, Japha, Nazareth, and Cana before turning back east to Capernaum."

"Yes, Captain. I will inform the others and deploy my team for a night perimeter."

9

PROPHET IN HIS OWN TOWN

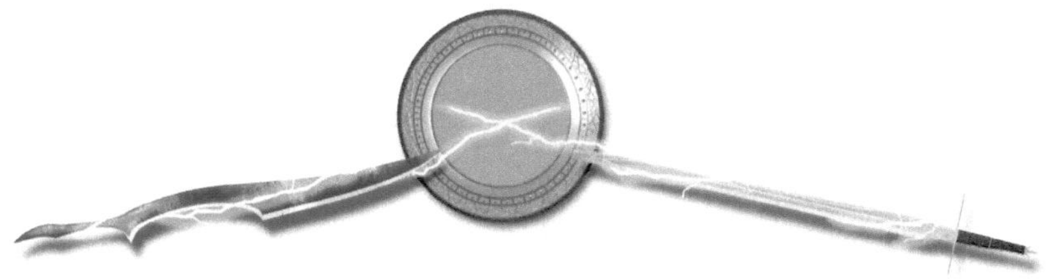

Battle minus 2.5 years

Elric stood on the brow of the cliffs at Nazareth and gazed off over the lands below. He said to Zaben standing beside him, "This is where Luchek drove the horse off the cliff and forced Joseph to sell his home." He shook his head. "Those were difficult days."

"With every mission we have to adapt to the countermoves of the enemy," Zaben said.

They stared out with distant eyes.

"Of course," Elric said, "you had your own difficulties in Egypt in those days."

Zaben bit his lip. "All part of the plan."

Elric crossed his arms. "Luchek . . . I knew him as Luminir. He was in my choir. It makes my heart ache."

Zaben nodded. "I have contended with many I knew from the Ministry of Prophetic Administration before the Rebellion. It is never easy."

Jenli flew up from behind and landed without a sound. "Captain, the King is entering the synagogue now."

"Good."

"And, sir, there is enemy presence in the synagogue. They have attached themselves to a number of the people, and they did not flee when the King entered. Shall we drive them out?"

Elric turned to Zaben.

Zaben bit his lip and said, "It may prove instructive to see their intentions."

"Agreed. This is the first time they have dared to get this close. Let's go."

Elric unfolded his wings and shot toward the synagogue with Zaben and Jenli close behind. The three landed at the front entrance and drew their swords. A small crowd of people clustered near the doorway, straining inward. Timrok stepped up to Elric.

"Sir," Timrok reported, "a beaelzur captain, two lieutenants, and six warriors. Can I—"

Elric held up his hand. "Not yet. Follow me."

Elric stepped through the crowd and the front wall, flanked by Timrok, Zaben, and Jenli. Inside, people filled the room shoulder to shoulder. Up front, in the seats of honor, Yadid, Shalev, and Raziel sat with their regal priestly robes. Half a dozen scribes occupied other seats of distinction. The chief priest, Zeev, stood before the bimah table, reading a prescribed passage from a scroll. Jesus, surrounded by no more than eight of His disciples, sat near the back.

In the Middle Realm, the demon captain huddled behind Zeev, whispering noxious words. The words floated like yellow vapor around Zeev and disappeared into his spirit. Hiding behind Yadid and Shalev, the two beaelzur lieutenants sank their claws into the unsuspecting rabbis. The other six beaelzurim clung close to the scribes and elders. A regional elzur warrior stood over Raziel with his wings forming a canopy of white over him. Every one of the demons released a steady barrage of poisonous words into the Middle Realm. Every one kept a terrified set of evil red eyes fixed on the Son of Man. The arrival of Elric and three elzur lieutenants caught only a passing glance from the demon captain.

Timrok's team stood ready with swords drawn. Like a mountain avalanche on the edge of release, Prestus, Chase, Nalyd, and Micah each occupied a corner of the room. Kylek held the position a short sword's length from Jesus. Jenli, Timrok and Zaben fanned out to the sides of Elric. The resolute eyes of all the angelic warriors elevated the tension in the Middle Realm, and every spirit remained motionless. A single twitch could unleash a barrage of violence.

Elric eyed the demon captain. *What is your play here? What is your intent?*

All the traditional elements of the service continued in the Physical Realm like a passing fog. Elric's focus stayed locked on the enemy. *A direct attack on the King? With so few? Are there hordes waiting at a distance? Waiting for a cue? Will we receive the flame of vengeance? Will the King Himself speak a word and vanquish them? Does He even see them? Does He—*

Jesus stood.

Every eye in the Middle Realm followed His every move. He approached the bimah table. An attendant stepped forward and leaned in close. Jesus whispered something to him, and the attendant nodded. A moment later, the attendant returned with a large book, which he placed on the table. Jesus thanked him with a smile and a nod.

"The book of Isaiah," Jesus announced to the assembly.

Jesus flipped through the parchment pages of the book. He stopped and smiled with His finger on a page and a twinkle in His eye.

He read from the book with a clear voice, solid and authoritative. "'The Spirit of the Lord is upon me, because He anointed me to preach the gospel to the poor. He has sent me to proclaim release to the captives, and recovery of sight to the blind, to set free those who are oppressed, to proclaim the favorable year of the Lord.'"

He closed the book, gave it back to the attendant, and sat down.

Every eye in the synagogue fixed on Him—every eye in the Physical Realm, every eye in the Middle Realm. No one made a sound.

He said, "Today this Scripture has been fulfilled in your hearing."

A collective gasp emptied the air in the room.

"He just claimed to be the Messiah!" the demon captain roared. His words blanketed the humans with flames. "It's blasphemy!"

A murmur spread throughout the people. They all turned to each other and whispered.

"What did he just say?"

"How can this be?"

"Is this not Joseph's son?"

"The Messiah doesn't come out of Nazareth, does He?"

The other demons echoed the captain's words, and the energy wound into little tornadoes of fire spinning in the Middle Realm over each of the men of influence.

The rabbis all crossed their arms and scowled. The scribes shifted in their seats and stroked their gray beards.

Jesus glanced at Raziel, who returned a half-hidden smile.

Over the buzz, Jesus spoke out, "Truly I say to you, no prophet is welcome in his hometown. But I say to you in truth, there were many widows in Israel in the days of Elijah, when the sky was shut up for three years and six months, when a great famine came over all the land; and yet Elijah was sent to none of them, but only to Zarephath, in the land of Sidon, to a woman who was a widow. And there were many lepers in Israel in the time of Elisha the prophet; and none of them was cleansed, but only Naaman the Syrian."

"It is an outrage!" the demon captain called out. "This man is a blasphemer and a deceiver! Will the Messiah not come to the people of Israel?"

"Blasphemer!" the other demons echoed.

"He must be killed!" the demon captain shouted.

"Kill Him! Kill Him!" the other demons chanted.

Their fiery words sizzled in the Middle Realm, energized dozens of tornadoes, and filled the air with thick sulfurous smoke.

Zeev, Yadid, and Shalev jumped to their feet with shock and indignation emblazoned across their faces.

"Who do you think you are?" Zeev shouted with a pointed finger.

"Blasphemer!" the demons railed.

"Enough!" Elric commanded. "Drive these traitors out!"

Elric leapt toward the beaelzur captain with his sword high above his head. The floating composite elements of his blade swept through the air like tongues of fire with the glowing blue energy in the gaps whirring. At the last moment, the blade elements sprang together into a powerful wedge and crashed down onto the demon captain's waiting sword. Sparks exploded at the collision. The demon faltered to one knee under the weight of Elric's blow. Elric followed with a wide horizontal arc directed at the demon's neck.

The demon captain bounded upward, deflected Elric's blade with a sideways parry, unfolded his wings, and shouted, "Retreat!"

The demon captain disappeared through the roof in a blur of blackness. Other black streaks shot upward.

Elric glanced around to assess the damage done in the Physical Realm. In less than a heartbeat, a hailstorm of plasma fireballs pounded through the ceiling toward the humans. The fiery darts contained words of destruction: "Kill Him," "Blasphemer," "Destroy the liar."

Elric blocked two of the blasts with his shield, but the deluge smothered the rest of the room.

"Finish them!" Elric shouted.

Timrok yanked the bindings tight over the mouth of a demon who still had yellow smoke gushing from a chest wound. Timrok kicked him over and launched upward using the fallen beaelzur's face as a springboard. He sliced through four fireballs with his two blades on his way through the ceiling. Jenli, Zaben, and Timrok's team followed.

The barrage stopped in a moment, but the air in the Middle Realm had already coalesced into a giant cyclone of flames and smoke driving through the spirits of the men. Hundreds of smaller tornadoes peeled off the main vortex. Red lightning flashed. Elric squinted and braced against the torrent.

The men in the room shook their fists and shouted at Jesus. Four large temple guards seized Jesus by the arms and shoulders and pushed Him toward the door. Zeev, Yadid, Shalev, and the scribes pressed close behind, shouting, pointing, and shaking their fists.

Raziel and Jesus' disciples yelled over the mayhem, "Stop this!"

"We should listen to Him!"

"Let's hear all He has to say!"

The enraged mob shoved them aside and charged toward Jesus in a feverish stampede. They pushed Him outside and drove Him toward the city gate.

"Stop!" Elric shouted toward the crowd. "Peace! Be still! Release Him!" His words formed powerful balls of plasma, but the fiery cyclone above the mob devoured the light like insignificant leaves in a gale. Only tiny shards of light in the Middle Realm reached some of the men's spirits. None of it penetrated.

The angelic team regrouped with Elric in the air above the stampede.

"Keep trying to reach them," Elric called out. "And make sure the enemy does not return."

A hailstorm of light from the team rained down on the mob.

A maelstrom of fire and smoke swallowed the bolts of light.

None of the team's words penetrated the men's shells of darkness.

Driven by the fire of the demon's words, the men pushed Jesus out the city gate toward the cliffs. With fists clenched, they threw dirt in the air and shouted.

"Away with him!"

"Kill him!"

"Purge Israel of all liars!"

"Throw this blasphemer off the cliff," Zeev shouted over the din.

"Off the cliff!" echoed the scribes.

With the irrational assembly pushing from behind, the strongmen muscled Jesus forward toward the cliffs.

Elric looked at the closing span between the wave of men and the edge of the cliffs. He grimaced at the cyclone of fire engulfing the mob. *We cannot stop this!*

A single slap of his wings and he plunged downward toward the cliff edge. He landed and turned toward the mob. With his sword stretched out level with the ground, he commanded, "Blindness to the King." A horizontal blue disc of light exploded outward and expanded like a circular wave in a pool of water. It swept across the crowd, who continued pushing forward.

The strongmen lost their grips and stumbled. Turning in frantic circles, they yelled, "Where did he go?" "Where is he?"

Jesus, free from their clutches, spun around and walked away from the cliff toward the city gate against the flow of the mob. The people jostled around Him, oblivious to His presence, still pressing forward.

"He's gone," reverberated through the crowd.

"He was just here."

"Where did he go?"

"He disappeared."

He passed through their midst and continued walking at a composed pace without looking back. Timrok marched in front of

Him. Jenli marched behind. Timrok's team formed tight flanks with swords drawn.

Zaben landed beside Elric and sheathed his sword. "The Woodorian Slip. I haven't seen that maneuver for a while."

Elric smiled. "Extreme, but effective."

The crowd slowed to a stop and milled about in disarray. The officials combed through the mass with exasperated gestures and shouts of "Where is he?"

Jesus passed through the city gate.

Elric said to Zaben, "Keep Him hidden in the camp until tomorrow morning. We will leave Nazareth tomorrow. Send some disciples to collect Mary. It will be safer for her to begin traveling with us."

* * *

Elric and the four lieutenants gathered in the corner of Mary's house while the disciples James and John helped Mary pack by the light of olive oil lamps.

"The events of this afternoon were most disturbing," Elric said.

"The people . . . " Jenli said, "They couldn't hear a word from us."

Timrok ran his hand through his wild, bushy hair and shook his head. "Even after we dispatched the enemy, the crowd continued under the enemy's control."

"Mob blindness," Elric said. "Not an uncommon tool of the enemy. With the right environment in the Middle Realm, it only takes a few people to entrap the entire group. Once it starts, they become lost to our leading and all rational thought."

Elric crossed his arms and clenched his jaw. The four lieutenants' gazes dropped to the ground.

From a back room, John's voice cut into the weight of the moment. "No, Mary, only pack what you really need. We'll be traveling and living out of tents. You don't want to carry anything that may become a burden."

Elric smiled.

"Actually," Zaben announced, "this is exactly the event we needed to see."

Elric raised his chin, and the other lieutenants turned their attention to Zaben.

"The enemy has revealed his intent," Zaben continued. "Until now, the King has been primarily reaching the common people. He brings healing to their bodies and hope to their souls. They have been almost uniformly receptive. It is difficult for the enemy to counter this, especially when they fear coming too close to Him." Zaben paused. "But . . . there was one place where we saw resistance."

"In the temple during Passover," Jenli said. "The religious leaders."

Zaben nodded. "The enemy recognized this and has built his strategy around it. Today was their first test battle—control the chief priests and scribes; fill the air with religious division; and use the elders to lead the people into mob blindness."

"It was very effective," Jenli said.

"But now we know their strategy," Zaben said with a glint in his eyes.

"We must devise a counterstrategy of our own," Elric said. "Another event like today is unacceptable."

Timrok rested his hands on his sword handles. "We go on the offensive. We drive the enemy away from the religious leaders and win them for ourselves."

"A major effort," Elric said with a pensive head shake. "It would take many more warriors than we have, and these men will not be easily won. The strongholds of religious tradition and pride are firmly entrenched."

"True," Zaben said. "But I agree with Timrok that we need to focus on the religious leaders. Only . . . " Zaben bit his lower lip and raised his eyebrows. "We shall be more subtle in our approach. Allow the enemy to think his plan is proceeding according to his intent."

Elric crossed his hands behind his back and let slip a smug grin. "And now, from the one who brought us the Esther-Mordecai-Haman campaign . . . " He gestured with his hand for Zaben to continue.

Zaben smiled and gave a single head nod. "We need not win all the leaders, only a select few. Those who are already seeking truth."

"Raziel, here in Nazareth," Jenli said.

"And Nicodemus in Jerusalem," Zaben answered. "They are out there. I believe the King has reserved a remnant and has already been speaking to them. We need only identify them and secure them. The enemy will continue to strengthen their hold on the chief leaders. The Son of Man will continue to gain support of the people. The enemy will feel threatened by the leaders who are loyal to the King and will seek opportunity to remove them—perhaps expel them from the synagogues, perhaps something more severe. Whatever the edict, there will come a time when the enemy will make a significant move."

Zaben paused. Elric gazed into Zaben's calculating eyes and waited.

"But," Zaben continued, "we will be waiting with thousands of supporters who will rise up and rebel against the religious leaders—not against Rome—against the religious establishment."

Elric nodded. *I can see where this is going.*

Zaben continued, "The Roman governors, fearing riots and desiring to keep the peace, will step in, remove the chief elders, and our select men will take their place. This leaves us with unified control over the Sanhedrin and support of all the people."

Jenli picked up the plan. "Who will promote our twelve generals into strategic positions and rally for a new King."

Timrok finished. "Who will lead His army to topple Rome and establish His kingdom in Jerusalem."

Elric chuckled. "Using Rome to set up the conditions that will lead to their own fall—it does have a Haman-like irony. I like it. It is a good plan. We begin immediately. All who are currently assigned to the twelve generals will divide their efforts. Continue to see to their safety and appointed connections but move ahead in our travels and search out leaders who can be reached. Isolate them from the enemy and bring them to the King. Lacidar, your team stays with the prophet John. Timrok, your team stays close to the Son of Man."

Zaben, Jenli, and Lacidar nodded.

Timrok stroked his beard and scowled. "This is fine for a long-term strategy, but how do we prevent a repeat of today's events?"

Elric crossed his arms and stared straight ahead. "We control the atmosphere. Do not allow the enemy to gather near groups of leaders. Do not allow them to speak to the crowd. Drive them off. Keep them quiet. We cannot prevent them from speaking to the leaders they own, but we will force them to do their work behind closed doors—away from the people."

Mary, James, and John shuffled out the front door with arms full of baskets and bags. The room in the Physical Realm fell dark and quiet.

"We move at first light tomorrow," Elric said. "Send scouts forward to Cana."

"In His service."

10

EVIDENCE OF THINGS NOT SEEN

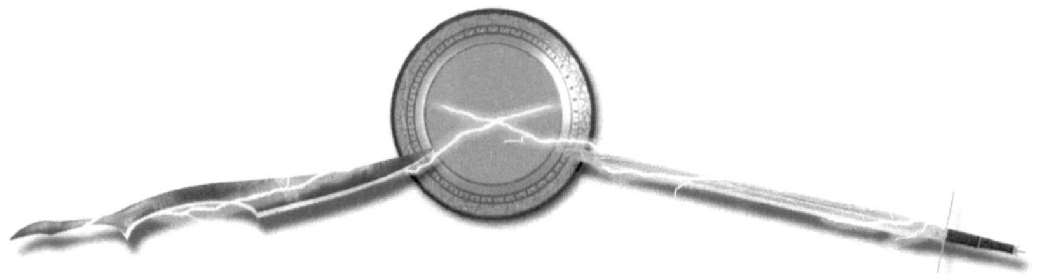

Battle minus 2.5 years

Elric landed on the bow of the boat and took in a deep breath of the cool lake air of Galilee. His wings folded away.

"Captain," Jenli called out, making his way to the front. "Welcome aboard." He motioned with his hand at the human crew. "It's hard to keep a fisherman off the water."

"Indeed."

"How are things at the camp?" Jenli asked.

"Quiet. For now. The Son of Man is sleeping. The disciples are all sleeping—except, of course, these four. The crowd of followers is settled in for the night. We are anticipating the arrival of a large number of people from all around the region tomorrow. Word about His healing of the royal officer's son in Cana has spread like wildfire.

And many of these people saw the signs He worked in the temple during the Passover. Everyone wants to see Him and hear Him."

"Well," Jenli said, "the two sons of Jonah and the two sons of Zebedee shall bring in a catch to help feed those who come."

Elric smiled at the men working on the boat that swayed beneath his feet. Peter manned the tiller, and Andrew and four hired crewmen prepared the nets. Brondor walked beside the boat, just beyond the wake. His sword remained sheathed, but his eyes sparkled with vigilant light. Another boat glided along the same course an arrow's shot away. Onboard that boat, James and John, their father Zebedee, and three other hired hands made ready for a night of fishing. Near the center mast, Christov and Carothim stood by their charges, James and John.

"I never tire of seeing the word of the King produce its effect," Jenli said, pointing at the nets. "His promises work their way into the Physical Realm in so many different forms, but to me, nothing compares to these nets."

In the Physical Realm, at Elric's feet lay a pile of weathered, wet, and utilitarian netting—brown and tan braided cord interlaced to form a standard gap mesh for fishing. The men worked together and spread them out flat. In the Middle Realm, the mesh shimmered with a soothing, cool light and hummed at frequency too low for ears. Thin filaments of energy wound around every cord, and tiny pulses of light shot up and down the strands. Constant motion, perpetual power. At every intersection of the mesh, colliding pulses of light shot tiny sparks knee high into the air. A mass of utilitarian netting—empowered by a promise of the King.

Elric nodded. "The Lord will command a blessing on everything you put your hand to." His words floated down over the nets, and the network of filaments surged with extra energy. The pulses moved faster and glower brighter. The sparks shot higher. The whole heap of netting coursed with energy.

Jenli laughed. "Ha ha! Over a thousand years, and the word is as active as the day He spoke it. The fish, of course, can't see it. But they are drawn to it. The men do the physical work. The King causes the increase. It's one of my favorite things to watch."

With the sun well below the horizon and the shoreline disappearing into the darkness behind them, Peter called out, "This looks good. Let's start here."

Andrew and another crewman dropped the mainsail, and the boat drifted to a stop.

"Any chance we're going to catch anything tonight?" one of the crewmembers grunted, reaching for his side of the net.

"Probably not," answered one of the others.

Andrew hoisted his side of the net and said with a strained voice, "No moon tonight. We all know what that means."

The men's words coalesced over the nets into a black storm cloud in the Middle Realm. Tiny black droplets fell from the cloud like a fine mist of tar, smothering the nets. The filaments of light grew weak and slow. The shimmer of energy waned to a dim glow.

Elric shook his head.

"On three," Andrew said. "One, two, three."

Splash. The net sank into the deep. Even through the darkness of the water, Elric could still see the faint glow of the nets.

Splash. A net from the other boat hit the water.

The men waited. Peter lit an oil lamp and hung it from the mast. A light appeared on the other boat, casting a warm glow over the crew and a serene reflection off the surface of the water.

"I don't know what it is about nights with no moon," Andrew said. "The catch is always small."

His words floated out over the water and rained tiny black droplets which sank like stones into the water over the net. Deep below, the faint glow from the net became fainter, barely visible now.

More waiting.

"What do you think of this Jesus of Nazareth?" Andrew asked Peter.

"There is something about Him," Peter said. "He commands healing, and people are healed. With a single word, He casts out demons. I've never seen anything like it. But more than that, every time He speaks my heart burns within me."

Andrew nodded.

"I don't know how to describe it," Peter continued. "There is life, truth, excitement, expectancy. I must admit, I don't understand half of what He is saying. The depth is beyond me."

"His eyes," Andrew said. "I feel like He sees right into my soul."

"There *is* something about Him," Peter said. He stood up. "Let's pull this net in and see what we have."

The six men lined up from bow to stern, reached out, and grabbed a handful of netting. Together they hoisted up and in. Up and in. Water splashed, netting scraped against the wooden hull, and the men grunted with each pull. The last section of net pulled into the boat with one final heave. There on the floor of the hull lay a heap of netting. And two small fish.

Peter untangled one from the net, held it in his hand, and shook his head. No larger than the palm of his hand, the fish flopped and squirmed. Peter tossed it back into the water. He freed the second fish and threw it overboard. "Raise the sail. Let's move to a different spot."

With the water splashing against the bow again, the men went to work spreading out the nets. The energy of the King's word had all but vanished from the nets. Natural, wet cords replaced the filaments of light. Empty space between the mesh replaced the luster of promise.

"And this is one of the most frustrating things to watch," Jenli said to Elric. "Promises of the King being made of none effect by the unbelief of men. How can they not see the power they release, especially in their words?"

Elric scowled. "They can't. It's not possible. They can only relate to the natural world."

"I know," Jenli said. "Still . . . "

"Okay," Peter called out from the stern. "Let's try here."

The boat glided to a stop. *Splash.* Men waited. The allotted time passed. Dark, empty nets piled back into the boat.

They moved to a different spot on the lake. The men pulled up empty nets.

They moved again. They dumped lifeless nets back into the dark water. Peter stretched side to side with his hands on his lower back and let out an exasperated groan. He slumped down onto a wooden plank seat.

"I don't understand it," Peter sighed.

"It's really not a surprise," Andrew said. "The catch is always small on a moonless night."

"But the Master told us to come out tonight and bring in enough to feed a large crowd tomorrow. Why doesn't God provide? We're doing what He told us to do."

"I don't know."

Elric and Jenli stood near the mast with their arms crossed.

"Do you ever wish you could exercise faith for them?" Jenli said.

"All the time," Elric answered. "It's hard enough to watch the King's promises nullified. But they almost always impugn the King's honor as a result. This is most difficult."

Peter rose. The other men stood. They pulled in empty nets. They raised the sail and moved to another spot.

And another. And another.

Finally, with the night spent and spirits low, both boats retreated back to shore.

* * *

The morning sun shone on Elric and Jenli's backs, but their giant frames cast no shadow on the shore beside the Sea of Galilee. Elric positioned himself on the other side of Peter's beached boat while Jesus taught at the water's edge. On the hill leading down to the water, hundreds of people gathered, and more arrived every minute. Timrok's team patrolled throughout the crowd. Zaben stood guard at the highest vantage.

With a determined gait, Timrok passed through the mass of people pressing in. He wore a scowl and had a palm on each of his swords. His brisk march ended beside Elric, and he snapped back around, facing the crowd. "I don't like it," Timrok said, eyeing the people.

"Oh, I do," Elric replied with a smile. "The word is good. The King is touching many. Just look at the power of His word piercing through and changing hearts. Satan's kingdom suffers loss at every word."

"But the people," Timrok grunted, "They are crowding in from every direction. And the King is backed up to the shoreline. There is no escape route should the enemy mount an attack."

"The enemy is keeping their distance. The King's presence is too much for them. And these people . . . " He scanned across all the faces. "They are all hungry for truth and life. It is not the King who needs an escape route."

Timrok released a "hmph" and continued examining the crowd.

Jenli gave Elric a smile and folded his hands behind his back.

"There!" Timrok said, pointing into the crowd. "Tenth row back. On the left. None of the King's words are penetrating his strongholds. His eyes have no light at all. And he wears a dagger on his belt."

Jenli pulled his ledger from his tunic and flipped through the pages. He stopped on a page, his finger pointing to an entry. "Marcus. Of Cana. A farmer. Not possessed."

"He doesn't need to be possessed to be a puppet of the enemy," Timrok said. "He is a threat, and we are hemmed in." He drew one of his swords halfway.

"One man," Elric replied. "Just have one of your team . . . "

Kylek stepped through the crowd and stood between the man and Jesus. He drew his sword and stuck the tip of his sword into the ground. Facing the man, with his hands resting on the handle of his sword, Kylek locked eyes and became still as a rock.

Elric laughed. "It seems your team has already spotted him."

Timrok pushed his sword back into its sheath. "They are well trained."

Elric smiled and rested his hand on Timrok's shoulder.

Jesus stopped speaking. Elric, Timrok, and Jenli turned toward Him.

"Peter," Jesus called out. "Peter, come here."

Peter scampered over from the pile of nets.

"Peter, the crowd grows large, and it is becoming difficult for the people to hear. I would like to use your boat."

"Yes, Master. Of course."

Jesus got into the boat with Simon Peter, and Andrew pushed them away from the shore. With the water up to his waist, Andrew gave one final shove with his legs and pulled himself up into the boat. Peter steered the boat out a little from shore and dropped the anchor. Jesus sat down.

The people filled in the open space all the way up to the water's edge, and Jesus continued to teach.

Timrok clapped his hands together once and announced, "Well, that should do it."

Elric and Jenli laughed. Elric said, "The King is driven by love for these people, but He is no stranger to tactics."

Three hours passed, and Jesus finished His lessons. He told the people to remain nearby while He acquired a load of fish. He said to Simon, "Put out into the deep water and let down your nets for a catch."

Simon answered, "Master, we worked hard all night and caught nothing, but I will do as You say and let down the nets."

On the beach, Elric unfolded his wings, expanded them upward, and launched toward the boat. His feet landed on the bow and his wings tucked away just as Andrew finished raising the sail. A mild breeze filled the sail, and the boat slipped through the pleasant waters. Jenli landed near the mast. He motioned to Elric and pointed at the nets.

The nets coursed with energy in the Middle Realm. Every strand of the mesh pulsed with light shooting up and down the length of the filaments. Sparks shot outward at each intersection. It looked exactly as it had at the beginning of the night before. Alive with promise.

Elric nodded and smiled.

With the wind blowing in his hair, Peter said, "Master, I don't understand. We went out last night at your word. Why didn't the Lord provide?"

Jesus paused a moment and said, "The kingdom of God is like . . . a landowner who has entrusted a fertile plot to his servant. He gave his servant seeds for all kinds of crops and went about his business. If the servant does not plant the seeds and tend the garden, is it the fault of the landowner if the servant does not reap a harvest?"

Peter's eyes darted left and right. He looked down into the hull of the boat. He brushed the hair out of his face and gazed out over the water. Finally, he said, "But we did work. We worked hard all night."

Jesus smiled. "You tilled the soil. But you did not plant the seed."

Peter's face scrunched up. He glanced over at Andrew who answered with a perplexed shrug.

"The word of God is the seed," Jesus continued. "It will always produce a crop when allowed to germinate and grow. But it is spirit. You must lay hold of it and bring it into the natural."

"But, Master, how?"

"Do you not know?"

Peter gazed out over the water for a long minute. He turned back toward Jesus. "Faith?"

Jesus nodded. "Faith is confidence in what we hope for and assurance about what we do not see. It brings substance to that which already exists in the spirit." He turned to Andrew. "Drop the sail."

The boat drifted to a stop.

"Is there a promise for provision that you know?" Jesus asked.

Peter and Andrew stared at each other with blank expressions.

"Does it not say in the book of the law that the Lord will make you abound in prosperity?"

Peter and Andrew nodded.

The words of promise hung above the nets in a layer of perpetual shimmering sparks.

"Do you believe this?" Jesus asked.

Andrew shrugged. Peter stuttered, "Well, yes, I suppose, but—"

Jesus stood up. "Is the word of God true, or is it not?"

"It is," Peter said.

"Then believe it. Exercise your faith. Take the promise which is spirit and bring it to pass."

Peter and Andrew looked back and forth at each other while the energy of Jesus' words soaked into their spirits. A spark lit in Peter's eyes. He stood up. "I do believe," he said. "God will provide according to His word."

Andrew stood. "God will provide."

Their words coalesced in the Middle Realm with the words of the promise and exploded into lightning bolts which shot downward into the nets. The nets shimmered and pulsed. The speed of the lights racing through the filaments quadrupled. The sparks whizzed clear out of the boat. The vibrations of the humming energy pounded against Elric's chest.

Jenli shouted, "Ha ha! Yes! Yes!"

"Let down the nets," Jesus said.

Splash.

Elric smiled at the ball of fire spreading out in the depths. "This is going to be good," he said.

After a short wait, Peter said, "Let's pull them in."

Peter, Andrew, and Jesus lined up and gave a heave. Up and in. Up and in. The first three pulls were not a problem for the short crew. The fourth pull stopped them cold. They put their backs into it and hoisted together.

"Aghrrah!" Peter expelled with a massive pull. "What is . . . aghrrah . . . this? . . . aghrrah . . . I've never . . . aghrrah . . . seen a load . . . aghrrah . . . this heavy . . . aghrrah."

"Peter!" Andrew shouted with a strained voice. "The net! It can't handle the weight! It's starting to break!"

"We need help!" Peter exhaled through gritted teeth. "Hold the nets. Hold the nets."

Turning back toward shore, Peter flailed his arms and jumped up and down.

Elric pulled his sword. Holding it at a diagonal angle, a glinting light flashed once. A beacon from shore flashed back.

After a few moments, James and John waved back from the beach. Peter waved and thrashed. After another few moments, the Zebedee boat with a full crew launched. Its sail billowed full.

"They're coming," Peter said, grabbing a fist full of net and leaning back. "Help is coming."

"Brondor!" Elric called out.

In an instant, Brondor appeared from behind.

"Secure the net," Elric said.

Brondor stood on the water above the net and spoke the word "strength" into one hand and "resilience" into the other. Two large balls of plasma energy appeared, one in each hand. He smashed them together. The energy exploded into a huge shining blue blanket, which he directed downward into the water. It reached the depths below the net with Brondor grasping the four corners above the water. He gathered the corners together and cinched them tight as though securing the contents of a large bag.

Minutes later, the other boat arrived.

"What's the problem?" James called out across the closing gap.

"The catch is too big," Peter answered. "We can't pull it in. And the net is breaking."

Zebedee steered the boat up beside Peter's boat. With grappling hooks, the crew of six pulled upward on the net from the opposite side.

"Good! Good!" Peter shouted. "Be careful with the net!"

The net held together. It neared the surface, and the first wave of the catch heaved up and into Peter's boat. Fifty large fish flopped around the feet of Peter, Andrew, and Jesus.

"Good!" shouted Peter. "Again! One, two, three . . . aghrrah!"

Fish filled the hull up to their knees.

"One, two, three . . . aghrrah!"

The level of fish rose above their thighs. With the boat riding low from the weight, water splashed in over the sides.

"Peter!" Andrew shouted. "The boat will sink if we take on any more!"

"Pull the catch your way," Peter shouted to the other boat. "We're full!"

The nets heaved up into Zebedee's boat. Up and in. Up and in.

"We can't take any more," John yelled. "We're starting to sink!"

"Hold on!" Peter called back. He looked at the last of the fish in the net. He turned to Andrew and said, "One more pull, and we'll have the full catch."

"We dare not," Andrew answered.

"It will be fine," Peter said. To the other boat, he yelled, "We'll take this last haul. You head back to shore!" To Andrew and Jesus, Peter said, "On three. Here we go . . . "

"Peter!" Andrew shouted. "We'll sink!"

Peter looked at the water coming in over the sides. He paused. He groaned. "Maybe you're right." Gathering the netting from his end, Peter fumbled forward toward Jesus through the mass of fish. He shoved his clump of netting toward Jesus and said, "Master, grab here. Lock your arms around here and brace yourself." He reached for the netting by Andrew. Pulling it tight and straining back, he brought it within Jesus' reach. "And take this here. Do you have it?"

Peter waded to the mast and rose the sail. "We're going to drag the remainder of the catch back to shore in the net." He grabbed a wooden bucket and tossed it to Andrew. "You bail!"

The boat cut through the water and turned toward the shore. "Master," Peter called out from the tiller. "If the strain becomes too much, call for help."

Jesus nodded.

Jenli jumped over and took hold of the net just in front of Jesus.

Brondor walked beside, still holding the net together.

Elric spoke the word "float" into his hand and held it against the hull. The wooden hull took on a thin coat of light and raised four inches in the water.

Andrew bailed.

Within minutes, both boats reached the shore. Groups of men rushed out and pulled the boats up onto the beach. A group pulled in the net dragging behind. The crews of both boats pushed through the fish and jumped over the sides.

On the shore, Jesus told the men, "Unload the catch and give them to the people to eat."

Peter, Andrew, James, and John, along with the rest of the crew, gathered around Jesus—wet, still breathing hard, and eyes wide. Peter dropped to his knees and said, "Go away from me, Lord; for I am a sinful man!"

Jesus raised him up and answered, "Do not fear, from now on you will be catching men."

11

KINGDOM AUTHORITY

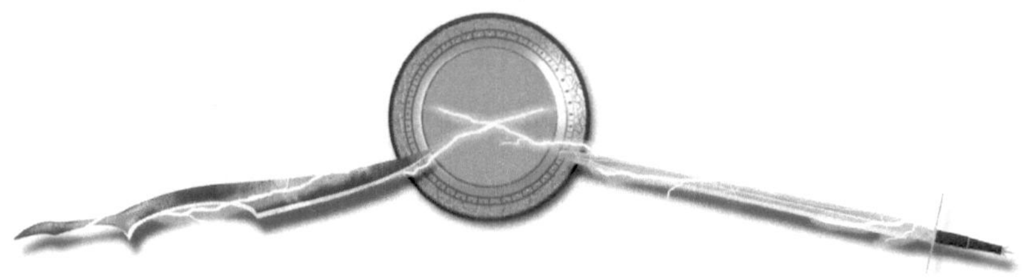

Battle minus 2.5 years

Sabbath day. *What difference does it make?* Daniel slumped against the back of the synagogue at Capernaum with a full flask of wine and slid down to the smooth limestone pavement. His eyelids drooped down, and the flask tipped up. He swallowed hard and long. *All the miserable days are the same. At least today we're in Capernaum, and maybe I can get some rest.* For whatever reason, this is where Levi seemed the most quiet. With the night's catch unloaded, enough wine to numb the senses, and the shade of the northeastern side of the tall limestone edifice of futility, Daniel could disconnect enough to actually sleep.

"We should go," Vorsogh whispered in Daniel's right ear.

"Go to sleep, Levi," Daniel grumbled. He took another long drink. "I am."

Fear percolated up from the inner darkness and prickled his skin. He pulled his sleeves down and crossed arms, but the fear grew and set him on edge. He glanced outward at the people passing by—not at their faces, just the moving feet. More people than usual. *Of course, it is a Sabbath.* They just passed by without giving him any notice.

"We need to go now," Vorsogh demanded.

"What are you afraid of, Levi?" Daniel whispered. "These people are nothing." He pulled the hood of his cloak over his head and buried his face. "Go to sleep."

Even with the quickening pace of the drum beat pounding fear inside his chest, the black fog settled in over his brain and he drifted off into darkness.

A place of nothingness—no light, no feeling, no time.

"Aughh!" Daniel screamed in the sudden awakening of consciousness.

"Quiet!" insisted the voice in his right ear.

Terror paralyzed his every frayed nerve. Opening his eyes felt like prying open solid iron doors. In his face—the foundation corner of some building. He craned his neck around from the rigid fetal position he found himself. The back side of the synagogue. *That's right, we're in Capernaum.*

He stretched out his legs, but they recoiled like a startled snake back to the fetal position.

"Stay still!" demanded the voice.

Fear, deeper than any emotion he had ever known, gripped his bones. Stronger than the pain, stronger than the despair, stronger than the hatred—panic raged through his whole being. His body began to shake.

He rolled over onto his back, quivering like a scolded dog.

"Stop moving," growled the voice. "We must not be seen!"

With every drop of strength he could summon, Daniel forced himself to a sitting position. "Levi, what are you so afraid of?"

"We must not be seen! Quickly, we must go. We must go now!"

Still shaking, Daniel clawed up the wall to his feet. Everything in his flesh wanted to run—to escape the unknown mortal danger somehow connected with the synagogue. Instead, he stumbled to the corner of the building. With terror pounding in his throat, he peeked around the corner.

A sizable crowd spilled around the southwestern corner of the building from the steps leading up to the entrance porch. Even from this distance, the whispers in the crowd floated to his hiding spot.

"I've never heard anyone like him."

"He's not like the other rabbis."

"He teaches as one with authority."

"Who is he?"

"Jesus. Jesus of Nazareth."

Daniel ducked back around the corner, panic screaming from within.

"We must go!" Levi urged. "Quickly, before He comes out!"

"Jesus," Daniel mused. "I knew a Jesus in Nazareth when I was a boy. The son of Joseph and Mary. I wonder—"

"Now," Levi said. "Escape quickly while we can."

"Escape? He's not dangerous." He snuck another peek around the corner. "It would be interesting to see him."

"No! We must not!"

"I'm going to go look. Just to see what he looks like." Daniel took a step.

"I will not permit it," Levi growled.

Daniel shuddered and clutched the wall. He took another step. The familiar fog of darkness descended into his brain.

"No!" Daniel barked. "Let go of me!"

The fog lifted—just enough. Daniel blinked and shook off a little more fog. He trudged forward, shaking, twitching, and fighting the flood of terror. With every labored step, the resistance grew. With every increase in opposition, his defiance against Levi mounted.

"I don't know what it is you fear," Daniel muttered through gritted teeth, "but I am going to see who this man is."

He approached the edge of the milling crowd. One by one, the people saw him and backed away with mortified expressions. He didn't care. The only thing that mattered was doing the one thing Levi would have him *not* do.

He reached the porch steps, stark white and insurmountable. Stopping to catch his breath, he gaped at the top step and shuddered. He turned toward the people around him. A man with wide eyes put his arm around his wife's shoulder and pulled away. A small boy hid behind the legs of his mother. The buffer zone around him grew.

He grunted and turned back to the steps. He couldn't control the shaking, but with clenched teeth he forced one foot up the first step. Then the next.

At the top of the steps, he braced his shoulder against the front wall and fought for his breath. The world seemed to be spinning. The black fog tore through his brain like a tornado. Every nerve in his body burned. Any moment now, he would surely explode in a blazing inferno.

A commotion to the left. People emerged from the front entrance and spread out onto the limestone-paved porch. And then . . . Jesus.

Daniel leapt forward. As though watching himself from a distance, his body contorted like a cornered wild animal. Shaking and writhing, he screamed, "Let us alone! What business do we have with each other, Jesus of Nazareth? Have You come to destroy us? I know who You are—the Holy One of God!" His voice, low and guttural, echoed across the porch with an inhuman rasp. Daniel put his hand on his throat and gasped at the sound that just came out of his mouth.

The crowd around Jesus parted, leaving Him with a direct line of sight with Daniel. Daniel's heart pounded.

Jesus turned without a startle and said, "Be quiet and come out of him!"

In an instant, Daniel found himself convulsing on the pavement. The black fog crushed his consciousness within two hammering heartbeats.

And then, darkness.

* * *

Vorsogh emerged from Daniel's body, thrashing and shrieking. Timrok waited for him from behind, flanked by Prestus and Chase in front.

"Take him." Elric commanded.

Prestus and Chase raised the tips of their swords against Vorsogh's neck and stretched his chin up high. Vorsogh started to extend his wings, but Timrok seized them with his hands. Pulling the leathery bat wings together in the center of Vorsogh's back, Timrok clamped them in place with one hand and produced a bundle of pulsing cords in the other. With a single flick, the cords of light wrapped around the writhing demon, cinched tight, and immobilized him neck to foot.

"You have no right!" Vorsogh squealed. "This man is mine! You can't send me to the abyss for this! He invited me to—"

Elric signaled for Timrok to cut off the tirade, and in an instant, a band of gleaming light covered Vorsogh's mouth. Timrok pulled the band tight until it set in hard against Vorsogh's back teeth. He yanked one notch tighter.

Elric stepped forward with his hands folded behind his back. He moved in face to face. Elric's emerald eyes twinkled with living light. Vorsogh's eyes, sunken deep within their boney sockets, quivered with pale red panic.

"The earth is the *Lord's*," Elric said with a cool, controlled tone. "And the Son of Man is come to take back that which was lost. The kingdom of God is at hand. Your days are numbered."

Elric took one step back and turned his eyes toward Timrok. "Remove this traitor from the presence of the King. Take him far from here."

"In His service." Timrok hoisted Vorsogh by the cords in the center of his back, unfolded his wings, and shot up through the porch overhang.

* * *

Daniel opened his eyes to a sea of amazed faces looking down at him, flat on his back.

"Look," someone said. "He's opening his eyes."

"I think he's all right," someone else said.

Light flooded in from everywhere. Daniel squinted. The brightness of the day seemed somehow . . . brighter, cleaner, sharper. He took a deep breath. The air almost felt sweet within his lungs. It filled his head with an expanse of clarity. No fog. No hatred. No anger. A little confusion—*What just happened? What's going on?*

A single face emerged amid the mix of faces. A young man. Maybe thirty. Short beard and brown hair. Eyes that could pierce his very soul. A bright smile. An extended hand.

Daniel reached up for the hand, and Jesus pulled him to his feet.

"What is happening to me?" Daniel asked.

Jesus took Daniel's hands and turned them palm side up. He gently passed His thumbs over the raised scar lines on Daniel's forearms. "The enemy has held you in bondage for many years. Your father in heaven knows your pain. Today, the power of God has delivered you. Be free and walk in the light."

Jesus turned and crossed the porch toward the steps. The crowd followed with whispers buzzing about.

"What is this? A new teaching with authority! He commands even the unclean spirits, and they obey Him."

"He must be some kind of prophet."

"From Nazareth?"

The voices tailed off with the crowd, and Daniel found himself alone on the porch. He sat at the top of the steps and looked out over the city below. Just beyond the buildings lay the Sea of Galilee, shimmering in the sunlight. Birds sang their songs. Such a beautiful day.

He sat by himself. Alone. He turned each way and found only the deserted porch entrance to the synagogue. Strange how quickly the crowd left. Amazing how lonely alone is.

"Levi? Levi, are you there?" he whispered.

He already knew the answer.

Now what?

12

FIRST MINISTRY TOUR

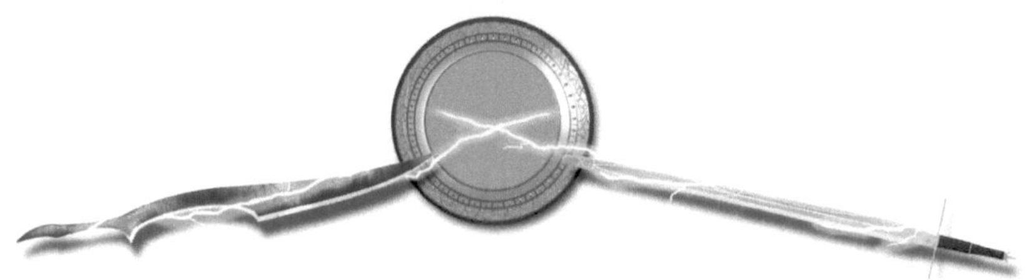

Battle minus 2.5 years

Elric, Zaben, and Jenli gathered on the roof of Peter's house, overlooking the open courtyard in the center. The busy Sabbath had become calm, and evening brought a welcome quiet. The crowd that followed Jesus from the synagogue had dispersed—some to their homes, some to the tent village by the lake at the edge of town. In the courtyard below, Jesus sat in a chair near the unlit firepit with six young children. The youngest sat in His lap. The oldest draped against His shoulder under His right arm. The others sat on the ground with captivated faces. Peter, Andrew, James, and John clustered near the doorway to the main living area, watching Jesus with the children. Philip and Bartholomew watched from across the courtyard just below Elric. Half a dozen women moved throughout, tending to things.

Philip's voice, though low, floated up to the angels gathered on the roof through the calm evening air. "It's just the story of the first Passover," he said, "which these children have heard many times."

"Why does it sound so different when He tells it?" Bartholomew said.

"I don't know. It's almost like He was there. It's more than a story."

Lacidar alighted on the roof behind Elric, Zaben, and Jenli. The three turned and smiled.

"Good," Elric said, "We are all here. We should move inside."

Elric flashed his blade eastward. A single flash answered from a rooftop down the street.

Elric, Zaben, Jenli, and Lacidar dropped through the roof into a large, open room. The room, well suited for large gatherings, sat unoccupied except for some storage crates stacked against one wall. Elric brought up the war map, which filled the room with light and energy in the Middle Realm.

Timrok emerged through the side wall.

Elric nodded to Jenli, who pulled his ledger from his cloak and thumbed through the pages.

Jenli read aloud, "Possessed man at the synagogue delivered, boy healed of palsy, Peter's mother-in-law healed of fever, three others healed of fevers, man healed of tooth abscess, and a woman healed of chronic cough. It was a good day. The people are responding to the word. Reports of His works are spreading quickly, and the people are filled with expectation."

"Lacidar," Elric said, "Report from the Jordan?"

Lacidar answered, "The prophet, John, continues to preach with power. The Kingdom advances every day."

Gazing into the war map, Elric said, "Enemy pressure to silence John continues to build."

"Yes," Lacidar said, "but short of a full-scale campaign within the house of Herod Antipas, I see no way to stop it."

"We do not have the resources to break that stronghold," Elric said, rubbing his chin. "And I have received no orders for a change of course for John. Maintain your operations. Stay vigilant."

"Yes, sir,"

With a flash, like silent lightning, Grigor appeared in the room through the ceiling. Elric and the four lieutenants blinked and turned toward the sleek logirhi.

"A word of the Lord," Grigor announced. "The Son of Man is to complete a circuit through the towns in the region of Galilee and make known the Kingdom. He will begin this trip after Sabbath next."

"In His service," Elric said.

"By His word." Grigor lifted his wings and disappeared.

Elric stared at the war map with his hands folded behind his back. The four lieutenants joined him with pensive eyes and pursed lips.

Zaben broke the silence. "Galilee? If we had stayed in Jerusalem another month, we would surely have garnered enough support to raise a sizable army. Instead, we travel about in a land of obscurity."

"Good," Timrok said, palming his sword handles. "Give me ten shepherds or fishermen with the power of the Spirit over an army of a thousand trained soldiers who rely on their own swords."

"It should be no surprise," Elric said. "The King's heart is always toward the poor, downtrodden, and marginalized. And remember His word to Isaiah the prophet, 'the land of Zebulun and the land of Naphtali, by the way of the sea, on the other side of Jordan, Galilee of the Gentiles. The people who walk in darkness will see a great light. Those who live in a dark land, the light will shine on them.' This is where we are supposed to be."

"You are right, of course," Zaben replied. "Sometimes my zeal for the mission . . . "

Elric put his hand on Zaben's shoulder. "Kindle the zeal, remember His word. The day we look toward is coming. He will bring it to pass as we execute His will on earth."

"In His service," Zaben said.

"In His service," the other lieutenants echoed.

* * *

Elric waited beneath a giant oak outside Sepphoris and watched the sun rise. To his right, Jesus—barely visible from this vantage—knelt alone atop a nearby peak. Timrok and his team—conspicuously visible—held defensive positions halfway up the hill. Continuous streams of light gleamed upward and rained downward on the mountain in the Middle Realm—a spectacular display that had become the normal morning routine over the last month of traveling throughout the villages of Galilee.

Peter, James, and John sat on large rocks at the base of the hill near the footpath leading up.

Straight ahead—the gates to the city of Sepphoris. Tomorrow, Jesus would go into the synagogue there and teach on the Sabbath as usual. The last four meetings in synagogues resulted in skirmishes with the enemy. Tomorrow, Elric's team would almost certainly see battle again.

To the left, the temporary tent encampment of followers still slept. Soon, hundreds of people would be up and looking for the Son of Man.

Zaben and Jenli approached from the direction of Sepphoris, flying low and silent. They landed in front of Elric without a sound. Their wings tucked away.

Zaben spoke in a low voice. "Captain, our scouts found among the men here no leaders who can be easily reached for the Kingdom."

Jenli flipped through his ledger and said, "All the priests and elders are in the hands of the enemy. Every one has strongholds too thick to penetrate. It is even worse than the last city."

Elric crossed his arms and let out a long breath. "We shall see. The Spirit can break through, even where we cannot. Once they see His mighty works and hear the truth, we may still win some. Certainly, the people will receive His word."

Zaben shrugged his shoulders. "I hope you are right. Sepphoris is the city where Judas the Zealot and his army were defeated by the Romans. These people are wary and full of fear. They will not be quick to join a cause."

"The King is not yet rallying an army," Elric replied. "He is bringing life and healing to the broken and hurting. Man always needs this. The people will respond."

With the sun now in full array, the camp stirred. Within an hour, a crowd of a hundred people gathered and milled about the outer edge of the camp, looking for Jesus. Someone spotted Him on top of the hill, and the crowd moved toward the base. Peter, James, and John held them back at the path entrance. More people gathered. Men, women, children. Old and young. The crowd grew to two hundred. Three hundred. The closest followers—thirty men, including the rest of the inner circle of twelve—pried their way to the front and helped Peter, James, and John.

"Look at this," Elric said to Zaben and Jenli. "Faith is strong. Expectation is high."

In the Middle Realm, the atmosphere above and around the people sparkled and glowed. The energy from the people's faith stretched out like a magnet, bending all the light inward toward their spirits and bodies.

"Even they can sense it," Jenli said. "You can see it in their eyes."

The crowd became silent. They pressed forward, craning in toward the mountain path.

Jesus appeared on the path and stopped next to Peter, James, and John.

A wave of whispers swept across the crowd, followed by a hush. No one moved.

Suddenly, a woman carrying a small child burst through the front rows of the crowd and cried out, "Master, my daughter is very sick with a high fever. Would you heal her?"

Jesus smiled and answered, "Bring her here to me. Do not fear. Only believe."

He placed His hand on the girl's forehead, and a shimmering blue cloud of energy surrounded her in the Middle Realm.

"I do believe," the mother said.

At the mother's word, the cloud of energy plunged into the girl's spirit and disappeared into her flesh.

The little girl's eyes brightened. The pallor of her face turned flush. With an energetic twist, she squirmed out of her mother's arms and landed on her bare little feet. The mother bent down, wrapped her hands around the girl's head with her palms on the girl's cheeks, and pressed her lips against the girl's forehead.

"The fever's gone," the mother breathed. She stood and shouted, "The fever is gone! My daughter is healed!" She hopped up and down and spun around to the crowd. "She's healed! She's healed!"

She turned back to Jesus and said, "Thank you, Master, thank you!"

Jesus smiled and said, "Your faith has made your daughter well. Go in peace." To the crowd, He announced, "Prepare your heart. The kingdom of God is at hand."

The crowd erupted. People laughed and hugged and pointed and grabbed hands and slapped shoulders. Many jostled forward, worming their way to the front. The thirty close followers formed a barrier line and held the people back while those along the front line waved frantic arms and called out for attention. Jesus motioned for Peter, who took another woman with a child by the hand and led her up to Jesus.

Elric crossed his arms and said, "The people are desperate for a deliverer."

"Yes," Zaben said, "but will that translate into the will to fight when the time comes?"

"We shall see."

Shouts from the front rose above the crowd noise. "My son is healed! He did it! Praise God! He did it!"

A collective gasp seized the crowd, and the people hugged and slapped shoulders.

An hour of miracles passed while Elric, Zaben, and Jenli observed from the under the oak tree. Healing power from the Throne—active and radiating from the Spirit of the Son of Man. A word spoken by the Son of Man—blazing with energy into the Middle Realm. That word in the Middle Realm—pulled into the recipient's spirit by an act of faith. The flesh in the Physical Realm—responding to the spirit. Healing. Every time. And every time a person was set free from some physical bondage or affliction of the enemy, Timrok spun and danced atop a large boulder near the King. The rest of his team remained as stoic as possible for the sake of appearances, but even they let a little celebration slip with each victory.

Timrok just finished a piece of fancy footwork when Elric nudged Zaben and pointed toward the back of the crowd. "Not everyone is excited to see the Kingdom advancing," he said.

Three scribes from town huddled a stone's throw distance from the back of the crowd. All three wore disapproving scowls and crossed arms. Behind them, a small demon hunkered low. Never raising his eyes toward the light at the front of the crowd, he wrapped his long, bony talons around the scribes' shoulders, shielded his own face with a black, leathery wing, and raised up just enough to whisper words into the air. His words swirled around the scribes' heads like thick tornado clouds of sulfur. The energy absorbed into the scribes' spirits, their dark strongholds acting like thirsty sponges.

Two rabbis held positions just outside the city gates. Two beaelzurim sheltered behind them and fed their spirits with poisonous lies.

Zaben shook his head and replied, "Yes, I see. Still, they keep their distance."

"They are becoming more bold," Elric said.

"They can't stop this," Jenli said, gesturing with his hand toward the blazing light enveloping the crowd. "And tomorrow, in the synagogue, we will be careful to clear out the enemy before the King arrives. We will not have a repeat of Nazareth, even though they—"

"Unclean!" rang out from the crowd of people. To the left, the people at the back of the crowd parted, backing away and clearing an open path.

A single man hobbled forward. His bare feet dragged across the dirt—feet covered with red and white lesions. Two disfigured stubs bulged out on his left foot where two toes should have been. He forced his right foot forward, revealing a missing toe on that foot. Mottled red skin with flakey white scabs scarred his neck, extended up the side of his face, and swallowed half his ear. Off balance, he flailed one arm with fingers contorted and misshapen. The other arm stayed pinned to his side.

A small vile demon back-stepped two paces ahead of the man and spewed a barrage of noxious poison from between his jagged teeth. "Stop! Go back home! Now! This Man cannot help you! The things you hear of Him are all lies. You can't be here. You are unclean. You are unworthy. Look at the way the crowd is looking at you. You only add shame to your pain. It is not lawful for you to come amongst the people."

The words shot through the Middle Realm like flaming meteors, pummeling the man with every strained breath. He flailed his arm again, and then again.

The crowd opened a wider path. "Unclean!" echoed across the people. "A leper! Unclean!"

"He won't help you," the demon continued. "It is unlawful for Him to touch you. He probably won't even allow you to come near. You're not worthy. Your own sins have caused this, and God wants you to suffer. Go home. Turn around now and—"

Flash! Like a lightning strike, Prestus hit the ground one step ahead of the demon. His sword swung around in a blur of light. The demon's sword met his. *Crash!* Sparks exploded through the air of the Middle Realm. Two efficient parries and Prestus ran the demon through. With yellow sulfurous smoke still streaming from the demon's chest and back, Prestus bound him head to foot with cords of light, toppled him to the ground, and put his foot on the demon's neck. He glanced up toward Elric.

Elric nodded once and called out, "Take him far from here. His lies have no place here."

Prestus grabbed the bindings at the demon's back, unfurled his wings, and disappeared over the horizon.

The man hobbled on.

Christov landed next to the man and said, "Strength and courage." The words formed a shimmering blue plasma ball, and Christov pressed the energy into the man's spirit. He put his arm around the man's shoulders and walked with him.

The crowd stayed divided with a wide berth for the leper. Men and women shielded their noses and mouths with their tunics.

Children hid behind their mothers and covered their faces with their mother's skirts. Cries of "unclean" died out, and a tense silence gripped the crowd.

The man hobbled on.

The line of disciples controlling the crowd at the front drew in tight in front of Jesus and pulled tunics up over their noses and mouths. They shuffled their feet and shot anxious glances at the leper and then back toward Jesus.

Jesus stood still with His hands behind His back.

The leper approached the front, and the line of disciples fixed desperate eyes on Jesus while tightening their face coverings.

Jesus said to the disciples, "Let him draw near."

The disciples pulled back, divided to each side, and scrambled to a safe distance.

With no one separating them, the leper struggled forward toward Jesus. Jesus remained still and watched him approach.

"Look at His eyes," Jenli said. "Have you ever seen such true compassion?"

Elric smiled. "Not in a man."

Finally, the leper limped two more steps and dropped to his hands and knees. With his face low to the ground and his matted hair dangling down into the dirt he said, "Lord, if You are willing, You can make me clean."

Everyone in the crowd held their breath and stared. The disciples stood frozen.

Without hesitation, Jesus stepped forward and knelt down in the dirt. He reached for the man's shoulders and drew him up to a kneeling position.

The people gasped.

Jesus' eyes locked on the man's face as though they were the only two people there. "I *am* willing." He grabbed the man's forearms—right in the middle of the leprous skin. "Be cleansed."

In the Middle Realm, a flood of light rushed from Jesus' Spirit into the man's spirit. From under Jesus' hands, clean pink skin emerged on the man's arms. The fresh skin spread down toward his hands, leaving no trace of leprous scars. The man gulped for air and kept turning his arms from one side to the other with wide, stunned eyes. His fingers uncurled, each joint aligning in perfect, unswollen straightness.

He leapt up and erupted in uncontrollable laughter.

Jesus stood and watched with a satisfied smile.

The man patted his neck with his fresh, clean fingers and touched the brand-new skin spreading up his face. He reached for his ear. A full, pink lobe emerged beneath his fingers. A fountain of tears streamed from his eyes, and his laughter grew into hysterical shouts.

The disciples, with tunics still covering their faces, edged inward. Their eyes shone with a mix of wonder and fear.

The man ripped open his tunic at the neck, revealing his bare chest. Clean. Lesion-free.

The disciples drew in closer.

The man lifted the tattered bottom of his tunic, and the fresh skin stretched down below his knees and over his feet. Toes straightened, and distorted nubs became full toes.

"Look at this! Look at this!" he shouted, hopping on one foot and holding the other up in the air while turning circles in the dirt.

The disciples dropped their face coverings and laughed and clapped.

The man lunged toward Jesus and wrapped Him in a tight embrace. He repeated over and over, "Thank you. Thank you. Thank you."

Tears streamed down Jesus' face. He buried His face in the man's neck and held his embrace for a long time.

The disciples laughed, gawked at each other, and wiped their eyes.

The man pulled back and looked Jesus in the face. "Master . . . what can I ever do . . . "

Jesus dabbed His eyes, and his face became solemn and fatherly. "See that you tell no one; but go, show yourself to the priest and present the offering that Moses commanded, as a testimony to them."

The man paused a moment, then nodded, then hugged Jesus again.

Leaping and spinning, he ran back through the part in the crowd. "Look at me! I'm clean! He healed me! Look at me!"

The people still held their distance, but many clapped and waved.

Elric turned and caught Zaben wiping his eyes. Elric laughed and slapped his back.

"The man is not being quiet," Zaben said. "Shall I send one of my team to help him remain silent?"

"No. The King has done a great thing for him today. It is only natural for him to express his joy."

The man approached the city gate. The three beaelzurim with the scribes and rabbis near the gate flittered off. The three scribes covered their mouths with their tunics and stepped back. The two rabbis turned and walked the opposite direction as though they had important business elsewhere.

The crowd closed back in and pressed even closer to Jesus.

Elric crossed his arms. "The Son of Man—the express image of the Father. Never again will men question the King's willingness to heal."

Zaben nodded. "We have always known it, but it is incredible to see a vessel of flesh pull the spiritual reality into the natural realm."

"Every day He amazes me anew."

13

DIRECTION

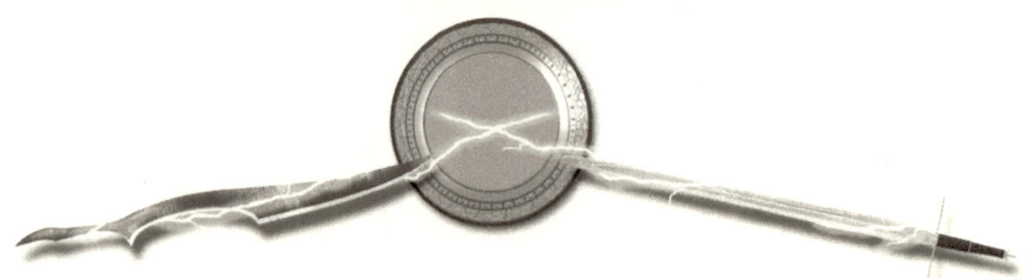

Battle minus 2 years

Daniel strolled beside Joel, his fishing boat captain, up the main dirt street of Ein Gev. With the night's catch loaded for market, the gear stowed, and the sun just coming up, they sauntered at an easy pace. Sparse early morning foot traffic made for a quiet, easy walk.

Daniel continued his story. "But I always thought that it was the spirit of my brother, Levi. He was killed by the Romans when I was young. It sounded like him. And he knew me."

"A demon," Joel said. "Really?"

Daniel nodded. "That's what they say. I don't know. He was always with me. I could always feel his presence. There were times, especially at the beginning, when I was really glad he was there. I thought it was Levi, and I was so alone."

Daniel shook his head and sighed. "But there was a darkness about him. Deep inside I knew something was wrong. Hatred, fear, shame, anger—evil thoughts."

They passed an opening in a stone-faced building with stairs leading down into shadows. A man lay passed out in the corner of the alcove at the bottom of the stairs. Daniel paused and glanced down through the entrance. "Always taking me places I shouldn't be." He continued walking. "And then there were the times when he . . . just took control."

"What do you mean?"

"It was like a dark fog would fill my mind. And when it lifted, I wouldn't know where I was. Or what I had done. Sometimes I could tell I'd done . . . terrible things."

"While you were awake?"

"Sometimes. Or asleep. Sometimes I would go to bed and then wake up with . . . well, I could tell there were terrible things."

"I had no idea. You always seemed so distant and full of sorrow, but I would never have thought any of this. I just thought it was too much wine."

"I love being on the water. I always have. He usually let me have that. Probably just so I would appear mostly normal. But even then, he was always there."

"And now?"

"He's gone. I'm all alone."

"You sound sad about that."

"No. No, it's good to be free from his control. My thoughts are clear again. I can actually tell they are my own thoughts. And I don't live in constant fear and anger. Here's my street."

They turned left onto a narrow side street. The continuous line of dwellings on each side formed a stone and mudbrick city canyon. Daniel and Joel continued up the path a short distance. Daniel stopped and sat on a stone windowsill and leaned against the closed wooden shutters. He pulled out a pouch and shook four dates into his hand. Popping one in his mouth, he offered two to Joel.

"Six months now," Daniel said. "I've been free for six months." He pointed toward the door beside him. "I'm even living in a house now."

Joel took a bite of a date. "And it all started in Capernaum. What did the prophet do to make the demon come out?"

"He just told it to come out."

"That's amazing. Who has that kind of authority?"

Daniel shrugged. "His name is Jesus. He's from Nazareth. I didn't get a chance to hear him teach or anything because he and all the people just left. I don't know what his message is. I don't know if I'll ever see him again. All I know is, somehow, he set me free. And now here I am, my house swept and put in order."

* * *

"There you are," Vorsogh breathed through clenched teeth. From a rooftop across the street, he had a clear line of sight to his old home of flesh, Daniel, who sat outside his home talking with Joel.

"And look at you now, living in a house and carrying on your life without me. You have no idea the torturous six months I have endured. Wandering around the desert. No assignment. No commander willing to bring the shame of a disembodied lieutenant under his dominion. No purpose. No rest."

He exhaled a long stream of yellow smoke. "But I knew I would find you here."

He checked the rooftops. He scanned through narrow eyes up and down the street. No elzurim in sight.

"So empty. So vulnerable. You will be mine again," he hissed. "And this time, I will be so powerful you'll have no ability to resist."

He stretched his leathery bat wings and rose into the air.

"I will be back."

* * *

Battle minus 1.2 years

Elric surveyed the afternoon operation just outside Capernaum from a large outcropping of boulders between a hill and the approach to the shoreline. Jenli and Zaben flanked him on each side.

Jesus sat atop the hill overlooking the Sea of Galilee with a hundred of His closest followers gathered in a tight half ring on the gentle slope. Another several hundred filled the lower parts of the rise. Small stands of trees along the sides and around the back formed a natural boundary, and Jesus' voice carried across the organic amphitheater.

Like five massive stone statue sentinels, Timrok's team provided an imposing inner boundary around the King. Glowing with white-hot energy and weapons drawn, their presence sent an unmistakable message to any impetuous enemy spirit.

Typical with meetings like this, the beaelzurim kept their distance. As the seeds of light shot out from Jesus' words toward the people, the demons didn't dart among them trying to pluck the seeds away. Instead, they hunkered down a safe distance away and waited to get the people alone. Hundreds of glowing red eyes peered through the shadows from behind the trees. Elric gritted his teeth. Zaben and Jenli's team formed loose lines along the tree line, but only for appearances. There would be no enemy encroachment with the King this close.

Regional elzur warriors worked amongst the people, focusing the seeds from the King and speaking words of faith and encouragement. The Middle Realm buzzed with energy and excitement.

"It's good to be back in Capernaum," Jenli said. "These last three weeks have been a needed rest for the disciples."

Zaben replied, "Yes, but we could be reaching so many more if we were still moving about."

"The people are coming," Jenli said. "Word has spread throughout the whole region. Every day the crowd here grows. They are coming in from as far as Tyre . . ."

Elric only half listened to the two lieutenants. Something to the right caught his eye. At the very bottom of the hill, off to the side, stood a single sycamore tree. Leaning against it, by himself—Matthew. His distinctive publican garb set him apart from the common people, as did his fresh-shaved face and clean skin and hair. Kaylar stood beside him with one wing cupped behind Matthew's head, amplifying the words coming down from the top of the hill.

"Captain," Jenli said. "Sir, do you agree?"

Elric pointed toward Matthew. "Why does Matthew stay so far away?"

"Safety," Jenli answered. "Although Kaylar has done all he can to encourage him to move forward. We could keep him safe."

"Where is his Roman guard?" Elric asked.

"Matthew persevered against his service," Jenli said. "A Roman guard draws conspicuous attention, and Matthew seeks a more discreet presence. He has been sneaking away in the afternoons and listening from the border all week."

A steady stream of light seeds flowed from the top of the hill, reached Matthew, and entered his spirit.

Elric nodded. "He is receptive to the word."

Jenli flipped through his ledger and skimmed several pages with his finger. "He is ready. All it will take is a personal call from the King."

"The last of the twelve generals," Zaben said.

Elric crossed his arms. "We will see that the Son of Man passes by Matthew's tax collection booth some time before we leave for the Passover festival. You are sure he will be able to walk away from his position and material status?"

"He will," Jenli said. "In fact, we will encourage him to bring the Son of Man into his house and serve a grand dinner to mark the beginning of his new life."

Elric laughed. "Eating with a tax collector. In the tax collector's house. This will certainly stretch the boundaries for the other disciples."

"And catch the notice of the religious leaders," Zaben said.

"Good, good," Elric said. "I like it."

* * *

Battle minus 1 year

In the war room in Capernaum, Elric and the lieutenants examined the war map. The amount of activity, interconnected timelines, and furious pace throughout the map was dizzying—even for these seasoned warriors. Each one gawked into the multiple layers of swirling colors with stunned expressions and unblinking eyes.

Elric broke the silence. "Two weeks," he said. "Passover. It's almost time to begin the trip to Jerusalem. There is much we need to navigate."

"Too much," Zaben said. "This trip is beset with peril. I recommend we stay here in Galilee during the festival this year."

"He will not miss Passover," Elric said. "He cannot."

Zaben shook his head. "But we dare not march into Jerusalem with all these followers. There are hundreds."

Jenli flipped to a page in his ledger. "One thousand three hundred and forty-two."

"Over a thousand!" Zaben said. "This will appear to the Jewish leaders—and the Romans—like an army marching on Jerusalem. And this is no army. They are neither trained nor armed. The twelve generals haven't been officially commissioned yet. This will present itself as an insurrection."

"Good," Timrok said. "Let's get the battle started. We will prevail with the King leading."

"But this isn't the plan," Zaben said. "We are waiting for the religious leaders to overplay their position such that the Romans remove them and then our select followers can step in with the support of the people. We are not prepared for this yet."

"War plans evolve," Timrok gruffed. "If this march leads to—"

Elric stopped Timrok with an upraised hand. With a calm voice he said, "What is our status for religious leaders on the side of the King?"

Jenli flipped through his journal. "It is not good." He turned a few more pages. "Malachi in Cana. Boaz in Japha. Of course, Raziel in Nazareth. Yigal in Garis. And Shmuel in Gennesaret."

"And probably Nicodemus in Jerusalem," Zaben added. "This is not enough."

Elric crossed his arms and nodded. "I agree. And the timing is not right to provoke a battle now. To the best of my understanding, there is still more work to accomplish." He gazed into the war map and paused. "Ideas, then. How do we bring the King into Jerusalem without causing undue attention?"

Several moments of contemplation passed.

"Send envoys ahead," Lacidar said. "Alert the leaders and officials that we are coming, but that it is a peaceful following."

"Split the people into smaller companies," Timrok said. "Stagger their arrivals."

A bright flash enveloped the room. Elric squinted. He reopened his eyes, and Grigor stood in their midst. His wings folded away without a sound.

"A word of the Lord," Grigor announced.

Elric waved his hand, and the war map disappeared. He nodded to Grigor.

"The Son of Man will send his disciples on to the festival without Him," Grigor said. "Without His presence, the crowd will disperse and not arrive in Jerusalem together. The Son of Man will travel to

Jerusalem alone and enter without notice. Once there, He will teach and perform signs that the people may believe."

"In His service," Elric said.

"By His word," Grigor replied. He lifted his wings and disappeared.

Alone again with the lieutenants, Elric raised his chin and said, "Word from the Throne is a welcome treasure. We have clarity. We have our orders."

14

DARKNESS PASSING OVER

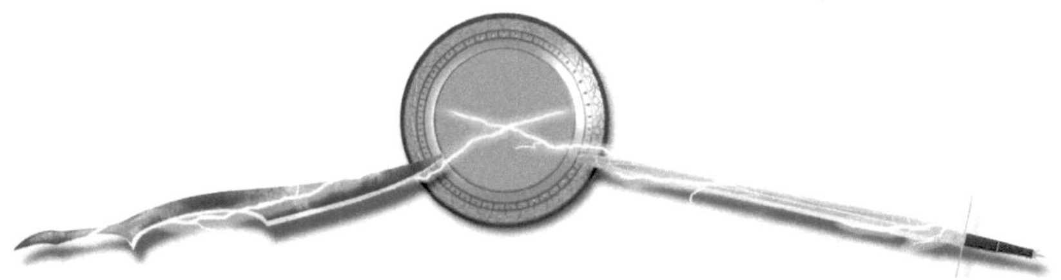

Battle minus 1 year

Vorsogh flew low over the barren desert, far from Marr's jurisdiction and far from all the distractions of the King walking around on the earth in a shell of flesh. None of that mattered. Only one thing mattered—reclaiming his old host, Daniel.

But he couldn't just reenter after the humiliating defeat in Capernaum. He would need to come back with an irresistible show of power. He needed reinforcements. He needed more—

There!

He swooped down and landed in front of a small beaelzur warrior wandering the desert floor. The small demon shrieked and made a wild swing with his jagged sword. Vorsogh swatted the blade aside, grabbed the demon's wrist, and pressed his blade against the lesser demon's neck. Outmatched in size and power, the small warrior had no chance against the mighty lieutenant.

With his neck stretched as far as he could, the little demon spit toward Vorsogh and exhaled a stream of sulfurous smoke through his flared nostrils. "Who are you, and what do you want?"

"I will ask the questions," Vorsogh snarled. "What are you doing out here? Are you on assignment?"

"I have no charge. I am my own master."

"Everyone has a master. To whom do you answer?"

"No one!"

Vorsogh pushed the edge of his blade closer. "Who?"

"No one!"

Vorsogh lowered his blade but held firm to the demon's wrist. "You have recently lost a host and have nowhere to go. Am I right?"

The small demon twisted and pulled his arm against Vorsogh's unrelenting grip. "So what? Leave me alone."

Vorsogh released his grip and took a step back. "Would you like a new host?"

Rubbing his wrist with his other hand, the demon said without raising his eyes from the ground, "Do you propose some kind of arrangement?"

"I do."

"Tell me."

"My name is Vorsogh. I, too, recently lost my host. I am going to reclaim him. But I will do so with great power and authority. I seek others to help me create an unstoppable presence. He is mine, but you could share in this glory."

"Then I would answer to you?"

"Of course. But you would have flesh again which, together, we would master."

"Where is he?"

"On the far side of the Sea of Galilee, in the Decapolis region."

"Galilee? I hear the King of Hosts is there! We dare not go anywhere near there."

"He is working out of Capernaum. We are safe in Decapolis."

"It sounds dangerous. What if He finds us? It will take more than the two of us to resist Him."

Vorsogh smiled. "I already have thirty-one others."

"Thirty-one? How many are you—"

"I told you—an unstoppable presence. I will return with a thousand if I can assemble as many."

"Where are the others?"

"I have a holding place until I can collect enough. Come, I will show you. And you can help gather more forces. You will feel the prickle of wind against human skin again soon."

* * *

In a large inner room in the heart of the temple complex in Jerusalem, a dozen chief priests gathered for an emergency meeting on the second day of Passover. Caiaphas, the high priest, leaned back in his chair behind the large stately table and folded his hands on his chest under his white beard. Two of his advisors stood close behind.

The dark wood-paneled walls had stacked rows of inset alcoves filled with hundreds of scrolls and books. Wall sconces provided warm, bright light and accentuated all the items of status—gold and silver chalices and plates, intricate tapestries, and the breastplate with the twelve stones of Israel hanging in the corner.

Enormous beaelzur captains, constricted in size for the space, pressed shoulder to shoulder along all four walls. The sulfurous vapors from their heavy breaths mixed with the layer of smoke hanging in the Middle Realm. From the ceiling to chest-level, the smoke obscured their grotesque faces, revealing only their smoldering red eyes.

Marr stood behind Caiaphas with his hands resting on the man's shoulders. Before him stood Asherah. Behind Asherah, on either side, Molech and Yarikh stood with arms crossed. Dozens of small beaelzurim clung to the priests and flittered around the room through the haze.

One of the priests addressed Caiaphas. "We all know this man. He has been at the Pool of Bethesda for thirty years."

"And how is it that he now walks?" Caiaphas asked.

"Jesus of Nazareth, whom you have heard much about, raised him up."

Another priest added, "On the Sabbath! And he told the man to carry his bed mat!"

Marr shouted, "An outrage!"

All the demons in the room echoed Marr's charge.

Caiaphas raised his eyebrows and stroked his beard.

Another priest spoke up in a sheepish voice. "We cannot deny that a notable miracle has occurred. Is it possible Jesus could be a prophet? Or even the Promised One?"

His words shot into the Middle Realm as packets of light, but they bogged down in the haze like stones in thick mud. The little demons pounced on them in a frenzy, slashing them with their blades and crushing them with their hands.

"This man is *not* the Promised One," Marr roared. "He is a madman from Nazareth."

"Not the Promised One!" shouted all the demons. "Not the Messiah!"

The fiery darts accelerated through the haze and sank into the men's layers of darkness with ease.

"No," Caiaphas said with a contemplative tone. "I think not. The Messiah clearly does not come out of Nazareth, and we know this man and his family are from Nazareth."

Marr nodded and shot a puff of smoke through his nostrils. The other demons continued to feed the haze. "Not the Messiah, not the Messiah."

"But," the priest with the sheepish voice said, "he is working undeniable miracles. Truly he has great power." He swallowed hard and cleared his throat. "A man could not do these signs apart from the power of God."

The demons smothered his words within a heartbeat, and six dark warriors surrounded him, pressed in close, and engulfed him in a firestorm.

"Lies!"

"You are confused!"

"You should be ashamed of your ignorance!"

"Silence, you fool!"

Marr thundered, "This is *not* the power of God! His power comes from Beelzebul!"

"He has a demon!" chanted the demons. "Beelzebul! Beelzebul!"

Hundreds of fiery seeds shot into the men's spirits.

Caiaphas sat forward and gripped the edge of the table with both hands. "We know he is *not* from God because he does *not* follow the traditions of the elders. He breaks the law, and no man of God would do such things." He sat back. "There is only one explanation. He has a demon. He draws his power from Beelzebul."

The priests all nodded and scowled.

One of the priests said, "What are we to do about him, then? He is drawing many to himself. He will draw away all Israel if we do not stop him."

"Kill Him!" Marr hissed. "Destroy the Son of Man."

One of Caiaphas's advisors leaned forward and whispered something in his ear. Caiaphas nodded once.

"He must be silenced," Caiaphas said, rubbing his brows.

One of the priests grumbled, "He violated the Sabbath! The Law of Moses condemned a man to death for picking up sticks on the Sabbath—a lesser offense than this."

"Kill Him!" the demons echoed. "Kill Him!"

"He should be stoned!" a Pharisee shouted.

Caiaphas shook his head. "We are under the hand of Rome now. It would take consensus of the Sanhedrin and the judgment of Pilate. I do not think we have sufficient grounds."

"But something must be done," one of the priests said. "He is a threat. Surely you see this."

"Yes. He is a threat." Caiaphas leaned forward with his forearms crossed on the table. "We must catch him in a clear violation of the law. I want him under constant observation. Every word he speaks.

Every movement he makes. Every act he does. He is a man—he will make a mistake. And we will be there to catch him in it."

The priests nodded.

"Further, I want you to assemble teams of learned elders to test him in his sayings. Test him in matters of the law—both the Law of Moses and Roman law. Set traps that he will fall into."

The priests nodded.

One of the priests asked, "And what of the people? How do we keep them from following him?"

"Fear," growled Marr. "Control them with fear."

Caiaphas took a deep breath and paused. He turned to his two advisors who bent over for a private consultation. They whispered and nodded, and Caiaphas turned back to the priests.

"Jesus is a threat to our people and our traditions. Anyone who follows him has rejected their heritage and will be cut off from Israel. This includes the whole house of Israel, from Sidon to Beersheba. Make this word known in every synagogue."

Caiaphas shifted in his seat and eyed each priest in the room. "And . . . make it clear that enforcement of this edict will be most severe amongst the leaders. Priests, scribes, rabbis—shall be made a public display if they err in this matter."

The men all filed out of the room, leaving Caiaphas alone.

The beaelzurim in the room held their place and focused on Marr.

"These men are weak," Marr said with a slow, disgusted cadence. "They have murderous hearts, but they fear losing the approval of men. Increase pressure on them. Promote strife between their factions—make them compete against each other for who can create the most resistance against the Son of Man."

"And the people," he continued, "I want them so full of fear of shame and hardship that none would dare to follow Him."

He looked at Asherah. "The leaders here in Judea are almost universally ours, but you must take care not to lose any to the enemy."

To Molech and Yarikh he said, "The enemy has been actively seeking to win leaders in your regions. Destroy these men. Remove them from the synagogues, strike them with sickness, cloud their minds with fear and confusion, entangle them in scandal."

Molech said, "And what of the prophet John at the Jordan? He continues to draw many, and he points them all toward the Son of Man."

"Destroy him. Why do you wait?"

"It will take a large assault. The King's host—"

"Destroy him."

"Yes, master."

Marr gave a dismissive flick of his hand and said, "Go. You all have much work to do."

15

LAW'S STING

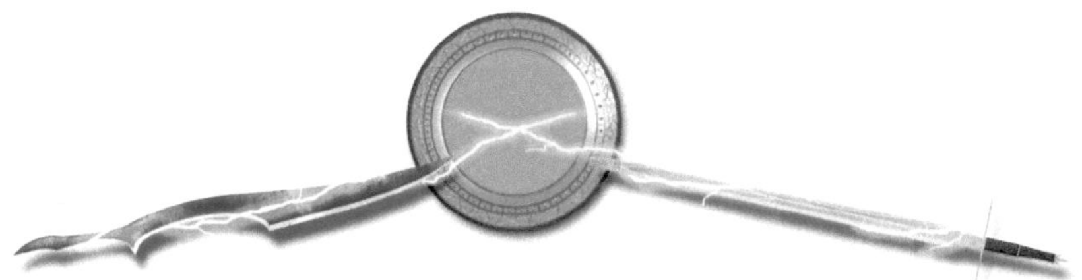

Battle minus 1 year

From behind a stone balustrade on a high inner wall of the temple grounds, Zaben, Christov, and Carothim peered down across the Court of Israel. Day four of the Passover was complete, night had settled in, and a group of six men had gathered under a portico, behind the pillars, and away from the light of the court torches. The men talked in hushed tones, glancing over their shoulders and pausing their conversation when anyone passed too close.

Four of the men, rabbis from Judea, had strong layers of black spiritual armor. Helmets of darkness, along with breastplates, shoulder guards, and belts provided formidable strongholds in the Middle Realm. One of the men, David, a priest from Ekron, had an equally formidable stronghold of light. The gleam from his helmet and breastplate illuminated the spiritual air around him. Joseph, the sixth man, was a priest from Arimathea and a respected member of the council. He had a patchwork of light and darkness covering his chest, but his helmet had a consistent, faint glow.

Three small beaelzur warriors worked amongst the men, darting from one to another and filling the spiritual air with a layer of noxious smoke.

"But I think you do not understand the significance of the edict," one of the rabbis said to David. "The council *will* put you out. You will be cut off from Israel."

His words shot toward David like flaming arrows.

The demons shot their own. "Think of the shame on you and your entire family. What will you do? Where will you go? You should fear for your very life!"

All the fiery darts bounced off his breastplate with no effect.

David shook his head. "I do not believe this. They would not go so far." He turned to Joseph. "You are on the council. What do you hear from the elders?"

Joseph wrinkled his face and rubbed his brow. "They certainly appear committed to this decree. I do not fully understand it. They are greatly troubled. They are afraid of Jesus and His teachings."

"But why?" David said. "You have all heard Him. He speaks words of life. My heart burns within me at every word."

"Lies!" shouted the demons. "He speaks lies and goes against the traditions of the elders! He breaks the Sabbath. He is dangerous."

"I have heard him," one of the rabbis said. "I find him offensive and divisive."

"I agree," said one of the other rabbis. "He appears to me a madman, full of presumption."

More fiery darts hurled toward David.

David answered, "He speaks with authority. It is not presumption if what He says is true."

"The chief priests and elders do not agree," one the rabbis said. "It is dangerous for you to think this way."

The three demons pummeled David with more attacks. "You are greatly mistaken. Are you wiser than the chief priests? You are a fool!"

On top of the court wall, Zaben turned and ducked behind the stone banister. "I can watch this no longer. We must get down there and drive the enemy off."

"But sir," Christov said, "our orders—"

"Our *mission* . . . is to win individual leaders. This man will be in our camp if we can separate him from the enemy."

Carothim said, "I agree with Christov. We should be patient. If we engage the enemy now, we will expose our intent with David. It will be safer to reach him when he returns to Ekron."

"You may be right." Zaben spied back into the court below.

David continued his case. "And what of all the miraculous signs He is working? When the Christ comes, He will not perform more signs than those which this man has done, will He?"

"He is not the Messiah!" screeched the demons.

One of the rabbis said, "These signs only make him more dangerous. It misleads weak-minded people."

The demons shot continuous streams of firebolts at David. "The man has a demon! He is dangerous! Not the Messiah!"

Another rabbi added, "I think he works these signs by Beelzebul."

Zaben pulled his sword from its sheath and growled, "Enough. This has to stop."

He pounced downward into the court, only half-opening his wings at the last moment to land. With a single stroke, he ran his blade through the chest of one beaelzurim. He pulled his sword back amid a cloud of yellow smoke and wrapped the stunned warrior with cords of light.

The other two demons shrieked and lunged toward Zaben in a frenzy. Zaben smashed his shield into the face of one while locking blades with the other. He leapt back and spun, his blade cutting a sizzling horizontal arc. The two demons recoiled just enough for Zaben's blade to miss their torsos by a hair. They lunged again.

Flash! Flash! Two bolts of light shot down from the shadows above.

Christov's feet pounded into the shoulders of one demon. Carothim's sword drove through the forehead of the other. In a single heartbeat, both beaelzurim lay immobilized on the ground, bindings of light from their mouths to their ankles.

Zaben nodded once to his warriors and stepped over to David.

"You are right about Jesus," Zaben said. His words formed clouds of light that spread outward toward the men. "He is the Messiah. Take courage and do not believe their lies."

None of his words penetrated the hard shells of the four rabbis, but all the light entered David and Joseph.

He continued. "Do not fear the threats of the elders. Follow the Son of Man. Believe His—"

Smash! The world went black.

Zaben opened his eyes—flat on his back, too weak to move, with an enormous beaelzur captain's foot crushing his neck and smashing hard against his chin. Bindings constricted his arms, chest, and legs.

He glanced left. Carothim lay on his side, bound, and under the foot of another dark captain.

He glanced right. Christov was down.

The three small demons, unbound, cackled and scudded around.

The demon captain above him said, "Not a wise move, Lieutenant." His low voice rumbled through Zaben's chest. "You cannot have this man. Now I will destroy him before your eyes."

Zaben tried to squeeze out a "no," but the captain's foot pushed harder against his chin.

The captain spoke the words "I take from you the breath of life" into his right hand where the words rolled up into a pulsing ball of fire. He pressed the fireball against David's back. The plasma sparked and sizzled on contact with David's armor of light, but the demon twisted and rammed it inward. Most of the energy dissipated in the ricocheting sparks, but some of it passed through into David's spirit.

All the demons watched David and waited.

"And even if the council decides to . . . " David stopped. He gasped and reached for his chest.

"What is it?" Joseph asked. "What's the matter?"

"I . . . don't know. Can't . . . catch my breath."

The demon captain grunted, "My work here is done." He gave Zaben's neck another shove with his foot and flew off into the darkness along with the other captain.

The three small demons danced around David, laughing and clawing at him.

"Are you all right?" Joseph asked.

"I . . . don't . . . know. I've . . . never . . . "

Joseph said, "Come. I'll help you to a physician." He put David's arm around his own shoulder and propped him up. "Quickly! Let's go!"

The two stumbled off across the court, followed by the three demons who shot a steady torrent of darts. "You'll never make it! You are going to die! There is no hope!" The troop rounded a corner, and their voices faded into the distance.

Zaben sighed and looked straight up at the night sky.

How did I not see them coming?

He closed his eyes and sighed again. With each breath, the bindings constrained his rising chest. With each constriction, his thoughts reached out toward David and his own struggle for breath.

If I could just get to him. I know I could save him. It's not too late. If I could just—

"Well, what happened here?" a voice above him said.

Zaben opened his eyes.

"Timrok! Quickly, loose us!"

Timrok sliced through Zaben's bindings, and Zaben bounded to his feet. He picked up his sword and freed Carothim while Timrok released Christov.

"Hurry!" Zaben shouted. He unfurled his wings and blasted upward. Timrok, Christov, and Carothim followed close behind.

"There!" Zaben shouted amid the flurry of wings. He pointed down toward David and Joseph.

The four landed in a flash near the two men as they hobbled toward the temple infirmary door. The three demons brandished their weapons and stepped forward for a fight. Timrok pulled his two swords and swung them around in a dizzying flourish. Carothim and Christov planted their feet and leveled their blades. Zaben gritted his teeth, lifted his sword from his shoulder, and took a step forward.

The three beaelzurim stopped and glanced toward each other and then back at Zaben.

One of the demons said, "It matters not. Death has already been dealt, and no physician can stop it now. You have lost this battle, just as you will lose the war."

The three flew off over the temple wall, tittering all along their erratic paths.

Carothim and Christov sheathed their swords and looked to Zaben.

"Carothim," Zaben said. "Block the door. Christov, go inside and deafen ears to any outside calls."

The two nodded and moved into position.

Joseph reached for the door with one hand while bolstering David up with the other. The door wouldn't open. Joseph looked up at the infirmary sign beside the door and tried again. It still would not open. He knocked. He knocked again. He pounded hard and called out with a desperate cry, "Help! We need help!"

Zaben drew close and said, "Take him to Jesus. Jesus will heal him."

Joseph pounded on the door again. "Help us! Please!" He turned his head toward David and asked, "How are you doing?"

"Not . . . well. Getting . . . worse. I can't . . . "

"Yes, you can. Keep fighting. Come, I have an idea." Joseph wheeled David around and headed for the temple gate.

Zaben smiled and said to Timrok, "We're going to bring David to the King. Would you like to help with the escort?"

"It is always an honor to bring someone to the King."

With Timrok in the lead and Carothim and Christov on the flanks, Joseph left the temple grounds and wound through tent encampments of the Passover pilgrims. Through the whole trip, Zaben rested his hand on David's back, speaking strength and hope and peace.

Finally, they made it to Jesus' tent. The two men went inside while the warriors in white waited outside.

"David will be a strong asset when the time comes," Zaben said.

Timrok nodded. "It appears Joseph is also ready for the Kingdom."

Zaben laughed. "Yes, especially after this meeting. Thank you for your assistance."

Timrok slapped Zaben's shoulder, chuckled, and meandered off into the camp.

An hour passed, and David and Joseph emerged. Both of their spirits glowed, and their eyes twinkled. Their voices had a lilt of excitement and wonder as the strolled down the tent aisles accompanied by Zaben, Carothim, and Christov.

"I had heard of the miraculous healings," Joseph said. "But until now, I had not yet seen one."

David did a little skip. "I felt the power surge through my body. The power of God flowed through me and healed me. They can argue all they want about doctrine and law, but I know that I was touched by God. Did you sense His love as He spoke with us? His true compassion?"

"Yes. I have to say it was nothing like I have ever experienced."

"I am fully convinced," David said. "This has to be the Promised One."

Joseph looked around with a nervous scan. With a lower voice he said, "Be careful what you say. The edict of the council has been made known, and you never know who may be listening."

"I don't care who hears. What can they do? Put me out of the synagogue? I will go and follow Him. He has the words of life, not the elders."

They turned down a dark aisle and came face to face with a ragged-looking man. His hair and beard were matted and filthy. Clothes stained and tattered. Eyes wild. The man revealed his hands from behind his back, and in his right hand, the blade of a dagger flashed.

Zaben leapt between the man and David and Joseph. Carothim and Christov pulled their swords.

Backing away, Joseph said, "What do you want? If you seek money, we have none. We just came from working in the temple all day and we have no money pouches."

"I do not care about money," the man said. His voice sounded gravelly and inhuman. "I am a sent one."

"Sent?" David said. "Sent for what purpose?"

"Aaaugh!" screeched the man as he charged at David.

"He is possessed!" Zaben shouted. "It is the enemy!"

Zaben drove his sword through the man. An angry demon spewed out the back, but the man continued forward. The demon flopped on the ground, rolled twice, grabbed his sword, and bounded toward Zaben. Zaben met his blade with a crash. Sparks shot through the spiritual air. The demon jumped straight up and dove downward. Zaben spun and swiped the descending blade away. During his spin, he saw Carothim and Christov both engaged with enemy warriors of their own. *An ambush!* He blocked a strike with his shield. He swung again. The demon flipped backward, landed, and sprang into the sky. With a flurry of bat wings, he disappeared.

Silence.

All the enemy warriors were gone.

Carothim and Christov stood motionless with swords still at the ready.

The possessed man was gone.

Joseph was gone.

David lay motionless in the dirt.

Without a sound, a shimmering angel appeared and landed next to David. Zaben's eyes met his, and Zaben's head dropped in defeat.

David stood up out of his body. With a confused expression, his eyes moved from Zaben to each of the angels standing by. "Am I . . . dead?"

Zaben put his hand on his shoulder and nodded. "Brave and faithful servant of the King, your fight is complete. Go now with my friend. He will take you to a place of rest. The King Himself awaits your arrival."

The two disappeared into the sky like fading stars.

The energy of David's spilled blood rose from the ground and swirled waist-high in the Middle Realm. It coalesced and dropped back down to the ground as a large spiritual stone. Zaben turned his gaze from the fading stars to the stone, walked over, and sat down on it.

"You were right," Zaben said to Christov and Carothim. "I should have waited. It was shortsighted and lacking in wisdom."

Christov said, "You had no way of knowing the enemy would—"

"But I usually can anticipate their moves. How is it that I was so blind?"

Christov and Carothim had no answer.

"It's this mission," Zaben said. "There is so much at stake, and we receive so little guidance. I think my zeal for the mission sometimes clouds my vision."

"We are all zealous to see that day," Carothim said.

"Yes," Zaben said. "And it can't come soon enough."

Zaben stood. "Go make a search for Joseph. See to his safety and bring me word."

Christov and Carothim nodded and raised their wings.

"But," Zaben interrupted. "Be discrete. Joseph may still be reachable, and we do not want to lose him."

"In His service."

16

BATTLE FOR JOHN

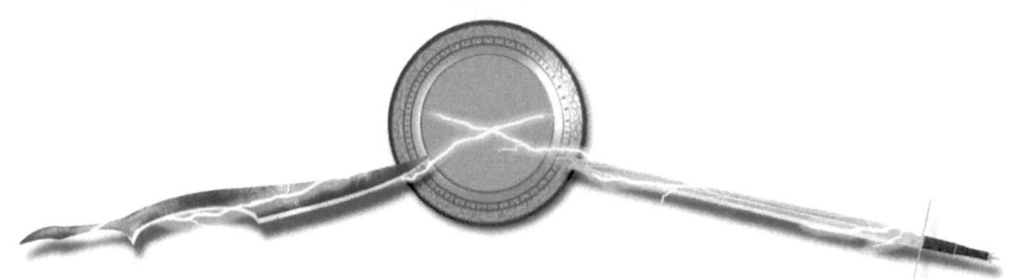

Battle minus 1 year

Elric and Jenli walked together ten paces behind Jesus, James, and John, who kept pace with the caravan of several hundred men, women, and children. From their location in the middle of the company, Elric could barely see the determined gaits of Simon and Andrew in the lead position. Timrok, on the other hand, was large and conspicuous up front.

"I am not surprised to see Simon taking us by the way of the sea instead of through Samaria," Jenli said.

Elric laughed. "Yes, the Son of Man is letting him set the course."

"As much as I enjoy Passover, I am glad to be out here away from the temple," Jenli said.

"Mm," Elric replied with a slow head nod. "The concentration of enemy forces was like none we have encountered so far."

"Still, He was not arrested. Nor any of his followers."

"Yes, the team executed well. When your team and Timrok's did the Wittucian flanking maneuver, the enemy couldn't respond, and the men couldn't lay their hands on Him. Very effective."

Jenli laughed. "Three times!"

"I suspect, though, that if we have to go back to the temple again under our current rules of engagement, the enemy will not be so easily hindered."

"Hopefully, next time we will be coming behind the unstoppable sword of the King."

"Yes. The day we all—"

A single light streaked low across the horizon and approached the caravan like a bolt of lightning. Stephanus emerged from the bolt in front of Elric with a flash and shouted before his feet reached the ground, "Captain, the prophet John! We are under siege!"

"How many?"

"Thousands!"

Elric drew his war trumpet and sounded three clear blasts.

In an instant, every one of Timrok, Zaben, and Jenli's teams stood in a tight formation before him with the three lieutenants shoulder to shoulder in front.

"The enemy has come for the prophet John," Elric announced. "Lacidar is under siege. We go to reinforce him. Timrok, leave two warriors here with the King. All other blades—to war!"

Elric leapt into the air and flew as fast as his wings could pound.

The Jordan river appeared ahead, and flashes of light, flames, and smoke in the Middle Realm pinpointed John's location. Elric dropped altitude and skimmed only feet above the ground. Advancing toward an overlooking hill, he alighted on the back side and crawled to the crest on his elbows. Zaben crawled on his left, Timrok and Jenli on his right.

In the valley below, a horrific battle raged. Hundreds of elzurim fought desperate hand-to-hand battles across the encampment against an advancing horde of demons closing in from all sides. Thousands of furious fireballs blazed inward against the defenders. Sparks shot high into the Middle Realm, and a heavy layer of smoke choked the spiritual air of the valley.

In the Physical Realm, dozens of people meandered about the camp, oblivious to the conflict. A group of about a hundred men sat listening to the prophet John by the river.

"Captain," Zaben said, pointing up a path that led into the valley. "Roman soldiers."

A detachment of ten soldiers and an officer approached. The tips of their spears gleamed in the sunlight and rose and fell in unison with the cadence of their march.

"Captain," Timrok said, pointing to a hill on the opposite side of the valley. "Molech."

The huge beaelzur commander and his entourage oversaw the battle from their superior position.

In the center of the conflict, Lacidar and his team held a tight perimeter around John, but they would not be able to hold off the onslaught much longer.

"We can surely overcome," Timrok said. "We concentrate around John and push the enemy back."

"There are too many," Elric said. "If we simply join the fight, we will be overrun with the rest."

"A distraction," Zaben said. "Remember when King David went up against the Philistines in the Valley of Rephaim?"

"Yes! Good plan," Elric said. "Timrok—take Stephanus, the rest of your team, and two more to fill out your team—and join Lacidar. The rest of us will circle around behind the Roman soldiers, create the sound of a mighty army in the Physical Realm, and shine the light of a thousand warriors of the King in the Middle Realm."

Timrok grimaced. "Your troop will not stand long against this horde when they turn to challenge you."

"We need not stand long. We only need to give you enough time to move John. Start by hiding him tent to tent. Then sneak him out a back way. The enemy will be blind to your movements because they will be too focused on mine."

Timrok nodded.

"Go!"

Timrok motioned to Nalyd, Micah, and Kylek with a single wave. He pointed to Stephanus, Lorr, and Jerem with quick deliberation. He pulled his two swords, and the small team dove down into the mayhem without hesitation.

Elric paused, shaking his head at the reckless abandon of the warriors he just sent into terrible danger.

Zaben said with a reassuring tone, "They will secure John—once we draw the enemy away."

"Let's go," Elric said.

Ducking back below the brow of the hill, Elric took flight and led the rest of the team down, away, and around until they reached the back side of a hill just behind the detail of Roman soldiers.

He turned to the team.

Jenli. Zaben. Four from each of their teams. Ten altogether.

So few.

He lifted his chin and commanded, "The sound of a mighty army. And the light of a thousand hosts of heaven!"

He clapped his hands, and a huge plasma ball formed between them. Each of the team did the same. Together, they all rubbed the outer layer of energy, squeezing and twisting the plasma. A flood of light erupted high into the Middle Realm, and the reverberation of a huge marching army echoed through the Physical Realm.

Elric called out above the rising pitch, "Jenli—survey!"

Jenli opened his wings and lifted straight up, hovering just high enough to see over the hill. He watched only a moment and landed like a stone.

"The Roman soldiers are continuing their course," he shouted over the noise. "They have not slowed nor turned to right or to the left."

He moved his mouth closer to Elric's ear but continued to shout. "But the enemy is coming!"

"How many?"

"A great multitude. Perhaps all of them."

Elric nodded. To the group he yelled, "Prepare yourselves!"

The first wave of demons broke over the knoll. Only forty. Fast and furious.

Elric's team met them with a war shout and resolute steel. Each elzur warrior dispatched three, four, five demons at a time. Blades clanged, shields crashed, and sparks burned through the air.

Just as the first wave of demons got off the ground, regained their strength, and prepared to reengage, the second wave washed over. Hundreds.

"Draw back!" Elric shouted as he cut one demon down. "Pull them away, but don't get captur—"

Zzzt crash! A massive force smashed into his back left shoulder. Fiery pain shot down his left arm, and the momentum of the hit spun him around. As he wheeled around, he saw them. Hundreds more coming in from behind. And hundreds of fireballs already in the air. Shouts from his team rose above the sizzle of the missiles.

"Captain! They've flanked us from behind! They are—aughh!"

"Look out!"

"There are too many to—argh!"

"We can't—"

The barrage of the first volley blazed through their line, and the second volley followed within a single breath. A ball of plasma streaked toward Elric. He strained to lift his shield, but his weakened left arm still hung numb and useless. At the last second, he slashed with his blade and split the fireball in two. One half shot off to the left. The other grazed his right shoulder, sending him careening backward. Off balance, with both arms paralyzed with pain, he blinked hard, trying to regain focus. His vision cleared just enough to see the fireball coming right at his face. *Zzzzt.* Red—pain—black.

Elric opened his eyes—flat on his back, nothing but blue sky above him. Lingering sulfur burned his eyes, and he blinked the welling water away until it ran down the side of his face. He tried to move his arms. They stayed pinned to his sides.

He was bound.

He rolled to his side. Strewn across the ground lay all ten of his team, bound and motionless. One of them managed to sit upright while still bound. Jenli.

Jenli looked all around and said, "Captain? Captain, are you all right?"

"Yes." Elric struggled against the bindings, but they held tight. "Although that battle did not last long. I wonder if it was enough time for Timrok and Lacidar to secure John."

"Sir, if you can, sit up. You need to see this."

Elric rolled onto his back and sat up. He glanced over to Jenli and followed Jenli's eyes toward the trail.

"Oh no," Elric sighed.

The demon captain Khilaf led a small procession over the hill and down the trail which passed right in front of Elric. Khilaf marched in front, followed by four beaelzur warriors, followed by five elzur warriors bound waist to neck, followed by four more beaelzur warriors. The angels trudged forward in single file with bindings tying each one to the next. Their heads hung low, and despair filled their eyes.

Khilaf didn't speak a word but shot a haughty glance toward Elric.

Elric gritted his teeth.

Khilaf smirked and continued his march.

"Captain." Zaben had sat up. "Sir, one of those warriors is Lorr."

"Shhh."

The detail passed beyond earshot, and Zaben whispered, "Why would they take Lorr?"

"Why would they take any?" Jenli said.

Elric's head dropped low. "To shame me. That was Captain Khilaf. That entire show was for me."

"Sir, look." Jenli said.

Another procession crested the hill and came down the path—another demon captain with a squad of ten beaelzur warriors followed by a detachment of Roman soldiers—with John. John had thick ropes binding his hands behind his back, but he walked with stalwart steps and bright eyes. A small group of John's followers appeared at the top of the hill and watched the detail fade into the distance. Then they retreated like lost sheep back into the river valley.

Elric called out to the team, "Can anyone break loose a hand through his bindings? If you can, you could roll to one of our weapons and cut one of us free."

"No."

"No."

"No."

"If only we could simply translate back into the King's Realm," Zaben said.

"Bindings bind," Jenli said. "We can't change physics."

"Of course, I know this. But aren't there times—"

"Captain," Brondor shouted. "Incoming!"

A single light approached from the north, high and descending fast. A shining elzur warrior alighted next to Elric and announced, "Captain, I am sent to release you and your team."

Elric rolled to his side away from the warrior, and the bindings snapped loose on his back from his shoulders to his feet with a single slice of the warrior's dagger. Elric filled his unconstricted chest with air and let it out with a sigh. He jumped to his feet and said, "Thank you."

Elric picked up his sword and went first to Zaben. The unknown warrior moved to Jenli, loosed him, and started toward Christov.

Back on his feet, Jenli stopped the warrior and said, "Luxor? Luxor, is that you?"

"Jenli!" Luxor shouted. "My old lieutenant!"

Jenli formed a plasma ball of "joy" and moved to combine it with Luxor's energy. Luxor didn't form his own plasma ball but put his hand up and pressed Jenli's energy between his hand and Jenli's. The ball exploded and sent a shower of joy droplets across the field. Jenli and Luxor laughed.

"Captain," Jenli said, "It's Luxor! He was on my team stationed in Nazareth back before . . . our mission. You may recall, he and Deenr were taken by the enemy."

Elric finished loosing Emms and walked back toward Jenli. The rest of the team collected their weapons and gathered around.

Elric smiled and said, "Luxor, it is a happy surprise to see you. I am anxious to hear your story, but I'm afraid right now we need to see to the rest of the team. Come, let's free our comrades."

Elric lifted off and headed for the river valley.

Below, in the Physical Realm, the peaceful Jordan slipped southward without a care. A small tent village beside it sat undisturbed. A few hundred people milled about with nothing to do and nowhere to go.

In the Middle Realm, hundreds of bound elzurim littered the battlefield.

It appears the beaelzur forces have all moved out.

Near the water's edge lay a large concentration of fallen warriors. "We'll start there," Elric called out. "Free our team and work your way outward."

The team dove in unison.

"There were too many," Lacidar groaned as Elric landed and cut through his bindings. "We lost John."

"I know," Elric answered. "I had hoped our diversion would be enough for you to get John out."

Timrok stepped up. He picked some black binding remnants off his shoulder and flung them aside. He slid his swords back into their sheaths. "Your diversion worked, captain. You emptied the whole valley. Only . . . there wasn't enough time. The enemy reengaged almost immediately."

Elric's left eye twitched twice, and he nodded.

Zaben, Jenli, and Luxor rejoined the gathering.

"There's more," Timrok said. "I lost Lorr." He picked up Lorr's sword and shield and handed them to Zaben. "I'm so sorry."

Zaben bit his lip and nodded once.

"It was Captain Khilaf," Lacidar said. "After the battle, he walked through and picked five warriors who were fighting here close to John. I think he was purposely looking for warriors who might have been on our team."

Elric nodded. "He was sending me a message."

He looked around the battlefield. Most of the elzurim had been freed, and they all moved off toward their charges or other missions. The rest of Elric's team stood in disciplined ranks at parade rest—minus Prestus and Chase, who Timrok had left with the King's caravan.

And minus Lorr.

"What's next?" Lacidar asked.

Elric crossed his arms and closed his eyes. After a moment he answered, "Our duty to John is not complete. The enemy may have taken him, but he still belongs to the King."

Timrok palmed his sword handles. "A mission to break him out?"

"Perhaps. Eventually. But we first need to find where they have taken him and formulate a plan." To Lacidar he said, "Take your team and learn what you can. If you find him, stay with him and keep him encouraged. I suspect you will be deep within the enemy's headquarters, but they have no authority to prevent you from ministering to him. Though they try to block you, enforce the King's authority, and they will have to comply."

"Yes, sir."

"Only do not overstep your authority or do anything beyond direct ministry to John. Give the enemy no grounds to bring a sword against you."

Lacidar nodded.

"The rest of us . . . we must return to our posts with the Son of Man and His twelve generals immediately. We continue back to Capernaum."

"Sir," Jenli said, "may Luxor stay with us for now? We are down a sword."

Elric paused a moment and nodded. "For now. Until we find a replacement for Lorr."

17

CHOSEN

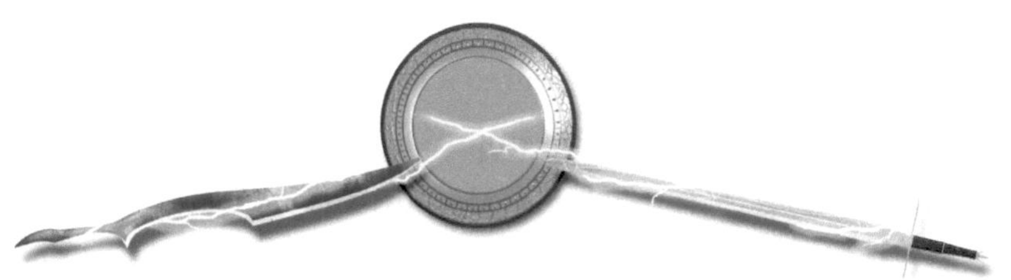

Battle minus 1 year

Just north of Capernaum, just at the base of a hill, just before sunrise, Zaben landed next to Elric.

"Good morning," Elric said, not taking his gaze off Jenli, who sat cross-legged an arrow's shot away down the gentle slope. Jenli remained still as a stone with his dagger in his hand, facing east.

"The King is still here praying?" Zaben asked.

Elric turned toward the top of the hill. Showers of light beamed down on Jesus, who knelt in the predawn stillness as He had since sunset. Timrok stood just outside the columns of light, feet shoulder-width apart, arms crossed, and enlarged to the full extent of his frame. "Yes," Elric said. "The Father has been speaking to Him all night."

"What is He saying?"

"I do not know. Let's find out."

Elric waved to Timrok, who unfurled his wings and made a graceful glide down the hill. In an instant, Prestus appeared at the top of the hill and took Timrok's position next to Jesus. Timrok finished his glide, landing in front of Elric and Zaben.

"Captain," Timrok said.

"Good morning," Elric said. "A full night of prayer. It seems there is a word from the Throne. Were you able to hear any of it?"

Timrok nodded. "He is about to start another ministry tour. But more than that . . . " A huge grin erupted from behind Timrok's bushy mustache and beard, and he bounced on his toes like an excited child. "He has been given confirmation of the names of the twelve. He will make the appointments today."

"Finally," Zaben said, "the preparation of the generals for the King's army begins."

The sun broke over the horizon, and Elric turned to the east.

Still sitting below on the slope, Jenli took his dagger, held the blade up to the fresh rays of the morning sun, and scraped the edge of it across his cheek and chin. He repeated on the other side. Then he moved to the top of his head.

"Why does he do that?" Timrok asked, crossing his arms.

Zaben crossed his arms. "This is a good question."

Jenli finished shaving all the stubble on the top of his head and returned the dagger to the holder strapped to his ankle. He stood, turned, and walked toward the gathering.

Elric smiled and crossed his arms. "You can ask him now."

Jenli stepped up to three sets of crossed arms and staring faces. Looking a little uncomfortable, he said, "What?"

Elric laughed. "Timrok has a burning question." He turned to Timrok. "Go ahead, ask."

"Why do you do that?" Timrok said.

"What?"

"The whole . . . " Timrok ran his hand over the bushel of unkempt hair on top of his own head and around his face. "Shaving everything."

Jenli smiled. "I used to keep my hair long."

"It was beautiful," Elric said. "Dark black, long, straight, and flowing."

"Before the Rebellion." Jenli's smile melted away, and he became solemn. "But then . . . " He stopped. His eyes welled up. "Then, during the Rebellion, while we were executing the order to banish the traitors from the King's Realm, I grabbed one of the rebels from behind. My ninth or tenth one. Before I could translate to the Middle Realm, he reached back and took fists full of my hair and wouldn't let go. He flipped me over his back, still holding my hair, and we ended up face to face."

Jenli wiped both his eyes with his sleeve and paused for a breath. "I knew him. We were good friends. I will never forget his eyes. All the light—gone. Nothing but empty hatred." He stopped for another deep breath. "I pulled him close, wrapped my wings around us and translated. Once in the Middle Realm, the transformation of his body happened fast. It was like his skin was on fire. He was screaming and writhing, and he couldn't let go of my hair. He kept trying to pull away, but his fingers were so contorted with pain, he couldn't untangle my hair from his fists. He was so close, the sulfur from his breath burned my eyes. I couldn't see."

Jenli took two slow breaths, tears streaming down his cheeks. "I translated back before the transformation was complete."

Elric put his hand on Jenli's shoulder.

"He was my friend," Jenli said with a crackling voice.

"That was a hard day," Zaben said.

Jenli wiped his eyes again. "Before the Rebellion, my hair was a glory to the King. After that day, it seemed only an impediment to our new roles in the Kingdom. I shaved it all off. And I will continue to do so until the Kingdom is restored."

Timrok sniffled, wiped his eyes, and wrapped Jenli up in a brawny hug. He stepped back, still holding Jenli's shoulders and said, "It is an honor to serve with you."

With a cheerful lilt, Elric said, "Timrok, tell him your good news from last night."

Timrok slapped Jenli's shoulders twice and stepped back. "The King will appoint His twelve generals today! I heard this word directly from the Throne."

Jenli managed a bittersweet smile. "This is great news. The Day of the Lord draws near."

Motion at the top of the hill. Elric turned.

Jesus stood, picked up a small kneeling blanket, flung it over his shoulder, and started down the hill.

Timrok's team formed a tight perimeter around Jesus and marched with Him, their swords out and ready. The troop passed by Elric and the lieutenants.

Elric stepped out behind the troop and followed along. Zaben, Timrok, and Jenli joined.

"Zaben," Elric said as they walked, "we still need to identify a replacement for Lorr. This is your team—have you considered anyone?"

"Not yet."

"How about Luxor?" Jenli said.

"He has proven useful these last few weeks," Elric said. "But I leave this to you, Zaben."

"I don't really know him," Zaben said. "What strengths does he bring to the team?"

Jenli answered, "He was certainly a faithful warrior while on my team in Nazareth. Good with a sword. And . . . he has a keen eye for strategy. Not as visionary as you, of course, but I do think he would complement your team well."

"What about his time of captivity?" Elric asked.

"He does not speak of it. I do not even know how he escaped."

"That's not unusual," Elric said. "Those that do break free are never able to tell their tale. The pain of being separated from the King is too much to bear. How is he now? Is he able to take on the load of this mission?"

"I think so. He seems . . . slightly distant compared to before his captivity. And his eyes look duller. But, considering all he's been through, he appears strong and ready to serve."

"Very well," Zaben said. "I choose Luxor for my team."

"Good," Elric said. "He can have Lorr's sword and shield. And he can begin immediately. Who was Lorr's charge?"

"Judas."

"Brief Luxor on our mission and introduce him to Judas. I expect that, after the King appoints the twelve today, we will begin another ministry tour soon. So, Luxor needs to assume his role quickly."

"Yes, sir."

* * *

From the cave where Vorsogh had been gathering beaelzur recruits, a black mist floated out in the Middle Realm. Silent, thin, and opaque, it propelled forward inches above the ground—fast enough to cross the vast wilderness in a day, but not so fast as to capture the attention of any observant spirit. Minutes passed before the final wisp of dark mist left the cave. An entire legion of stealthy demonic energy swept across the wilderness floor toward the eastern shores of the Sea of Galilee.

The mist reached the northeastern boundary of the Decapolis region. Unnoticed, unchallenged.

It rolled into Ein Gev at the third watch of the night. With a slower pace, it floated through the streets, morphing around buildings, driving toward its goal.

Here and there, dogs barked. Birds fluttered away.

Down a narrow side street, where the continuous line of dwellings on each side formed a stone and mudbrick city canyon, the mist piled up outside one home. Finally, the last of the dark vapor joined the silent cloud.

The cloud boiled in place for only a moment.

Then it all disappeared through the front wall.

* * *

From a dead sleep, Daniel sat bolt upright and screamed.

Terror gripped his entire being, and he struggled to breathe. His eyes strained through the darkness.

"Who's there?" he squeaked out through a constricted throat.

Silence.

Though thick with night shadows, the room looked empty. No unwanted intruders. And yet . . . there was a presence. An unseen presence. A presence that felt . . . familiar. A presence that . . .

"Levi? Levi, is that you?"

In his right ear he heard a voice from the past. "Hello little brother. Did you miss me?" The voice seemed familiar, but it almost sounded like a chorus of voices, melded together.

"I know you're not really my brother. And I . . . I thought you left."

"I had no choice. But now I am back."

"You feel different. Heavier. More—"

"Powerful? Yes, I am a thousand times more powerful than before. You are mine, and I will not be driven away again."

18

THE KING'S WAYS

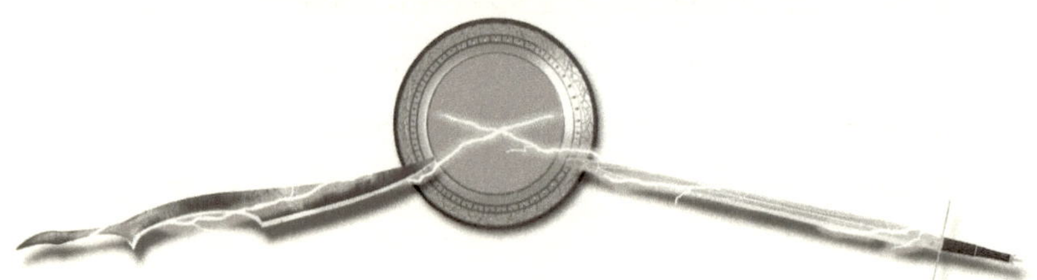

Battle minus 1 year

Elric stood back from the war map at Simon's house in Capernaum and let the lieutenants study the movements for themselves. Zaben chewed on his lower lip and pointed at different features in the map to himself as though calculating his next twenty moves. Timrok rocked heel to toe, his hands behind his back, examining all the swirling motion. Jenli went back and forth from his ledger to the map and back to his ledger.

Jenli jotted something in his book, shook his head, and said, "So many appointments, connections, protection details, countermoves. With everything concentrated around the Son of Man, the pace is unlike anything I've ever seen."

Elric kept his place in the back. "Do not concern yourself with extraneous details. All the other elzurim have their assignments. Keep your teams concentrated on the King and the twelve generals." He stepped forward. "As you can see, we are about to begin another tour of Galilee and the surrounding regions. But first, tomorrow, the Son of Man will spend one more day teaching here. He will work from the mount overlooking the Sea of Galilee as before. Expect the largest crowd we have had so far. The Son of Man will have much to say concerning the Kingdom. After tomorrow, we move out."

Jaeden and Ry dropped through the ceiling and landed beside the map.

"Pardon the interruption, Captain," Jaeden said. "We bring news from Lacidar."

Elric motioned with his hand, and the map disappeared. "Excellent. It was my hope to hear something soon."

"John is being held in Machaerus, where Herod Antipas currently resides. John is in chains in the palace prison." Jaeden said. "Lacidar is with him."

"What charges are levied against him?" Elric asked. "Is there to be a trial?"

"No official charges yet," Jaeden answered.

Ry added, "Herod Antipas fears John's influence over the people and that he might raise up a rebellion. But John's denouncing of Antipas's marriage to Herodias is his unspoken offense."

"He will likely be charged with sedition," Jaeden said, "for these are the words being spoken to Antipas by the enemy."

"A capital offense," Timrok said with a grimace. "We need to break him out."

"By force?" Zaben said. "Do his followers have the strength to attack Machaerus?"

Jaeden shook his head. "I think not. It is a citadel on a high rocky hill surrounded by deep ravines."

"Visibility in all directions," Ry said.

Jaeden said, "Ninety-foot walls."

Ry said, "Heavily fortified."

Elric motioned with his hands. "We all agree a frontal assault is not practical. Can we reach Antipas himself?"

Jaeden shook his head and scowled. "The King is speaking to him continually. But the enemy blocks almost all His word. And the light that does get through never gets past his personal strongholds."

"Someone close to him, then," Zaben said. "His wife, siblings, counselors?"

"Surely not his wife," Ry answered. "Her hatred for John is very strong."

"There is Herodias's daughter," Jaeden said. "She is young and impressionable."

Ry nodded. "And perhaps the centurion who brought John in. While a loyal soldier, he appears sympathetic to John's case."

"Do you have freedom to move about within the palace?" Elric asked.

Jaeden shrugged and gave a half nod. "There are many beaelzurim there. Molech keeps his seat wherever Antipas resides. However, many people come and go. And there are elzurim who travel with their charges. So, it is possible to move about, but our authority there is restricted."

"This is sufficient," Elric said. "Try to get close to someone who might provide an opening to speak to Antipas. Look for opportunities. We must reach him."

"Yes, sir," Jaeden and Ry answered in unison.

"And make certain Lacidar keeps John encouraged. We will surely see him freed."

"In His service."

* * *

From the shoulder of the hill overlooking the Sea of Galilee near Capernaum, Zaben gazed out over the multitude gathered to hear the Son of Man. Thousands sat on the slope, pressed in tight and straining for every word coming from the top of the mount.

As usual, sinister sets of red eyes peered in from the darkness of the tree lines on each side. Zaben gave a little chuckle. *Full of bravado when the King is unseen. Full of fear when He is present in the flesh.*

As usual, floods of light in the Middle Realm streamed down through Jesus and washed over the crowd. Yet, even though immersed in the waves of pure light, much of the word glanced off the people's hard shells.

Zaben shook his head. *They can tell He speaks words of life, and they are drawn to Him. But they hear so little. So many strongholds.*

Luxor stepped up from behind and stood to Zaben's left. "A large crowd today," Luxor said.

Zaben nodded. "The largest one yet."

"This could be the foundation of a sizable army."

"Not counting the women and children, it is a good beginning."

"I am confused, though," Luxor said. "'Blessed are the meek' are not words to rally an army."

Zaben smiled. "Welcome to the team. We have our orders, but the King executes on His timetable and according to His ways. He is always more interested in hearts than battle plans."

"Still, there is going to be a battle?"

"Eventually. We know very little."

"Is it true that He has mortal flesh?"

"Just like every other man. Except His Spirit is alive. He must accomplish His mission as a man—He is bound by His word."

"But that means . . . "

"That is why we are here. Our primary mission is to protect the King. The enemy cannot touch Him directly, but He can be reached through the hands of men."

Zaben pointed at the small group of men closest to Jesus. "And these are our secondary mission. The twelve generals. When the King does raise up His army, these will be the leaders."

"There has been no military training, even for these," Luxor said.

"Heart first. I expect the rest will come later."

Simon the Zealot and Judas sat together, off to the side of the others. Zaben motioned toward them and said, "You have not had long to get to know Judas. But what is your assessment?"

"He has no love for Rome," Luxor said. "He is ready for a liberator to lead Israel out of bondage. Not as militant as the Zealot, but he is cunning. He seems to have an eye for strategies."

"Good. That will be a useful strength for a general."

Jesus' booming voice interrupted as He continued His teaching. "You have heard that it was said, 'You shall love your neighbor and hate your enemy.' But I say to you, love your enemies and pray for those who persecute you, so that you may prove yourselves to be sons of your Father who is in heaven; for He causes His sun to rise on the evil and the good, and sends rain on the righteous and the unrighteous."

The crowd stirred at this, another saying that challenged their hearts and their understanding of the King. Zaben eyed the disciples. Most appeared captivated and amazed. Judas fidgeted and whispered something to Simon.

"It seems the Son of Man's sayings are difficult for some," Luxor said.

Zaben nodded. "Heart first. Remember, it is easy to let zeal for the mission cloud one's vision." He paused. "I know." He paused again. "Just keep him focused on the King. The seeds of faith will bear fruit in season."

19

WE ARE LEVI

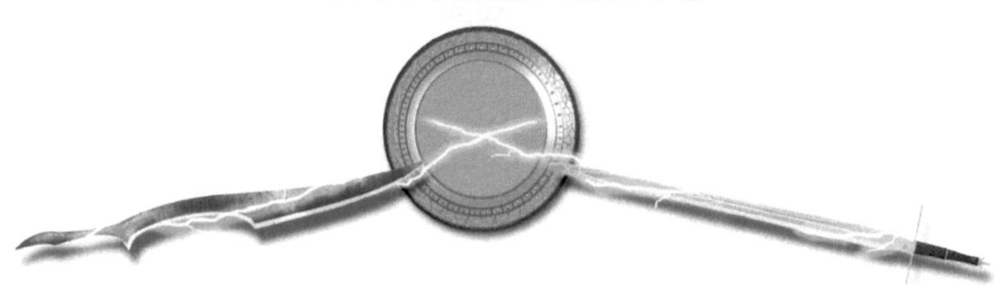

Battle minus 1 year

Daniel gripped his left wrist with his right hand. *The shaking won't stop!* He gripped his right wrist with his left hand. He knit his fingers together. Nothing stopped the uncontrollable shaking. His head twitched. A shudder shot from his head to his feet like a jolt of lightning.

"Levi," he stammered. "Are you doing this to my body?"

No answer. Only fear—fear boiling up from the pit of his stomach until it clung to the roof of his mouth. He clenched his teeth to keep it contained. He shot uneasy glances around the room of his empty house.

What am I so afraid of? He made another frantic scan. *Everything.* And mixed with the fear—hatred.

I remember this feeling of hatred before—when the evil spirit was with me, in me.

But this time it was heavier. Like the weight of a thousand generations of resentment multiplied within a thousand bitter hearts.

He shuddered again and watched his shaking hands as though they belonged to someone else. A blanket of darkness descended over his thoughts, and the world began to fade.

"No!" he shouted, jerking his head around to drive back the fog. "Let go of me! It's almost dusk, and I need to get down to the fishing boats."

No voice answered. But the fear escalated to terror. And the hatred erupted into rage. And the curtain sank lower and lower, squeezing his consciousness, and crushing . . . all light . . . from . . . his eyes . . . until . . .

* * *

A man lumbered through the night shadows down a less-traveled street in Ein Gev. He muttered a steady stream of unintelligible words under his breath, interrupted by brief bursts of shouting and shaking his fist. He carried no lamp in his hand. He carried nothing at all— except unseen baggage of fitful delirium.

A man and his wife approached from the opposite direction but diverted to the other side of the street and quickened their steps as they passed. The husband kept checking over his shoulder, and the wife clung to his arm.

The man paid no notice to the passing couple.

A dog barked from the shadows of a side alley. The crickets became silent.

The man stopped in front of an opening in a stone-faced building. The opening led downstairs to a small unlit alcove. On the left side of the alcove, a warm yellow glow escaped through the rough cracks and edges of a thick wooden door, which muffled raucous voices and laughter from within. He stepped through the opening, down into the dark, stone-walled stairwell.

The dog stopped barking, and the crickets resumed their chirping.

The room behind the door at the bottom of the stairs was square, with dank, plastered walls and just enough light to see how much wine was left in the bottom of a cup. Ten square wood tables with their chairs filled the space. One wall had a full-length stone slab counter at standing height. Behind the counter, shelves held dozens of clay pots and pitchers of various sizes and shapes. Large clay vessels, much too large to move by hand, lined the wall below the shelves.

Two dozen men occupied the tables, each with a large cup of wine either in his hand, at his lips, or on the table. Tables of four. Tables of two and three. One table with six crowded around for a lively game of knucklebones. Every time the bones rolled, the group erupted in shouts of joy and disappointment, and the jingling of coins followed. Some tables had loud arguments; some had riotous laughter; some had private, solemn solitude.

Business was good for Ezra, the man behind the counter.

The door opened, and a man entered from off the street, muttering something unintelligible under his breath. Ezra watched him come in, but none of the other patrons looked up. A very large man with huge muscular folded arms, a grim stone face, and watchful eyes stood in the corner near the counter and followed the newcomer with his eyes.

The man off the street stepped up to the counter. "Wine," he said. His voice sounded low and gravelly with overtones that made it sound like a chorus of voices. "Full strength, undiluted."

"I have to charge extra for full strength."

"Just bring it."

The man stood at the counter and drank his wine by himself, never looking at the other people. The strong drink went down fast. He thumped the empty cup on the counter and said, "Bring another."

As Ezra filled the cup from a flask, another man approached the counter with two empty cups. "Two more, please," the man said.

Ezra reached for another flask and went to work.

The man turned to the lone man at the counter and said, "Daniel! I'm surprised to see you here. Aren't you working tonight?"

Without looking up from his cup, Daniel growled, "We are Levi."

The man gave Daniel a friendly bump on the shoulder with his hand. "That's funny. Did Joel give you the night off?"

Daniel pushed the man's hand away with a violent sweep of his arm. He turned his head and locked eyes. "We are Levi."

The wild malevolence in Daniel's eyes and the unearthly rasp of his voice made the man back away. He dropped three coins on the counter, took his cups of wine, and returned to his table. He whispered something to his friend at the table, and the two stole uneasy glances at the back of Daniel at the counter.

Daniel thumped his empty cup on the counter and said, "Bring another."

Ezra said, "You should slow down, friend."

"We are not your friend. Bring more wine."

"You have not paid for the first two yet. Perhaps you should pay your bill before I bring you any more."

"We owe nothing to you insignificant mortals."

Ezra eyed the strongman in the corner. The man nodded.

"I'm afraid I must ask you to leave," Ezra said.

"You have no authority over us. Bring more wine."

Ezra nodded to the strongman and motioned with his hand toward the door.

The strongman stood a full head and shoulders above Daniel, and his arms were as big around as Daniel's thigh. He put his hand on Daniel's shoulder and said, "Let's go."

Daniel grunted and swiped the strongman's hand away.

The strongman grimaced, locked his jaw, stepped forward, and wrapped his huge arms around Daniel's chest from behind. He started to lift Daniel off the ground, but Daniel thrust both elbows back into his gut with a surprising *whump*. The man doubled over, out of breath and dazed. Daniel took hold of him at his biceps, lifted him above his head, and tossed him across the room like a sack of barley. The strongman flailed through the air, smashing three tables, toppling six men, and landing in a heap against the back wall.

Every man in the room jumped to his feet. The six on the floor got up. With a tense silence, they all looked at Daniel, then at the strongman who was picking himself up, then back at Daniel.

With teeth bared like a cornered animal, Daniel snarled, "We hate you. We will kill you all."

Back on his feet, the strongman shouted, "Get him!"

Three men made tentative approaches. Daniel tossed each aside with ease. One got up and wiped the blood from his broken nose. One split his lip. He spit out a mouthful of blood, and a tooth landed in the puddles of blood. The third stayed seated with his back to the wall where he landed and supported his left arm with his right hand.

"Now!" someone yelled.

All at once, the strongman and the rest of the men converged like a pack of enraged wolves. Swinging their fists and driving inward, the men attacked.

Daniel landed a single blow to the center of one man's chest, and he flew backward as though kicked by mule. He grabbed one man's hand and bent his wrist until it snapped. One attacker went low for Daniel's leg. Daniel took hold of his head, swung the man around, and took out five others.

Not one could land a solid hit. Not one could grasp his arm or hand. With the strength of twenty men, Daniel dispatched every one that came within his reach. Men shouted angry curses, moaned agonized cries, and roared through desperate assaults. Daniel anticipated every move, countered every hit, and inflicted pain with every contact.

The attackers drew thin with more and more of them lying disabled on the floor. The strongman wiped the blood away from the cut above his eye and prepared for another charge.

Crash!

A large clay pitcher shattered on the back of Daniel's head, sending wine and chunks of pottery flying across the room. Daniel crumpled to the ground. Ezra stood behind him with the remains of a pitcher handle in his hands.

The men pounced on Daniel, unconscious and face down in a pool of wine and blood. Four men pinned each of his arms to the ground, two on each arm. Four more took his legs.

The strongman called out to Ezra, "There is rope in the back room. Bring it out, and I'll tie him up before he wakes."

The strongman just finished binding Daniel's hands behind his back with thick rope—double wound and cinched tight—when Daniel stirred. Daniel kicked both his legs free, sending those four men falling backward. The strongman drove his knee into Daniel's back, but Daniel rolled, kicked out the strongman's legs from behind, and leapt to his feet.

The men backed away.

Daniel strained against the ropes, but his arms stayed pinned behind his back.

Flat on his back, the strongman sat up. "This fight is over," he said. "You are bound, and I am taking you to the Roman authorities."

Daniel showed his teeth like a wild animal. He shouted, "Araugh!" and pulled his hands free. The rope snapped as though it was made of wet parchment.

Daniel tossed the remnants of the rope in the strongman's face, turned, and walked out the door.

The room lay in shambles. Busted tables, broken pottery, spilled wine and blood. Unanswered questions filled the air. What kind of hatred would drive a man like that? Where did he get such unnatural strength? How do you stop him? Where would he strike next?

20

SECOND MINISTRY TOUR

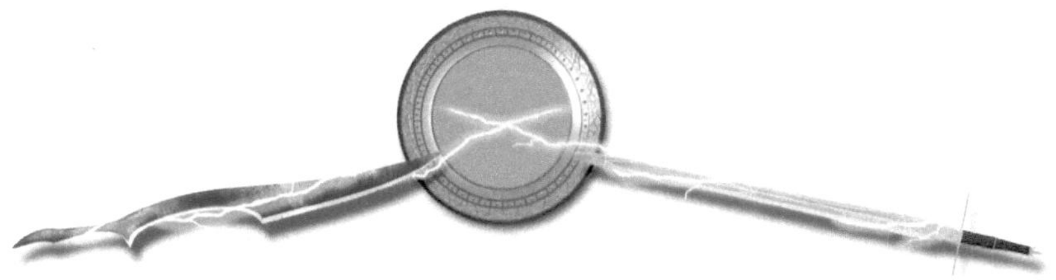

Battle minus 11 months

One month into the second tour of Galilee, on the outskirts of the nomad encampment just outside Cana, Elric finished a conference with Grigor and left Grigor waiting under a tree. Elric rejoined Zaben, Jenli, and Timrok.

"One more day here in Cana," Elric said. "Then we move south to Nain."

"Are we stopping anywhere along the way?" Zaben asked.

"No. The Son of Man has an appointment in Nain." Elric turned to Jenli. "I need you to go ahead of us for a special detail. It is time critical. You will leave immediately. Go see Grigor for details."

"Yes, sir." Jenli turned and took a step toward Grigor.

"And Jenli," Elric said.

Jenli stopped.

"I think sleep will be the simplest solution."

Jenli responded with a blank expression.

"And be at the city gate at noon in three days."

Jenli nodded and continued toward Grigor.

Three days later, Elric and Timrok walked in front of the southbound caravan as it approached Nain. Behind them, the Son of Man and the twelve, traveling light. Close behind them, another fifty on foot. Behind them, at a distance, the full mass of the caravan with wagons, beasts of burden, tents, supplies, and hundreds of followers.

The teams of Timrok, Zaben, and Jenli formed disciplined columns all along the entourage, and enemy engagements were few.

Ahead, Elric spotted the northern city gate. He checked the sun.

"Almost noon," he said. "We should see . . . yes, there."

"A funeral procession?" Timrok said.

Just passing out of the city gate, in the Physical Realm, a sizable crowd followed an open-top wooden coffin borne on the shoulders of six men. A single veiled woman walked behind the coffin. Even from this distance, the wails of the mourners rose above the noise of the caravan.

"Yes," said Elric.

"Is this why we are here? Is this the Son of Man's appointment?"

"It is. This is the only son of a widow. He was only in his teens."

"But it is a funeral. What more can He do now other than offer comfort? Unless He plans on . . . "

Elric smiled.

"Yes! This will get the enemy's attention."

The enemy. In the Middle Realm, the funeral procession looked like a small battlefield. Dozens of beaelzurim swirled through the people, shooting flaming arrows of sorrow, hopelessness, and anger. Thick clouds of noxious words choked the whole atmosphere around the procession. A demon lieutenant walked with the mother with his bat wing draped over her head. From above, showers of light—filled with words from the Throne—rained down on the people. Words of strength, peace, encouragement, hope. But none of the light could break through the darkness. The people embraced the pain and breathed in the lies of the enemy. Several elzurim fought to break through to the mother, but their attempts were repeatedly thwarted.

"Almost every funeral I have seen looks like this," Elric said. "Death is the final victory for the enemy. And it almost always leads to further victories for the enemy among the living."

"Haha," Timrok said. "But this one will be different."

"There is Jenli," Elric said. "Good."

Jenli approached from another direction, away from the commotion of the procession. In his arms, the form of a man's spirit lay draped, limp and motionless. Jenli met up with Elric and Timrok and walked with them.

"It appears everything went according to plan," Elric said, looking at the man in Jenli's arms.

"Mostly," Jenli said. "At the moment of his passing, I met him and immediately caused him to sleep as you suggested. I agree that this will result in fewer complications."

"But . . . " Elric said.

"But the enemy contended with me. Though the boy would have gone to Abraham's Bosom in Sheol, Satan has legal rights, and the local beaelzur principality was not willing to let me hold him here."

"How did you prevail?"

"Commander Kai. He came and enforced the King's command. The enemy had to relent."

The caravan drew closer to the funeral procession. They would cross paths soon.

"Captain," Timrok said, "Shall I drive the enemy away in preparation for the arrival of the King?"

"With the King Himself present, I doubt that will be . . . " Elric paused. He looked over at Timrok and smiled. "Yes. Lieutenant, take your team and drive away these traitors."

Timrok gave a little hop and said, "Yes, sir!" He drew both his swords and gave a flash toward the back.

Five lights streaked forward. Timrok leapt into the air, and six bolts of lightning smashed into the funeral procession. Timrok's fight did not last long. The beaelzurim spotted the Son of Man approaching, and they scurried away before He could get close.

Jesus and the twelve met up with the procession. He spoke with some of the mourners as they walked and learned of the widow's loss.

He caught up with her, walked alongside, and said, "Do not go on weeping."

And He came up and touched the coffin, and the bearers came to a halt.

The whole procession stopped. The crowd from the caravan gathered around. The mourners quit wailing, and the assembly became quiet.

Jenli stepped forward and laid the boy's spirit back in his body.

Jesus said, "Young man, I say to you, arise!"

A blast of light exploded in the Middle Realm. And from the middle of the light, the boy sat up.

"What's going on?" the boy said. "Where am I? What is all this?"

Shocked at the movement, the coffin bearers almost lost control. They steadied the box and lowered it to the ground. Jesus took the boy's hand and helped him step out. He gave him back to his mother and said, "The Father has turned mourning into dancing for you. He has untied your sackcloth and encircled you with joy."

"Look at this!" the mother squealed. "He's alive!" She hugged him and shook him with tears streaming down her face. Her mourner's veil ripped from her head and fell into the dirt. She couldn't stop laughing and hugging him.

The crowd from the procession mobbed around.

"Is it true?"

"How can this be?"

"He's really alive!"

Jesus slipped away from the crowd and headed back up the trail from which they had just come. The twelve followed but kept gawking back at the living boy in the middle of the crowd. The crowd of followers in the caravan stood around in awe.

"A great prophet has appeared among us!"

"God has visited His people!"

Zaben stepped up to Elric, Jenli, and Timrok. "That's it? We came all the way down here for this one widow?"

Elric laughed. "Does this surprise you?"

"No. Still, it is no way to raise an army."

Elric laughed again. "His ways are higher than our ways. I love what He is doing."

"Taking back territory from the enemy," Timrok said. "Enforcing His kingdom."

"Where to next?" Jenli asked.

"I do not know yet," Elric said. "We'll just keep moving through Galilee, taking back territory from the enemy. One soul at a time."

* * *

The clouds hung low over the Decapolis town of Hippos, providing a welcome respite from the blazing sun for the vendors and patrons on the street market. It was a busy afternoon. Meats, clothing, vegetables, wine, fruits, tapestries—colorful booths packed both sides of the lane. The patrons filled the lane, elbow to elbow. People squeezed by each other, turning sideways and lifting their baskets over their heads. The chaos had a natural rhythm, and consistent buzz filled the air.

"Stop!" rang out above the buzz. "Thief!"

A ragged-looking man with a pouch stuffed with dates in his left hand broke away from a vendor stand and pushed through the crowd.

"Stop that man! He is a thief!" the vendor yelled.

People looked around.

The man plowed through, knocking the unsuspecting down as he went.

"Somebody stop him! Stop him! Thief!"

The thief approached two large men in the center of the lane and turned his shoulder to burrow between them. The two men stood their ground and grabbed the thief.

"Where are *you* going?" one of the men said.

The thief made an inhuman grunt and swung his left arm, catching one man mid-chest. The man flew backward and crashed into a cart with containers filled with grain. The grain spilled all over the ground, and the cart collapsed beneath him. The thief grabbed the other man with his free right hand, lifted him off the ground and flung him across the lane. He flew twenty feet, above the heads of the crowd, and smashed through a cart of greens.

The thief reeled around, hissing at the people, who backed away with perplexed eyes. He snatched a skin filled with wine hanging from the awning of a vendor to his right and growled, "We hate you. We hate you all."

He rushed forward, and the people stepped aside—those that could. Those that couldn't got plowed over. He reached the end of the marketplace lane and disappeared.

* * *

Jaeden and Ry entered the Machaerus compound with Judah and Reuben, two of the prophet John's closest disciples. Jaeden put one hand on Judah's shoulder. Ry kept his on Reuben's shoulder. Both elzurim left their swords sheathed. Two simple warriors with their human charges. No threat. No cause for alarm.

A Roman soldier led Judah and Reuben down long, grand halls with majestic columns. Staff and officials of the state passed by and milled about. Roman sentries stood at doorway openings.

Jaeden and Ry passed high-ranking beaelzurim—commanders, captains, even one general. Their presence drew sneers and hateful glances, but Jaeden and Ry kept their eyes drilled forward and avoided all appearances of engagement.

They turned down one final hallway with a door and two sentries at the end of it. One of the sentries unlocked a large lock, rotated an iron arm to its open position, and pushed the thick door open. They stepped into a darker space. The walls, made of common stacked gray stone, had none of the grandeur of the rest of the palace. They stopped at the top of the landing, and the door swung shut behind them. The iron arm clanged into place on the other side of the door. Another guard met them on the landing and took over the lead.

Down the wide stone staircase into the dungeon they descended. They turned left past rows of solitary iron door cellblocks, then right down another line of cells. Desperate moans from the hopeless unseen echoed down the hallways and did not pause at the heavy tromping of two Roman soldiers and shuffling feet of two outsiders.

They stopped in front of an iron door with no window.

Jaeden and Ry stayed outside with their charges to maintain appearances.

The cellblock soldier clinked through a set of keys, found one, and opened the door. He stepped back and let Judah and Reuben enter. The door clanged shut, and the two soldiers waited outside.

Jaeden and Ry looked at each other, nodded and passed through the front of the cell wall.

They walked into a room thick with sulfurous smoke in the Middle Realm. They coughed and squinted through the haze.

From somewhere within the fog, a dark figure with a raspy voice spoke to John. "And he hasn't extended his arm to deliver Israel. This man is not the Messiah at all. Which means your whole life was a waste. And what is your reward? Prison. You will die here. For nothing! Nothing!"

A demon captain!

Jaeden and Ry spotted Lacidar, bound and stuffed in the corner of the cell. His resonar lay beside him. Jaeden and Ry both reached for their swords, but Lacidar shook his head. They pushed them back into their scabbards and stood in front of Judah and Reuben, face to face with the captain.

"Oh, we have visitors," the demon said in a sing-song voice. "Are you come to vanquish me?"

Without a word Jaeden and Ry crossed their arms and stood firm.

"I'm fine," John said to Judah and Reuben. "They are giving me food and water, and I have not been mistreated."

"Have there been charges filed yet?" Judah asked.

"I do not know."

"They can't continue to hold you without cause, can they?" Reuben said.

"It's Herod."

"What can we do?" Reuben asked. "Surely there is some official that we can plead your case before."

"I don't know." John buried his face in his hands and began sobbing.

Judah knelt beside John and put his hand around his back. Reuben put his hand on John's shoulder.

"I'm sorry," John said between breaths. "I'm sorry. It's just . . . this place. It's so lonely and full of hopelessness. Sometimes I wonder . . . "

"What?"

"Nothing."

"What?"

"Do this for me. Find Jesus, wherever He is and ask Him this: 'Are You the Coming One, or are we to look for another?' Please. Find Him. And bring me word quickly."

"Yes, master. We will."

Judah pounded on the door. It opened, and he and Reuben went out.

Jaeden and Ry lingered a moment and looked over at Lacidar with determined eyes. They glanced back at the demon captain and turned to leave.

As they passed through the cell wall, the captain's raspy voice continued, "Those two will never make it back here. Even if they do find Jesus, they will probably be killed by a Roman soldier or a bandit. It doesn't matter because you already know the answer. He is not the One . . . "

21

UNCHAINED

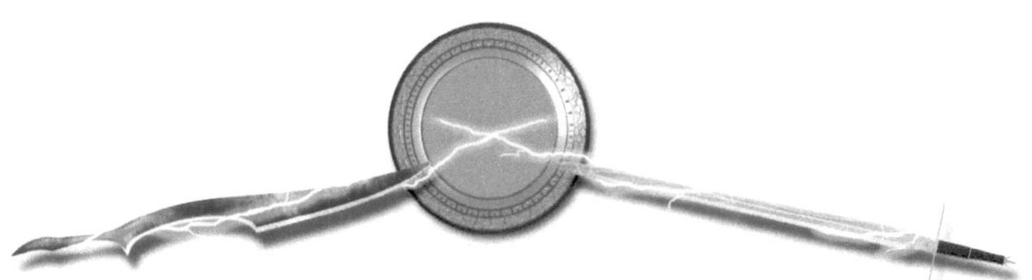

Battle minus 11 months

Gergesa, on the eastern shore of Galilee, like most of the Decapolis region, had long since abandoned traditional Jewish customs for pagan traditions and values. Secular mixed with the sacred. Pigs grazed on the open hills by the sea, and legs of ham hung beside lamb and goats in the marketplace.

The meat quarter filled the far southern end of the marketplace, with vendors on both sides of the wide lane. Stacks of raw pork, lamb, and fish created a wall of pungent air at the entrance of the lane. Just north of the meat quarter, colorful displays of fruits and vegetables lined the produce quarter. Above that, the grains quarter. And then the textiles on the north end. The width of the lane disguised the large number of people shuffling through the dirt street, but the cloud of dust rose high on the busy afternoon.

Through the dust, through the malodorous meat quarter, a disheveled man stumbled up the market lane. He muttered a steady stream of unintelligible words under his breath, interrupted by brief bursts of shouting and shaking his fist. His eyes, wild with malice, darted from person to person with frantic hunger. The patrons created an uneasy bubble of space around him and watched him with wary side glances.

He made a move toward a young woman with a basket of fruit coming from the opposite direction but then veered away.

"Not this one!" the man grunted to himself.

The woman skittered away to the far side of the lane, and the man continued up the dirt path. He came upon three women with their backs to him in the produce quarter. He turned in toward them.

"No!" he grumbled. "I hate all of these."

He cut hard left and continued up the grain quarter, growling and shouting, "No! Why do you fight us? Why do you fight me? I am your master!"

He passed two more women.

"No! No!"

He slapped his face with multiple blows and yanked at his matted hair. Men passed by, but he gave no notice to any of them.

A young woman with her mother pulled a scarf from a vendor rack. Both women, oblivious to the strange man staggering up the street, admired the scarf. The young woman held the bright purple silk against her cheek and nodded. The mother stroked it with her hand and smiled.

Slam! From out of nowhere, without a warning, the crazy man pounced on the young girl like a hungry lion. They toppled onto a stack of rugs. The girl screamed and flailed, but the man pinned her down with ease.

The mother screamed and threw herself onto the man's back, yanking at his shoulders and pulling him off with all her strength. The man grunted and flung one arm around. The force of his blow lifted her off the ground and sent her flying backward into the scarf stand. He used his free hand to grab the bottom of his tunic and rip it off over his head. He had nothing on underneath. He then used both hands to tear at her clothes.

A small crowd gathered, wary and shocked at the audacious spectacle.

"Help!" screamed the mother, untangling herself from the pile of chaos. "Somebody do something!"

Two men from the crowd jumped forward and reached for the attacker. With a single thrust, the attacker kicked one man over the heads of the growing crowd like a mule would launch an empty bucket. The other man received a backhanded fist to his jaw, flew ten feet to the side, and landed motionless in a cloud of dust.

"Help! Help!" the mother shrieked. "Stop him! Help!"

Five more men stepped forward. One by one, each met unhuman power that dispatched them like pesky flies. Between the interruptions, the wild man continued to tear at the girl's clothes.

"Help! Help!" the mother continued, pushing her way through the mass of onlookers.

Another man flew through the air and plowed through the mob.

"What is this? What's going on?" A man's booming voice rang out from the back of the throng. "Make way! Move aside!"

A detachment of five Roman soldiers.

"Move! Move!" the officer shouted, pushing his way forward. His four spearmen pressed the people back with the shafts of their spears and created an open lane for the officer to pass through. He stepped over a man lying unconscious in the dirt and continued inward toward the source of the disturbance.

The officer shook his head at the naked man on top of a screaming girl with half her clothes ripped off.

"You!" the officer shouted. "Enough of this! Get up!" He stepped up and grasped the man's shoulder. "I said get up!"

Smash! The man's fist hit the officer so hard, it dented his breastplate and lifted him off the ground. The officer landed on his back gasping for air.

In an instant, the four spearmen advanced. One thrust his spear toward the man, but the man intercepted the tip and used the spear to vault the soldier over the people's heads. Another took hold of a foot but received a mule kick from the other foot. The third came in close, raised his heel and prepared to kick the man over, but the man snagged the soldier's foot and flipped him backward.

Tromp, tromp, tromp, tromp. The heavy cadence of ten Roman soldiers in double-time step rumbled down the street. They surrounded the man at a safe distance and leveled their spears. The one remaining spearman from the original squad nodded to the others and said, "Together! Ready . . . now!"

Eleven sharp iron spearheads thrust forward in unison and made contact with bare flesh from the man's thighs to his neck. The man reached for one of the nearest spears, but the other ten pressed hard enough to draw blood. The man tried rolling, but every movement drew more blood. He lay still, growling like caged animal.

The Roman officer stepped up, brushed the dirt off his arms and dented breastplate. He reached into one of the soldier's packs and pulled out a set of thick iron chains. He handed them to his squad member and ordered, "Chain this man. Make it tight. Make it hurt."

The soldier started with chains around the man's ankles. The man tried to resist, but the spearpoints drove deeper. Next, the soldier chained the man's hands behind his back.

"Stand him up," the officer said.

Two of the soldiers reached under his arms and hoisted him up while the others kept their spearpoints pressed close against vulnerable flesh.

"Turn him around," the officer commanded.

The two soldiers took hold of his shoulders and rotated him around. The others formed a tight circle all the way around with their spears always on the edge of drawing blood.

A woman standing nearby covered the girl with a shawl, helped her up, and hurried her over to her hysterical mother. The two women stayed tight in each other's arms, sobbing.

The man's wild eyes shot between the officer and the people in the crowd. Those closest in the crowd backed up. The man panted and hissed and bared his teeth like a wild dog. The crowd backed up more.

"You are . . . very bold," the officer said in a composed, superior tone. "Attacking a woman in the middle of a busy street. Surely, you did not think you could prevail?"

The man sneered and growled with guttural voice, low and breathy, "You are merely humans."

"I see," the officer said. "What is your name?"

The man hissed.

"Tell me your name."

He hissed again.

"Tell me now."

The soldiers pressed their spearpoints harder against his skin.

"We are Levi," the man snarled.

"Levi," the officer said. "You are going where *humans* go who break the law—prison."

"We hate you," the man shouted. "We hate all of you. Why should the King regard you as anything but dead dogs? You have all transgressed the law. You all deserve death. We will bring you down to the pit where you belong."

"Let's go," the officer said.

The man screeched, "Aaraugh!" He pulled against the chains around his wrists, and the iron links bent and gave way. With the loose length of chain in his free hand, he spun in place and slapped all the spears away, ripping them out of the soldiers' hands and shattering the shafts of some.

The crowd gasped and scrambled backward.

He took hold of the chains around his ankles and busted them loose.

"We are not your prisoner!" he shouted. "You are ours!"

He bolted toward the officer, shoved him flat on his back, leapt over him, and ran down the street, howling, "We hate you!"

He reached the end of the lane and turned toward the Sea of Galilee. He disappeared over the hill, headed in the direction of the caves and tombs overlooking the sea.

22

UNBOUND

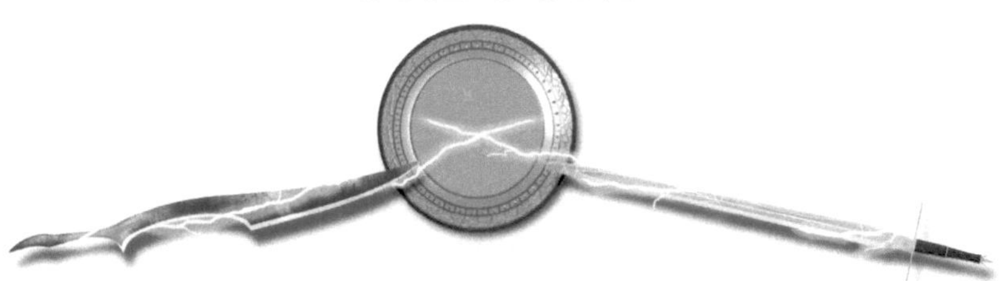

Battle minus 10 months

Elric watched over the gathering just outside of Garis with Jaeden and Ry. The morning had proceeded like so many of the others on this tour of the Galilean towns. With a thousand people thronging to see the Son of Man, they had to stay on the outskirts of town. The teaching time had finished, and now the sick and lame flocked through in hopes of receiving a healing. And just like every other time, showers of mercy and love rained down in the Middle Realm and transformed into physical healing for every one Jesus touched.

"Look," Elric said to Jaeden and Ry, "Judah and Reuben are about to speak to Jesus on behalf of John."

"I hope it is a strong word," Ry said. "John's pain is great."

"Listen," Elric said.

Jesus answered and said to them, "Go and report to John what you hear and see: those who are blind receive sight and those who limp walk, those with leprosy are cleansed and those who are deaf hear, the dead are raised, and the poor have the gospel preached to them. And blessed is any person who does not take offense at Me."

Elric smiled. "He answers from the prophet Isaiah."

"I hope this is enough for John," Jaeden said. "You should have seen him in prison. I think he would have had strength enough to stand, if not for the enemy."

Ry added, "Lacidar is not able to minister, and the beaelzur captain is pounding John with continuous lies."

"He had little chance," Jaeden said.

"There is always hope," Elric said. "This is a good word for John."

"Judah and Reuben are already on the trail back to Machaerus," Jaeden said. "It will take us a week to reach John. By your leave, Captain, we must return to our charges."

"Yes, of course. If you are able, tell Lacidar . . . wait, listen. Jesus is talking to the crowd about John."

"What did you go out into the wilderness to see? A reed shaken by the wind? But what did you go out to see? A man dressed in soft clothing? Those who wear soft clothing are in kings' palaces! But what did you go out to see? A prophet? Yes, I tell you, and one who is more than a prophet. This is the one about whom it is written: 'Behold, I am sending My messenger ahead of You, who will prepare Your way before You.' Truly I say to you, among those born of women there has not arisen anyone greater than John the Baptist! Yet the one who is least in the kingdom of heaven is greater than he. And from the days of John the Baptist until now the kingdom of heaven has been treated violently, and violent men take it by force. For all the Prophets and the Law prophesied until John. And if you are willing to accept it, John himself is Elijah who was to come. The one who has ears to hear, let him hear."

"Now *that* was an encouraging word for John," Ry said. "Why did He not say this for Judah and Reuben to hear, that they might report this to John?"

Elric laughed. "Because He is the Lord, and He knows what John needs. He knows that John will recognize the prophecies of Isaiah. The Spirit will quicken them in his heart and bring *true* joy and encouragement. These other words would only speak to his flesh. I believe John will be encouraged."

"Yes, sir," they both replied.

"Go. Protect your charges. Make sure John receives this word."

"In His service."

"And . . . if you are able, tell Lacidar we will be coming for him."

* * *

In the late still of the night, behind the tents of the encampment outside the Galilean town of Rumah, Elric, Zaben, Jenli, and Timrok met under the moon shadows of a large tree.

Elric spoke with hushed tones. "We still await an opportunity we can use to develop a plan to free John. However, I believe he needs our help now. I cannot continue to allow this beaelzur captain to attack the faith of this great prophet. John is strong, but the enemy is relentless. It has been ten days since John's disciples brought him word from the King. It is time we intervene."

"What is your plan? John is being held deep in the enemy's stronghold," Zaben said.

Elric looked at Timrok and said with a cunning smile, "We . . . just attack."

"Yes!" Timrok exclaimed—a little too loudly. He glanced around into the shadows for listening ears.

"Sir?" Zaben said.

"It will be a precise strike. We only need to disable this one captain and free Lacidar. They are alone in one room. We need not engage any other forces. We're not there to break John out, only to provide relief to John until we do."

Zaben nodded. Timrok beamed.

Elric continued. "We gather high above the palace, make ourselves as small as possible, and shoot directly into the room like a bolt of lightning as silently as possible. We subdue the captain, bind him, and keep him confined there. We loose Lacidar. Then we exit like we came in. The entire mission will be complete in less than a minute."

"Who's on the team?" Timrok asked, palming his sword handles.

"A small team. Myself . . . and Timrok."

"Yes!" Timrok exclaimed—this time in a whisper. "When do we go?"

"Right now," Elric said. Turning back to Zaben and Jenli, he said, "Give us an hour. If we are not back by then, come in after us. And bring reinforcements."

Zaben and Jenli nodded.

"Let's go." Elric unfolded his wings and shot into the sky with Timrok close behind.

Moments later, Elric and Timrok hovered high in the stratosphere. Even though from this vantage the whole sphere of the earth spread out before them, their target—one room in the palace dungeon in Machaerus—lay directly below.

"Ready?" Elric said as he pulled his sword from its sheath.

Timrok pulled both his swords. "Ready."

"Go!"

Two tiny filaments of light streaked downward, no larger than a spark and no brighter than a distant star. In less than a blink, they blasted through the ceiling of John's cellblock. Within that same blink, their feet touched the ground, they expanded their frames to the height of the room, their wings folded away, and their swords raised to the ready position.

Elric blinked and squinted. Intense white light flooded the room.

What is this? We didn't create this light!

Joyous music bounced off the walls. And the sweet aroma from the King's court permeated everything.

His eyes adjusted, and he glanced around the room.

John lay on his floor mat with his hands extended toward heaven, singing softly.

No demon captain.

Lacidar stood in the corner, playing an exhilarating tune on his resonar. "Captain! Timrok!" he said. "It is great to see you!" He stopped playing and stepped forward.

Elric couldn't hide the bewilderment from his face. "We are here to . . . set you free." He lowered his sword.

Timrok let his swords swing down to the ground. "And bind up the enemy."

Lacidar laughed. "John has already done this!"

Still bewildered, Elric asked, "What happened?"

"John received a word from the King. Two of his disciples sought Him out and brought the word back."

"Yes, yes . . ."

"The word made his faith come alive! He has done nothing but sing praises every waking moment. The presence of the Spirit has been strong upon him. The demon captain could not stand before him. John's praises drove the enemy away, and they do not dare to come close. Even my cords melted away. I have been free to minister and join his song!"

Elric sheathed his sword. "Excellent. This is good. Timrok, it appears our work here is complete."

Timrok slid his swords back into their sheaths and sighed.

"We are still waiting for an opportunity to free John," Elric said to Lacidar. "But we will get him out."

"I'm sure we will," Lacidar said. He strummed his resonar and smiled. "Until then, we will fill this place with praise."

Elric smiled, put his hand on Timrok's shoulder, and unfurled his wings.

"Watch for us. Be ready." Elric said.

Lacidar nodded.

Elric and Timrok disappeared through the ceiling.

23

LIVING AMONG THE DEAD

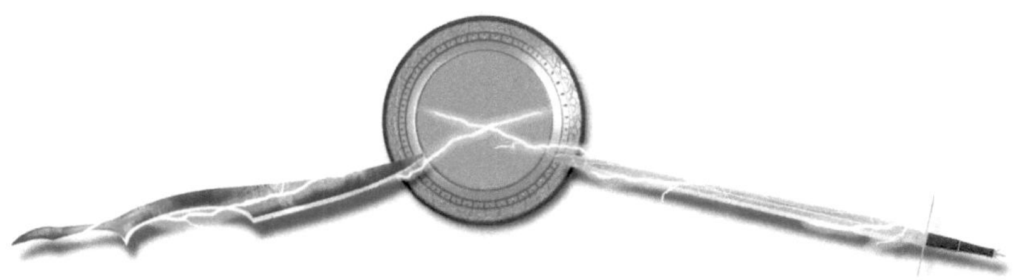

Battle minus 10 months

Daniel awoke to something uncomfortable in the middle of his back. He rolled to his side and reached back.

A rock? Why is there a rock . . .

He was lying on the ground, in the dirt.

Where am I?

He sat up. A thick, musky, rottenness filled the air. He focused through the darkness. The walls appeared to be stone. Like a cave. And carved out in the stone—ledges—with bodies! Dead, wrapped bodies! All around!

It's a tomb!

He leapt up and shuffled toward the light coming from around a corner. He turned the corner and bolted toward an opening to the outside. He burst into the daylight, squinting in the blazing sun and gasping for breath.

The vast Sea of Galilee spread out in front of him. The beaches lay some distance below—too far to hear the waves hitting the shore. To the right, more caves. Probably tombs. To the left, more tombs.

And a pig! Dead and rotting on the ground outside his cave. Its entrails had been ripped out and lay in a pile with thousands of flies swarming all around. Hunks of its flesh had been torn away as though peeled off by a wild animal.

A breeze whistled by and brushed against his skin. All of his skin.

"Aaugh!" he gasped aloud.

Where are my clothes?

Suddenly he realized everything hurt.

His feet. He looked down. Bare, cut, scabbed, and blood stained.

His back. He felt with his hands and twisted to see what he could. It was like a dozen deep cuts on his back from his thighs to his neck, half healed with thick scabs.

His forearms. Fresh cuts on top of old wounds, jagged and rough, as though made by a sharp rock.

All over his body—scrapes, cuts, bruises, dried blood.

I'm hungry. I feel like I haven't eaten in days.

He glanced at the dead pig and grimaced.

"Levi?" he said. "Where am I? What have you done?"

An empty silence answered.

"I know you are there," Daniel said. "I can feel your presence. Levi?"

The chorus of voices answered in his right ear, "Yes, my brother, we are here."

"What have you done?"

"The question is, what have *you* done? You are an evil man, guilty of many heinous crimes. We have brought you here to keep you safe."

Daniel buried his face in his hands and muttered, "I . . . I don't remember anything."

"That is best."

"How long have I been out here? Without clothes?"

"What does time mean when you live among the dead?"

"How long?"

"Two moons."

Motion from below caught his eye—a man coming up the trail from the shore. Unkempt hair, tattered clothes. Daniel hid himself just inside the cave entrance.

"Who is that?" Daniel asked, peeking around the corner.

"We do not know his name," came the answer in his right ear. "But he is one like us. Only not nearly as powerful. He lives here, too, and brings us water from Gergesa."

"Levi . . . I want you to leave. I want my life back."

Shooting pains of anger shot through his body, and he began to shake and convulse.

"You have no life without us. Nobody wants you. You are hated and without value."

"I want you to leave!"

A guttural laugh percolated from his belly and rattled in his throat. "You are ours. We will never leave!"

He could feel himself slipping away again.

"No! No!"

The dark fog descended over his consciousness.

* * *

Battle minus 9 months

A small troop of disciples and Jesus passed through the gates of Nazareth on their way back to the nomad camp just outside the city. Timrok and his team led the way. Jenli and his team guarded the left flank. Zaben's team had the right flank. Elric and Zaben walked behind.

"That was a most disheartening Sabbath service," Elric said.

"Not surprising, though," Zaben answered. "Last time we were here, they tried to kill Him."

"Yes, by not allowing any of the enemy into the synagogue this time, the enemy was not able to stir up the religious leaders. Still, so much unbelief among the people."

"These people all knew Him growing up. And His whole family. Most have not seen the mighty miracles, and they only know Him according to the flesh."

Elric nodded. "It is true."

"Perhaps tomorrow they will come out, witness the miracles for themselves, and believe," Zaben said.

"We shall see what tomorrow brings."

The next morning, Jesus stationed Himself on a hill, and the crowd of followers gathered around. Several hundred of His regular followers sat down, hungry for more words of life. Almost a hundred from Nazareth came out. Another fifty from surrounding towns joined.

Elric, Zaben, and Jenli stood on another hill overlooking the crowd. The Son of Man began teaching, and the showers of light rained down in the Middle Realm as always.

"Look at this," Jenli said. "We have not seen this much darkness before."

The people from Nazareth all carried dark clouds of unbelief that radiated outward from their personal strongholds. The clouds coalesced over the entire assembly and formed a canopy that blocked most of the seeds of light from reaching the people. Even those receptive to the words became hindered by the veil of darkness.

"This is the same thing we saw yesterday in the synagogue," Elric said. "And this is not the direct work of the enemy—it is the people themselves."

Zaben bit his lip and grimaced. "Once the miracles begin, this cloud will lift."

Later, the teaching finished, and the disciples stood to manage the queue of sick and afflicted who needed healing.

"Six?" Jenli exclaimed. "Only six people are coming forward for healing? In a crowd this size?"

"It takes faith to expect a healing," Elric said. "There is no expectancy here."

The first lady in the line started jumping up and down. "I'm healed! I'm healed! Praise God! Thank you, thank you!"

Murmuring swept through the crowd.

"Listen to the people," Zaben said.

"Who is that woman?"

"She's not from here. How do we know she's not just putting on a show?"

"What was her ailment?"

"A persistent cough."

"A cough. That is nothing."

"What is *this* man's problem?"

"Back pain."

"It is easy for him to say the pain is gone. I cannot see a difference."

Elric shook his head. "There will be no miracles here today."

* * *

Battle minus 8 months

Jesus and the twelve, along with the women, wove through the streets of Capernaum on their way to the shore. The rest of the traveling followers would be waiting there for another day of teaching. Elric and his team formed their usual perimeter.

Prestus flew in low and fast from a side lane. He landed in front of Elric.

"Captain," Prestus reported, "a Roman centurion approaches. He appears to be headed toward the King."

Timrok appeared. His wings folded away.

"A Roman centurion," Elric said to Timrok.

Timrok nodded.

"Is he coming with a squad of soldiers?" Elric asked.

"No, sir. He is alone."

"Curious," Elric said. "This does not seem like a threat. Let him come." He turned to Timrok. "Nevertheless . . . "

Timrok nodded, raised his wings, and disappeared. Prestus followed him.

Moments later, a Roman centurion—flanked by Timrok and Prestus—intercepted the group of disciples and Jesus. "Teacher!" he called out from behind the group. "Teacher!" he shouted louder.

Jesus stopped and turned. All the disciples stopped. The centurion moved toward Jesus. He wore his full battle uniform with his sword clinking against his leg as his walked. The disciples, looking wary, parted and created an uneasy aisleway for the soldier. The centurion stopped in front of Jesus. Timrok, with both swords drawn, stood between the King and the soldier. Prestus stood behind. Chase, Nalyd, Kylek, and Micah formed a barrier between the soldier and the disciples.

The centurion knelt on one knee and bowed his head. "Lord, my servant is lying paralyzed at home, terribly tormented."

Jesus took hold of the centurion's arm and lifted him up. He smiled and said, "I will come and heal him."

Without lifting his eyes, the centurion replied, "Lord, I am not worthy for You to come under my roof, but just say the word, and my servant will be healed. For I also am a man under authority, with soldiers under me; and I say to this one, 'Go!' and he goes, and to another, 'Come!' and he comes, and to my slave, 'Do this!' and he does it."

A small sphere of light appeared in the Middle Realm just above the centurion. It grew until it became a massive fireball, pulsing and humming. Sparks and little bolts of lightning shot outward from within the rising energy.

Jesus raised His eyebrows and looked at the man with amazement. Jesus said to those who were following, "Truly I say to you, I have not found such great faith with anyone in Israel. And I say to you that many will come from east and west, and recline at the table with Abraham, Isaac, and Jacob in the kingdom of heaven; but the sons of the kingdom will be thrown out into the outer darkness; in that place there will be weeping and gnashing of teeth."

And Jesus said to the centurion, "Go; it shall be done for you as you have believed."

At the word "Go," the energy ball shot off in the direction of the centurion's house, sizzling and roaring as it went.

Elric laughed, leapt into the air, spun three times, and landed with his arms stretched upward. "Yes!" he shouted. "Yes!" To Prestus he said, "Go back with the centurion and celebrate with him and his family. Fill that house with joy and singing!"

"In His service," Prestus said with a smile and a single nod.

Grigor landed in front of Elric as the group of disciples continued on their way. "A word of the Lord," he said.

Elric, still smiling, replied, "Yes?"

"The Son of Man will teach here again today, but tonight He must cross the lake for an appointment in the Gerasenes."

"In His service."

Grigor smiled. "By His word."

Elric turned to Timrok and said, "It has been a very good month back here in Capernaum. I can't wait to see what happens on the other side of the lake."

24

WAVES OF DESTRUCTION

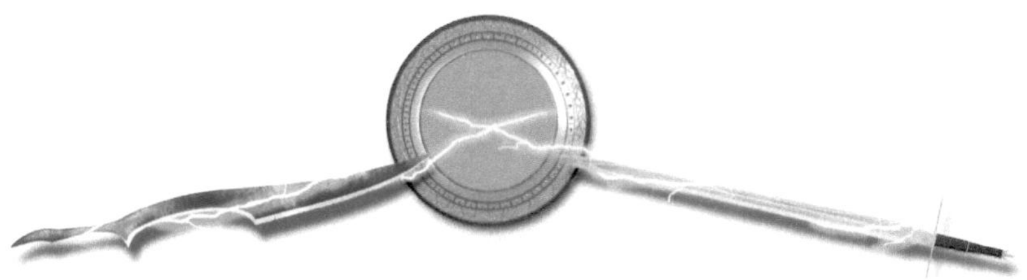

Battle minus 8 months

Molech and ten of his beaelzur captains stood on the far northern edge of the Sea of Galilee in the third watch of the night. A gentle breeze made for a quiet night on the lake, good for peaceful sailing.

A small demon flittered up from the south and landed before Molech. "Now," the demon said.

"You are sure?" Molech growled. "The Son of Man and all twelve of His inner circle are in the boat?"

"Yes, master."

"And they are in the very middle of the lake? In the deep, far from shore?"

"Yes, master. And more—the Son of Man is asleep in the stern."

Molech let out a sinister cackle. "Fools. I am surprised the Son of Man would allow Himself to be so vulnerable. Tonight, He will pay the price for His folly."

Molech clapped his hands together. "Unleash the winds!" he commanded. "Let the sea rage under our fury!"

He and all ten captains spoke the words "mighty winds" into their hands, and giant flaming energy balls formed. They stretched the plasmas until they became towering vertical disks. Then they all blew into the disks. Streams of air entered one side of the disk with the strength of their breath and emerged on the other side with the power of a hurricane gale. Whitecaps spread across the sea. The waves grew. Soon, swells over twenty feet high thundered across the face of the deep. The winds drove southward, engulfing the entire lake.

"Stronger!" Molech shouted. "Stronger!"

* * *

The bow of the ship with Jesus and the twelve disciples pitched high into the swelling wave. *Crash!* The water broke over the bow and flooded the deck. *Crash!* The bow heaved downward on the back side of the wave and then rose again to meet the next towering wall of water. *Crash!* Peter manned the tiller, straining hard to keep the bow pointed into the oncoming waves. Some men manned the oars, pulling hard to help. But in the black of night, the waves seemed to come in from every direction. The boat rolled left, and water poured in over the side. It rolled right, and more water flooded in. *Crash!* Water gushed in over the bow. All other hands manned buckets and bailed as fast as they could while clutching anything they could find to keep from being thrown from the ship.

All other hands except for the Son of Man—who slept in the stern, seemingly unconcerned about the mortal danger of the imminent swamping of the ship.

* * *

Elric kept his feet planted on the bow of the ship and rose and fell with every violent pitch as though he was part of the hull. Calm and composed, he watched the waves and held his balance with effortless control. A canopy of light engulfed the ship in the Middle Realm—energy from the Throne, untouched by the tumult in the Physical Realm.

Elric glanced back at his team.

Every one of Jenli and Zaben's team had firm grips on each of the twelve generals. None of them would be going overboard.

Prestus and Chase walked alongside the ship, one on each side with their hand on the top side rail. They held the ship above water and prevented it from rolling too far either direction.

Nalyd, Kylek, and Micah stood on deck and sloshed water out as fast as it came in with simple commands into the Middle Realm.

Timrok appeared in front of Elric, hovering before the bow of the ship. He jostled his wings to stay eye to eye with Elric as the boat heaved. "Captain, this tempest is the work of the enemy. Molech and ten of his captains are creating this."

"I am not surprised," Elric shouted over the gale.

"Shall I take my team and put an end to their treachery?"

Elric laughed. "No. Let them rage. We can easily deliver this ship through any storm the enemy brings. You can help on deck. The men bailing are growing weary."

"Captain," Zaben called out from behind. "The men lose heart. They are fearing for their lives. I think they are going to wake Jesus."

"We cannot prevent that," Elric called back. "I had hoped they would trust in the King's provision. They are not doubting our ability—but His."

Moments later, Jesus appeared from the stern onto the tossing deck. He reached for some rigging and steadied Himself.

He spoke in a loud voice, "Hush, be still."

In the Middle Realm, His words melded into eleven giant arrows of light with flaming tips. They shot northward at the speed of light with a mighty roar. In an instant, the wind died down and it became perfectly calm.

He said to the disciples, "Why are you afraid? Do you still have no faith?" He turned and went back to the stern and closed the hatch.

The men became very much afraid and said to one another, "Who, then, is this, that even the wind and the sea obey Him?"

Timrok stepped up the to the bow and said to Elric, "I would have liked to have seen Molech being crushed by the word of the King."

Elric laughed. "The enemy is full of bluster, but they cannot stand before a single word from the King."

* * *

"Yaahaa!" screamed Daniel into the gale-force winds.

He stood thigh-deep in the Sea of Galilee just below the cave tombs in the dark of night and waited for the next wave. The sea rose and slammed a wall of churning water against his bare chest. He braced against the impact and howled a maniacal laugh.

The voice in his right ear shouted, "Feel the power! Unrestrained fury!"

Smash! Another wave crashed into his chest.

"Aaah haaah haaah haaah!"

The roar of the wind drowned out his screams.

Smash!

"This is what power feels like," the voice said. "This is what we bring to you, little brother."

In an instant, the winds died. The waves receded. The water became still as glass. Complete silence fell over the beach.

"What happened?" Daniel whispered.

"I don't know."

Daniel said, "It stopped as quickly as it started. I've seen storms before, but that was like nothing I've ever seen."

He stepped out of the water and stared at the steep climb back up to the tombs. "I don't feel like climbing back up to the cave, I think I'll sleep here on the beach tonight."

He glanced around the beach. His tomb-mate, who still didn't have a name, must have followed him down here and had already lay down on a patch of sand.

* * *

A pleasant breeze breathed across the black waters. The men hoisted the sails, someone hung a lamp from the mast, and Peter turned the boat back toward its original destination.

Elric motioned for Jenli and Timrok, who stepped up to the bow.

Elric said, "Take your teams and scout out the Gerasenes. We do not know the appointment the Son of Man is sent to keep. And we do not know what enemy forces we will face there."

Timrok and Jenli gathered their teams and disappeared into the darkness, flying low just above the water.

After an hour of peaceful sailing, Timrok and Jenli returned. They alighted on the deck behind Elric at the bow.

"Sir," Timrok began, "we think we have identified our appointment. There are two men, alone on the beach, who are possessed. One of them appears to have many demons."

Jenli finished flipping through his journal, pointed at an entry on a page, and nodded his head. "One of the men we have seen before. Remember in Capernaum, when the King cast a demon out of the man at the synagogue?"

"His name was Daniel?" Elric said.

"Yes, this is the man."

Timrok sneered. "And the vile traitor's name was Vorsogh."

"Yes," Jenli said.

Elric shook his head. "This means Vorsogh returned to Daniel with additional beaelzurim. Do you know the numbers?"

"No, sir. It appears to be many."

Elric crossed his arms and nodded. "I agree—this is our appointment. Go back and keep these two on the beach. We should be there shortly after sunrise."

"In His service."

* * *

Daniel awoke with the sun blazing in his face. He squinted and sat up. The water still looked like glass, and the seagulls provided the only sounds. Out on the lake, a large boat glided along with just enough wind to keep its sails filled. It looked like its course could be . . .

It's headed here! It's going to land on this beach!

He could see the men on the deck. About a dozen.

I should get back to the cave. I can't be seen like this.

He glanced back at the men on the boat. He hadn't seen anyone from beyond the caves for a long time. It gave him a sense of detachment, like the rest of the world continued on while he stayed trapped in his solitary pain. It only made the pain worse.

Suddenly, terror seized him. He glanced again at the men in the boat and shuddered.

Fear gripped his bones. Stronger than the pain, stronger than the despair, stronger than the hatred—panic raged through his whole being. His body began to shake.

I know this feeling. This is how I felt in Capernaum when Jesus was in the synagogue.

"Levi, what are you afraid of?"

"We must leave," the voice said.

"Is it Jesus of Nazareth? Is Jesus on that boat?"

"We must go now!"

"If it's Jesus, I want to see Him. Let's just stay here and—"

Slam! The fog of darkness crashed over his mind like an avalanche. There was no resisting. Daniel was gone.

* * *

Timrok stood with both swords drawn in front of Daniel between him and the trail up to the tombs. His team formed a tight circle around him.

"Step aside," the chorus of voices growled through Daniel's clinched teeth.

"The King has an appointment with this man," Timrok said. "And I am here to see that He keeps it."

"You have no authority here."

"We are here to claim authority. The King will regain that which has been stolen."

"You and your insignificant team are no match for us. We have the strength of a thousand!"

Timrok laughed. "Then come out of the man and fight us."

"Grrr!"

"Give us a hundred. I love a good fight."

"Grrr!" Daniel fell to the ground, convulsing and twitching and shrieking in terror.

25

WAVES OF GRACE

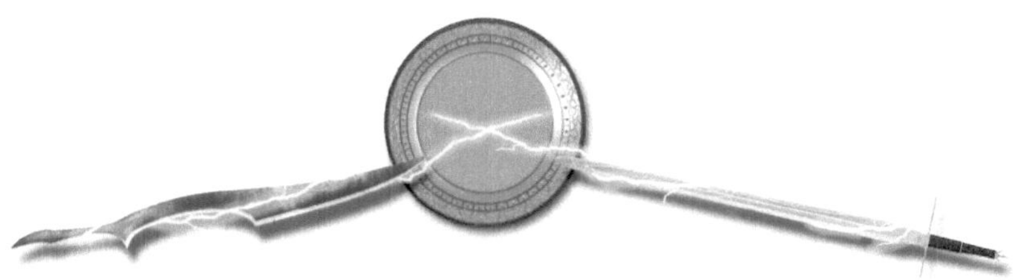

Battle minus 8 months

Elric landed on the beach as the boat reached the shore. To the left, Daniel writhed on the ground, surrounded by Timrok and his team. To the right, another man paced and shouted and yanked at his matted hair. Jenli and his team kept him in place. The man picked up stones and threw them at the disciples as they came ashore. The disciples dodged left and right and backed away.

Undeterred by the volley of stones, Jesus stepped toward the man. Jenli's team deflected the rocks' trajectories, and they all fell short.

Jesus called out, "Come out of him!"

The man fell on the ground, writhing and groaning.

"Come out, and torment him no more!"

A demon leapt out of the man, extended his wings, and lifted off the ground in a frantic attempt to flee the presence of the King. In an instant, Jenli snagged the tip of his left wing and slung him back to the ground. Brondor bound him with shimmering cords of light.

Elric ordered, "Take him far from here."

Brondor lifted the demon by the back of the cords and disappeared over the horizon.

Three of the disciples helped the man up and kept their arms around his shoulders while Jesus moved toward Daniel.

"Come out of the man, you unclean spirit!" Jesus commanded.

Daniel stood up and spun around toward the trail. Timrok leveled his swords at him. Daniel spun back around and hissed.

"Come out!"

Daniel convulsed and screeched, but then bowed with his eyes to the ground. He shouted with a loud voice, "What business do You have with us, Jesus, Son of the Most High God? We implore You by God, do not torment us!"

"What is your name?"

A guttural growl rumbled in Daniel's throat. "My name is Legion, for we are many."

"Your days of tormenting this man are through."

"What are You going to do? Please do not send us to the abyss! We beg you! Will you torment us before the time?"

"You will come out."

"If You are going to cast us out, send us into the herd of pigs."

Elric turned and looked at the hillside behind them at a distance. A very large herd of swine grazed on the open range.

"Go," Jesus commanded.

In a flurry of bat wings, high-pitched shrieks, and a blur of frenzied motion, a thousand beaelzurim fled Daniel's body and shot toward the herd of pigs. Daniel shook as though being shredded by every talon that ripped through the boundary of his flesh. For several seconds, the shaking continued. The last demon left, and Daniel collapsed on the ground.

"Is he dead?" one of the disciples asked.

Jesus knelt beside him and placed His hand on Daniel's chest. He closed His eyes. Showers of light rained down on them.

Jesus opened His eyes and said, "Daniel. Daniel, wake up."

Daniel opened his eyes and blinked. "Where am I? What happened?"

Jesus took hold of his hand, stood up, and said, "Get up."

Daniel pulled himself up with help but required additional support for his weak and unbalanced legs.

Jesus turned toward the disciples. "Did anyone bring an extra change of clothes?"

"I did," shouted James.

"Please bring them here. And bring, also, some food and water."

An enormous tumult shook the mountainside behind them. Squealing pigs and thousands of tramping hooves echoed across the hill. In a thick cloud of dust, the whole herd rushed down the steep bank into the sea and drowned in the waters.

One by one, thousands of terrified beaelzurim emerged from the water and raced off.

The herdsmen ran away, headed toward the city.

With Daniel clothed, Jesus had him and the other man sit with Him on a large boulder.

"Here," Jesus said. "Daniel, Barak—eat some bread and figs. You need the strength."

They ate and drank and looked at Jesus with quizzical eyes.

"How do you know my name?" Barak asked. "And how is it that you would come to this very place and find us? Why are you here?"

Jesus smiled. "The Father sent me."

"Why?"

"For *you*. If one sheep from the flock is lost, will not the shepherd go and search until he finds it and then bring it home?"

"But you don't know what I've done." Daniel's voice cracked. "Terrible things. Things that can't be spoken of."

Barak nodded.

"The Father knows. But He loves you. He has always loved you."

Tears streamed down both the men's faces.

Jesus continued, "The enemy has held you in bondage for many years. But because of the Father's love, He has declared release for the captives and freedom for the oppressed. This life of enslavement and pain was never His intent for you. It was all from the enemy. The enemy comes only to steal and kill and destroy; I came so that you would have life, and have it abundantly."

The men sobbed and laughed and wiped the tears with their sleeves and struggled to breathe between the sobs.

Daniel took a drink from a waterskin and calmed his breathing. "I remember, when I was very young, my father would talk about the Messiah who is to come. He will have great power and will save Israel."

Barak gasped and pointed toward Jesus. "Those demons called you the Son of the Most High!"

Jesus smiled.

"The Messiah will also have the power to heal," Daniel said. "If you are He, then could you also heal a deaf ear?"

"What do you believe?"

"I believe you are He who is to come."

A bright cloud of energy formed and swirled near Daniel's right ear.

Jesus smiled, reached out His hand, covered Daniel's right ear, and said, "Be it done according to your faith."

Flash! The cloud of energy shot into Daniel's spirit, and a warm glow emanated back out.

Daniel yanked at his ear. "I can hear! Somebody say something!"

Barak, with eyes wide and mouth hanging open, blurted out, "Daniel? Daniel, can you hear me?"

Daniel jumped to his feet and spun around. "Yes! Yes! I can hear! I haven't been able to hear with this ear since I was a boy!" He grabbed Jesus' hands. "Thank you!"

"You should eat more. Here, your body needs the nourishment."

"Captain," Timrok called out to Elric. "A large crowd approaches. Hundreds. They are coming from Gergesa. I count at least fifty beaelzurim among them. This could become a fight."

Elric answered, "Timrok, pull your team back and circle around from behind. Remain hidden until needed. Zaben and Jenli, form your teams into ranks between the King and the incoming forces. I doubt the enemy will come too close to the King, but they need to know we are here."

While the people on the beach talked, Elric's warriors sprang to action. Within moments, a formidable wall of angelic power stood between the enemy and the Son of Man.

Elric took a place with Zaben on his left and Jenli on his right. He drew his sword. "Watch," he said. "The Son of Man is going to turn this on the enemy's head. Once the people of the town see these two men, they will believe in Him. The whole town will be saved."

"We are about to see," Jenli said.

A large mob came over the hill and descended onto the clearing beyond the beach. Jesus, along with Daniel, Barak, and the twelve climbed up to meet them.

The two ranks of angels marched in front of the Son of Man.

The fifty demons spotted Jesus and scattered backward. They shrieked and hid their faces and lurched toward the back of the crowd. Some took off and flew away. The ones that stayed ducked low behind the people.

A man stepped out from the crowd and called out in a loud voice, "Who are you, and why are you here?"

Jesus answered, "I am Jesus of Nazareth. I have come to declare to you the kingdom of God."

The man shouted back, "You are a sorcerer, and you have come to destroy us!"

The crowd echoed his charges with raised fists, pointed fingers, and loud accusations.

James and John stepped forward between the crowd and Jesus.

"People of Gergesa," James called out above the restless murmurs. "Listen to my words. Do you know these two men? They lived among these tombs and terrorized your town. They were oppressed of Satan, having many demons. Look at them now. They have been set free. They are in their right mind and have been made whole."

"By the power of evil!" the man shouted.

John raised his voice. "This is the power of God! This is the administration of His kingdom. His kingdom is a kingdom of life, not destruction."

"Then why did you destroy all our pigs?" one of the herdsmen yelled.

"It was the enemy who drove your herd into the sea," John answered.

"At your word," shouted another one of the herdsmen, pointing at Jesus. "We saw you speaking to the evil spirits!"

"Sorcerer!" rang out from the crowd. "Away with you! Sorcerer!"

"Leave our country," the lead man from the crowd shouted. "We do not want your magic here. We implore you. Leave us and do us no more harm."

Jesus nodded and raised one arm in the air. He stepped between James and John with His hands on their shoulders. He passed between them and addressed the crowd. "I leave your country at your request. But know this, truly the kingdom of God has come nigh to you, and you did not receive it."

He turned and headed back toward the beach. His disciples followed. The mob became quiet and watched the retreat.

"That is it?" Jenli said. "Will He not defend His case?"

"He is the King," Elric said. "He does not have to defend Himself to anyone. And He never forces Himself on those who reject Him."

Daniel ran and caught up with Jesus. "Master," he said as they walked, "can I come with you?"

"Now is not the time for you," Jesus answered. "The Son of Man must suffer many things, and you will not have the strength endure it."

"But I want to be your disciple."

"You will be." Jesus climbed into the boat. "You must trust me."

Daniel followed Him waist-deep into the water. "I do trust you. Let me accompany you."

Jesus reached down and put His hand on Daniel's shoulder. He smiled and locked eyes. "Go home to your people and report to them what great things the Lord has done for you, and how He had mercy on you."

Daniel nodded. "Yes, Lord. I will. Thank you."

Elric, Timrok, Zaben, and Jenli gathered at the edge of the water and watched the crowd disperse over the hill. Behind them, oars splashed in the water and knocked against the side of the boat.

"It makes my heart ache to see men reject the King," Elric said.

Zaben bit his lip and nodded. "Fear mixed with unbelief is a powerful tool of the enemy."

Daniel passed through the middle of their group and headed toward the trail.

Timrok said, "At least Daniel and Barak received deliverance."

They all nodded.

A flurry of wings made Elric look up. An elzur warrior approached and landed.

"Lieutenant Théodor!" Elric said with a surprised laugh. He spoke the word "joy" into his hand, and a sizzling ball of energy formed.

Théodor formed an energy ball of "grace."

The two smashed their hands together, and joy and grace rained over the whole beach.

"I have been sent to minister to Daniel," Théodor said. "He is my new charge."

"Very good," Elric said. "He will need your strength."

Théodor eyed the boat slipping out into the deep. "This is some assignment you have."

Elric laughed. "You could not begin to imagine." He locked forearms with Théodor and pulled him close. "The time is near. Soon the King will set all things right."

26

WHOSE FAITH

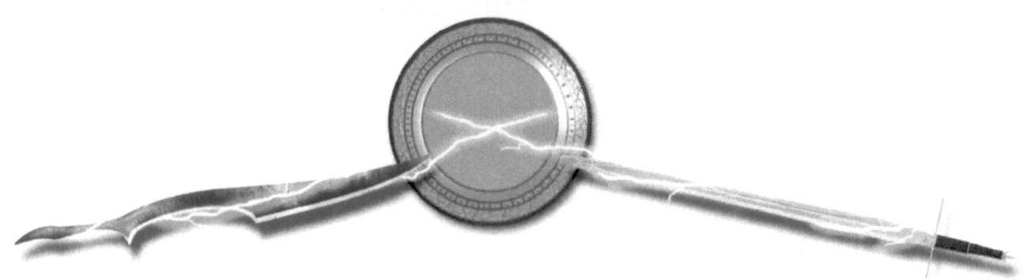

Battle minus 8 months

Elric floated to a soft landing on a rooftop in Capernaum overlooking the shore. His wings tucked away, he folded his arms, and he surveyed the area. To his right, the boat with the Son of Man and the twelve generals approached from their excursion across the sea. To his left, a street leading through town, flanked by buildings in tight rows with their plaster-covered stone fronts. From all around, people moved toward the shore.

Elric chuckled to himself. *Word spreads quickly.*

From the nomad encampment outside of town, from the side alleys of town, from the street below, from the beachfront in both directions—hundreds of people swarmed toward the incoming boat.

The twelve generals and the Son of Man stepped onto the land and into a mob of followers pushing close, calling His name, and reaching out for a touch. The twelve did their best to forge a way through the mass, but the crowd kept them pinned near the water's edge.

Jesus didn't try to push past the people but reached out and touched hands and spoke with each individual. He would grab a hand, hold it, look into their eyes, and smile. Then He would say the thing needed by that person: "Bless you." "The Father loves you." "It is time for you to lay aside the bitterness you hold against your mother." "Come, follow me." "The Father knows your pain. Seek His face and find peace."

"Teacher!" a loud voice shouted over the crowd. "Please, let me through. I need to see Him. It cannot wait. Master!"

Grigor alighted on the roof next to Elric without a sound. "A word of the Lord," he said.

Elric turned. "Yes?"

"This man is Jairus, a synagogue official. His daughter is about to die. The King will raise her back to life, but we must have someone with her at her passing and keep her close. You will not have to hold her long."

Elric nodded. "In His service."

Grigor disappeared.

Jairus had somehow made his way through the crowd and had thrown himself down at Jesus' feet. With a cracking voice he said, "My little daughter is at the point of death; please come and lay Your hands on her, so that she will get well and live. Please come to my house, for she is too ill to come out. Please, I beg you."

Jesus lifted him up and put his arm around his shoulder. "I will go to your house. Do not fear."

Elric signaled for Jenli, and Jenli appeared.

"This man's daughter is about to pass," Elric said, "but the King will restore her. Go and be with her. She will not be separated from her body long, so this time simply wrap her in a cloud of white light until He calls her back."

"Yes, sir."

"And Jenli, bring your team—in case the enemy tries to oppose you as they did in Nain."

Jenli lifted his wings and disappeared.

Jesus and Jairus started up the street, but the mob moved with them and continued to press in from all sides.

Elric hopped to the next rooftop with a single flap of his wings. It was an amazing spectacle from this viewpoint. The Son of Man shimmered with intense light in the Middle Realm. A cloud of energy from the Throne radiated from within and enveloped everyone near Him. *How is it possible these people can handle the King Himself and live? I cannot imagine walking up and touching even the footstool of His throne.* He remembered all the times he had stood in the inner court before the throne, with the coals of fire, the flashing lightning, the rolling thunder, and the glory cloud up to his knees. *And yet, all this power has no effect on them in the Physical Realm. They touch Him. But they . . . wait, what is this?*

A woman, veiled and frail in the Physical Realm, squeezed between the shuffling crowd toward Jesus from behind. She never raised her eyes or spoke a word. Other than her determination to catch up with Him, she looked no different from any of the others in the crowd. But in the Middle Realm, her presence created a reaction with the cloud of light surrounding the King—as though her spirit was a powerful magnet, drawing the energy in. Eruptions of light shot outward from the King like solar flares from the sun and bent toward the woman.

She reached Him, just barely, and an explosion shook the Middle Realm.

Jesus stopped.

"Who is the one who touched Me?" He said. "Who touched My garments?"

The people around Him took a step back and answered with blank, perplexed expressions. They shook their heads and looked around at each other.

Peter leaned in and said, "Master, the people are crowding and pressing in on You."

But Jesus said, "Someone did touch Me, for I was aware that power had left Me."

Several tense moments passed. Finally, a meek voice spoke out, just above a whisper. "It was me."

The crowd parted, and the woman stumbled forward. Hesitant and trembling, she dropped to her knees before Him. Without lifting her eyes, she said, "Master, forgive me. I have suffered from a chronic hemorrhage of blood for twelve years. I have seen many physicians, and I have spent all I had to get well. But they did not help at all. In fact, it has become worse. I was desperate and had lost all hope. But then I heard about you. I heard that you have the ability to heal with just a word or a touch. I believe this word, and I believe that you carry the power of God. I knew I did not stand a chance to get your attention, but I thought to myself—if I could just touch His garments, I will get well. I did, and immediately the flow of blood dried up. I can feel in my body that I am healed."

Jesus took her hand and pulled her to her feet. "Daughter, your faith has made you well; go in peace and be cured of your disease."

Elric crossed his arms and laughed. *Of course. It's as simple as faith. The King's power is always there, but it requires faith to pull it from the Middle Realm into the Physical. This is the first time I've seen someone access the King's provision without the Son of Man having to exercise* His *faith.*

A man from up the street wove his way through the crowd and came to Jairus, standing near Jesus. He said, "Your daughter has died; do not trouble the Teacher anymore."

Jairus buried his face in his hands and broke down, weeping.

Jesus put His arm around his shoulder and said, "Do not be afraid any longer; only believe, and she will be made well. Come, let us go to her."

Elric smiled. *The Son of Man* will *have to exercise His faith for this one.*

They reached Jairus's house to find it surrounded by mourners. Elric flew past the wall of darkness in the Middle Realm created by the hopeless wails of the grieving people and landed in an inner room. There, just above the lifeless body of a young girl, the girl's spirit lay suspended in midair in the Middle Realm enveloped in a bright cloud of light.

Elric smiled at Jenli, who fed the shimmering cloud with pulses of energy from his hands.

"She sees only the light," Jenli said. "And she cannot hear through the cloud."

Elric nodded. "The King is here now. He will speak a word."

"Death and life are in the power of the tongue," Jenli said.

Elric crossed his arms as Jesus entered the room with the girl's parents and Peter, James, and John. He smiled and said, "And in the light of the King's face is life."

* * *

Battle minus 6 months

The water in the seaport of Sidon rested in the serene predawn quiet. Beyond the harbor, the Mediterranean Sea stretched out in a lazy fog with the horizon not quite visible yet. The masts of a dozen large sea-faring ships sleeping in the harbor swayed and dipped with a slow, gentle cadence.

Elric, Jenli, and Zaben left the north end of the nomad encampment and strolled along the water's edge. Jutting out to the left into the harbor, a rocky point lay just ahead. Jesus sat alone on the point, praying as usual. Timrok stood full-sized between the main shore and the King. The light glowing from the Son of Man and raining down upon Him in the Middle Realm would have made a powerful beacon for traveling ships, but none of its radiance pierced into the Physical Realm.

Elric signaled for Timrok. In an instant, Timrok joined the group, and Kylek took his place on the rocky point.

"It has been two months since we left Capernaum," Elric said as they continued to stroll. "This is as far north as we are going. The King will finish here today, and tomorrow we begin to work our way back down to Galilee."

"It has been a good journey," Zaben said.

"Tyre and Sidon both have been more receptive than some of the Galilean towns," Jenli said. "Many of the people have chosen to follow Him. Our traveling group continues to grow."

"Still, none of these are warriors," Zaben said.

Timrok huffed, "Yet."

Traveling low and fast, a light approached from the south. Like a puff of wind, Stephanus appeared and landed in front of Elric. "Captain, I bring news from Machaerus."

"Excellent. Did Antipas respond as we hoped?" Elric asked.

"No. At first, everything went according to plan. We reached Dominic, the regional governor of northern Perea. He does not care about the prophet John's well-being, but towns in his region had profited from all the travelers who came out to see John at the Jordan. We spoke to Dominic for weeks. Finally, he wrote an entreaty to Herod calling for John's release and to challenge the legality of holding him without formal charge."

"Good."

"Interestingly," Stephanus continued, "Herod fears John. He recognizes John is a holy man. He even brings John into his court and listens to him speak. We thought that this official request would be enough to sway him. But he is heavily influenced by the enemy. Molech himself directs his decisions. So John remains in prison, and Dominic is being removed from his position."

Elric shook his head and looked at Zaben. "We need another plan."

"Have we made any progress reaching anyone in Antipas's inner circle?" Zaben asked.

"Only Herodias's daughter, Salome," Stephanus said. "She is young, and she has a soft heart. BaeLee has been speaking to her whenever the enemy leaves her alone. She believes John is innocent and should not be in prison."

"But she has no influence in state affairs," Elric said. "How can we use her to reach Antipas? Especially under the close eye of Molech. We do not want to endanger her also."

Zaben bit his lip, and his eyes darted back and forth. Elric could see the moves and countermoves playing out in Zaben's calculations.

"Antipas is impulsive," Zaben said. "And proud. Given the opportunity, he would make a grand gesture to demonstrate his power. We need him to make such a gesture to Salome, preferably in front of other people so he cannot back out, even though Molech may demand it."

"Antipas has a birthday in two weeks," Jenli said, holding a ledger open with his finger on a page.

Zaben nodded his head. "An opportune day. It will be expected that the king host a large banquet and create a spectacle of entertainment events. Is there any presentation Salome can make? Does she sing or play an instrument?"

"She is a beautiful dancer," Stephanus said.

"This may be our chance," Zaben said.

"It will be a dangerous mission," Elric said. "We'll need warriors in the room to speak to both Salome and Antipas at the right time. Molech's court will be filled with beaelzur officers."

Stephanus said, "Our full team—Ry, Jaeden, BaeLee, Kelsof, and I—have been working within the stronghold all these months. We can enter with a human charge without raising alarm."

Elric crossed his arms and raised his chin. Finally, he nodded. "Let's get John out."

27

AN OPPORTUNE DAY

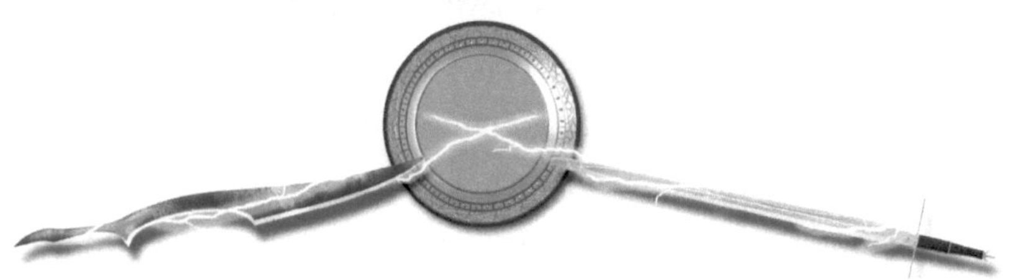

Battle minus 6 months

The main banquet hall of the palace on the rock fortress of
Machaerus filled with hundreds of honored guests. Nobles and
military commanders, leading people of Galilee—all the elite
gathered to celebrate the birthday of Herod Antipas. The head table
faced inward toward the expansive hall. On the left and right, long
tables stretched the length of the room, leaving a large vacant area
in the middle. Long, flowing curtains adorned the walls. Their deep
maroon hue added to the elegance and royalty of the hall. An army
of servants swarmed around the tables carrying trays and pitchers and
an endless supply of food and wine.

Roman soldiers stood like statues at the entrance, near the head
table, and at regular intervals along the walls.

Antipas sat at the center of the head table in a chair with a conspicuously high back. With its ornate engravings and gold-plated accents, it sent a clear signal to all those gathered. He drank his wine and laughed with the high-ranking officials at the head table.

His wife, Herodias, and the rest of his immediate family, along with extended family and lesser subjects dined in the adjacent hall.

A gala event in the Physical Realm—complete with a steady stream of entertainers filing in and out and performing their arts in the center of the room.

In the Middle Realm, a cloud of gloom hung heavy in the air from the ceiling halfway down to the floor. Molech's throne rested high above the head table just behind Herod's chair, and Molech cast a distant gaze over the assembly with disdain. Demon captains lined the walls—three between every Roman soldier. Molech's top two captains stood on either side of his throne. Several dozen smaller demons flittered about, fueling arguments over nothing, propagating lies about everything, and encouraging overindulgences in food and wine, especially the wine.

Four audacious elzur warriors had entered with their charges, but they all looked familiar and posed no immediate threat. They each stood behind their person and avoided unnecessary contact.

Molech let out a long, audible sigh. Yellow smoke escaped through his teeth and mixed with the toxic atmosphere. "These people," he groaned. "They have no perception of the gravity of the hour. This frivolous . . . " he made a rolling gesture with his hand toward the festivities in the hall, "assembly means nothing." He shouted, "Nothing!"

He rested his elbow on the throne armrest and propped his head up with his hand. "The Son of Man gathers more followers every day. Soon, there won't be a single place in Galilee that hasn't received a touch from the King. And now He's back from the coastal region of Tyre and Sidon and is working in Bethsaida. Even twelve of His followers have gone out without Him and performed signs and taken authority over *my* warriors in *my* domain." He formed a fireball in his right hand and then crushed it with a closing fist. The energy exploded and shot sparks and smoke out between his fingers. "If only I could have prevailed two months ago when I had Him out on the Sea of Galilee. My storm should have swamped that boat. He was mine!"

"At least you have the prophet John," the captain on his right said.

"Ha!" Molech shouted. "And what has this accomplished? The Son of Man continues. He has made no attempt to free John."

"Then kill John," the captain sneered.

"If I had my way, John would have already passed through my fire. But Antipas is weak. The fool fears John. Though I command John's execution, still Antipas . . . "

A commotion on the floor in the middle of the room brought all action in the Middle Realm to a stop. Molech glanced up with furrowed brows.

A small musical troupe began a song, and a young girl moved to the center of the room. Shadowing her every move like a spiritual glove, an elzur warrior followed along—or led the way—it was difficult to tell.

"Master," one of the captains said. "It is Salome, Herodias's daughter."

"I know who it is, fool! What is this presumptuous puppet of the King doing with her?"

"Dancing . . ."

They danced—spinning and floating across the floor with graceful flowing motion.

One of the elzurim in the room launched an energy ball of "beauty and grace" into the air, and tiny sparks showered down on all the guests. The conversations stopped. All eyes turned toward the dancing girl.

"What is happening?" Molech growled.

The dance continued. Several minutes passed, and all the demons stood frozen with their swords drawn and eyes fixed on the bold display. Then, the song finished, Salome took one final spin, and she bowed with elegant style.

Another one of the elzur warriors exploded an energy ball on the ground, and warm light of "adulation" rose through the people.

The guests all applauded. Some stood. Then they all stood, clapping and smiling and shouting their praises.

Tiny beads of light shot from somewhere toward Herod at the head table. Like a single strand of individual raindrops, the energy was almost imperceptible—but Molech spotted it. *What are these words, and how long have they been reaching Herod?* Molech leapt down from his throne and stood between the stream of light and Herod. The light hit Molech.

"Grant her a request?" Molech shouted. He followed the stream back to one of the elzur warriors off to the left. He pointed and roared, "Silence this pest!"

In an instant, a demon captain's blade from behind pressed tight against the intruder's neck, and the stream stopped.

The applause died down, and Herod, still standing announced to Salome, "Ask me for whatever you want, and I will give it to you."

"Silence, you fool!" Molech rumbled. "You do not know what she may ask."

Molech's words smashed into Herod like a hammer. He fell backward into his chair. Looking a little embarrassed, Herod glanced around at his guests, who were now all watching him. He sat up and stretched his neck and said with a crackling voice, "Whatever you ask of me, I will give it to you, up to half of my kingdom."

Molech growled.

All eyes turned back to Salome.

The elzur warrior had his wing covering the girl as he spoke to her.

"No!" roared Molech. "Somebody stop this!"

The closest demon captain jumped, grabbed the angel by his wing, and slammed him to the ground in a high, swift arc. The angel sprang back to his feet, pulled his sword, and shouted to Salome, "Release John! Say it! Be strong!"

The angel's words coalesced and swirled toward Salome.

Molech thundered, "No! John is dangerous! John is an enemy!"

Molech's words blasted toward Salome and intercepted the angel's words, twisting into a mass of jumbled energy with sparks flying in all directions.

Salome stood with her mouth hanging half open and a confused look on her face.

The angel battled with the demon captain, spinning and leaping and staying one step ahead of the stronger warrior. The other three free elzurim in the room jumped into the fight. The fourth warrior on the left broke free and joined the others. Now five brazen elzurim formed a perimeter around Salome.

"Enough of this!" Molech roared.

Every demon in the room converged on the five. War shouts rang out and sparks flew, but the clash lasted only a moment.

"Bind them all," Molech commanded.

The captains bound the elzurim and piled them together in a heap in the center of room.

"Where did Salome go?" Molech called out with tension in his voice.

One of the demon warriors answered, "She has gone out to confer with her mother."

Molech sat back on his throne and smiled. "Good. Very good." He turned to the captain on his right. "Go and make sure Salome comes back with the correct request."

Minutes later, Salome returned to the hall accompanied by a hulking demon captain. She wore a pained look in her eyes, and she walked with tentative, reluctant steps. She stopped in the center of the room where she had completed her performance. The room became silent as death.

She spoke the words as though reading them from a script. "I want you to give me at once . . . the head of John the Baptist on a platter."

The guests gasped.

Antipas breathed, "Oh no."

"Ha ha!" Molech shouted. "Finally! You have given an oath before all these people. You must grant this request!"

Antipas looked around at all the dignitaries and military leaders who stared at him, waiting for his answer. He hesitated another minute and then finally looked over to the head centurion. Antipas nodded and gestured with his hand.

The soldier marched out with brisk disciplined steps.

"Yes!" Molech boomed. "You, you, you, and you—go and be sure this thing is accomplished."

Four massive demon captains marched out behind the Roman soldier.

Herod sat back in his chair and took a long drink of his wine. The guests talked only in whispers, and tense anticipation hung heavy in the room. Salome stood alone, fidgeting with her dress and her hair and never lifting her eyes above the floor.

Several more uncomfortable minutes passed.

From the pile of elzurim in the center of the hall, one of the warrior's bindings broke free like the release of a coiled spring. The angel lifted his wings and shot straight up through the ceiling.

Several demon warriors raised their swords and unfurled their wings.

Molech looked up and said, "Let him go. The coward."

The demons lowered their weapons and tucked their wings away.

A nearby captain walked over to the pile and kicked the dagger out of the hand of one of the bound angels. "Clever," the captain grumbled. "That won't happen again."

Motion at the entrance to the hall. All the guests turned. Herod looked up and set down his wine goblet. Salome faced the entrance.

Molech stood. The head centurion, flanked by two soldiers, marched in step into the hall. The centurion carried a round platter with a silver domed cover.

Behind the soldiers, four demon captains pressed a bound elzur lieutenant forward at sword point. One of the captains carried some kind of stringed instrument—probably the property of the pathetic lieutenant.

The soldiers halted in front of Salome. The centurion handed the platter to Salome, who took a moment to adjust to its weight. Then, the centurion lifted the cover.

John the Baptist's head. Eyes still open, frozen in a state of terror. Mouth half open and full of blood. Blood dripping off the platter onto the floor.

The guests gasped. Some covered their eyes.

Salome glanced at the macabre gift on the platter for only a moment. She turned her head away and nodded. The centurion replaced the cover.

"John the Baptist is dead!" Molech called out in triumph. All the beaelzurim cheered.

Salome moved toward the exit with slow, careful steps trying to keep the dripping blood from falling onto her dress. The demons chanted in unison with sinister grunts and pounded their steel blades against the ground as Salome made her lonely procession out of the hall.

Salome exited and turned toward the adjacent hall. The demons erupted again into a long celebration of shouts, chants, and banging steel.

Boom! Flash! The room became engulfed in brilliant white light.

Molech squinted through the scintillating glare. In the center of the room, two figures appeared, shining even brighter than the blinding light of the explosion. One appeared to have the stature of an elzur captain. The other had two flashing swords. Like a whirlwind, the two warriors' blades whirred. In a moment, in less than a heartbeat, they disappeared.

The light dissipated, and Molech's eyes adjusted to the room. All the demons stood frozen and silent, rubbing their eyes. The four bound elzurim were gone. The bound lieutenant and his instrument were gone.

Molech laughed. He raised his arms with clenched fists. "John is dead!"

The celebration in the Middle Realm continued.

28

BREAD

Battle minus 6 months

Near the water's edge of the Sea of Galilee just outside Bethsaida, Jesus and the twelve disciples, along with the women, gathered around six of John the Baptist's disciples. Tears filled every eye in the circle. The women sobbed the loudest, but the men who had started off with John before following Jesus wept as hard as them. The Son of Man's chest rose and fell with each sob, and He wiped the steady stream of tears off His cheek with His sleeve.

"And then we came in and removed his body," Reuben said.

Judah gritted his teeth. "They executed him right there in the cell. No notice. No preparation."

"And we buried him in a proper tomb," Reuben said.

"At the whim of girl!" Judah grumbled. "How does that happen?"

Jesus wiped His eyes and put His hand on Judah's shoulder. "You men, go with our sisters here back to the camp and get some breakfast."

As they walked off clutching one another, Jesus said, "Simon, bring your boat around. Let us come away by ourselves to a secluded place and rest a little while."

Without a word, Jesus and the twelve loaded into the boat, and they launched. They sailed south along the eastern border, staying close to land. No one spoke. The heavy weeping became quiet tears squeezed from the marrow of their shock. Everyone moved with slow, labored motion. Jesus pulled the hood of His cloak over His head and stared out at the water sliding by.

Elric stood at the bow of the boat with Lacidar. They, too, watched the water without discussion.

After a long while, Lacidar finally broke the silence. "I would like to take my team and stay with John's disciples for a season. They need the encouragement."

Elric nodded. "It is less than six months until Passover. We'll need you back before then."

"Yes, sir." Lacidar unfolded his wings like unwrapping a bandage and glided off over the calm water.

Moments later, Timrok landed on the bow. He spoke with a quick, practical tone. "Captain, the people on the shore saw the boat leave and have presumed your destination. They are running ahead on foot and will be there waiting. Sir, there are thousands. They are coming in from all the surrounding villages."

"All looking for a touch from the King," Elric said. "The good news of His mercy is spreading everywhere. This is not unexpected."

Timrok glanced around the boat. "Are these men prepared to minister to so many?"

Elric smiled. "Surely, the Son of Man is. He sees the Father's will beyond the flesh. These others . . . will find strength from the Spirit as they focus on the needs of others."

"There is a mountain there with much grass at the base—well suited for teaching and ministry."

"Good. Have your team set up a perimeter."

"This is already done."

Elric nodded. "We will be there shortly."

Timrok took off and headed for the shore.

The boat came around a small peninsula and spun hard left toward a secluded cove with a sandy beach, perfect to run aground. Elric caught the first glimpse of what awaited them—thousands of people on the grassy base of a small mountain, just beyond the waterfront.

The twelve reacted.

"Look at all those people!"

"Where did they all come from?"

"How did they know where we were going?"

"I thought we were going to get some time alone to rest."

Jesus' voice rose over the grumbling. "Sheep need a shepherd. The Father loves all of these. Come, let us share the good things of the Kingdom."

With the help of the twelve, the Son of Man burrowed His way through the crowd and climbed the mountain to a place where He could be seen and heard by all. He sat down. He taught. He healed many. The heaviness of the loss of John became lost in the joy of restored bodies and changed lives. The day grew long, and still the crowd lingered.

The twelve came up to Him and said, "This place is secluded and it is already late; send them away so that they may go into the surrounding countryside and villages and buy themselves something to eat."

Without hesitation, Jesus said, "You give them something to eat."

They glanced at each other with perplexed expressions and then back down the slope at the thousands of people spread out across the grass.

Jesus turned to Philip. "Where are we to buy bread so that these people may eat?"

Philip shrugged and answered, "Two hundred denarii worth of bread is not enough for them, for each to receive just a little!"

"How many loaves do you have?

They all answered with blank looks.

"Go look!"

The twelve dispersed into the crowd.

In the Middle Realm, a single glowing bundle of energy drifted downward in front of Elric. It floated like a gentle snowflake and landed on the ground at Elric's feet. He picked it up and held it in the palm of his hand. He smiled. He motioned for Jenli, Zaben, and Timrok.

"Jenli, Zaben," Elric said. "Gather your teams and bring them here. The King is about to accomplish a great work."

Several minutes later, the twelve disciples returned.

Andrew said, "There is a boy here who has five barley loaves and two fish; but what are these for so many people?"

Jesus said, "Bring the loaves and fishes to me. Put the people into groups of hundreds and fifties, and have them recline to eat. They should start fires to cook the fish. And bring back with you each a basket with a cloth cover."

The twelve dispersed again, and Elric turned to his team. "The King is going to provide food for these people," Elric said. He opened his hand and held the energy snowflake out for the team to see.

All their eyes sparkled, and childlike joy spread across their faces.

"Are we making manna?" Jenli asked.

"Not exactly," Elric said. "It appears this will be more like the days of the widow in Zarephath. The King wants to use the thing they have in their hand. And it appears He intends to do the multiplication through the hands of the disciples. So, each of you needs to go out with your charge as they distribute the food. You know what to do."

They all nodded.

The twelve disciples returned, and Andrew handed Jesus the basket with the five barley loaves and two fish. Jesus lifted the cloth covering, looked in, smiled, and re-covered the basket.

He looked up and said, "Father, thank you for your provision. We receive it with joy. I bless this bread and fish. I bless every one who partakes."

A flurry of energy packets floated down in the Middle Realm, and Zaben, Jenli, and their teams bounced around, laughing and catching the floating flakes in midair. Elric gathered a handful and moved next to Jesus.

Jesus reached into the basket and pulled out a loaf from under the cloth covering. He broke it and smelled the fresh center. Smiling, he the handed the two halves to Simon.

Elric took a bundle of energy and pressed it into Jesus' basket. The moment it touched one of the barley loaves inside the basket, it transformed from spiritual energy into a physical barley loaf.

Jesus handed Simon another loaf. Elric pressed another handful of light into His basket, and a loaf multiplied.

Jesus handed Simon one fish. Elric smashed his energy into the remaining fish, and the spiritual energy transformed into a fish.

Jesus handed Simon another fish. Another fish appeared under the cloth in His basket.

Two loaves and two fish for Simon. Jesus turned to Andrew and handed him one loaf. Then a second loaf. Then a fish.

The twelve gasped and looked at each other.

"Were there not only two fish?"

"Where did the third fish come from?"

Jesus didn't react but handed Andrew another fish as Elric continued to transform the spiritual provisions into the Physical Realm. Two loaves and two fish for Andrew.

Jesus handed James one loaf. Then a second loaf.

The disciples gasped again.

"That is six loaves! There were only five!"

Jesus handed James a fish and said, "As you give these out to the people, do as I have done." He handed James another fish. "Keep your basket covered by a cloth. Take only one loaf and one fish at a time. But give each group as much as they want." He handed John one loaf. Then a second. "Freely you have received. Freely give."

One by one, Jesus distributed two loaves and two fish to each of the twelve. One by one, Elric replaced the issued food with spiritual provision from the Father. And one by one, the faith of the Son of Man pulled the provision into the Physical Realm. The disciples stood dumbfounded.

Jesus said, "Now, you go feed these people. The hour is late, and they are hungry."

The twelve dispersed, each accompanied by one of Zaben and Jenli's team. The angels all carried handfuls of light and continued gathering more from the gentle snowfall in the Middle Realm.

Elric stayed by Jesus and watched the distribution. Peter pulled the third loaf from his basket and looked back up the hill with astonished eyes and a beaming smile. Jesus smiled back and motioned for him to keep going. The initial wonder of it turned into a realization of the magnitude of the task to be accomplished, and Simon's pace accelerated. Each of the twelve had the same reaction.

Except Philip.

Motion stalled at the group where Philip had gone. With defeat weighing down his shoulders, Philip trudged back up the hill. Jennidab walked beside. They reached the place where Jesus sat.

Jennidab said to Elric, "Captain, I—"

Elric stopped him with a raised hand and said, "I know."

Philip flipped back the cloth covering of his basket and showed his empty basket. "Master, I can't do it."

Jesus smiled at Philip and said, "No, you can't. Apart from me, you can do nothing."

"Did I do something wrong?" Philip asked. "Am I supposed to say some special word?"

"This is not a magic trick. Do not place your faith in your own abilities. You must see past the flesh. Look at the others."

Philip glanced down the hill at the steady distribution of food happening among the groups of people.

Jesus continued, "Do these other disciples have some power or ability that you do not have?"

Philip shrugged.

"This is not about power or ability. It is about the love of your heavenly Father. He wants to provide for His people, and He chooses to meet their needs through other people. The provision is already there, but you need to access it through faith in *Him*. Faith that *He* will accomplish that which He has spoken. Give me your basket."

Jesus put two more loaves and two fish into Philip's basket and covered them with the cloth.

"Do you believe the Father cares for these people and wants to meet their needs?"

"Yes, Master."

"Have I not told you the Father's will?"

Philip nodded.

"Then trust me. Have faith in your heavenly Father. Go do the work of the Kingdom."

"Yes, Master."

Philip turned and went back to his group. He handed them a loaf. Then a second loaf. Then a third loaf. He looked back at Jesus and grinned. Jesus nodded.

Elric surveyed the panorama, crossed his arms, and smiled. The smoke of over two hundred small campfires lit up the grassy foothills between the mountain and the shore as afternoon turned into evening. Every group contained someone who had received a miraculous healing, and everyone sat around their campfires, eating barley loaves and roasted fish and listening to the stories of healing and restoration.

With their duties in the field complete, Jenli and Zaben joined Elric.

Timrok landed next to them and said, "The enemy has kept their distance. There was nothing they could do to stop this. It feels like we are gaining momentum."

The twelve finished eating, and Jesus asked them, "How many did you feed?"

They conferred together, with Matthew keeping the tally. Matthew answered, "About five thousand men. Plus the women and children."

With a satisfied smile, Jesus said, "Good. Very good. Gather up the leftover pieces so that nothing will be lost."

So, they gathered them up and filled twelve baskets with pieces from the five barley loaves which were left over by those who had eaten.

Judas reported, "Master, the people are beginning to rally together. They intend on declaring you king."

"Yes!" shouted Timrok.

Simon the Zealot added, "There is even talk of taking you by force if necessary. The people are desperate for a deliverer. And they believe you are the Prophet who has come into the world."

Zaben looked to Elric. "Is the time really now?"

Elric furrowed his brows and shook his head. "I do not think so. I have heard nothing."

"My time is not yet come," Jesus said.

Elric gave a confirming nod to the three lieutenants.

"These people see only according to the flesh," Jesus said. "They seek temporal things like bread for their stomach. They do not yet perceive the true bread of life. I will turn them aside. But you, go back to the boat and cross over to the other side. I will send the crowd away and stay here alone to pray for a while. Then I will meet you at Capernaum."

James asked, "How will you get there? You do not have a boat, and it is a full day's walk around the northern end of the lake."

"The Father will provide a way."

"But Master," Simon said, "It will be dark soon and the wind is building. Would it not be better to spend the night here and cross over together in the morning?"

"Do as I have spoken."

29

WAVES OF FAITH

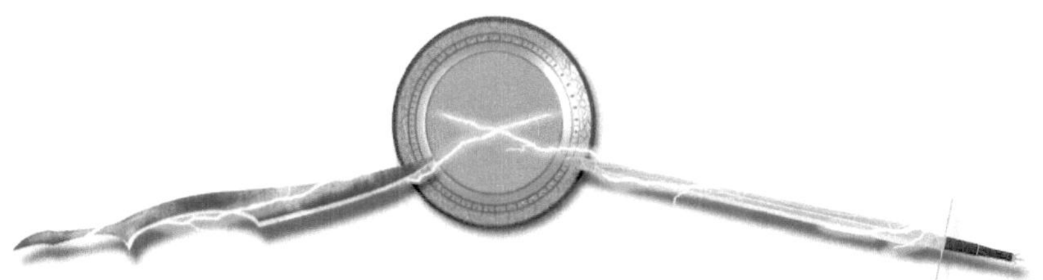

Battle minus 6 months

At the fourth watch of the night, Jesus stood at the edge of the water with a strong wind blowing in His face. The whitecaps of the waves glowed under a partial moon and pounded out a cacophony of violent opposition. The last eight hours on the mountain after Jesus dispersed the crowd had been quiet, but the development of a howling wind brought Him down to the shore.

Elric held his position near the King with Timrok's five warriors in a tight perimeter around them. A steady stream of light poured down on the Son of Man. *What is He about to do? He is receiving something from the Throne.*

Timrok landed in front of Elric. "Captain, I have made a thorough search. These winds are natural and not a direct attack from the enemy."

"What *is* the status of the twelve generals?"

"They are over three miles across the sea, but they are laboring hard against the wind. Jenli and Zaben's teams are upholding them and giving them strength, so they are safe. But without the physical presence of the King, they are near despair."

Elric crossed his arms and nodded. "*That's* what the Son of Man is contemplating. His heart is going out to the disciples, and He is awaiting direction from the Throne."

"Is He going to calm the waves?"

"I do not know. That would be the most . . . wait . . . look at that!"

The ground around Jesus' feet shimmered and sparkled with energy in the Middle Realm. A bright blue aura of plasma enveloped His feet up to His ankles and radiated downward.

"What is that?" Timrok said.

"I'm not sure," Elric said, "but I may have an idea. Remember when Elisha made the axe head float?"

"Were you there for that?"

"No, but I heard about it. The King made the water displaced by the axe head change density such that the buoyancy of the iron was sufficient for it to float and remain on the surface. And look at that. That's exactly what I would expect in the Middle Realm for such a provision."

"Bending natural laws," Timrok said with extra excitement in his voice. "We do not see this very often. Do you think the Son of Man can see this in the Middle Realm?"

"I doubt it. The Father wants Him to *walk* by faith."

"Walk *on* the water? As a man?"

"Just like any other man, the faith to believe in the Father's ability is easy. It is the faith to believe you have heard the Father's word concerning a matter—that is the difficult part."

Timrok shook his head. "The Son of Man always hears the word from the Father."

"Still," Elric said, "He must walk by faith. No one has ever—"

"Sir! There He goes!"

Jesus took a step into the water. Only half of His foot submerged as though buoyed up by the water itself. Like the hull of ship, His foot cut through the water and sustained His full weight. He took a moment to find His balance and took another step. The waves crashed against Him, submerging His knees and splashing up to His waist. He braced against the impact and held His balance. He took another step. Another wave slapped against Him. He took another step. With each step, His stability improved and speed increased. After walking twenty yards into the sea, He established a steady rhythm of using the rising swell of a wave to step over the crest and march forward against the contrary winds.

Elric, Timrok, and Timrok's team marched alongside. One mile passed. Then two. By mile three, Elric spotted the rest of the team at work with the boat carrying the twelve. He flashed his sword into the darkness and received an answer flash from Zaben. Near mile four they caught up with the boat.

"What is He doing?" Timrok called out over the wind and waves. "It looks like He is going to pass right by!"

"I don't know," Elric answered. "He said He would meet them on the other side. Perhaps He is going on ahead to meet them there." He looked over at the twelve straining against their oars and looking tired and desperate. "Perhaps He is waiting for them to call on Him for help."

A scream of terror echoed across the water from the boat. "Aaaugh!"

"Aaaugh! What is that?"

"It is a ghost!"

Twelve squeals rang out. All rowing stopped.

"A ghost!"

Jesus called back, "Take courage, it is I; do not be afraid."

Elric could feel the twelve sets of eyes straining through the darkness and the stunned bewilderment in their silence.

Finally, Peter shouted, "Lord, if it is You, command me to come to You on the water."

And He said, "Come!"

The instant Jesus said "come," the same cloud of energy in the Middle Realm surrounding His feet appeared on Peter's. Peter got out of the boat and walked on the water and came toward Jesus. Andrew jumped from his position in the boat to the tiller where Peter had been working and kept the boat pointed into the wind. All the others clutched the side of the boat and watched with amazement.

Jenli moved out with Peter and stretched out his hand toward him.

Elric yelled, "No, Jenli. Let him walk."

Peter managed to find his balance and took several steps. A wave smacked against him, and he tottered from the impact. He straightened up and took another step. Another wave hit him. He stayed upright, but he sank into the water up to his knees. The glow of the energy in the Middle Realm at Peter's feet remained as strong as Jesus', but his waterline rose like a ship that had taken on water. Another wave crashed into him. He submerged up to his waist.

With panic in his voice, he screamed, "Lord, save me!"

Jesus reached out with His hand and took hold of him, and said to him, "You of little faith, why did you doubt?"

With his arm around Jesus' shoulders and his feet on top of the water, Peter and Jesus made their way back toward the boat.

Just before they reached the boat, a swirling vortex of light appeared in front of the boat in the Middle Realm. Millions of individual sparks spun around the ring, making multiple revolutions before spiraling inward and exploding in a final flash of light at the center. The size of the ring began as small as a plate and expanded until it was larger than the boat. The individual sparks spinning inward flashed in the middle of the ring and created a pulsing, dazzling eye at the center of the vortex. The reverberation of the sparks had a low frequency like the long rumble of thunder, and its roar rose above the sound of the wind and waves.

Timrok yelled above the noise, "Captain, is that a time-space—"

Kaboom!

In an instant, when Jesus' feet entered the boat, the nose of the boat stretched forward to a pinpoint at the eye of the vortex, followed by the body of the boat, followed by the stern, until the whole boat— and everyone in it, men and angels—disappeared into the vortex. The next instant, the vortex collapsed inward on itself and disappeared. The sea became still and smooth as glass.

Elric, Timrok, and Timrok's team stood in the middle of the sea with the moon reflecting off the still water in perfect silence.

Elric's hands dropped to his sides. "Yes. I have not seen that since the days of Elisha."

"I have never seen one," Timrok said. "Where did the Spirit take them?"

"I do not know."

A small light approached from the west, traveling fast just above the surface of the water. It grew larger as it drew closer. Suddenly, Zaben appeared. His wings tucked away.

"Captain," Zaben said, "The boat has come to land at Gennesaret."

Timrok said, "Did the men see all this? That was amazing!"

"No," Zaben answered. "One second, we were out here amidst the raging sea. The next, we were near the shore, and the sea was calm."

Elric smiled at Timrok and the team. He raised his wings and said, "We go to Gennesaret!"

30

RESTITUTION

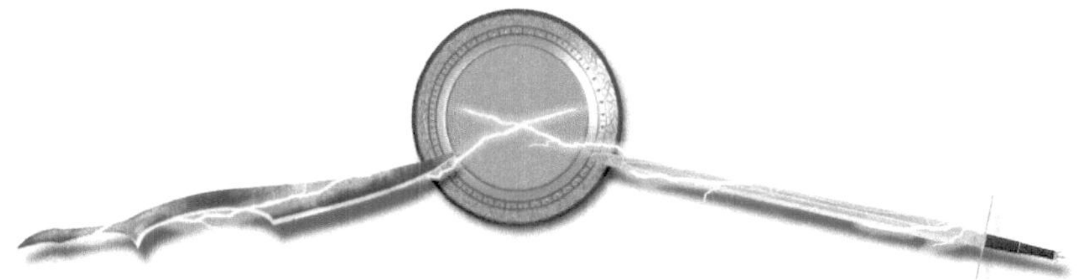

Battle minus 6 months

Daniel wandered up a less-traveled street in Ein Gev. He stopped in front of an opening in a stone-faced building that led downstairs to a small alcove. *This is the place.* His stomach did flip flops, and his heart pounded in his throat. He paused a moment, swallowed hard, and took a deep breath. With steady, determined steps, he descended. On the left side of the alcove, he opened a thick wooden door and stepped in.

The man behind the counter spotted Daniel, stopped pouring a drink, and shot a nervous glance over to the strongman at his post.

The strongman stepped forward and intercepted Daniel before he could reach the counter. The strongman took an imposing stance but raised the palms of his hands to a half-surrendered position. "We don't want any trouble. Please find another place to—"

"Please," Daniel interrupted with as contrite a tone as he could offer. "I am not here to cause trouble."

The strongman glanced back at the man behind the counter. The man gave a tentative nod. The strongman turned sideways and let Daniel pass but followed at a safe distance.

Daniel stepped up to the counter. "My name is Daniel. Are you the owner of this place?"

"Daniel? You are sure it's not Levi?"

Daniel let out a long sigh. "I was a different person last time I was here—a person I am not proud of. But I have been set free from that life, and I am here to make restitution for the damage I caused."

"My name is Ezra. I am the owner."

Daniel dropped a pouch full of coins on the counter. It made a hefty metallic clink. "I don't know how much damage I caused, but this is two weeks' pay. I hope it will help."

Ezra lifted the pouch and felt the weight. "This is very generous. I'm sure it is enough." He set the pouch back on the counter. "What happened to you?"

Daniel smiled. "I'm glad you asked. For most of my life, I was tormented by an evil spirit. I thought it was the spirit of my brother Levi, but it was actually a demon."

Ezra's eyes grew wide. "Levi—that explains . . . a demon?"

Daniel nodded. "Then while I was in Capernaum after a fishing trip, a man named Jesus, a prophet out of Nazareth, cast the demon out with a single command. It was the first time I was free for as long as I can remember. I settled here in Ein Gev and was doing well. Then one night it returned—only it wasn't alone. It brought a thousand more evil spirits with it. They took complete control, and I don't remember much after that. I regained consciousness in the tombs outside Gergesa."

Daniel rolled up his sleeves to show the deep scars all over his forearms. Ezra and the strongman winced.

"Their sole objective was to cause pain and destruction. Not only to me, but to anyone within my reach."

The strongman fingered the large, raised scar on his own forehead.

"Then one day, the same man Jesus showed up on the beach near the tombs and cast all the demons out. They are completely gone."

"How?" Ezra asked.

"By the power of God. He told me God loves me and that He knew my pain and that He wanted me to be free."

"That's amazing!"

"And there's more. I had been deaf in my right ear since I was a young boy. He touched my ear and healed it! I can hear!"

"Who is this Jesus?"

"I don't really know. But I do know that He has the power of God. And He sought me out to save me. I believe He is the promised Messiah."

"The Messiah?"

"Many others who have heard Him and seen His works are saying the same thing. I tried to join his disciples and follow Him, but He said for now that should go back to my home and tell everyone the good things God has done for me. So, I am retracing my steps through the Decapolis, telling my story, and trying to make restitution where I can."

"I have never heard such a story," Ezra said.

The strongman said, "If I had not seen you before—with the unnatural strength you had and the sheer hatred in your eyes . . . and now—I would not have believed it."

"It is all true. God delivered me. Now I have a hope and a future."

"I need to meet this Jesus," Ezra said.

"I do too," said the strongman with eyes full of tears.

* * *

Battle minus 4 months

From a flat rooftop an arrow's shot away from the synagogue in Capernaum, Zaben watched the mass of people stream away. Hundreds of grumbling conversations rose through the unsettled air.

"This statement is very unpleasant; who can listen to it?"

"Eat his flesh? Drink his blood?

"How can this man give us His flesh to eat?"

"Nothing like this has ever been spoken in Israel. Cannibalism? It is unthinkable."

"He has said difficult things before, but this is too much."

"I am done following him."

"I had hoped that he was the one. I'm going back to my home."

Luxor landed next to Zaben. Looking down at the people he said, "We are losing many followers. What is the Son of Man doing?"

Zaben shook his head. "I do not know."

"Do you understand what He meant when He said, 'The one who eats My flesh and drinks My blood has eternal life, and I will raise him up on the last day'?"

"It has to have spiritual meaning."

"Why does He not explain it more fully so these will not leave?"

Zaben bit his lip and scowled. "Perhaps He is reducing the number of His army as He did with Gideon."

The people continued to file out of the synagogue with shaking heads and grumbling lips.

Luxor leaned forward with his arms resting on the waist-high ledge of the plastered roof border wall. Looking out beyond the people as though straining into the future he said, "Do we know His strategy for the final campaign?"

Zaben sighed. "It remains a mystery. Even to us. So, we continue to work toward our plan and wait for the right time."

"It seems to me that we have sufficient numbers now," Luxor said. Looking down at the people dispersing, he continued, "The longer we wait, the more difficult the battle."

"There have been opportunities for Him to step into His role as King already, but He withdraws every time. What do you suggest we do? Raise up the Roman army against Him?"

"No, of course not. But according to your plan, we are waiting for the enemy to overplay a move against the leaders who are loyal to the Son of Man so the people will rise up against the religious establishment. And then the Romans will step in and remove the religious leaders, making way for the rise of our new leaders—and the establishment of a new king."

"Yes?"

"Why do we wait? Why not force the enemy to move now?"

"How? This would require us to incite the religious leaders to evil schemes. We could never—"

"No," Luxor interrupted. "No, we only perform works of the Kingdom. However, what if the opportunity to establish the Kingdom is at hand, and we miss it because we are waiting for the *enemy* to move? What if the Son of Man is waiting for *us* to bring it to pass?"

Zaben chewed on his lip and gazed out over the rooftops of the city.

31

MOUNT HERMON

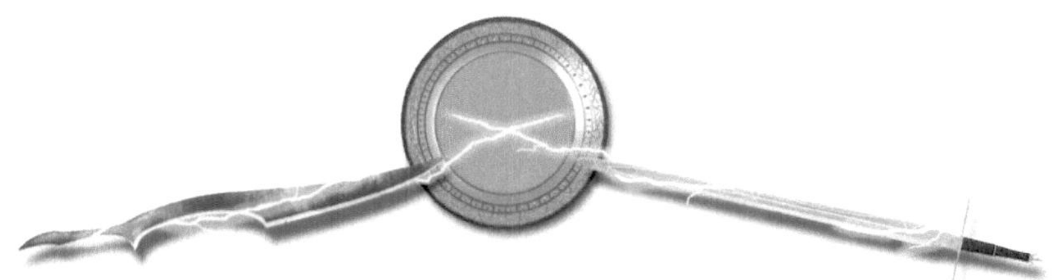

Battle minus 1 month

Elric lay face down on the ground at the base of Mount Hermon, just north of Caesarea Philippi. Behind him, his entire team also lay prostrate—all in precise ranks with their swords laid out on the ground in front of them. The radiance of the light enveloping the entire mountain in the Middle Realm washed over them with the same heaviness Elric knew from the outer courtyard in the King's Realm.

Jesus had taken Peter, James, and John up the mountain with Him while the other disciples remained in Caesarea Philippi. And, as instructed by Grigor, Elric and his team stayed at the base. As much as Elric wanted to see the moment when Jesus revealed His true glory—which was the purpose of this operation—it was only for Peter, James, and John.

He could hear nothing from them now that they had hiked miles up the trail. And though he dared not lift his eyes to the mountain, he couldn't keep his mind from racing.

This is it! This is it! The King is taking on His true form. This is the day we have awaited since the Rebellion. No enemy will stand before Him now. Finally, He will vanquish His foes and establish His kingdom on earth. What is going on up there? What is He saying to them? Any moment now . . . Michael and the Mighty Ones will appear. I wonder if the enemy is seeing—

Flash!

The radiance of the light in the Middle Realm exploded into a brilliance Elric only knew from the King's inner court throne room. The immensity of it took his breath away. It took his thoughts away. The presence of the King and His glory became his only conscious awareness.

A booming voice thundered from the top of the mountain, "This is My Son, My Chosen One; listen to Him!"

Elric closed his eyes and pressed his face harder into the ground.

In the next instant, the cloud of light disappeared. The heaviness of the glory lifted.

Elric waited. He lifted his head and looked around. A light breeze rustled the leaves of the nearby trees. Birds chirped. The late afternoon sun sank low. He sat up and looked up the mountain. Nothing. He looked up toward the heavens for Michael. Nothing. He picked up his sword and stood, sliding the sword into its sheath.

One by one, the rest of the team rose to their feet. They remained in their ranks and glanced at each other with confused eyes. They looked toward Elric.

"Stand at ease," Elric announced. He motioned for the lieutenants.

Zaben, Jenli, Lacidar, and Timrok circled in close.

"What happened?" Timrok said. "I thought He was going to—"

"I did, too," Jenli said. "I thought this was it."

Zaben shook his head. "I wasn't sure. He is supposed to start His campaign from the Mount of Olives, accompanied by a great earthquake according to the prophet Zechariah."

"That's right," Jenli said. "Then, what *was* this?"

"A declaration," Elric said, crossing his arms. "A turning point. I think this was more than a sign for these three men. I think it was an announcement that the King is about to take His place."

Lacidar said, "Do you think the enemy saw?"

"They saw," Timrok said as he grasped his sword handles.

Elric nodded. "This changes everything. We must increase our vigilance and be ready for anything. The enemy will surely make a move soon. The Passover is only a month away. Perhaps this festival will mark the fullness of times."

"Sir," Timrok said as he looked up the mountain trail, "what of the King, Peter, James, and John?"

Elric lifted his chin. "It seems clear the King has the form of the Son of Man again. We should resume our posts. Zaben and Jenli, your teams can return to their charges. Timrok, you and your team will accompany me up the mountain. Lacidar, it is good to have you back. With the increased danger, I would like you and your team to join Timrok and double the security around the King."

32

COMING FORTH

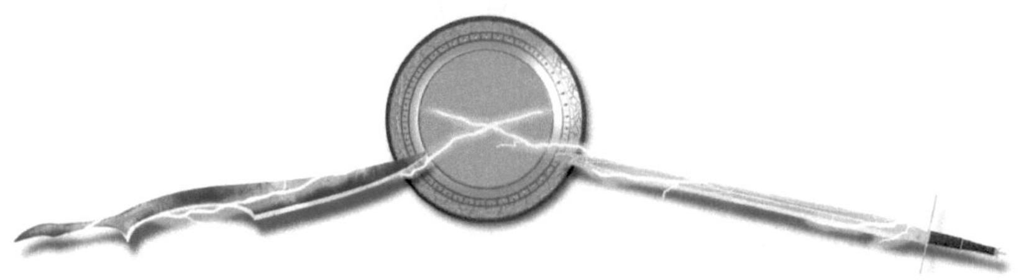

Battle minus 2 weeks

"*L*azarus, come forth!"

Jesus' voice rang out across the clearing in front of the tomb where Lazarus had been laid four days prior. The people had gathered from the small town of Bethany where Mary and Martha, the sisters of Lazarus, lived. Mourners from Jerusalem, less than two miles away, added to the crowd. Over a hundred mourners watched with incredulous eyes hidden behind black veils. Another hundred mixed with the crowd—Jesus' disciples and followers—who watched with sadness and wonder. In the Physical Realm, hopelessness and pain weighed heavy on the weary people. And though the sun shone with its unchanging radiance, it seemed distant and irrelevant.

In the Middle Realm, Elric stood behind the Son of Man and off to the side where he could see the entrance to the tomb. He waited with his hands on his hips and a smile on his lips. Timrok and Lacidar's teams formed a barrier between the crowd and the Son of Man, each with one wary eye on the people and one eye on the tomb. The brightness of the sun paled in the brightness of the Son.

A rumbling from within the tomb shook the spiritual ground. Black smoke shot outward in every direction. Two massive black bat-like wings emerged from inside the tomb upward through the cave ceiling. Two more burst through the knoll on each side. Then, amid flames and billowing sulfur, the great dark cherub rose through the stone hillside and covered the entire tomb—Satan himself. Towering over everything, his burning eyes locked onto the Son of Man.

Elric leapt between Satan and the King with his sword drawn and ready for battle. His entire team formed tight ranks behind him. He felt insignificant before the mighty cherub, but if Satan wanted a fight, he would give it to him.

Satan made no acknowledgment of Elric and his team. He growled, "This is not legal! The keys of death and grave belong to *me*!" His words increased in intensity and pace. "No man can be released from Sheol—whether in Hades or Abraham's bosom—without my will. You cannot have this man! I forbid it!"

Elric wanted to glance back at Jesus to see His reaction, but he kept his eyes—and his blade—trained on the enemy. *I wonder if He can see and hear this. What is He going to say? What is He going to do?*

Shafts of light penetrated through Satan's clouds of darkness from within the tomb. Lazarus hobbled out, still bound hand and foot with wrappings and a cloth wrapped around his face. He passed through Satan and stood in the open clearing.

Jesus said to the people standing by, "Unbind him, and let him go."

Satan roared. He spewed a tempest of flames toward the King. Elric braced for the blast and sheltered behind his shield. With the firestorm wrapping around his shield, he glanced around at the rest of his team. They managed to stay on their feet behind their shields, but the force of the shockwaves pushed them backward. Timrok, with no shield to screen himself from the blast, planted his feet and faced into the blast in sheer defiance. His eyes squeezed shut, and the gale pulled all his wild hair tight against his face and head.

"I will kill you!" Satan thundered. "And the inheritance will be mine!"

The flames stopped, and Elric peeked over the top of his shield. Satan lifted into the air like a giant dragon, released a haunting screech, and disappeared over the hill in the direction of Jerusalem.

Did the blast affect the King? Or Lazarus? Elric spun around.

Jesus embraced Lazarus and laughed with Mary and Martha as though none of the maelstrom in the Middle Realm even happened.

Elric laughed and slid his sword into its sheath.

The crowd of people buzzed with excitement and pressed in close to see and touch Lazarus.

Elric drew backward, away from the crowd. The lieutenants followed. Elric reached his hand out toward Timrok and pinched out a smoking ember smoldering on Timrok's beard. Timrok gave an embarrassed smile and brushed out his smoking beard. Then he patted down the rest of his hair.

"Word of this is sure to reach the religious leaders in Jerusalem," Elric said.

"They already are looking for opportunity to seize Him," Jenli said. "Where do we go next? Even coming here was a risk."

"Perhaps we should pull back and remain hidden for a time," Lacidar said.

"Retreat?" Timrok grumbled. "The King never retreats."

"Not a retreat," Lacidar said. "A strategic pause. There is no dishonor in waiting for the right time."

Elric nodded. "The King will not hide His light from His people. However, it may be prudent to avoid the religious leaders right now."

"What of the festival?" Zaben asked. "Passover begins next week. Surely the King will not miss Passover?"

Elric shrugged. "I have received no direction. For now, let's move out to the country near the wilderness, to the town of Ephraim."

Timrok rested his hands on his sword handles. "These are treacherous times."

* * *

Marr and his ranking officers packed the dark wood-paneled office of the high priest at the temple complex in Jerusalem. Toxic smoke filled the air in the Middle Realm and smothered every ray of light from the Throne that tried to reach the men in the room. The men—Caiaphas, the chief elders, and a dozen high-level priests and scribes—met for an urgent council to discuss the recent news of the resurrection of a man in Bethany.

"What are we doing?" one of the priests said. "For this man is performing many signs. If we let Him go on like this, all men will believe in Him, and the Romans will come and take away both our place and our nation."

"I agree," echoed a scribe. "He is doing more than just disturbing a few people. He threatens our religious heritage, our nation, our very way of life."

"How do we stop him?" one asked.

Marr answered without hesitation. "Kill Him!" His words formed fiery darts that penetrated every man in the room. "I have had enough of subtlety and schemes to ensnare Him. Just kill Him."

All the demons chanted in unison, "Kill, kill, kill."

One of the senior elders said, "Every time we try to trap him in some point of the law, he turns it around and makes us look foolish before the people. I think we need a more direct approach."

This sparked a flurry of debate amongst the men.

"He needs to be eliminated."

"Kill him? The law forbids the killing of an innocent man."

"He leads the people astray. He is guilty of incitement to rebellion."

"It is murder."

"Imprisonment then."

"This will only embolden his followers. He needs to be killed."

"But we can't just—"

"We have to! The Romans will—"

Caiaphas stood and lifted his hands. The room became quiet. With a calm, authoritative voice he said, "You know nothing at all, nor do you take into account that it is expedient for you that one man die for the people, and that the whole nation not perish." He sat down.

"That is right," one of the senior elders said. "It is not murder. It is the necessary sacrifice of a single man for the sake of an entire nation."

An advisor standing behind Caiaphas's seat announced, "It is settled, then. Jesus the Nazarene is to be executed. Seek opportunity to take him into custody and accomplish this judgment."

"Let us do it now," a priest said. "Where is he?"

One of the priests standing in the back said, "No one knows. After he left Bethany, he has not walked publicly."

"He cannot stay hidden long," one said. "The Passover begins next week."

Caiaphas said, "Circulate these orders—if anyone knows where he is, he is to report it, so that we might seize him."

Marr sat back on his throne and let out a long stream of smoke from his nostrils. "This ends soon. Soon, the Son of Man will be dead, and we will assume our rightful places in a new kingdom."

A small snake in the corner of the room shot its forked tongue in and out and watched the men file out of the high priest's chambers. It paused a moment and slithered off through the back wall.

* * *

With Joel, the fishing boat captain, at the tiller and Daniel seated beside him, the boat sliced through the peaceful predawn waters back toward Ein Gev. The remaining four crewmembers sat midship with the load of fish and piles of nets at their feet.

In the Middle Realm, Théodor was the only elzur warrior onboard, and he stood beside Daniel, enjoying the quiet night on the lake. For almost eight months now, Théodor served with Daniel, and none of the legion had threatened to reenter his charge. He fought with the typical resistance when Daniel traveled throughout the Decapolis sharing his testimony, but none ever tried to exceed their bounds.

"I don't know," Daniel said to Joel. "I can't get past this feeling that I need to be doing something else."

"What else can you do?" Joel said. "You have visited every city in the region and told your story to everyone who would listen. You even repaid people and businesses for damages."

"I just . . . I don't really know much about this Jesus. All I can do is tell what happened to me."

Théodor jumped in. "That's right! There is power in the word of your testimony. More power than great learning."

Daniel continued. "I would really like to follow Him and be a disciple. Learn His teachings. Experience more of His power."

"Then do it," Joel said.

"I can't. Not yet. He said it was not time for me."

"When will the time come?"

"I don't know. It still feels like the time isn't right. Like there is unfinished business."

"As I said, I don't know what else you can do."

Daniel gazed out across the water, unable to see into the darkness beyond the warm ring of light cast by the lantern hanging from the mast. "There was something He said to me there on the shore that day. It has been pulling at my mind for months."

"What? What did He say?"

" 'Go home to your people and tell them what the Lord did for you.' "

"Yes, and you have done that."

" 'Go *home* to *your people*.' The Decapolis is not really my home. My family is in Nazareth. I ran away from home when I was very young."

"Then it seems clear what you must do," Joel said.

"Listen to him," Théodor said. "This is the King's word to you."

"It's not that easy. Actually, my father disowned me. My older brother hates me. There is a lifetime of pain and resentment. I don't know if I can."

Théodor said, "Forgiveness, restoration. This is the King's will. Be strong."

"I think you can," Joel said. "And I think you should. Just consider it all—Jesus came and sought you out; He delivered you; He healed you; He gave you this specific command; He continues to remind you of His word. I think the One who was able to deliver you is also able to give you the strength you need. Strength to forgive. Strength to face your father."

"That's right!" Théodor said. "This is the King's word to you!" Théodor smiled at Joel. *I have been telling Daniel this for months. It's always more effective when the King delivers His word through another person.*

"But what if my father doesn't receive me?"

"What if he does?" Joel said.

Daniel continued staring off into the distance.

"Do you want to know what else I think?" Joel asked.

Daniel nodded.

"I think that when you take care of this unfinished business, you will experience a release to go and follow Jesus the way you want."

Daniel turned and looked Joel in the eyes. Joel smiled.

"Maybe you are right," Daniel said.

"He is right!" Théodor said. "It is time for you to go home. Do not delay any longer."

Daniel looked back over the water. "All right. I will do it. When we get back, I'll help get this catch unloaded. Then, I'll pack up and head back to Nazareth."

Joel grabbed Daniel's shoulder and smiled. "You are a good man, Daniel. I think the Lord has great things in store for you."

33

EASTERN GATE

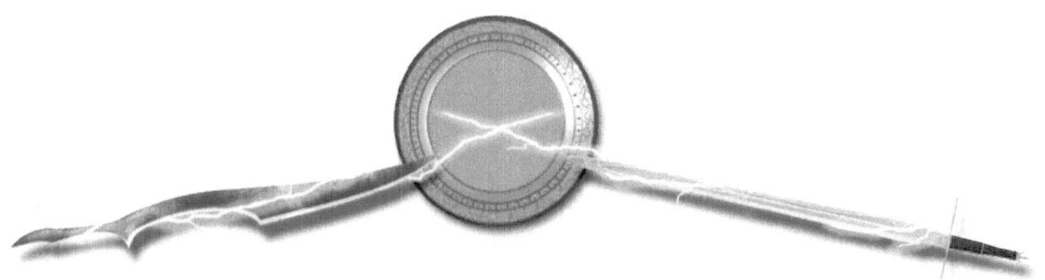

Battle minus 5 days

Saturday evening, while Jesus and the twelve dined at the home of Lazarus, Martha, and Mary in Bethany, Elric and Zaben conferred outside in an open field.

Zaben continued his thoughts on strategy. "We have been waiting for the enemy to overplay some edict against leaders or people in the synagogues—which will trigger an uprising of the people against the religious establishment."

"Yes?" Elric said, curious about the next thoughts.

"I am beginning to think that the trigger might be the Son of Man himself."

"What do you mean?"

"The people love Him. They continue to be drawn to Him. They are ready to make Him king. Imagine what will happen if we go into

Jerusalem for Passover—into the temple—and the religious leaders make a move against Him."

"The people will probably riot." Elric said.

"Yes. And then the Romans step in to keep the peace, the agitators are removed, our leaders take their place, and the way is made for a new king."

"Hmm. They already wish to seize Him by force," Elric said.

Zaben nodded. "Does He plan on going into Jerusalem publicly?"

"I have not received any direction yet."

A silent flash lit the field where they stood. Grigor appeared. His wings folded away. "Captain," Grigor said. "Gather your team for an announcement."

Elric nodded to Zaben, who took off toward the house. Elric shot a flash of light from his blade toward the tree line at the perimeter of the area. A light flashed back. Seconds later, a flurry of wings converged on Elric's location in the field. Elric checked over his shoulder. Four lieutenants in a tight line directly behind him. Twenty warriors in smart ranks behind them. All at attention.

Elric smiled and turned back to Grigor. "All present."

Instead of stepping forward to make his announcement, Grigor moved to the side and took a step back. A fine white mist appeared in front of the assembly. It grew in size and increased in depth. It became brighter and brighter until Elric had to squint. Still brighter. Brighter. Then, it receded. Elric focused into the evaporating mist, and there before them stood a massive form. An archangel. Blazing white—too white even for the Middle Realm. With silver eyes!

Gabriel! This can mean only one thing! It took all the discipline Elric could summon to keep from leaping into the air.

"Faithful warriors of the King," Gabriel began. His voice rumbled with power and authority. "Tomorrow the Son of Man enters Jerusalem as the promised King, the son of David, the Messiah of Israel."

Yes! Yes! How long Elric had waited to hear these words.

Gabriel continued. "The host of heaven will herald His arrival, but the men of earth will not hear or see. You will march in the procession behind the King." He paused. "Are there any questions?"

Elric gritted his teeth. *I have a thousand. But I would surely not speak even one.*

From somewhere in the ranks behind, Elric heard a voice call out.

"Master Gabriel, when He enters Jerusalem, will that mark the beginning of the final battle?"

Elric's heart sank. *We all know the deep mysteries of the King are revealed only as needed. After all these years of diligent patience, who would have the audacity to be so direct? Who would actually ask Gabriel—*

"Luxor," Gabriel said. "The one who replaced Lorr after he was taken by the enemy—you are new to the team and ambitious. The King recognizes your role in this mission." Gabriel scanned over the whole gathering. "I know you are *all* desirous of the day."

Elric relaxed a little. *Perhaps Gabriel will tell us something new.*

Gabriel continued. "But this mystery remains sealed. I can tell you this—the Son of Man still has work to complete before He sits on His throne. Any other questions?"

Silence.

Gabriel looked at Elric. "You have your orders."

"In His service," Elric answered.

"For His glory," Gabriel said. He wrapped his wings around his body and disappeared in a fading mist.

Grigor stepped up into his place. He proceeded with the typical facts-only decorum of a logirhim. "There is a man in Bethphage named Jonathan, son of Judah. He lives just off the main street after you enter the village."

Elric glanced back at Jenli, who flipped through a ledger. Jenli stopped on a page and nodded. Elric turned back to Grigor.

"He has a donkey, and the donkey's colt, on which the King will ride tomorrow."

Elric nodded. "To fulfill the word of the prophet Zechariah."

"You are to give Jonathan a dream tonight. The sign to him to release his donkey and the colt are the words 'The Lord needs them.' Prepare Jonathan for this word."

Elric nodded.

Grigor continued. "The chief priests in Jerusalem seek to kill Lazarus for the word of his testimony. It is best if he does not enter Jerusalem with the Son of Man tomorrow. You will not have to assign any of your team for his protection because the King is dispatching two additional warriors to stay with him."

Elric nodded.

"Do you have any questions for *me*?" Grigor said.

"For the procession," Elric said, "do we wear ceremonial white?"

Grigor took a deep breath and let it out slowly. "No. Your warrior gear is most prudent." He continued, "Resistance will be extreme in Jerusalem. Expect zealous attacks from the enemy. Remain strong. Keep the King safe."

"In His service."

"By His word." Grigor paused a moment and smiled at Elric. He looked past Elric at the rest of the team, still in disciplined ranks. He raised his wings and disappeared with a single flap.

Elric spun around. He eyed the troops with a stoic face. He waited. He could sense the pent-up energy in the ranks. He waited. He could sense they knew he knew the excitement he kept restrained by holding them at attention. So, he waited a little more. Finally, he issued the command, stern and curt, "Dismissed."

The ranks erupted with an explosion of sound and motion. Half of the warriors shot straight up like comets, shouting joyous exclamations. Some did acrobatics. Some danced. One flew laps around the house in a blur. All laughed and shouted.

Jenli and Lacidar launched upward together in an interleaving spiral. Timrok danced on his toes with his arms in the air. Zaben leapt into the air with a shout, landed, and then bounced in place with a silly grin.

Seeing the reaction of all the others filled Elric with such joy and satisfaction that he just smiled and watched.

* * *

Battle minus 4 days

Sunday afternoon, Bethany. As Jesus and the twelve started down the road toward Bethphage, Elric and the team formed up on the road behind Him—Elric in front, followed by four lieutenants, four wide, followed by twenty warriors, four wide and five deep. They all wore their standard earthy battle dress, but their swords remained sheathed, and their shields hung on their arms by their sides. At Elric's signal, they marched. With their eyes locked forward, they kept a sharp formation in perfect step.

Large groups of people appeared on the road and joined the entourage as they made their way toward Bethphage.

Elric maintained his cadence but considered all the people joining the group. *They are coming out from Jerusalem and all the surrounding villages. These have heard about Lazarus and hope to see him and the Son of Man.* He studied them as they approached. No enemy forces amongst any. *These are supporters. No apparent threat.*

Jesus spoke with James and John. They nodded and ran ahead.

Going to get the donkey and her colt. Now we shall see if Jonathan will respond to Jenli's dream as planned.

Bethphage came into view. More people joined the assembly. Well over a hundred now. They reached the road leading off to Bethphage's city gate, and James and John stood at the intersection with a donkey and her colt. The procession came to a halt.

More people joined the crowd, and Elric could hear the excitement building.

"It's the prophet Jesus, who raised Lazarus from the dead!"

"And not only this, I saw Him give sight to a blind man."

"I saw Him cleanse a leper."

"And a heal a deaf man."

"And cast out demons."

"He is going to enter Jerusalem through the eastern gate, as foretold of the Messiah."

"And riding on the foal of a donkey!"

"He really is the Messiah!"

"This is the Messiah!"

John laid his cloak on the colt, and Jesus sat. More people came running from the town.

"It's the Messiah! He's going to enter Jerusalem!"

Without a word, Jesus started forward.

The people ran ahead and threw their cloaks on the ground in front of Him. Others ran farther ahead and cut branches from leafy trees and palms and laid them down on the ground. Elric's troop resumed their march.

Excitement in the crowd continued to build. Still more people joined.

There must be at least three hundred, and more are coming. These people are so desperate for a deliverer. Elric let a small smile sneak through his disciplined bearing. *Today is the day! These people may have waited their lifetime for this day, but I have been waiting thousands of years.*

The Mount of Olives approached on the left.

This is it! The Messiah enters Jerusalem from the Mount of Olives according to the prophet Zechariah. A great earthquake will split the mount from east to west, and half the mountain will move to the north and half to the south.

The road came around the corner at the descent of the Mount of Olives, and there before them lay Jerusalem. The golden dome of the temple shimmered in the afternoon sun. The great wall and the eastern gate rose just beyond the Kidron valley.

In the Middle Realm, the host of heaven had already assembled and awaited the arrival of the King.

Elric gasped for air at the spectacle before him.

Angelic trumpeters with long sleek silver trumpets stood shoulder to shoulder at ground level on both sides of the road from the Mount of Olives all the way to the eastern gate. Above and behind them, rows of mighty elzur commanders. Above and behind them, in ascending layers as in a giant coliseum, myriads of angels hovered—all clothed in white so pure and bright that it made Elric squint.

At the sight of the King, in perfect unison, all the trumpeters snapped their trumpets up to the ready position. All the commanders extended their swords upward at an angle toward the road. Their blades glistened in the light.

The trumpets sounded. Just as on the day of the King's birth, the trumpet fanfare began in unison with a fullness so pure that the sound rolled up into multicolored light and echoed off every layer of the spiritual atmosphere. The fanfare broke into melodies and countermelodies and intricate rhythms. "Glory to God!" climbed up from the bottom layer. "Glory to God in the highest!" bounded back down. All the angels joined in the song, from the ground to highest level.

> Glory to God
> Glory to God in the highest
> The One who is and the One who was
> And the One who is to come
> The Almighty King
>
> Glory to God
> Glory to God in the highest
> The kingdom of earth shall be

The kingdom of the Lord
The Almighty King

Glory to God
Glory to God in the highest
The Son of Man, the seed of David
Shall sit on His throne
The Almighty King

Tears filled Elric's eyes, and he had to blink to see. The tears ran down his cheeks as he maintained controlled steps.

The people cried out from in front and behind.

"Hosanna!"

"Blessed is He who comes in the name of the Lord."

"Blessed is the coming kingdom of our father David."

"Hosanna in the highest!"

Elric's heart pounded. *Any second now. The earthquake is going to split the Mount of Olives.* He marched ten more steps. *Any second now.*

The praises continued in the Middle Realm and the Physical Realm, but no earthquake. Onward they marched.

Elric turned his attention to Jesus. *He looks almost sad. This is the most triumphant day I have known; the host of heaven rejoice; the people shout His praise—and yet He does not glory in this moment. This is more than humility. He is carrying a great burden. What is it?*

The Mount of Olives passed behind them, and the Kidron valley lie ahead. Still no earthquake.

Something more is happening than we know.

The procession climbed up the western side of the Kidron valley and began its ascent up the temple mount. The two mighty senturim at the corners of the outer temple wall lay face down with their arms outstretched and their massive swords on the ground.

The crowd of people, now thousands, squeezed in close around the path leading up to the eastern gate. They continued to declare, "Hosanna! Hail the coming King!"

Over the shouting mass, some Pharisees in the crowd called out to Him, "Teacher, rebuke Your disciples!"

Jesus replied, "I tell you, if these stop speaking, the stones will cry out!"

They reached the gate. Jesus paused a moment and scanned the high city wall from north to south.

Elric strained to see His face. *Is that a tear in His eye?*

Jesus continued forward. The moment He crossed through the gate, the whole assembly of angels stopped their song and disbanded in a blink. Elric didn't look back to see, but he caught glimpses of the myriads shooting off in all directions like silent shooting stars.

The crowd pressed through the gate.

Elric and his team marched through the people and entered the city. Behind them—the city wall. Before them—across the courtyard, the outer wall of the temple grounds. He brought the detail to a halt. Jesus dismounted and handed the reins to John, who walked the donkey and her colt to the side and lashed them to post.

The parade is complete. Time to go back to work. Elric turned to the team and announced, "Dismissed." To Zaben and Jenli he motioned toward the top of the temple wall. They and their teams unfurled their wings and moved to strategic positions. To Timrok and Lacidar he motioned toward the King. In an instant a tight perimeter around Him formed, and an outer buffer mixed amongst the crowd.

Elric followed Jesus and the disciples into the outer court of the temple. As Elric passed through the wall, he noticed the senturim back at their stations with vigilant eyes and stern faces.

Inside the temple court, the typical buzz of activity filled the air. Money changers and vendors conducted business. Pilgrims from all over shuffled about, making purchases at booths, pointing at the amazing architecture, greeting family and friends, talking with priests, listening to singers. The upcoming festival brought increased traffic, and the influx of people from the Son of Man and His disciples and the crowd did not disturb the already-chaotic atmosphere in the Physical Realm.

In the Middle Realm, every eye turned toward the King. Beaelzurim all throughout the court stopped cold and stared with terror.

Jesus stood still and looked around the court.

Much of the crowd from outside made it into the court and gathered under a portico and waited in silence. His disciples pulled in close to Him and waited in silence. Groups of priests and scribes formed and watched the Son of Man in silence from the shadows.

Elric fidgeted and scanned all the people looking at the King. *They are all waiting for Him to say something. What is He going to do? This could be it. This could be . . .*

Jesus spoke in a soft voice to the twelve, "It is late. We should return to Bethany."

Without another word, He and the twelve filed out of the court. The crowd of people stood around, not sure what to do.

Elric's mind reeled. *What? What is He doing?*

He motioned to the team on the wall and headed out.

34

MONDAY

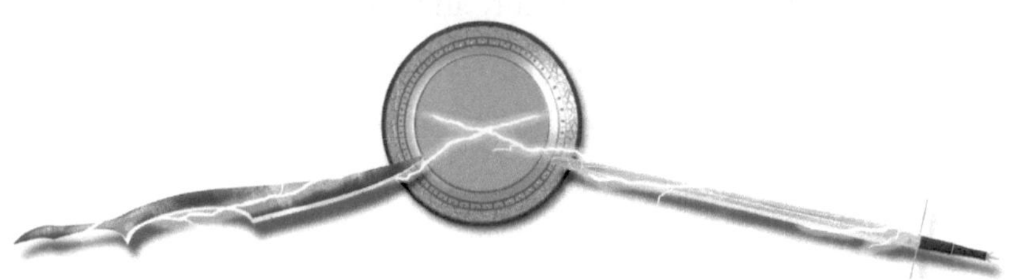

Battle minus 3 days

Monday morning, Elric and Zaben ducked behind the stone balustrade on the top of the outer temple wall in Jerusalem. A crackling bolt of lightning sizzled right over their heads and struck its target in the Middle Realm of the outer temple court. While the dark clouds boiled low in the spiritual air, frantic beaelzurim scattered in every direction to escape the storm pounding down upon them.

With every crack of thunder in the Middle Realm, Jesus cracked a whip in the Physical Realm. Under a clear blue sky, sheep and cattle stampeded toward the exit. Doves escaped from broken cages. Money changers scrambled for spilled coins.

Elric shouted over the tumult, "The King is cleaning house! We have seen this before!"

"Ha ha!" shouted Zaben. "And I am enjoying this as much as I did the last time!"

The storm in the Middle Realm raged just long enough for the Son of Man to clear the merchants and profiteers from the temple. Then came the cleansing rain in the Middle Realm.

With the last of the dove merchants scurrying away, Jesus shouted, "A house of prayer!" He punctuated His declaration with a final crack of His whip. He tossed the cords He was using as a whip onto a pile of broken bird cages and walked toward the nearest portico. Stopping at a place where the rabbis would sit and teach, He sat down and waited.

The people thronged to Him, eager for words of life or a healing touch.

"Now this is what I was expecting to see yesterday," Elric said. "Do you think the enemy will move against the King today?"

Zaben laughed. "Not today. There are none left in the temple complex."

* * *

Another emergency meeting of the chief council members convened after nightfall. Caiaphas leaned forward with his hands on his forehead and his elbows on his desk. "The whole world is going after him," he groaned.

Marr sat on his throne behind Caiaphas's seat and pointed his crooked finger at Asherah. "I do not want to hear excuses!" he railed. "Your failures today are—"

"My failures?" Asherah shot back. "The King Himself rained down fury from His Throne. None can stand against that. Not even you!"

"This storm lasted how long? Fifteen minutes? And yet the Son of Man remained undisturbed the rest of the day—performing miracles and drawing away even more supporters!"

"None of my forces could reenter the temple after the storm."

Marr sneered. "Could not, or would not? Are they so full of fear?"

"You were not there. You did not experience the terror of—"

"What of the men? Do you not have any men who can carry out your will without your direct leading?"

Asherah looked around at the men in the room. "They are weak."

"Then take Him tonight! Surely you can find men capable of accomplishing this deed."

"We . . . do not know where He is. He retreated at the end of the day, and we lost Him."

"Aaurgh!" roared Marr. "Then tomorrow! I presume He will enter the temple again tomorrow. When He does, you will seize Him. And this time, I will accept no failures."

A small snake appeared from the back of the room and slithered up onto Caiaphas's desk. Its black forked tongue darted in and out, and it raised its head toward Marr. "Oh wise and powerful prince of Persia," the snake cooed, "may I offer counsel?"

"*You*," snarled Marr, "would counsel *me*?"

Undeterred, the snake said, "I have knowledge of the enemy's plan."

"Tell me."

"The enemy wishes to remove the current religious leaders and install their own who will be supportive of a new king."

Marr chuckled. "An ambitious plan. But foolish. I own almost all these men. How could they hope to achieve such a thing?"

"By using the Romans."

"Ha! I own them, too."

"The people are very supportive of the Son of Man. They hang on His every word. Consider their reaction if you arrest Him in front of the people after He has just performed a miracle."

Marr sat back on his throne and breathed a long stream of smoke through his teeth. "They would probably riot."

"And the Roman army would . . . "

"Crush the riot and go after the ones who instigated it." Marr sat forward and eyed the small snake. "How is it that you know these things?"

"I travel about. I hear and see many things." The snake turned and slithered away.

Marr stood. "A new command—under no circumstance are you to take the Son of Man in the temple in view of the people. You must avoid a riot at any cost. You must find opportunity to seize Him by stealth, away from the crowd."

One of the priests in the room said, "What are we going to do about him? He has to be stopped."

Caiaphas answered, "You are correct; he has to be stopped. But we must take care not to seize him before the people. I fear they will riot. We should take him at night. Where is he staying?"

One of the priests said, "We do not know. He withdraws at night and stays hidden."

"Find a way to track him." Caiaphas said. "I want this affair settled before the start of Passover."

* * *

In a hidden inner room in Bethany, Elric and the lieutenants met.

Zaben addressed the group. "But the difference between the cleansing of the temple last time and this time is—this time, everything is prepared for King to assume His rightful place. The time is upon us."

Timrok grumbled, "And yet we retreat and hide."

Elric put his hand on Timrok's shoulder. "It is necessary for now. The enemy will make a mistake in the temple during the day, and then we will be able to fight. But at night, it is wise to avoid the religious leaders."

Jenli asked, "Has there been any new direction from the Throne?"

"No," Elric said. "We can assume He will continue to go into the temple during the day and withdraw at night. During the day, be ready to protect the King—eventually I expect there to be an attack, followed by a riot of the people. It will be challenging. If there is no attack, we need to be sure the King is not followed at the end of the day. Blind the eyes of the people. Distract the enemy. Divert the enemy. The King must disappear."

35

TESTING BY DAY

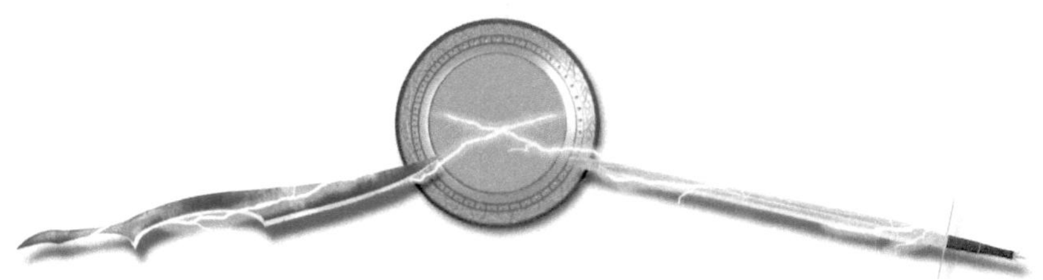

Battle minus 2 days

Tuesday morning, Elric entered the temple area before the others and surveyed the courtyard. The typical buzz of the outer court filled both the Physical and Middle Realms—minus the money changes and merchants, who were setting up just outside the temple walls and watching with worried looks for the wild man who turned their world upside down yesterday.

Already, groups of chief priests and elders gathered at several locations. One group, across the court under a portico, talked amongst themselves, unaware of the four demons who fed their spirits with a continuous stream of lies, judgment, and hatred. Two more formed on the left side behind the pillars, and enemy warriors worked hard on them. Another group waited to the right near the gate entrance.

The Son of Man entered, accompanied by the twelve. All the beaelzurim jumped and took cover behind the men. The demons continued to speak to their charges, but they made themselves small and peered over the men's shoulders. The demons behind the group on the right urged the men forward. "Go on! Challenge Him! He had no authority to do what He did yesterday. He is under the apprenticeship of none of the elders. He has no right to teach in the temple."

The group of elders stepped forward and intercepted Jesus. One of them called out, "By what authority are You doing these things, and who gave You this authority?"

Jesus stopped and turned to the group of men with long robes and gray beards and condescending eyes. He answered, "I will also ask you one question, which, if you tell Me, I will also tell you by what authority I do these things." He paused. The elders crossed their arms and waited. "The baptism of John was from what source: from heaven or from men?"

The men huddled close. They conferred together just above a whisper, but Elric stood close enough to hear.

"If we say, 'From heaven,' He will say to us, 'Then why did you not believe him?'"

But we cannot say, 'From men.' The people all regard John as a prophet."

Finally, the most senior elder turned and answered, "We do not know."

Jesus said to them, "Neither am I telling you by what authority I do these things." Without another word, He continued walking and took His seat under the portico. The disciples gathered in close and sat down. A crowd of people pressed in around Him. Jesus addressed the crowd. "But what do you think? A man had two sons, and he came to the first and said, 'Son, go work today in the vineyard.' But he replied, 'I do not want to.' Yet afterward he regretted it and went. And the man came to his second son and said the same thing; and he replied, 'I will, sir'; and yet he did not go. Which of the two did the will of his father?"

Someone answered, "The first."

Jesus looked out at the chief priests standing at the back of the assembly and said to them, "Truly I say to you that the tax collectors and prostitutes will get into the kingdom of God before you. For John came to you in the way of righteousness and you did not believe him; but the tax collectors and prostitutes did believe him; and you, seeing this, did not even have second thoughts afterward so as to believe him."

The group of elders who had challenged Him huffed and stormed away.

Elric smiled. *He certainly has no fear of these men. And look at the people. They can sense the authority of the King. And though the enemy has blinded the eyes of the leaders, even they can sense it. They fear it. They fear the people. The enemy is going to have to be very bold to try to move against Him here in the temple.*

Jesus continued teaching and telling parables.

Later in the morning, another group of priests approached. This time they came with several influential Herodians. Elric chuckled to himself at the way the enemy worked to embolden the men to try to trap the Son of Man but were too fearful to get close themselves.

"Teacher," one of the Herodians said, "we know that You are truthful and teach the way of God in truth, and do not care what anyone thinks; for You are not partial to anyone. Tell us then, what do You think? Is it permissible to pay a poll-tax to Caesar, or not?"

Jesus shook His head as though amazed at the futility of their malice. "Why are you testing Me, you hypocrites? Show Me the coin used for the poll-tax."

They brought Him a denarius.

He turned the coin to one side, held it up to them, and said, "Whose image and inscription is this?"

"Caesar's."

Then He said to them, "Then pay to Caesar the things that are Caesar's; and to God the things that are God's."

The challengers' faces fell, and their jaws dropped. They left Him and went away.

Elric laughed. *Do these mere men really think they can trap the King, the creator of the universe?*

Jesus continued to teach. Throughout the day, the Pharisees, chief priests, and elders interrupted and tried to catch Him in some point of the law. Every time, He sent them away humiliated and frustrated.

Near the end of the day, Jesus finished with a final parable. "Listen to another parable: There was a landowner who planted a vineyard. He put a wall around it, dug a winepress in it and built a watchtower. Then he rented the vineyard to some farmers and moved to another place. When the harvest time approached, he sent his servants to the tenants to collect his fruit. The tenants seized his servants; they beat one, killed another, and stoned a third. Then he sent other servants to them, more than the first time, and the tenants treated them the same way. Last of all, he sent his son to them. 'They will respect my son,' he said. "But when the tenants saw the son, they said to each other, 'This is the heir. Come, let's kill him and take his inheritance.' So they took him and threw him out of the vineyard and killed him. Therefore, when the owner of the vineyard comes, what will he do to those tenants?"

"He will bring those wretches to a wretched end," they replied, "and he will rent the vineyard to other tenants, who will give him his share of the crop at harvest time."

Jesus said to them, "Have you never read in the Scriptures: 'The stone the builders rejected has become the cornerstone; the Lord has done this, and it is marvelous in our eyes'? Therefore I tell you that the kingdom of God will be taken away from you and given to a people who will produce its fruit. Anyone who falls on this stone will be broken to pieces; anyone on whom it falls will be crushed."

* * *

After spending the evening alone on the Mount of Olives, Jesus and the twelve snuck back to Bethany, to the house of Simon, who used to be a leper, because they had received word that men had been dispatched to watch the house of Mary, Martha, and Lazarus. Elric and the lieutenants met in a stable behind Simon's house while the rest of the team stayed concealed around the perimeter.

"It is becoming more difficult to remain hidden," Elric said. "We need to find another place to stay tomorrow night. Avoiding Bethany would be wise."

"What is it going to take before the chief priests make a move against the King?" Jenli said. "He had some very harsh words for them today, and yet they did not even *try* to seize Him."

"They are too afraid," Timrok said.

"I think they are more afraid of a riot than of Him," Jenli said. "And there were times when it almost seemed like the enemy was holding them back because they knew it would spark a riot."

Lacidar said, "Do you think they know our plan?"

"It is hard to say," Elric said. He paused. "Did anyone else hear His parable about the vine growers today? In it, He said the vine growers threw the son out of the vineyard and killed him."

Timrok let out a "humph." He followed with, "First of all, it is merely a parable, for the sake of revealing a spiritual truth. And more importantly, that could never happen. They may *want* to kill Him, but we will not let that happen."

"Of course," Elric said with a contemplative tone. He looked over to Zaben, who hadn't spoken a word and whose gaze seemed distant. "Zaben, what do you think?"

Zaben remained lost in thought.

"Zaben?"

"What?" Zaben said with a startled jump.

"What is it?" Elric asked.

Zaben chewed on his lip and shook his head. "Nothing. I was simply thinking through different strategic paths and trying to foresee possible difficulties."

"Anything new?"

"No. We will have to wait and see what the day in the temple brings tomorrow."

* * *

Battle minus 16 hours

Wednesday morning in the temple, with the crowds gathered around and pockets of chief priests and elders grasping for control, the testing of the Son of Man continued. He had just silenced a group of Sadducees, and a group of Pharisees approached.

Elric remained on edge. One of these encounters was sure to instigate an uncontrolled outburst. He eyed the enemy warriors with the Pharisees. They held back, but they looked ready to engage in an instant.

One of the Pharisees, a lawyer, asked Jesus, "Teacher, which is the great commandment in the Law?"

Without hesitation, Jesus answered him, "'You shall love the Lord your God with all your heart, and with all your soul, and with all your mind.' This is the great and foremost commandment. The second is like it, 'You shall love your neighbor as yourself.' Upon these two commandments hang the whole Law and the Prophets."

The Pharisees stroked their beards, nodded, and backed away.

Elric kept his hand on the handle of his sword. Still no advance from the enemy.

All day—teaching, testing, parables, testing, truths of the kingdom, testing. By early afternoon, the chief priests, scribes, Pharisees, Sadducees, lawyers, and elders stood around the outside of the crowd with their mouths shut and their arms crossed.

Jesus looked past the people and spoke to the elders. "But woe to you, scribes and Pharisees, hypocrites, because you shut the kingdom of heaven in front of people; for you do not enter it yourselves, nor do you allow those who are entering to go in. Woe to you, scribes and

Pharisees, hypocrites, because you travel around on sea and land to make one proselyte; and when he becomes one, you make him twice as much a son of hell as yourselves."

Timrok stepped up beside Elric. "This should evoke a reaction. Do you think He's trying to make them attack Him?"

"I do not think so," Elric said. "I believe He is telling them truth whereby they might repent."

"Woe to you, scribes and Pharisees, hypocrites!" Jesus continued. "For you tithe mint and dill and cumin, and have neglected the weightier provisions of the Law: justice and mercy and faithfulness; but these are the things you should have done without neglecting the others. You blind guides, who strain out a gnat and swallow a camel! Woe to you, scribes and Pharisees, hypocrites! For you clean the outside of the cup and of the dish, but inside they are full of robbery and self-indulgence. You blind Pharisee, first clean the inside of the cup and of the dish, so that the outside of it may also become clean."

Timrok chuckled. "Those do not look like the faces of men ready to repent."

"No, they do not." Elric said, palming his sword handle.

Jesus continued, "Woe to you, scribes and Pharisees, hypocrites! For you are like whitewashed tombs which on the outside appear beautiful, but inside they are full of dead men's bones and all uncleanness. So you too, outwardly appear righteous to people, but inwardly you are full of hypocrisy and lawlessness. Woe to you, scribes and Pharisees, hypocrites! For you build the tombs for the prophets and decorate the monuments of the righteous, and you say, 'If we had been living in the days of our fathers, we would not have been partners with them in shedding the blood of the prophets.' So you testify against yourselves, that you are sons of those who murdered the prophets. Fill up, then, the measure of the guilt of your fathers. You snakes, you offspring of vipers, how will you escape the sentence of hell?"

"That's it," Timrok said. "They're moving." He pulled his swords out and set his feet.

"Wait!" Elric said. "Look!"

A line of beaelzurim leapt in front of the men and formed a wall. They spoke frantic warnings into the air.

"No! Not here! Not now!"

"What about the people?"

"You do not want to start a riot!"

"Fear the people! Fear what they will think of you. Fear what they may do."

The men backed away. They threw exasperated hands into the air and paced back and forth like lions separated from their prey by a wall of glass.

Jesus continued, "Therefore, behold, I am sending you prophets and wise men and scribes; some of them you will kill and crucify, and some of them you will flog in your synagogues, and persecute from city to city, so that upon you will fall the guilt of all the righteous blood shed on earth, from the blood of righteous Abel to the blood of Zechariah, the son of Berechiah, whom you murdered between the temple and the altar. Truly I say to you, all these things will come upon this generation."

Zaben joined Elric and Timrok. He shook his head. "It appears the enemy knows our plan. Not only are they not provoking the men to riot, they are preventing it."

"Mm," Elric said, nodding.

Jesus stood. He picked up his shoulder bag. He called out, "Jerusalem, Jerusalem, who kills the prophets and stones those who have been sent to her! How often I wanted to gather your children together, the way a hen gathers her chicks under her wings, and you were unwilling. Behold, your house is being left to you desolate! For I say to you, from now on you will not see Me until you say, 'Blessed is the One who comes in the name of the Lord!'"

He stepped through the crowd and headed for the gate. The disciples jumped to their feet and hurried after Him.

"Deploy your teams," Elric commanded. "The King is on the move, and we need to hide Him!"

36

WEDNESDAY NIGHT

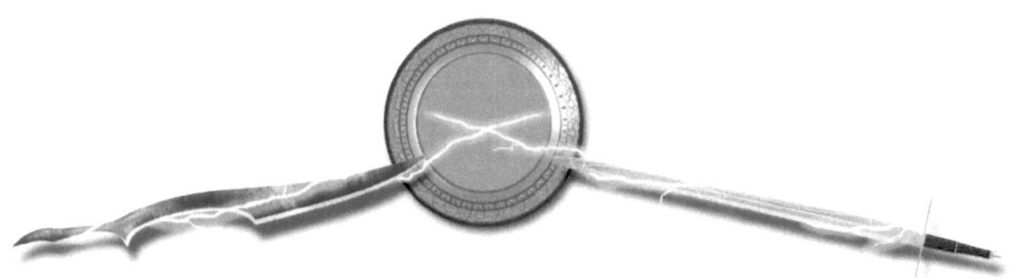

Battle minus 10 hours

The Day of Preparation for Passover would begin at sundown. The sun had not yet set over Jerusalem, but the shadows grew long, and the people bustled through the streets. In the lower city, south of the temple, rows of multi-level houses with their flat stone and mudbrick faces beckoned their residents home before nightfall.

Amid the motion on the street in the lower city, two men with hoods hiding their faces ducked into a house that had a lamp glowing on the windowsill of a second-story room. Minutes later, three hooded men from the other direction turned off the street into the same house. Two more men slid around the corner of a nearby house and entered the home of the glowing lamp. One of the men peered back toward the street through the open crack of the door for a moment. He pushed the door shut. Several minutes passed. Two more hooded men moved down the street with the cadence of the traffic, stopped, and shuffled into the house. After several more minutes, two more men with cloaked faces passed in front of the house. One of the men pointed at the second-story lamp. The other nodded. They looked up and down street, shielding their faces within the shadow of their hoods. They turned back and slipped into the house. The door clicked shut, and the lamp in the upstairs window disappeared. The window shutter closed.

On the street, the people moved along at a brisk pace, everyone heading to their own place.

* * *

The door closed behind James and Jesus at the house in the lower city of Jerusalem, and Elric paused outside to be sure none of the enemy had followed any of the disciples to their location. On the street, normal traffic in the Middle Realm—beaelzurim with their charges, elzurim with theirs. Brondor passed by from the left, Jessik from the right. Christov stood at the corner of the next street. On the rooftops—*Prestus, Chase, Kylek. The rest of the team well-hidden. Good. We're alone.* Elric turned and stepped through the front wall of the house.

Inside the house, Timrok greeted Elric. "Captain, all the disciples are here now. Peter and John have been here most of the day making preparations. The rest of the lieutenants are already upstairs. Zaben has brought Luxor."

"Very good," Elric said.

"I don't like being here in Jerusalem at night," Timrok said. "The chief priests and elders may be too afraid to take Him in public during the day for fear of the people, but alone at night . . . the chances of being spotted here in the city are too high."

Elric nodded. "Yes, but that decision was not ours." He put his hand on Timrok's shoulder. "Be at peace. We are all here and concealed for now."

Elric turned his attention toward the men in the room. Jesus and James had lowered their tunic hoods and stood with the owner of the house and his wife.

"Thank you for opening your home to us," Jesus said to the couple. He kissed each of them on the cheek. Holding the man's hand, Jesus said, "The blessing of the Father rests upon you and your house."

The man bowed his head, and Jesus and James walked up the stairs to the upper room. Elric and Timrok followed.

Elric moved ahead and passed through the upstairs door. Eleven disciples milled about a large table, knee high and surrounded by large colorful cushions. They talked with hushed voices. Jenli, Lacidar, and Zaben each stood like silent statues in three corners of the room. Luxor stood beside Zaben.

The door opened.

"The Master is here," Peter announced.

All the disciples smiled and breathed nervous laughs.

"Peace, peace," Jesus said, motioning with His hands. He smiled at the table and all its preparations and said, "Look at this beautiful table prepared for us by Peter and John. Come, let us recline and eat."

Everyone sat on the cushions, Jesus gave a brief prayer of thanksgiving, and the meal began. As usual with the inner twelve, He used the private time to teach. Elric gathered his inner team to one corner of the room—away from the mealtime conversation so they could strategize.

"What is our next move, Captain?" Jenli asked.

"I have received no direction," Elric replied. "After the meal, the King plans to leave the city through the Valley Gate and head up the Kidron Valley to the Mount of Olives. I do not know if He will continue on to Bethphage or just spend the night in the garden."

"And after that?" Jenli said.

Elric shrugged and shook his head.

"These are treacherous days, indeed," Lacidar said.

"I truly thought He would assume the mantle of King after His entrance to Jerusalem last Sunday," Zaben said.

"I did, too," Timrok said. "And I thought the clearing out of the money changers from the temple was His first step. But then He backed away and we've spent the last three days ducking and hiding when the crowds are gone. Hiding! Sneaking around like—"

Elric lifted his hand for quiet. "He is the King. He has a plan. He is not obliged to reveal His full plan to His servants. Our task has been, and continues to be, to protect His flesh from the enemy. We must not allow our expectations to cause us to lose focus. So, let us get back to . . ." Something across the room caught his eye. "What is Luxor doing with Judas?"

All the lieutenants looked. Luxor bent low and spoke private words into Judas's spirit.

Zaben cleared his throat. "Judas has a . . . special task . . . the Lord needs accomplished. Luxor is trying to build his strength. This is why I brought him with me tonight."

Elric nodded and turned back to the lieutenants. "We should take stock of the battlefield. We do not have time to examine the war map. I need your ground-level assessments. Who has the enemy reached? Let's begin with the Sanhedrin."

Timrok grimaced and said, "I fear they are all lost to the enemy."

"No," Jenli said. He pulled out his ledger. He flipped through several pages. "Nicodemus . . . Joseph of Arimathea . . ." He continued with several more names. Half a dozen others remained undecided. The enemy owned the high priest, Caiaphas, and his father-in-law, Annas.

For the next hour, they reviewed the chief priests, scribes, and lawyers while Jesus and the disciples ate. The overwhelming majority of the leading officials had been blinded by the enemy. Many of the people, however, were ready to name Jesus king and . . .

"Wait," Elric said. "What is He doing?"

The lieutenants turned.

Jesus had just stood up. He removed His outer garments and laid them aside. He girded Himself with a towel, poured water into a basin, and knelt in front of John.

"He is washing the disciples' feet!" Lacidar said.

Timrok's jaw dropped open. Jenli rubbed the stubble on the back of his head and scribbled notes in his ledger. Zaben shook his head and stroked his goatee.

Elric crossed his arms, smiled, and said, "Every day He amazes me anew."

In silence, the angelic team watched Jesus wash all the disciples' feet. Peter objected, but Jesus used the opportunity for more teaching and continued washing. After finishing, Jesus rose, put away the towel, and put His outer garments back on. He sat down and began teaching about what He had just done.

With furrowed brows, Zaben grumbled, "Why does He spend so much time with these lessons of humility and servanthood?"

Elric cocked his head and looked at Zaben with incredulous eyes. "He demonstrates the true nature of the Father, of course."

"Yes, but when is He going to do what He came here to do? When is He going destroy the enemy and establish His throne on the earth? We have waited three years now, and still He delays."

Elric's questioning eyes turned into a scowl. "And we will wait another millennium if He so chooses."

"What if He is waiting for us to *make* something happen?" Zaben said.

"No," Elric said with a flat, short tone.

"You have said it yourself," Zaben continued, "we are not receiving direct orders for everything. Because of the secrecy of this mission, He is expecting us to make decisions, to operate independently when necessary."

Elric, still scowling, gritted his teeth. "What do you suggest?"

Zaben paused a moment, glanced over at Luxor, looked at each of the rest of the team, and said, "Turn Him in to the religious leaders."

"What?" barked Lacidar and Jenli.

"No!" shouted Timrok.

Anger flashed in Elric's eyes.

"Force His hand," Zaben continued. "The Jewish officials . . . they can't touch Him. The King could obliterate them with the breath of His nostrils. He just needs the opportunity to face them, challenge them, defeat them. Then we challenge Rome."

"What you speak is betrayal," Timrok growled.

"You walk a very fine line," Elric said to Zaben. "Be careful not to cross it."

"It's not a betrayal if it's what He is waiting for us to accomplish," Zaben said.

Jenli shook his head. "Your keen eye for strategy has led you down a dark path."

Zaben backed away from the team and stepped over beside Luxor, just behind Judas. "I am right," he said. "This is the best path forward. I am tired of waiting, and I am ready to do what must be done. In fact, for the last several months, Luxor has been preparing Judas for this very task. Tonight, we help the King take His rightful place."

"What?" Elric shouted. "What have you done? This isn't the Lord's way!"

"It's *my* way," Zaben snarled back. "And I am right."

The light disappeared from Zaben's golden eyes, and they turned deep black. A dim, red glow emerged where the sparkling gold used to be.

"No! Zaben, don't!" Jenli shouted. He made a move toward Zaben, but Elric extended his arm and stopped him.

"It's too late," Elric said.

Zaben shrieked. The transformation began with his face. The skin turned ashen and pulled tight across his morphing visage—

sunken eye sockets, hollow cheeks, protruding cheekbones, and small boney spikes along his jaw line. Most of his hair disappeared like smoldering grass, and what remained became wiry and black. He held up his hands and watched them change color and wither into boney claw-like appendages with grotesque misshapen knuckles. He collapsed on the floor and writhed in agony as the rest of his body transformed. He extended one of his wings, but only a leathery bat-like wing emerged.

Lacidar stood with his hand covering his mouth. Jenli muttered, "No, no, no." Timrok watched through squinted eyes. Elric turned away. He had seen this happen to thousands of others after the Rebellion, and the pain of it was too much to bear—especially with one so close. Luxor smiled and cackled under his breath.

In the Physical Realm, Jesus groaned and buried His face in His hands.

John, who was leaning against Jesus' chest asked, "What is it, Master?"

"Truly, truly, I say to you, that one of you will betray Me."

The disciples looked at each other and questioned who it might be.

Jenli turned away from Zaben writhing on the floor and gaped at Luxor's apparent enjoyment of the spectacle. Jenli choked out, "Luxor, you are not really part of this conspiracy, are you?"

Luxor didn't respond. He placed his hand on Judas's shoulder.

"Luxor?" Elric demanded.

The smile left Luxor's face. He glared at Elric and the rest of the team.

Shhhboom! A flash of red flame exploded in the Middle Realm, blinding Elric and the team. The thick smoke of the explosion sank to the floor, and Luxor had vanished. In his place loomed the form of a dark cherub. His frame remained small enough to fit within the room, but his head reached to the ceiling, and his four wings spread out across the wall behind him.

"It's Satan!" Timrok shouted.

All four angels pulled their swords and took a battle stance.

Satan laughed. "Your weapons are useless against me."

"Where is Luxor?" Elric said, still brandishing his sword.

Satan gave a dismissive "humph" and replied, "He remains bound in my prison, of course."

Elric cocked his head and raised his eyebrows. "That means . . . you . . . you have been here . . . among us as Luxor this whole time? Deceiving Zaben?"

Zaben struggled to his feet, too crippled to stand fully upright.

Satan laughed again. "He has made his own choice." He pointed down at Judas. "And so has the man."

Judas and Jesus both dipped pieces of bread into a bowl of olive oil at the same time. Their eyes met. Jesus handed his piece of bread to Judas and said, "What you do, do quickly."

Elric's sword burst into a bright blue flame. Without hesitation, he lunged toward Satan. With one swift stroke, Elric brought his blade sizzling downward. Satan grabbed Zaben and thrust him forward into the path of Elric's blade. The flame of vengeance carved through Zaben, and he disappeared with a terrified cry and cloud of yellow smoke. Elric continued his swing in a continuous arc around a full circle and brought it whistling down toward Satan. Before his blade could reach its mark, Satan leapt and melded into Judas's body. Elric stopped short. He held his blade ready, but the flame flickered and died out.

Judas rose from the table, reached for his tunic, and scurried out the door. His footsteps thumped down the wooden stairs, and the other disciples whispered to each other.

The disciples' words seemed distant in the Physical Realm:

"Where is he off to?"

"Some kind of errand for the Master."

"Probably going to give some money to the poor."

"Right now?"

"I don't know . . . "

Elric let the tip of his sword swing down until it rested on the floor. "Timrok," he said.

"Yes, Captain?"

"Go quickly and try to stop Judas. With Satan controlling him now, there is probably little you can do, but make every effort."

"In His service."

Elric grabbed his arm. "And Timrok . . . don't get captured. We need you. Meet us in the garden."

"Yes, sir." Timrok disappeared through the ceiling.

Elric turned to Jenli and said, "Jenli, take your team and Zaben's team to the Garden of Gethsemane. Judas knows we plan to go there. He will probably try something tonight. Clear the area. Set up a perimeter. Look for a back way of escape. If we must, we will blind the men to the King as we did in Nazareth and slip out through their midst."

"With Satan here," Jenli said, "we may face more resistance from the enemy. A simple Woodorian Slip may be insufficient."

Elric took a deep breath. He glanced over at Jesus, still teaching the eleven. Elric took another breath and said, "The Lord will provide."

Jenli bowed his head, said, "In His service," and shot out through the side wall.

Lacidar alone remained with Elric in the Middle Realm of the upper room. They looked at each other with stunned faces without speaking a word. Elric glanced over to where Zaben had stood before he sent him to the abyss. The smell of rancid sulfur still hung in the air. Elric's chin fell to his chest, and he dropped to his knees. With both hands on the hilt of his sword, standing upright with the tip on the floor, he stayed on his knees and wept bitter tears for a long time. At one point, he looked up and noticed Jesus passing a cup of wine around to the disciples, but he didn't hear a word from the Physical Realm. He glanced over at Lacidar, who hummed a melancholy tune with tears streaming down his face.

"How did we miss it?" Elric muttered. "How could we be so blind?"

Lacidar shrugged and wiped his eyes.

Jesus stood up, followed by all the disciples. Elric jumped to his feet. Jesus began singing a hymn—an old traditional song of worship and dedication. The disciples joined. Elric and Lacidar joined.

The song finished, and the men all reached for their cloaks.

"It is time," Elric said to Lacidar. "Prepare your team and Timrok's team to move."

"In His service." Lacidar unfolded his wings and bolted straight up.

37

THE BATTLE BEGINS

Battle minus 5 hours

Timrok ducked behind a wall in the courtyard of the high priest's palace in Jerusalem two hours before midnight. He breathed out a long sigh. He couldn't stop Judas from reaching the palace. *Nothing worked—direct communication, the Roman soldiers on the street, the men at the palace gate, the dog, the men in the courtyard. Short of open conflict with Satan himself, I used every resource available.* And now, Judas had disappeared within the inner chambers. *I dare not try to follow Judas inside. I can only imagine the treachery happening behind those closed doors.*

He surveyed the courtyard. Half a dozen men milled about. A group of four priests passed through. Three men stood around a fire, warming themselves. Other than the one beaelzurim speaking to one of the priests who passed by, there didn't seem to be any other enemy forces.

With Satan here, there should be more enemy presence. He scanned the area again with a slow, careful sweep. *It's too quiet. Unless . . . unless even the enemy doesn't know of Satan's work with Judas . . .*

A small demon shot out through the front wall of the main chambers and streaked over the outer palace wall.

A messenger! Something is happening.

Two men emerged from the main front doors. The thick, heavy doors closed behind them, and the men pulled the hoods of their cloaks up over their heads and hurried across the courtyard and out the palace gate.

During the next period of quiet, Timrok only saw one small spirit in the form of a serpent slip out through the front wall and disappear into the shadows. Alone with his thoughts, Timrok replayed the events in the upper room.

Zaben . . . how could he do this thing? His eye for strategy has always led him to unconventional ideas, but to rebel like this . . . Tears welled up in his eyes. He brushed them away with his sleeve.

The roar of a hundred demon wings approached, and the air above the high priest's palace came to life. Like a swarm of bats, a horde of beaelzurim appeared, swirled around, and descended into the palace courts. Marr, the mighty prince of Persia, landed on the front steps of the main entry, flanked by the commander Asherah. No fewer than a hundred demons formed their entourage.

Timrok ducked low.

Marr barked orders, but Timrok couldn't hear from his hiding spot across the courtyard. At Marr's command, dozens of demons bolted out into the city. Molech arrived with his own entourage. Yarikh and his minions showed up. A mass of evil filled the court.

Men began to appear through the palace gate. Priests in ornate robes arrived first. Men with torches and swords tramped in. At least one of Marr's company met every man who entered the courtyard and spoke a steady stream of hatred and self-righteous indignation into their spirits. The air of the Middle Realm became rank with the poison of their words.

Within the first hour after the message went out, a dozen men had gathered. During the second hour, another twenty joined. The Roman soldiers arrived—a company of twelve marching in tight ranks with long spears resting on their shoulders. They fanned out into a single line around the perimeter and made their presence known to the growing crowd. The darkness of the enemy's words enveloped them all. By the fifth hour, over a hundred men crowded in near the front steps awaiting orders from the chief priests. Swords and spears glimmered in the light of the torches.

Marr gave a command, and Asherah, Molech, Yarikh, and hundreds of demons lifted into the air and headed east. Only Marr and fifty of his warriors remained with the mob of men.

They are headed for the Mount of Olives. I need to beat them there and warn our team!

* * *

Battle: 4:00 a.m.

Timrok flew at a furious pace toward the Mount of Olives, low and direct. The city whizzed below him in a blur—the outer wall—the Kidron valley—the Mount of . . . *Oh no!* Flashes of light and fire lit the air of the Middle Realm ahead. *The battle has already begun!* He pulled out both his swords and blasted into the fight on the ground.

He spun and leaped and wielded his swords in a blur. Within the first five seconds of joining the fight, he brought down ten enemy warriors. With so many to contend with, he couldn't take the time to bind those he disabled.

I need to reach the King! He slashed and spun and hacked his way forward.

He reached an area where eight of the disciples had gathered and fallen asleep. He spotted three of his warriors, Prestus, Kylek, and Micah, embroiled in the fight—each contending with two or three demons at a time. While the eight disciples slept, the sound of war shouts, clashing steel, and shrieks of pain filled the Middle Realm all around them. Sparks flew, fireballs of energy sizzled, and yellow clouds of sulfur hung in the air.

In a bounding leap, Prestus landed near Timrok and sliced through a demon attacking Timrok from behind. "Finally, we fight!" Prestus shouted.

"Ha ha!" Timrok shouted back, cutting another dark warrior down.

"Is today the day?" Prestus shouted. "Is the Day of the Lord finally come?"

"We shall see." Timrok surveyed the number of enemy warriors as he spun and sliced another enemy in half. *The numbers appear to be growing.* "I expect to see legions of the King's warriors and His Mighty Ones any time now."

"I hope so, because I'm not sure our team can prevail against so many."

The thought of this being the final battle filled Timrok with an excitement like he had never known. He leapt into the air with a back flip, hacked the head off one demon with one sword, thrust his other sword through the chest of another, spun a tight spiral and sliced off the arms of two others before he landed. "Let them all come. We will surely win!"

He bounded forward until he reached a place where the disciples Peter, James, and John had stopped and fallen asleep. Warriors from Zaben, Jenli, and Lacidar's teams fought all around. Enemy warriors nearby spoke heavy slumber into the air over the disciples. With a shout, Timrok leapt into the middle of them and sent them scattering.

Timrok glanced left. *Finally, there's the King.* A stone's throw away, Jesus knelt, deep in prayer in a place by Himself. Shafts of light from above illuminated the place where He knelt. Shafts of light from within Him beamed back upward. Timrok couldn't hear the words between the Father and the Son over the din of the battle, but the intensity of the moment glowed hot. None of the enemy dared to approach the ring of light, but they pressed in from every side.

And what's this?

Gabriel stood right behind Jesus, ministering to His flesh. Gabriel's hands pulsed with a blue glow, and he spoke words of strength. With a touch, all the energy transferred through Jesus' spirit and into His body.

Gabriel is here! Strengthening the King's flesh for the battle! This is it—this is the day! Surely Michael and all the host of heaven will arrive, and the King will crush the enemy.

"Yes!" Timrok shouted. He launched upward with a flip and a spin, taking out three more beaelzurim. Fueled by a zeal pent up for millennia, he doubled his speed and offensive. Like a wild tornado unleashed upon houses of straw, he swept all around the King and the three disciples, driving the enemy back and carving a swath of disabled demons. He maintained his pace for nearly an hour and didn't even notice that the numbers of enemy forces had more than quadrupled.

A light shot straight up into the sky. *It's Elric.* Most of the rest of their squad joined Elric in the air. Timrok glanced up and took down another demon. *That's good. Aerial combat provides the advantage of greater mobility. But I will stay as close to the King as I can.*

Between thrusts and swings, Timrok checked the battle above. *There are so many! The battle is turning!* Six demons grappled Chase to the ground and bound him chest to ankles with black cords of pulsing energy. Moments later, Brondor succumbed to the overwhelming numbers, shouting and writhing all the way to the ground where cords of darkness awaited him.

Bounding from stone to stone, Timrok hacked his way to Chase and sliced through his cords in a single precise swipe. Chase regained his weapon and flew to the nearby clearing where the eleven disciples remained buried in a fog of sleep.

What is happening? Why does the King delay?

He glanced over at Jesus, who had just stood up. Gabriel had disappeared. Jesus walked over to Peter, James, and John and woke them. He appeared calm and undisturbed, as though unaware of the battle raging all around.

What is He doing? Surely, He must know—

Elric's battle trumpet pierced through the noise. At the first blast, Timrok's heart leapt. *Yes! Reinforcements have arrived! The battle is . . . wait . . .* The trumpet call signaled retreat.

"What?" he shouted. "No!"

At the sound of the trumpet, all the rest of their squad shot up and away from the fight. Timrok held back for a moment, but all the other lights streaked across the sky, leaving him alone.

He raised both blades straight up. "Aughhh!" He rent another demon in two and blasted into the sky. Jeers of the enemy echoed from behind. He gritted his teeth and made his retreat. *Retreat! I can't believe . . .* He clenched his jaw tight, forced himself to look forward, and pressed on.

38

ALONE AND BLIND

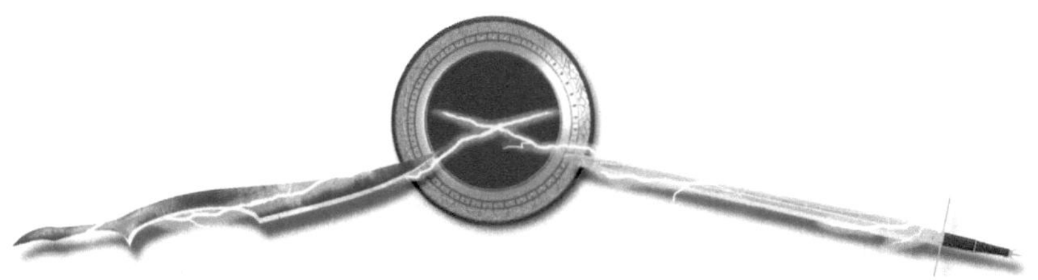

Battle: 4:30 a.m.

oments later, Timrok rendezvoused with Elric and the rest of the war-battered team in Jerusalem, hiding amongst the stone and mud buildings of the city. He followed Elric's cue and ducked under the cover of a stable for a private council. He crossed the threshold of the stall but paced near the entrance, watching around the corners. Inside, Elric and Jenli, knelt on dung-laden straw between two dusty cows.

"Where is Lacidar?" Elric asked.

Timrok checked outside. No sign of Lacidar.

Jenli looked to the ground and said with a low voice, "He was taken."

Timrok shook his head. A defeated sigh escaped his lips.

Elric said, "First we lose Zaben. Now Lacidar is taken. What is the status of your teams?"

Jenli answered, "The rest of Lacidar's team is all accounted for. I lost one warrior. Zaben's team lost two, plus Luxor."

"My team is intact," said Timrok. "But the King has fallen into the hands of the enemy! How could we retreat and leave Him there? We are warriors of the Most High. We could have stood against anything they—"

"No," Elric interrupted. "We would have all been taken captive, and the King would still be in their hands."

Timrok grumbled, "We could have stood. We could have—"

Jenli interrupted, "The captain is right. There were too many." He looked over at Elric. "Did you signal for reinforcements?"

Elric nodded.

"I don't understand it," Timrok said.

For several more moments, all three looked at the ground in silence. Movement! In the sky! Timrok squinted into the darkness. *What is that?* A black mist in the Middle Realm floated in above them and obscured the lights of the heavens. *Strange.* It rolled in like silent emptiness and grew thicker every moment. The mysterious cloud captured his attention, and the conversation inside the stable became distant.

Jenli's voice sounded filtered and peripheral. "What is our next move, captain?"

"The Sanhedrin," Elric answered. "If I am right, that's where they will take Him next. They need the approval of the elders to make their actions legal. Our immediate task is to secure the court and speak to the elders. We still have nineteen of us. Perhaps we . . . perhaps we can achieve His release through . . . ”

The black mist continued to creep in. *I've never seen anything like it.*

“What is it, Timrok?”

“You need to see this,” Timrok muttered, gazing upward.

A chill dropped like a blanket of invisible terror all around them. Elric and Jenli stood up and joined Timrok in the doorway. All three rubbed their arms with their hands and huddled at the threshold with only their heads poking out of the cover.

“What is that?” Timrok asked.

They all stood motionless and silent, gazing upward under the falling chill. Thick blackness crept across the sky.

Jenli said, “It’s like nothing I have ever seen.”

The fingers of darkness progressed, and a hollow emptiness replaced the distant stars and cut off connection with the heavens. *This isn't good. We can't be cut off from the King's Realm. Without power from Throne, we fight with only our own strength. Alone, in the enemy's territory . . . how can we . . .* All the air sucked out of Timrok’s lungs. His legs went limp, and he collapsed. He immediately fought his way back up, but it took all his strength to reach a kneeling position. *No . . . this can't be happening . . . this won't beat me . . .* He struggled through the weakness and made it back to his feet. Bent over and panting, he gasped, “What’s going on?”

Elric took a breath and looked upward. “Lord, what is this, and what would you have your servants do?”

Elric and Jenli climbed back to their feet. They waited for an answer from heaven. Nothing. They all returned to their cover in the stable and continued to wait. No logirhim with a message from the Throne appeared. Only a strange and lonely silence.

Elric asked, "Anything?"

Timrok shook his head.

"I have never . . . " Elric's voice cracked between faltering breaths, "never . . . felt this cut off from the King."

He turned to Jenli, "What are you sensing?"

"Nothing. There is nothing there at all. Before this . . . cloud of darkness . . . I was sensing pain—like the pain of a father watching the pain of his son. But now, there is nothing. Is this the enemy, or has the King pulled back His hand from us?"

"The truth is not apparent," Elric said. "I sense no malice in this cloud—only emptiness. One thing is certain—we are alone."

Elric's words carried as much dread as the darkness that surrounded them. Lone soldiers deep in enemy territory. Cut off from their source of power.

"How is that even possible?" Jenli whispered.

They all exchanged blank stares.

Elric dropped back to his knees with his hand grasping his sword hilt. He lifted his chin and said, "This changes nothing. Our mission to protect the King has not changed, and we must move forward."

Timrok nodded once.

"If we fail here tonight . . . " Elric's voice trailed off as though he didn't know how to finish the thought. "What *would* happen? What would happen if the enemy destroyed part of the Godhead? Is it possible?"

"If it wasn't, the Lord would not have charged us with this mission," Jenli said. "This is a question beyond comprehension. It is unthinkable."

"You can be sure the enemy is thinking of this," Timrok said.

Elric stood and said, "Then we must not fail. Rally your teams and prepare to advance on the courts of the Sanhedrin."

Timrok turned to leave.

"Wait," Jenli's arm blocked Timrok from exiting, and Jenli turned to Elric with a grim expression. "There is more we must consider."

"Quickly," Elric urged.

"What if it is actually the King's intent to die?"

Timrok wheeled around. "No! Not at the hands of the traitorous beaelzurim and sinful men."

"We have all heard His own words in these last weeks. He has been very unambiguous," Jenli said.

Timrok stood firm. "Not like this. If the King wishes to lay aside the frail flesh of man and take on an imperishable body to lead us to victory, He will do so in a manner of His choosing—with honor and sovereign will."

Elric rubbed his chin. "I agree. And if He intends to . . . die . . . why did He not change our orders?"

"How long has it been since we have received word from the Throne?" Jenli asked.

"Not since His entrance to Jerusalem," Elric replied.

"Is it possible the enemy is working to deceive us?" Jenli said. "What if the enemy has intercepted every logirhim message and is setting us up to fight against the King's true wishes?"

"Fight *against* the King?" Timrok said in a voice higher than usual. "We could not be so easily deceived."

"Could we not? How many of us lost close friends to the deception which led to the Rebellion?" Jenli said.

They each dropped their gaze and stared at the straw-covered ground.

"And," Jenli said, "tonight's events were completely unforeseen. We have been blind. And now this . . . " he gestured toward the rolling blackness. "I believe there is much more happening than we understand."

Timrok's tone became low and deliberate, "But if we fight against the King . . . "

"We will become His enemy," Elric finished. "We will become one of them."

"Fallen ones," Jenli said. "Cut off from the King forever."

Timrok's hands pulled away from his two swords, and he wiped them on the front of his tunic. Jenli placed both palms on his stubbled head.

"Surely the Lord would not condemn us for doing what we think is right?" Timrok said.

"Be careful," Elric said, "deceiving individuals to do what is right in their own eyes is exactly the tactic the enemy has used since the beginning. The only thing we can rely on is the word from the mouth of the King."

Jenli nodded. "And His words of late to his disciples have been contrary to our current direction."

Elric dropped back to his knees. Timrok could see the full weight of the moment pressing hard on his shoulders.

39

LIFE CHOICES

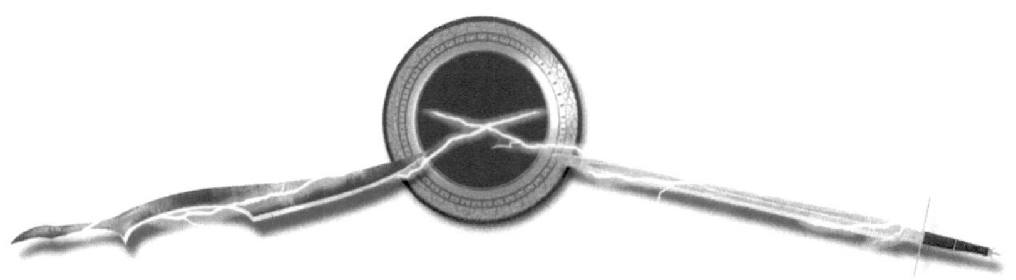

Battle: 4:30 a.m.

Alone in an animal shack, surrounded by an unknown darkness, cut off from their source of power, Timrok and Jenli awaited a decision from Elric. They looked at each other with desperate eyes only once and turned their gaze to the straw-strewn ground.

Elric stood and lifted his head. "My brothers, here then is what we have before us. If we do not attack and try to release the King, our mission has failed, and we do not know what consequences that will bring. The end is probably dire. If we do attack, we will likely be walking into a trap, and our chances of success are small considering we appear to be cut off from our source of strength. *And* if we attack, we could unwittingly play into the enemy's hands and possibly curse ourselves for all eternity."

Timrok took a deep breath and let his hands rest on his sword handles. "We will follow your orders to whatever end."

"We are with you," Jenli agreed.

"How did it come to this?" Elric pondered aloud. As he searched his heart for the right decision, he couldn't help but think back to when this whole campaign started. His thoughts took him all the way back to the beginning—before the King took on flesh, before this mission of mystery had been given to him. Back then, the plan seemed exciting—bold and audacious. Now, none of it made sense. Now, their way forward had become tangled by complications and choked by darkness.

Elric thought for only a moment, crossed his arms, and with a decisive tone said, "Our mission has not changed. We are going in there tonight to make sure the Son of Man is released. And in this goal, we *must* not fail."

Timrok nodded and crossed his arms.

"Captain," Jenli said, "if we are to do everything we can to secure His release, we need to consider contingencies. There are other paths besides a frontal assault."

Two men passed by in the alley beside the stable. They had no demon escorts, but the secret elzur council ducked low just in case. The men outside spoke in low night tones and headed somewhere of no concern. Even though the men couldn't see or hear them, the men's presence made Elric lower his voice.

Elric nodded. "Be brief—our time is short."

Jenli proceeded with an urgent pace. "Even if the meeting goes badly, I do not think the chief priests and elders will carry out an execution themselves."

Timrok shook his head. "You didn't hear what they were saying to the mob in the courtyard before His capture. The King will be stoned before daybreak!"

Jenli said, "I don't think so. They are the keepers of the Law. Those who are not bound to it in their hearts are at least bound to it for appearance's sake. No, they will not have blood on their hands directly. I think they will try to find a way to make the Romans do it."

Elric rubbed his chin.

Jenli continued. "Captain, let me take a small team to the palace of Pilate. In fact, Herod Antipas is in town, I could visit him as well—just in case."

"And do what? There is no time. The pieces are already in motion."

"I could speak to their spirits in a dream—give them a vision while they sleep. It's not much, but at this late hour, it may be our best hope."

"Very well. Do what you can with the Roman governors—then return to the high priest's palace as quickly as you can. Take two of your warriors with you. I can spare no more. Go. Go quickly."

Jenli spun around and disappeared through the side wall.

Elric turned to Timrok. "Are you ready?"

Timrok put his hands on his sword handles and smiled.

"You know we are heading into a trap," Elric said.

Timrok nodded. "The King will surely give us success."

Elric tried to force a smile. His left eye twitched twice. He gave a pensive nod. "Here is the plan," he said. "We will attack from four directions—four warriors on the sides, three on the front, five on the back. Take four of your team with you to the back. You will be the first to enter. Get in swiftly from the rear, take a passing assessment of the enemy's strength, engage briefly, and then draw as many as you can out the back. Have your warriors withdraw straight back. You come up through the roof and give us a report as you then join your squad. Once we see you and hear the state of the meeting room, I will rush the front with Zaben's two warriors. After we take the front, the sides will close in. Four of Lacidar's team will attack from the left. The right side will have two of Jenli's team, one of Lacidar's, and one of yours. Give us a few minutes to take control inside and bind most of the enemy. Then return with your squad through the roof, and together we will finish off the remaining forces. Then, we will be free to speak to the men of the Sanhedrin."

"It is a good plan," Timrok said.

"Go prepare the teams. We move as soon as everyone is ready."

"In His service."

Timrok disappeared through the wall, and Elric whispered under his breath, "Lord, provide success to your servants."

For the first time in his life, he wondered if the King could hear him through the empty darkness.

* * *

Battle: 4:45 a.m.

Elric stepped out of the stable with his sword drawn. He looked up at the thick, rolling darkness draped across the sky of the Middle Realm. Through the black cloud he saw nothing; he heard nothing; he felt nothing. He shivered from the chill and rubbed the back of his neck. He scanned the shadows of the nearby buildings until he spotted Timrok. Timrok nodded once. Without a sound, Elric motioned with his hand.

Ducking behind the night shadows of the city with stealth and caution, the troop advanced unseen. They could have been at the meeting hall in a moment, but they proceeded like a silent breeze—swirling around corners and whisping along walls. A squadron of six beaelzurim passed overhead on leathery wings in a loose, undisciplined formation. Elric disappeared into a wall and watched them fly toward the meeting hall. The squadron passed, and the angels resumed their advance.

Soon, their objective came into view. Elric motioned for the troop to wait, and each found a place to remain concealed. Elric surveying the surroundings—rooftops, alleys, the courtyard, the sky.

It's too quiet. Why are there no enemy troops? The oppressive presence of evil weighed heavy in the air, but where were they?

Here and there, men with ornate linen robes crossed the courtyard and entered the building through a tall double door with a grand rounded top. In the dead of night, the elders of Israel gathered.

Strange. The only movement here are these men.

He motioned for Timrok. Timrok slinked over and knelt beside Elric in the shadows.

"Notice anything?" Elric whispered.

Timrok grimaced. "A large horde of beaelzurim went with the mob of men to the garden. Perhaps they are still on their way back? Perhaps they have left the meeting hall unguarded?"

"Perhaps."

Four more men in priest's robes entered the building. Elric scanned the skies again. He scanned the courtyard.

"There is only one way to find out what awaits us inside," Elric whispered. "Are you ready?"

Timrok nodded.

"Have the teams fan out and get into position. As soon as you are in place at the rear, make your attack. We await your signal."

Timrok nodded and disappeared without a sound. Moments later, Christov and Carothim appeared from behind and crouched low next to Elric.

It took some time for Timrok's squad to steal around the back without detection. In reality, only minutes passed; but to Elric, those minutes stretched out like hours. The stillness pressed in. In the distance a dog barked. Crickets sang as though the night had no cares. Muffled voices of men inside the building added to the tension. The King would be arriving soon in the hands of determined men. There could be no retreat from this battle. The King must be released.

A battle shout of Timrok shattered the stillness. The familiar roar of Timrok's warriors rang out, signaling their charge from the rear. In an instant, shrill shrieks of demonic warfare echoed across the courtyard. Two of the Timrok's warriors shot out the back with a hundred dark creatures at their heels. It looked like two doves being chased from a bat's lair.

Two? Where are the other two?

Timrok emerged through the roof, but only up to his calf. Dozens of smaller demons shot up with him and swirled around him. He swatted the pests with his swords and struggled upward with his wings billowed and feverish, but several large hands attached to massive arms from below gripped his left foot and ankle.

"Thousands!" Timrok shouted. "There are too many! And *he's* here . . . the Prince of Pers . . . " Timrok disappeared—pulled down by forces from within.

Timrok's report brought an instantaneous response from Elric and the two warriors with him. With wild abandon, they exploded forward with fiery eyes and ready blades. Flashes of light bolted in from the sides.

All the anticipation of the ages, the work of the last thirty-four years, the excitement of the last three years, and all the uncertainty of the last ten hours—converged to this single moment of time. Within the next breath, he would know their fate.

40

CROUCHING AT THE DOOR

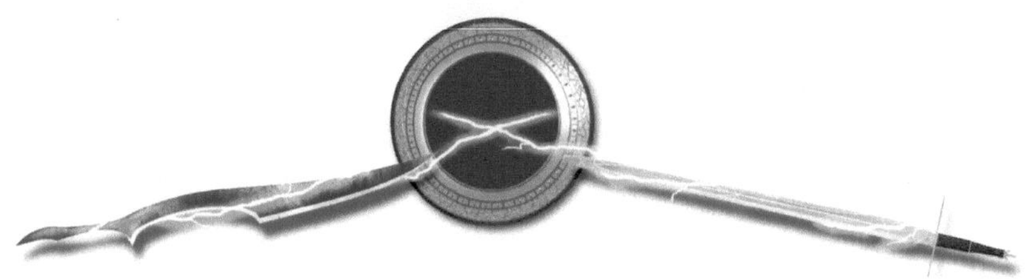

Battle: 4:45 a.m.

Elric and his squad passed through the front wall of the Sanhedrin meeting hall at full speed into a solid mass of evil. Elric's momentum stopped in an instant. Like a living wall of arms, a dozen leathery claws seized each of his arms and legs. Another dozen wrapped around his chest and neck. His sword clanged to the floor. Thick, black binding cords of energy wrapped from his ankles up to his neck. Before he even saw the inside of the room, he found himself immobilized and helpless. He blinked hard from the shock and looked around.

Thousands of beaelzurim of all ranks filled the space of the Middle Realm. Small impish snake-like demons darted about like flies. A whole company of battle-hardened warriors lined every wall, and hundreds of snarling demons perched in the corners of the ceiling like living gargoyles. Captains and lieutenants stood at the ready. A steady chaotic swirl of black wings churned above the men's heads amid a thick cloud of yellow sulfur smoke. And there, on a throne at the center of the back wall sat Marr, the prince of Persia himself, flanked by his commanders Asherah, Molech, and Yarikh.

Elric's two teams of angels from the sides burst through the walls. Like stones thrown into thick mud, their motion stopped in an instant. Their swords fell, unused, to the floor, and bindings fastened tight around their bodies. Timrok's two angels from the rear squad plunged in through the roof. A writhing mass of arms swallowed them up and dropped them, bound, to the floor.

It became silent, and all eyes turned toward Elric. He scanned the room for the rest of his team. Beside him near the front wall: Christov, and Carothim—bound. Timrok and his rear team: Prestus, Chase, Nalyd, Kylek—bound, but still struggling against the bindings. The left squad: BaeLee, Kelsof, Jaeden, Ry—bound. The right squad: Jessik, Jennidab, Micah, Stephanus—bound. In the corner of the room, Elric spotted the members of his team captured in the garden: Lacidar, Brondor, Emms, Xarjim—bound. Elric tried to take a deep breath, but the bindings constricted his chest. His left eye twitched twice. He dropped his head in defeat.

Two large demon captains hoisted Elric up by the bindings around his arms and ushered him forward before Marr.

The one sitting on the dark throne had a low, raspy, contemptuous growl. "Captain Elric, I believe?"

Elric gave no response.

"Yes, Captain," Marr continued, "I know you and your team. We all have known you from the day the King revealed Himself at the river Jordan." Marr looked around at the bound warriors. "It seems we are missing five. Wait, did I hear that you sent one of your own to the abyss for using Judas to betray the Son of Man?"

Elric's eyes welled up, and bitter tears streamed down his cheeks.

Marr sat back in his throne and chuckled. "That means there are really only four of your team missing. Tell me if I'm right—Jenli, Jerem, Kaylar, and Luxor? No matter. They will be captured soon, I'm sure."

Elric still remained silent.

Marr looked around again at Elric's team with a sneer. He shot yellow smoke out of his nostrils with a disgusted "hmph."

"This is it?" Marr said. "The Great King sends a pitiful band of puny warriors led by a mere captain? He has greatly underestimated my resolve."

Elric answered with a slow, defiant tone. "At the King's word, twelve legions of angels would crush you."

Marr looked indifferent. "Hmm," he said. "I have my own legions prepared. But more importantly, what is this veil of darkness between us and the heavens? Could it be that that we are cut off from the King's Realm? Could it be the King of heaven is blind to what is happening right now?"

Elric clenched his jaw and stared Marr in the eyes.

Marr continued. "No, I think there are no legions coming. I think your team was the Son of Man's last hope. His whole plan was flawed from the beginning. While He was in the heavens, we could not touch Him. Once He took on the flesh of man—"

"You still can not touch him," Elric shouted. "You have no authority."

"Yes, you are right," Marr said with a smirk, "but they do." He pointed a crooked talon at the gathering of men in the room. "He has submitted Himself to the order of mankind, and if these men so choose, they can accomplish that which *we* wish."

A wave of helplessness and despair washed over Elric in a way he had never known. He groped within for some way to answer the one on the throne. He gritted his teeth and said, "The Lord rebuke you."

Marr laughed and said, "We shall see." With a dismissive flick of his hand, he ordered the captains behind Elric, "Remove him from before my eyes. But keep him here. He must see what is to come."

The two demon captains lifted Elric and positioned him to the left of and just behind the throne. From there Elric watched the enemy do their work. Their words of self-righteousness, spite, envy, and hatred rested like burning coals on the spirits of every man in the room. Elric's plans of reaching the men before Jesus arrived had been dashed when he passed through the front wall. Now he watched all hopes of speaking life to the religious leaders being smothered before him. He wondered about the progress of Jenli's mission. For a quarter of an hour, he watched and wept.

41

THE GOVERNORS

Battle: 4:35 a.m.

Jenli, with Jerem and Kaylar, reached the palace compound of Pontius Pilate. They found a hiding place overlooking Pilate's palace courtyard and ducked low.

Jenli whispered, "As the Roman governor of this region, if the chief priests and elders want a Roman death sentence, it will need to come from Pilate."

Beaelzur forces were everywhere—mostly sentries and soldiers, an occasional captain and lieutenant. Numerous smaller demons skittered about.

"An enemy stronghold," Jenli said. "It will not be easy to reach Pilate."

Jenli remembered the time in the days of Herod the Great when he marched into this place with a blazing sword of vengeance and the prisoner Luchek. At that time, he faced thousands of beaelzurim. Tonight, the numbers looked fewer.

"Fortunately for us, it looks like most of their forces are out at the Mount of Olives. Still, a direct attack here is not possible. Stealth is our only option. I don't know what we'll find when we reach Pilate's bedchambers, so stay close. Let's move."

Avoiding the main courtyard, they slipped around the side along the outer wall and melted through the side wall into a vacant room. Opulent drapes, tapestries, and thick columns took on a warm glow from the flickering lamps. Jenli and his team passed through and glided around the corner to another empty room. They stepped down a short hall. Four demon warriors appeared around a corner, and Jenli's crew ducked into another room. Passing through the wall into the room, Jenli spotted two beaelzurim stationed there. He held out his arm, and they remained hidden in the wall and waited, watching the two in the room. The smaller demon in the room made some unsavory comment to the larger demon—probably a captain. The huge claws of the captain tightened around the writhing little insubordinate's neck and launched him across the room. Jenli almost felt pity for him.

Undisciplined, selfish brutes. Every one of them. The only thing they recognize is power, and the only thing they care about is increasing their own status and bringing destruction to the Lord's kingdom and to man. This is what the absence of God looks like.

With the coast clear, Jenli, Jerem, and Kaylar continued down the hall, passed through a large meeting room, and entered another vacant room. Making their way down a wide travertine corridor, the three sidestepped like dissipating vapors into thick marble pillars and waited for a small squad of demons to pass. Finally, on the right side of the hall, they reached Pilate's room. Directly across the hall—Pilate's wife's room.

Without revealing himself, Jenli pushed his head partially through the wall into Pilate's room. He pulled back and shook his head.

"No good," he whispered. "Four large sentries. "We will never be able to drive them off without revealing ourselves to rest of the compound, and I doubt we could draw them out long enough for me to give Pilate a vision."

I wonder . . . He crossed the hall to the other bedroom and poked his head in. He turned back toward Jerem and Kaylar.

"His wife has only one sentry." He paused and rubbed the back of his stubbled head. "We cannot reach Pilate directly, so we shall try to reach him through his wife. Here is the plan. Draw this one sentry out, pull him into Pilate's room, and engage him and the other sentries in there. Give me five minutes, then retreat and let them think they drove you out. I will sneak out before the wife's sentry returns, and they will never know we visited her."

Jerem and Kaylar smiled and nodded. Jenli hid himself in the wall. Jerem and Kaylar approached the bedroom on the left side of the hall.

* * *

Battle: 4:40 a.m.

Jerem and Kaylar walked through the wall, swords still sheathed, and stopped in the middle of Pilate's wife's room. The sentry looked shocked to see two of the heavenly host suddenly standing before him. He reached for his sword.

Kaylar turned with a half-grin to Jerem and said, "This is not Pilate's room."

The demon roared and lunged at them. His blade swung down toward them, and the angels both drew their swords in an instant and stopped his with a three-way crash of metal. Spiritual sparks flew in the dark room. They turned and shot across the hall and into Pilate's room with the enraged sentry snorting behind them.

In another instant, the two valiant warriors in white sparred with four more very surprised and very angry demons.

* * *

Jenli watched Jerem and Kaylar bolt across the hallway into Pilate's room with a beaelzur sentry one hot step behind. Jenli smiled. *These sentries may be strong and skilled with a sword, but Kaylar and Jerem have the prowess to carry on this fight as long as needed. Now, it's my turn to work.*

Jenli slipped into Pilate's wife's room. Kneeling beside her bed, he spoke words into the Middle Realm. "Jesus is innocent . . . have no part in His judgment . . . do not believe their lies . . . tell Pilate to release Him immediately." His words floated like translucent blue clouds and sank into her spirit.

Pilate's wife awoke with a start. She sat up and looked around her empty room. After a few seconds, she lay down and drifted back to sleep.

This is tricky work. If I speak too loudly, I wake her up and ruin the dream. If I don't speak loudly enough, she does not remember the dream. I need to find the perfect balance to make the dream real enough to remember when she wakes. This is the work for a messenger, not a warrior.

* * *

Across the hall, in Pilate's bedchamber, a heated battle raged. Seven figures turned, leaped, ducked, and performed unnatural acrobatics off the ceiling and walls of the room. Large blades crashed and clanked, sending yellow and blue sparks burning through the air of the Middle Realm all around Pilate.

In the Physical Ream, Pilate slept—although not well. He tossed to one side, then the other. He even woke up a few times for no reason. Although dark and quiet, restlessness stirred his room.

In the hallway, all remained calm. Lamps on wall sconces cast a quiet glow.

In Pilate's wife's bedroom, Pilate's wife slept. And dreamed.

* * *

When the allotted time had passed, Jerem and Kaylar allowed themselves to be pinned into a corner of Pilate's room. The five demon sentries had them now.

"We cannot prevail against these warriors!" shouted Jerem to Kaylar, "Quickly, retreat!" They both shot straight upward into the night.

"That's right!" came the jeers from below. "This is our palace, and you shall not trespass here!" They laughed and shouted other taunts, but by then, the angels couldn't hear them.

Jenli waited for them outside the palace walls. "Good work," Jenli said as they alighted in front of him. "The Lord has given us success. Let us now visit Herod."

* * *

Battle: 4:50 a.m.

Jenli, Jerem, and Kaylar landed on the roof of a house overlooking the compound of Herod Antipas. While palatial in form, these visiting quarters of the tetrarch of Galilee didn't begin to compare with the palace they had just left.

Jenli whispered, "I heard that Herod is in town for some matters of state. I hope he is here tonight."

Jerem whispered, "Why do we concern ourselves with Herod? He does not even have jurisdiction here. Do you really think he will have a hand in this?"

Jenli nodded. "I do not think it's a coincidence that he is in town at this particular time. I think the enemy has positioned him here just in case things do not go their way with Pilate. Since Jesus is known as a Galilean, Pilate may not want to judge His case. The enemy is creating every opportunity they can."

Jenli surveyed the area for enemy forces.

"This place is not nearly the stronghold of Pilate's palace," Jenli said. "Still, we use stealth. We shall do as before—sneak in, deliver a dream, sneak out. Let's go."

The three navigated the halls with only minor diversions and soon found themselves outside Herod's room. They stepped into the unoccupied room next door. Jenli made a clandestine assessment of

Herod's room. He pulled his head back through the wall, turned to Jerem and Kaylar, and shook his head.

"Four large sentries again," he said. "And we have no wife to speak to here. And worse, Herod is awake."

He rubbed the stubble on the top of his head as he thought. He looked back into Herod's room again. Herod sat at a table, working late by the yellow light of an olive oil lamp. He wrote on a papyrus and had several other scrolls open for reference. A dozen other rolled up scrolls stood on end at the back of the desk, leaning against the wall. On a table sat a carafe of wine and a half-full goblet, along with a plate with fruit and a partially eaten piece of meat. Two of the demon sentries stood on either side of the door. One stood at the foot of the bed. The other stood beside the governor. A large elaborate Persian rug hung on the wall. Three Roman spears, a broadsword, and a small round shield rested like sleeping sentinels in the far corner of the room. A light breeze tickled the heavy curtain hanging to one side of an open casement.

Jenli pulled back and gave a sly smile to his partners. "I have an idea. Spread out and see if you can find a scroll anywhere in the building that archives any of Jesus' activities. He has created much stir lately, so there are sure to be some documents somewhere. Herod has been intrigued by the Son of Man for some time. We will try to get him thinking tonight."

In an instant, the three disappeared in different directions. A minute later, they each returned with scrolls in hand.

Jenli scanned each scroll and settled on one with a smile and glint of hopeful satisfaction in his eyes. "Perfect," he said. "Return the rest."

Kaylar and Jerem slipped away and returned a moment later.

Jenli whispered. "I need you to charge the sentries. While you distract them, I will get this scroll into Herod's hands. A quick hit and go. In and out."

Jerem and Kaylar nodded.

"Give me enough time to get into position outside before you enter. Remember—engage quickly, engage them all, then get out. Here we go." Jenli disappeared with the scroll.

Jerem and Kaylar gave each other five counting head nods, brandished their silver blades, and burst into the governor's room. All four sentries shouted, pulled their weapons, and leapt toward Jerem and Kaylar. Sparks flashed. Steel sounded. A large gust of wind blew in through the window, flapped the curtain with a crack, and blew over all the scrolls on the desk. The gust even extinguished the lamp on the desk. In a wink, the two angels disappeared, leaving the sentries scratching their heads and looking confused.

Three lights flashed across the sky toward the high priest's palace, the meeting place of the Sanhedrin.

"Do you think he will see the scroll?" Kaylar called out as they flew.

"He will see it. I don't know if it will be enough, but we have done what we could. It is time to rejoin the others. I wonder if they have secured the meeting place yet."

* * *

In the late-night hours, a single freak gust of wind interrupted Herod's work in his bedchambers. He cursed under his breath, got up, and relit his lamp with a flame from the fireplace. He straightened up the strewn scrolls, and one lying half unrolled on the desk caught his eye. The title read, "Reported Acts of the Hebrew prophet, Jesus."

"What is this?" he muttered. "Interesting. A list of miracles this man named Jesus is said to have performed. Lame healed, blind receive sight, lepers healed, deaf hear. And what's this? A man brought back to life from the dead! Never has such a thing been seen in Israel. I've been hearing some of these things, but *this* is most interesting."

Herod continued reading the entire scroll which included a few of the key teachings of the prophet.

He seems to have done many good things. And his teachings are intriguing. Someday, I should hope to meet this man. Then I will see what magic he possesses. Perhaps he will perform a sign for me.

He rolled the scroll and set it aside.

Now, back to work.

42

THE GREAT PRIZE

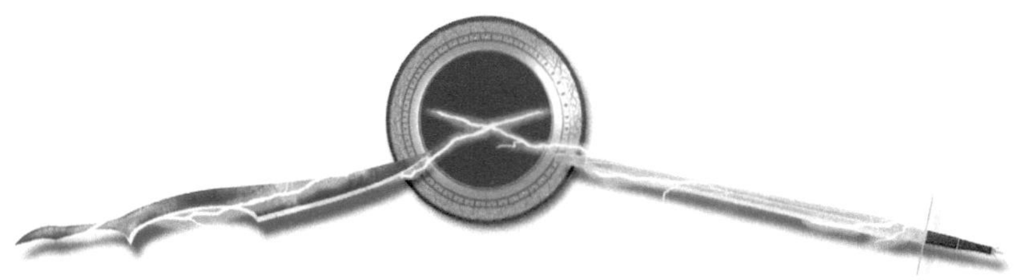

Battle: 5:00 a.m.

Without warning, Jenli, Jerem, and Kaylar blasted in through the roof of the Sanhedrin meeting hall. The impenetrable wall of evil near the ceiling enveloped them in an instant. Immobilized and bound, the three dropped to the floor with a thud. Elric breathed a long sigh of defeat.

Marr laughed. "Your failure is nearly complete," he called out to Elric. "This day, I will deliver to my master his great prize. We have awaited this opportunity for millennia. The time is finally here. And I will receive the praise due to me for my victory."

A small demon emerged through the front wall, wormed through the mass of beaelzurim at the perimeter, and jostled his way through the room to the throne. Bowing low, he said, "Master, the men have delivered the Son of Man to Annas for questioning."

"Good," Marr said. "Annas is a reliable servant for us. He will forward the Son of Man to Caiaphas, and Caiaphas will hear his elder statesman's position. There is still an hour before sunrise. It is time now to summon our lord." To the messenger he said, "Go. Find Satan and bring him here."

The messenger bowed again and disappeared through the front wall.

Half an hour later, a blinding red ball of fire exploded in the Middle Realm in the center of the room, followed by thick, black smoke. The smoke cleared, and the enormous frame of the great fallen cherub filled the back of the room. He spread two wings out along the ceiling, his wing tips each touching the side walls. He spread his other two wings out over the floor. He moved forward toward the throne, and his wings scraped the floor and ceiling from wall to wall, pressing in all the spirits on the ground and near the ceiling. Smoke surrounded his feet up to his knees, and the spiritual ground rumbled with each step.

Men in the room bristled, rubbed the bumps on the back of the necks, and looked around with confused, nervous expressions.

Satan reached the throne.

Marr stood and bowed. "My master," Marr said, "today I present to you the Son of Man. His protection has been removed, and He will stand before you at dawn." Marr stepped aside to the right of the throne.

Satan sat on the throne. For several long minutes he said nothing. Finally, he said, "Why does the King not attack to rescue the Son of Man?"

"He did," Marr said. "But we have defeated them."

Satan glanced around the room at Elric's team, bound and helpless. He turned to his left and locked eyes with Elric. Elric tried to maintain his stare, but the thought of his failure to recognize Satan's deception as Luxor overcame the only strength he had left, and he dropped his gaze to the ground.

"Yes," Satan said. "I see the Son of Man's security team. But where are Michael and the Mighty Ones? Where are the legions?"

"My lord—the veil of darkness . . . we have cut off the Son of Man from the King's Realm."

"*You* have created this veil?" Satan asked.

"I . . . assumed you brought this . . . my lord, it does not matter. The Son of Man is alone. This team was His only defense."

"Nevertheless, have your legions prepared."

"This is already done, my master."

The muffled sounds of a large crowd approached from the outside.

Marr grunted. "And now, He comes to us in bonds."

The door flung open, and the muffled sound of the crowd became crisp and loud. A large surge of men with clubs and swords and dusty robes mobbed into the room. They spoke with raised voices and jostled to all fit into the meeting place. Walking straight and strong, composed and quiet, the King entered. Every demon in the place fell deathly silent, lowered their eyes, and pressed backward. The great demon lord even averted his eyes, but in defiance he stood up and glared at the Son of Man. All the captured angels tried to fall to their knees, but their captors wouldn't allow it. Instead, they bowed their heads low.

An idea flashed in Elric's mind. It brought a small spark of hope and a twinkle in his eye. He lifted his head, opened his mouth, and sang at full volume.

"All praise to the King of kings!"

Every one of his team joined the second stanza with all their might.

"Praise Him for His mighty acts, for He is . . . "

Every demon in the room screeched and covered his ears. Half of them escaped from the room. The ranking demons shouted, "Stop this singing! Silence!" The captain and lieutenant demons near each of Elric's team grappled the angels' faces and covered their mouths. Before the host could finish the second line of the song, every one had multiple demon claws wrapped over their mouths.

Timrok resisted the longest. "For He is the awesome King. Forever we shall—" He, too, fell silent.

Elric had created the disturbance he had hoped for, but with everyone bound so securely, they couldn't break free and take advantage of it. Now each of them had bindings wrapped over their mouths. Elric's binding pulled like a tight bridle until it jammed against his back teeth.

The Jewish officers of the court pushed the King into the room, hands bound, with spear points forcing him onward. He complied with every demand and shove, and with the humility of a common man, He stood before the chief priest of Israel. Elric noticed bruising around His eye and blood on His lips.

They had the audacity to strike Him. I don't understand. How did my mission fail? How could I have let the King down? Here He is, the One who spoke the universe into existence—standing at the end of a spear and submitting to hostile men.

Elric couldn't bear to look at Him. He bit into the bindings in his mouth and closed his eyes.

* * *

Battle: 6:00 a.m.

The hearing before the elders of Israel began at sunrise. Jesus stood before Caiaphas. The chief priests and scribes sat in rows to the left and right with their ornate robes, distinguished beards, and judging eyes. The mob of men jostled shoulder to shoulder at the rear of the room, stretching their necks inward toward the proceedings. The main doors leading to the porch and the outer court stayed propped open so all the people could hear. A squad of Roman soldiers lined the steps outside.

An officer of the court whispered to Caiaphas and stepped aside. Caiaphas nodded. Several officers of the council raised their hands, and the room became quiet.

Caiaphas folded his hands. He lifted his chin and said, "Jesus of Nazareth, these men, having cause to arrest you, brought you to Annas, our former high priest and respected elder. He has found sufficient grounds for you to now stand before this council. Tell us, then, what are these teachings and strange doctrines by which you are troubling all Israel?"

Jesus answered him, "I have spoken openly to the world; I always taught in synagogues and in the temple, where all the Jews come together; and I spoke nothing in secret. Why do you question Me? Question those who have heard what I spoke to them; they know what I said."

One of the officers standing nearby struck Jesus on the face, saying, "Is that the way You answer the high priest?"

Jesus said, "If I have spoken wrongly, testify of the wrong; but if rightly, why do you strike Me?"

Caiaphas motioned to the officer, and the officer took a step back. Caiaphas said, "By your own words, we shall proceed. Officers of the court, prepare witnesses to testify before the council concerning this man and accusations by which he may be charged."

After several minutes of rustling and muted discussions at the rear of the hall, an officer stepped forward with a middle-aged man wearing a commoner's tunic and a salt-and-pepper beard. The room became quiet.

The man pointed his finger at Jesus and said, "This man defies the law of Moses. For I saw him doing work on the Sabbath."

Caiaphas nodded and stroked his beard. "How do you respond to this accusation?" Caiaphas said to Jesus.

Jesus gave no response.

"What work did you see him perform?" Caiaphas asked the witness.

The man straightened his back, lifted his chin, and said with a sneer, "He healed a lame man."

All the council members turned to each other and whispered. Caiaphas leaned over and conferred with a chief priest beside him. Turning back to the witness, Caiaphas said, "Are there any other laborious acts of work of which you can testify?"

The man's shoulders drooped, and he gave a sheepish nod. "No. Nothing else."

Someone in the back shouted, "He healed a blind man!"

"Quiet!" commanded one of the court officers.

"You are dismissed," Caiaphas said to the witness. "Bring forward another witness."

The crowd at the back rustled again. A man, a Galilean, slipped out of the hall to the outer porch. A rooster outside crowed once. Jesus bit His lip and closed His eyes.

43

BLIND JUSTICE

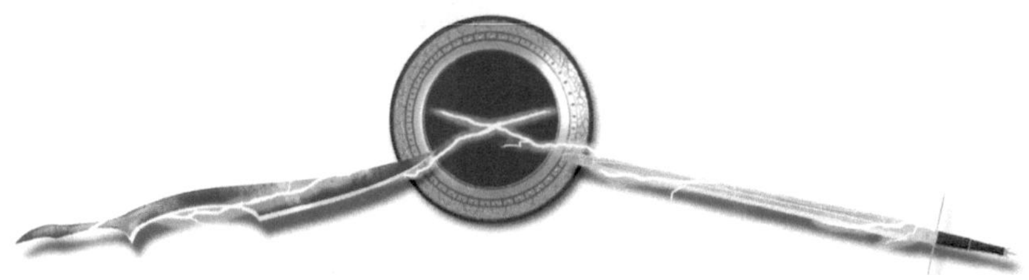

Battle: 6:45 a.m.

Elric could do nothing but watch the sham trial proceed. He looked at the members of the council, and his eyes filled with tears. Every member had two or three beaelzurim whispering lies and hateful poison into his spirit. *These men think they're in control, exercising their God-appointed duties to maintain order and the purity of their religion. They have no idea they are being used by the true enemy to accomplish the most heinous and traitorous deed since the dawn of creation.*

Satan sat on his throne, beside Caiaphas's prominent seat. The dark cherub leaned over on his left arm and spoke words into the air over the high priest. Like black clouds with flames smoldering within, the words settled on Caiaphas and sank into his spirit. Every time Satan spoke, Timrok rumbled and tried—in vain—to flex free from his constraints. Jenli looked over to Elric with distress in his eyes. Without a word, Elric could read his questioning eyes: "What is happening? Why is He allowing this? Why has He not called for additional forces?"

Elric had no answers. He just shook his head.

The last half hour and the parade of witnesses had not produced the results needed by the official council to warrant a death sentence.

"Enough of these petty accusations," Satan roared. "Somebody speak to a man and produce a charge worthy of death!"

All the demons in the back of the hall doubled their efforts with the men in the crowd.

Turning to the priest beside him, Caiaphas said, "This man is dangerous. We all know it. We finally have him in a place where we can do something to protect ourselves, our religion, and our way of life. But we cannot convict him on minor infractions of religious code. We need a charge that is serious enough to carry capital punishment."

Turning back to the crowd, Caiaphas announced, "Can anyone produce witnesses who can attest to a more serious crime?"

After some shuffling and quiet muttering, an officer escorted a man forward. He led the man by the arm until he stood front and center.

"So?" Caiaphas said. "Do you bring an accusation against this man?"

"Yes, master rabbi. This man, the one they call Jesus of Nazareth, killed my brother."

Timrok jerked so hard against his bindings he fell face first to the ground. The demon captains hoisted him back up. He shook his head and tried to yell, but the bindings around his mouth constricted his objections to the man's lie.

The crowd gasped. The elders fidgeted in their seats. Some stroked their long beards.

Caiaphas raised his eyebrows. "Really?" he said. "Tell us the details of the alleged murder."

"It happened just last week. Jesus was teaching and was surrounded by a large crowd. My brother tried to get in closer to speak with him, but his disciples wouldn't let him through. There was a fight. Then, all of a sudden, Jesus came in to break up the fight. He must have felt threatened because he grabbed somebody's knife and slit my brother's throat."

The crowd gasped. The council members looked at each other and nodded. Jesus remained motionless with His hands bound by thick, coarse rope. He gave no reaction at all.

"This is terrible," Caiaphas said. "Your loss brings grief to us all. You say there was a large crowd. Were there others who witnessed this tragedy?"

"Yes, master rabbi. I'm sure there were."

"Very good, thank you for your courage to come forward. We shall hear more of your testimony after we corroborate your account with other witnesses. Officers, please escort our friend to the inner chambers for now. Please go with these men. We will call for you shortly."

Turning to other officers, he said, "Bring in additional witnesses. At the mouth of two or three witnesses, this charge must be confirmed."

An officer stepped forward and said, "There are three prepared to testify."

"Good, good," Satan said.

"Very good," Caiaphas said. "Keep them in separate rooms and bring them in one at a time."

The first witness stood before the council. "Oh yes, I saw the whole thing," he said. "Jesus was in a complete rage and smashed the man's head with a rock. He would have killed others, too, if his disciples hadn't pulled him away."

Caiaphas rubbed his temples and said, "Bring in the next witness."

The second witness stood before the council. "He choked the man to death. It was the most horrible thing I have ever seen."

Caiaphas took a deep breath and said, "Next witness."

"Then, he cut the woman's throat with a knife," the third witness testified.

"A woman?" Caiaphas said.

"Well, that's what I was told."

"You did not witness the actual event?"

Nicodemus, one of the members of the council, stood up and shouted, "Stop this pretense! Every one of the charges we have heard this morning has been false and slanderous. This man is guilty of none of the things for which He is being charged. I don't even know what we are doing here."

Satan roared. His fists crashed on the arms of his throne and blasted rings of fire that filled the room. "Out! I want him out!"

Caiaphas stood up and shook his finger at Nicodemus. "You are out of order." He sat down but continued pointing his finger. "You are excused. Officers, escort Nicodemus out."

The officers led Nicodemus out of the hall, and the chief officer of the court motioned with his hands for order. The crowd became quiet.

Caiaphas rubbed his temples. With an exasperated tone he said, "Is there another witness who can testify to a different charge?"

Another officer stepped forward and said, "I have two witnesses who are prepared to testify."

"Bring them in separately," Caiaphas said.

The first witness took his place before the council and said, "This man stated, 'I am able to destroy the temple of God and to rebuild it in three days.'"

"Destroy the temple?" Caiaphas said. "This would be treason against our God and an insurrection against Rome! This is a serious claim." To Jesus he said, "How do you respond to this accusation? Do you plan to destroy the temple?"

Jesus remained silent.

"Bring in the second witness," Caiaphas ordered.

The second witness stood before the council. He testified, "We heard Him say, 'I will destroy this temple made with hands, and in three days I will build another made without hands.'"

Satan stood and thundered, "Enough of this! Ask Him if He is the Christ! Make Him say it with His own mouth."

The high priest stood up and said to Jesus, "Do You not answer? What is it that these men are testifying against You?"

Still, Jesus remained silent.

Caiaphas commanded, "I adjure You by the living God that You tell us whether You are the Christ, the Son of God."

The room fell deathly quiet. The shallow breathing of the men echoed like fading hope in Elric's ears. Caiaphas glared down at Jesus. Satan, still standing, flexed his fingers and made a fist. The men in the crowd stood like frozen statues. All the demons held their breath. The men of the Sanhedrin leaned inward, awaiting an answer.

Looking at the council seated around Him, Jesus said, "If I tell you, you will not believe; and if I ask a question, you will not answer."

All the council members shouted back, "Are you the Christ?" "Answer the High Priest!" "Are you the Son of God?"

A tense silence settled back over the hall.

With a voice calm and unthreatened, Jesus said, "I am; and you shall see the Son of Man sitting at the right hand of power, and coming with the clouds of heaven."

All the beaelzurim in the room covered their ears and cringed. Half of them escaped from the room as fast as they could.

The crowd of men gasped. The council members stood, covered their mouths, pulled at their beards, shook their fists, and shouted. Caiaphas tore his robes and shouted over the uproar, "What further need do we have of witnesses? You have heard the blasphemy; how does it seem to you?"

"Blasphemy!" They shouted. "He deserves death!" "Guilty!" "Death!" "Death!"

Several council members, including Joseph from Arimathea, remained silent, turned their faces away, and slipped out unnoticed amid the pandemonium.

Servants of the priests spat on Jesus, and others blindfolded Him. The servants and officers slapped Him in the face and beat Him with their fists, saying "Prophesy!" "If you are the Christ, tell us who hit you!" "Prophesy, oh Son of God!"

Satan sat down on his throne and smiled.

Elric hung his head and wept.

Timrok fell over on his face again.

All the demons who had left returned, and every evil spirit in the hall shouted, laughed, and rattled their swords together.

Caiaphas sat down and sighed.

The priest beside Caiaphas leaned in and asked, "Shall we take Him outside the city and stone Him?"

Caiaphas shook his head. "No," he said. "Lest we be become unclean for Passover. Further, we must take care not to be accused of exceeding our authority. We shall take him to Pilate to be crucified by Rome."

Over the mayhem, Caiaphas called out, "Officers, deliver this man to the Praetorium for the judgment of Pontius Pilate."

The crowd bustled out and left a corridor for the entourage to pass through. In the courtyard, groups of men and women stood around charcoal fires for warmth. Once outside, the officers stripped off Jesus' blindfold, and He squinted from the sun. Just then, a rooster crowed. Jesus turned, and His eyes stopped on Peter, who stood by a fire. Peter spun around and ran out of the courtyard, weeping as he went.

44

ROMAN JUSTICE

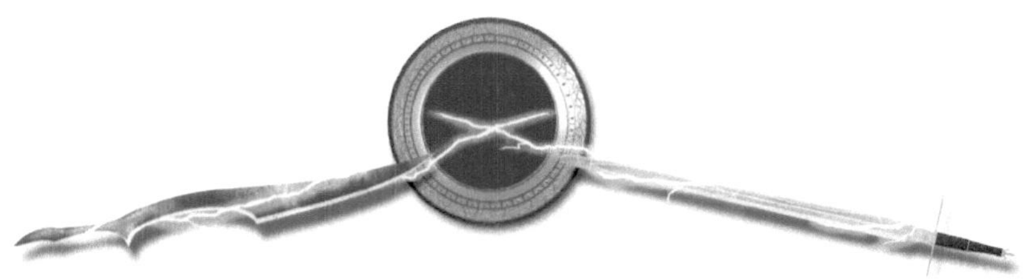

Battle: 6:45 a.m.

Satan led the parade from the high priest's palace to the Roman governor's palace. He walked in the very front with all four wings extended with dramatic flair. He carried his scepter, which sparked and rumbled every time it hit the ground. In the Middle Realm, legions of demons—thousands upon thousands—lined both sides of the street. They spread from the ground all the way up to the layer of darkness like spectators in a giant colosseum. They all shouted and shook their weapons in the air. Behind Satan marched Marr, Asherah, Molech, and Yarikh, all with swords raised in victory. Behind them trod the men in the Physical Realm—the squad of Roman soldiers, Jesus, the officers of the court, members of the Sanhedrin, and the crowd of men. Behind them, a spiritual platform borne on the shoulders of demon captains carried Elric and his team—bound, gagged, and helpless. A second platform carried all Elric's team's weapons and shields like a pile of trophies.

The regional elzur warriors gathered all around the outside of the procession, straining inward at the commotion. Questions rippled through the growing crowd of angels.

"What's going on?"

"Why is the enemy gathered like this?

"Looks like a victory parade."

"Who's down there?"

"It's the Lord! The enemy has captured the King!"

A trumpet blew, and thousands of angelic warriors charged the wall of demons from each side in a desperate, uncoordinated barrage. Their attack lasted only moments. With a wall so thick and dense, the defenses cut down each elzur warrior one by one, binding many, and chasing the rest away. The bound angels dropped like falling stars to the ground. Not one penetrated the wall, and the victory parade marched on to the Roman palace.

Elric looked up at the layer of darkness above them. *Still nothing. Still, the Son of Man does not call out. Still there is no answer from the Throne. How can this be?*

* * *

Battle: 7:00 a.m.

The procession reached the governor's palace, and the Jews all gathered in the outer courtyard.

The chief priest said to the Roman squad leader, "We are not able to enter the Praetorium, for it would make us unclean for Passover. Please summon the governor out here to the Pavement."

The soldier marched up the steps and disappeared into the palace. Satan walked up the stairs to the porch where he stood beside Pilate's judgment seat overlooking the vast courtyard known as the Pavement. Marr and his commanders took positions on the other side of the seat.

In the courtyard, the demon captains placed the platform carrying Elric and his team at the front of the Pavement near the porch. Elric strained his neck against the bindings, taking in all the surroundings. From here he could see all the proceedings. All the demons from inside the Sanhedrin meeting hall swirled around the men in the crowd, and all the legions of demons from around the parade route formed a new spiritual amphitheater wall around the palace.

The Roman squad leader reemerged and motioned to his soldiers. They shoved Jesus forward. He passed by Elric. Elric gasped at the sight—an open cut above one eye, blood from His nose matted on His mustache, and blood from His mouth matted on His beard. The soldiers led Jesus up the stairs and into the Praetorium. The large doors clanged shut behind them.

After several minutes, Pilate appeared through the governor's private door. He walked toward his seat on the porch overlooking the Pavement, squinting and rubbing his eyes. He sat, yawned, and squinted again as he looked out over the large mob of people below.

With a pained grimace of indifference, he called out, "What is all this, and why do you call such an assembly so early in the morning?"

Caiaphas stepped forward and bowed his head. "Honorable Pilate, respected governor and just judge, thank you for granting an audience this morning with your most humble servants. We bring to you today a man worthy of death for your judgment and sentencing."

Pilate yawned again. "What accusation do you bring against this Man?"

Caiaphas answered, "If this Man were not an evildoer, we would not have delivered Him to you."

Pilate rolled his eyes and motioned with his hand. With a dismissive tone he said, "Take Him yourselves, and judge Him according to your law." He stood up and turned back toward the door.

"But no . . ." Caiaphas called out.

Pilate turned his head and looked down at Caiaphas over his shoulder.

Caiaphas continued, "Honorable governor, he has already stood before the Sanhedrin and has been convicted of a capital offense. This is why we found it necessary to deliver Him to you."

Pilate turned back toward the crowd and crossed his arms.

Caiaphas continued, "We are not permitted to put anyone to death."

"Tell me His crime," Pilate said.

"We found this man misleading our nation and forbidding to pay taxes to Caesar," Caiaphas said.

A demon next to Caiaphas spoke into his spirit, "And He claims to be a king."

Caiaphas called out, "And saying that He Himself is Christ, a King."

"Hmph," Pilate said. "A king. Another insurrectionist. Very well, I shall question the man." He turned and entered the Praetorium through the governor's door.

Pilate's door closed with a low thump. The air became still in the Middle Realm. Satan motioned for Marr to go inside, and with a simple head nod, Marr disappeared through the front of the judgment hall. Satan held his scepter in front of himself with the tip resting on the ground and his two hands resting on the translucent black onyx skull crown. The fire within the skull glowed with silent malevolence.

Elric stared at the glowing skull at the head of the scepter during the silent minutes that passed. He had never considered the idea of Satan with unlimited authority. Everything good, everything honorable, everything that brings life—would be lost to evil, selfishness, and death. *It simply isn't possible. The King is the eternal, self-existent One. How can the one created usurp the creator? And, yet, this is happening. If it was told me, I wouldn't believe it. If Pilate returns a death sentence . . .*

The front doors of the Praetorium swung open, and Pilate marched out. Behind him came Jesus and the squad of soldiers. Marr followed the soldiers. Pilate sat on his judgment seat and looked out over the people. A hush fell over the air in both realms.

"I find no guilt in this man," Pilate announced.

The air in the Middle Realm erupted in shocked disapproval. "No!" "He must die!" "Kill Him!" "Death to the Son of Man!"

The air in the Physical Realm echoed the same message through the mouths of the men. "He is guilty!" "He deserves death!" The crowd shook their clubs and swords and spears in the air.

Pilate's judgment made Elric smile behind the bindings biting against his teeth. Elric looked around, waiting for the moment when the King would turn this all around. He glanced back at the platform with his team's confiscated weapons. He spotted his sword in the pile.

Satan shot a hateful glance toward Marr for his failure within the Praetorium and turned to Pilate. "Listen to the people," he said to Pilate. "This man is a threat to you. He is a threat to Caesar. He must die."

Pilate squirmed in his seat. Beads of sweat formed on his forehead.

Molech, standing behind Marr, formed an energy ball in his hand with the words, "Send Him to Herod." Amid all the shouting and chaos, he launched his fiery dart at Pilate, and it absorbed into his spirit.

The clamor of the crowd continued. The voice of one of the chief priests rose above the noise, and Pilate cocked his head and looked toward the priest. Pilate motioned for quiet. The crowd calmed down enough for him to hear, and he pointed at the priest. "You! Repeat your statement."

The priest spoke up in a loud voice. "He stirs up the people, teaching all over Judea, starting from Galilee even as far as this place."

"Galilee?" Pilate called out. "Is this man a Galilean?"

"Yes, yes," the crowd responded.

Pilate leaned back in his seat and smiled. "Galilee is not my jurisdiction. Herod Antipas must be the one to hear this case."

"No!" shouted Caiaphas, "But you, my lord—"

"Take Him to Herod." Pilate announced. "By chance he happens to be in Jerusalem now." He stood and left the porch before any more objections could be voiced.

Asherah turned to Molech with a hateful snarl.

"*My* man will see the job done," Molech said with a pompous lilt. "I have positioned him here just for this purpose."

* * *

Battle: 7:30 a.m.

The procession to Herod's palace lasted only minutes, but the victory parade in the Middle Realm carried on as though the death sentence had already been pronounced. Again, the crowd, their demon escorts, and Elric's team remained outside, surrounded by the myriads of beaelzurim all around. The chief priests and elders entered Herod's judgment hall, along with the Roman soldiers and Jesus—and Satan and Marr. Asherah, Molech, and Yarikh stood at the top of the steps in front of the main doors.

Elric listened to Asherah and Molech bicker.

"Pilate would have succumbed to the pressure," Asherah said. "If we had given him more time, he would have pronounced judgment."

Molech chuckled. "Herod isn't weak like Pilate. He will give us the sentence we seek."

"How can you be so sure?"

"He thinks Jesus may be John the Baptist, raised from the dead. He hopes to see a wondrous sign performed by Him. When he finds out that Jesus isn't John, and when Jesus doesn't perform any miracle, he will gladly listen to the charges of the elders."

For nearly half an hour, the crowd waited for a verdict from behind the closed doors. Finally, the doors burst open and Satan exploded out like a massive ball of fire. He alighted in the courtyard and stabbed his scepter into the ground. The Roman soldiers marched out with Jesus between them wearing a kingly purple robe. The Jewish elders followed close behind, upset and gesturing with their hands. Marr stepped out onto the porch beside his three commanders.

"What happened?" Molech asked. "What's going on?"

Marr shot a stream of hot yellow smoke from his nostrils. "Herod would not pronounce judgment. He mocked Him as king and is sending Him back to Pilate."

Asherah shot Molech a sarcastic smile.

Marr seized Asherah by his neck and lifted him until his toes barely touched the ground. "Pilate is under your charge. You are responsible for finishing this. Go prepare him now before we arrive."

Marr dropped Asherah, and Asherah huffed, "Yes, master."

Asherah turned to leave. Marr grabbed his arm. "Pilate is weak. Find an easy way out for him."

"Yes, master."

Battle: 8:00 a.m.

Another humiliating parade through the streets of Jerusalem brought Jesus back to Pilate's palace. Elric stood again on the vanquished platform at the front of the Pavement with his team, still bound and gagged. The elders of Israel and the mob of men filled the courtyard. Their demon escorts continued their frenzied message of death. Elric looked at the circle of beaelzurim stacked up all around them. *Has every demon on the planet arrived to watch this unbelievable spectacle?* The layer of darkness over the heavens hung low and showed no glimpse of light.

Pilate stepped out from the judgment hall and took his seat on the porch overlooking the Pavement. Asherah walked with him, speaking into his spirit with every step. Asherah stayed with him after he sat and took a position leaning over his left shoulder.

Pilate motioned with his hand for quiet and announced, "You brought this man to me as one who incites the people to rebellion, and behold, having examined Him before you, I have found no guilt in this man regarding the charges which you make against Him. No, nor has Herod, for he sent Him back to us; and behold, nothing deserving death has been done by Him."

The crowd stirred and became restless. The chief priests and scribes whispered to each other and looked nervous.

Asherah leaned forward and said to Pilate, "Offer the people a choice for the prisoner release. This way, the decision will be theirs, not yours. You can remain innocent in this case."

Pilate motioned for quiet again and said, "Now behold, tomorrow is the beginning of your Passover festival. As is my custom, I will release one prisoner to you in honor of your festival. Since I can find no guilt in this man, Jesus, I will punish Him and release Him."

Caiaphas called all the chief priests and scribes together and whispered something urgent to them. Elric couldn't hear what he said, but as soon as Caiaphas finished speaking, the elders fanned out amongst the crowd and relayed some message to all the people.

All the enemy spirits churned up the air in the Middle Realm with their wings and chanted, "Crucify, crucify, crucify!" The words spun up into hundreds of fiery tornadoes all across the crowd. Bolts of red lightning shot from one tornado to the next. Within only a few heartbeats, the energy of the lightning intensified the tornadoes, and they coalesced into a giant cyclone. Flames and smoke and sulfur and a cobweb net of red lightning swept through the spirits of every person in the courtyard.

Caiaphas called out to Pilate, "Away with this man, and release for us Barabbas!"

"Barabbas?" Pilate replied. "He is a convicted insurrectionist and a murderer! You would have me release to you a man deserving death over a man for whom no guilt is found?" The crowd became noisier, and he shouted over them. "Whom do you want me to release for you? Barabbas, or Jesus who is called Christ?"

Elric watched the cyclone of flames driving through the crowd. *The enemy has achieved mob blindness. Unless the King Himself puts an end to this, there will be no stopping this storm.*

"Release Barabbas!" the crowd cried out. "Give us Barabbas! Away with this man! Crucify Him! Crucify, crucify Jesus!"

"Why," Pilate yelled, "what evil has this man done? I have found in Him no guilt demanding death; therefore I will punish Him and release Him."

"Crucify Him! Crucify Him!" The individual shouts of the crowd merged and became a roaring chant. "Crucify Him! Crucify Him!" Over and over they shouted their chant and pumped their clubs, spears, and swords in the air with the cadence. Pilate motioned for order, but they continued chanting.

Elric looked at the Son of Man with desperate eyes. *If You are waiting for the moment of utmost gravity, this is it. Speak the word . . .*

Unable to be heard over the throng, Pilate motioned for the Roman squad leader. The soldier hurried up the steps and bent forward with his ear to Pilate's mouth. The soldier nodded and hurried back down the steps amid the incessant chants. He assembled his squad into two columns with Jesus between them and marched off to the left. The soldiers, with Jesus in His purple robe, disappeared around the corner of the building, and the crowd went wild with cheering and applause.

Asherah stood up straight behind Pilate, crossed his arms and smiled.

Satan strutted down the steps and followed the soldiers with his scepter held high.

Marr motioned for the demon captains in charge of Elric and his team to lift their platform and follow.

Elric winced. *Don't bring us in there. I can't watch this. Don't bring us in.*

The demon captains hoisted the platform up to their shoulders and followed the soldiers.

45

STRIPES

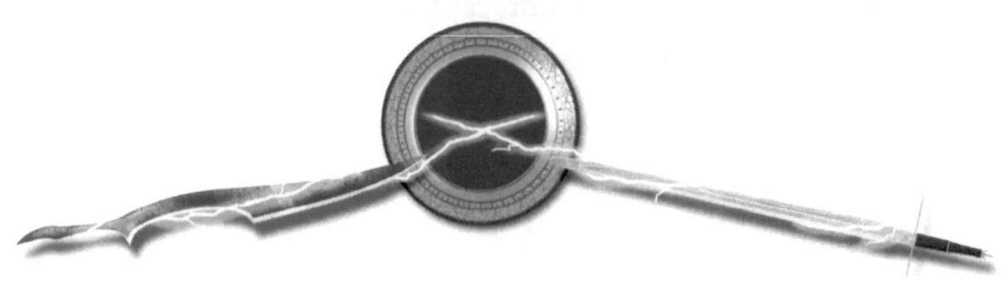

Battle: 8:30 a.m.

The demon captains carried Elric's team into a small open-air stadium behind the Praetorium and circled around the wooden post in the center of the dirt arena. They dropped the platform down on the far side with a careless thud.

"This should give you a clear view of His face," one of the demons graveled to the defeated angels on the platform.

Elric's heart sank. He cringed at the post directly in front of them—a thick log, ten feet tall, with a large iron ring near the top. The midsection of the post wore the battle scars of an active past and dried blood of countless victims.

Fine, stoneless dirt covered the smooth surface of the arena floor in the Physical Realm—perfect for marching, fighting, and soaking up men's blood. In the Middle Realm, thousands of large spiritual stones littered the arena floor—every one a memorial of a man's blood calling out to the King from the defiled earth. The beaelzurim on the ground had to step over, or on, the stones to move around the arena. Many of the stones had been piled up around the arena edges. Three small demons cleared away a dozen stones from around the post. Like tiresome rubbish, they picked up the stones and heaved them to the side.

Elric scanned the throng of beaelzurim surrounding them. From the floor of the arena, all the way up to the layer of darkness above them, thousands upon thousands pressed in to get a view. Thousands more packed onto the arena floor, leaving only a tight circle of open area around the post. A small brazen demon fluttered up and perched on top of the post like a vulture. Elric's eyes passed over the sea of faces, trying to find any he recognized. Surely he had fought hand to hand with hundreds of these over the eons, but none looked familiar. With all their snarling and contorted shouting, they all looked the same. He spotted Satan on the dignitary's platform. Marr stood beside him with Asherah, Molech, and Yarikh close behind. Elric continued his scan around the circle. *There*—Vorsogh, five levels up from the ground, shouting like a wild beast. *Not surprising to see him here.* To his left and three more levels up—*Luchek.* Hard to miss, with his disfigured right eye socket and dark blotchy scabbed skin. *My old friend Luminir. Look at you now.*

Seeing his old friend sent a shudder of pain into the pit of his being, and he wondered why he bothered looking at the faces of the enemy. He turned his attention to Physical Realm.

The entire Roman cohort of Jerusalem, 360 soldiers, marched in through an open corridor on the side. They filed in four abreast, circled all around the perimeter of the arena, halted, and faced inward. A fine cloud of dust from the tromping feet hovered just below knee level. A small detail emerged through the corridor entrance in two columns with Jesus walking between. At the sight of the bound prisoner, the whole Roman cohort yelled and jeered and shook their spears in the air. The detail commander led Jesus in to the center and stripped off His clothes in front of the post. The cohort cheered. The commander ran a rope through the ring on the top of the post, lashed one end of the rope onto the bindings around Jesus' wrists, and pulled the other end of the rope tight. The rope pulled Jesus' arms up until the skin stretched tight over His bare back. The cohort cheered louder.

Elric looked into Jesus' face and marveled. Jesus complied with every shove and demand. His face looked calm and resolute, as though He was in complete control. Elric saw no fear. No anger. No sign of hopelessness.

He has a plan. Any second now He is going to destroy the enemy with a single word.

The arena fell silent. The men standing on the dirt and the spirits all around held their breath.

The squad leader unrolled a parchment and held it at arm's length. His voice boomed across the arena. "The honorable Pontius Pilate, Governor of the land of Judea, by the authority of Tiberius, exalted Caesar of Rome and all its provinces, decrees this day that Jesus of Nazareth is to be punished for crimes against the state and its people. The crime: sedition, in that he claims to be the king of the Jews. The sanction: nonlethal punishment by means of flagrum."

The soldiers all laughed and pointed. "King of the Jews?" "This is a king?"

Cheers and shouting filled the air in both realms. Everywhere Elric looked—mindless hate in the faces of human and demonic soldiers. Suddenly, the cheers doubled in strength. *What?* Elric turned his head back toward the arena entrance. A lump formed in his throat. *The executioners.*

Two men, hulking muscular brutes almost seven feet tall, entered the arena shoulder to shoulder with grim, stone-cold expressions. Elric probed deep into their vacant eyes. *They each have a demon resident within.* Each held the wooden handle of a whip with four braided leather thongs. Along the thongs, small lead balls and sharp pieces of bone turned the simple whip into a "scorpion."

The demon throng went wild at the sight of the men with the whips. The two executioners moved into position behind Jesus, one to the left and one to the right, and the roar from both the Physical and Middle Realms became deafening.

Any second now. The King is going to break forth with vengeance. Any second—

With well-practiced precision, the executioner on the right raised his arm and swung his flagrum down. The thongs bit into Jesus' bare back. With a snap, the soldier ripped the whip back, tearing flesh away and sending blood into the air all around.

The demon horde erupted in victorious applause. The blood drops flew through the air, landing on everything and everyone near—in both realms. The first drops hit the small demon on top of the post. The instant the blood touched the demon, he shrieked, withered like a burning blade of grass, and exploded in cloud of yellow smoke, vanquished to the abyss. The spray of blood reached a wide circle around the post and splattered on another twenty demons. Each cried out in surprised anguish, shriveled and exploded. The yellow cloud from the vanquished spirits hung like poison death over the demons on the ground. Drops of blood landed on both the executioners, and the demons within them evaporated in a sulfurous cloud. The crowd of beaelzurim gasped and fell silent.

In the Physical Realm, Jesus cried out. The Roman soldiers cheered. The two executioners dropped to their knees as though overcome by dizziness or weakness. They each wiped drops of blood from their faces and staggered back to their feet. They looked dazed and confused, and they shook their heads, trying to regain focus. The executioner on the left slapped his face with his free hand and clenched his jaw tight with a scowl of determination. He raised his whip and brought it down on Jesus' back.

The circle of demons around the post pushed outward, away from the radius of flying blood, but another dozen of them turned into yellow clouds of smoke. The rest of the horde resumed their cheering.

Elric closed his eyes. He hummed a favorite praise song, but he couldn't block out the horrific sounds all around him. He felt a nudge from Lacidar beside him. He opened his eyes and turned his head toward Lacidar. With bindings still around his mouth, Lacidar motioned upward with his eyes. Elric looked up toward the blanket of darkness above.

What is that?

He squinted and strained to understand what his eyes saw.

That looks like cancer, a spiritual manifestation of the physical sickness, pouring into a giant bath.

He looked back at Lacidar with questioning eyes. Lacidar shrugged. He looked over at Jenli. Jenli shrugged. He looked over at Timrok. Timrok's gaze never broke away from the darkness above. Elric looked back up at the sky.

Heart disease, leprosy, blindness—all poured into the layer of darkness and swirled together.

It's like this layer of darkness is a giant container, and sickness is being poured into it.

An executioner took another strike.

Dementia, deafness, influenza, mental illness poured into the darkness. Elric scanned the demon horde—so transfixed on the torture happening below, they paid no attention to the phenomenon occurring above.

An executioner took another strike.

Boils, tumors, skin disease, spinal disorders poured into the darkness. With every stripe inflicted by the scorpion, a whole host of infirmities dumped into the strange container.

By the time the executioners finished, every malady known to man from the beginning of time swirled together in a giant bath of darkness hanging in the air above the Middle Realm. Elric couldn't take his eyes off the layer of darkness. The Physical Realm, where the soldiers wove a crown of thorns and beat it onto Jesus' head while they mocked and spat on Him, seemed like a distant dream—like the pain of a lesser reality. The reality of the strange spiritual phenomenon happening above captured all his attention and kept him transfixed.

What is all this? What does it all mean?

46

FINAL JUDGMENT

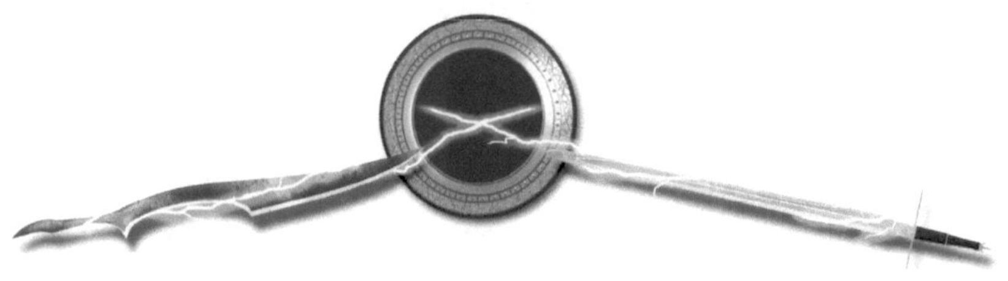

Battle: 8:45 a.m.

Pilate paced in his back room in the Praetorium, awaiting word from the soldiers that the scourging had been completed.

This man is innocent, he thought. *I cannot deliver Him to be crucified. And there is something about Him—something elusive that troubles my soul. I know there is more to this man—*

There was a knock at the door, and a soldier appeared. He announced, "The prisoner has been punished according to your orders. He is on his way back here now."

Pilate nodded. He took a deep breath and headed outside to the Pavement. The crowd of Jews had grown, and the potential for a riot made his stomach churn. *Surely, they will be satisfied when they see him scourged.* He reached the judgment seat on the porch overlooking the Pavement. He stopped and motioned with his hand for quiet.

His voice echoed across the Pavement. "Behold, I am bringing Him out to you so that you may know that I find no guilt in Him."

The crowd stirred and murmured but stayed under control.

A young page ran across the porch and handed a scroll to Pilate. "A message from your wife," the page said.

"Not now," Pilate said. He sat and rubbed his forehead.

"It is an urgent message. I was told my lord would want to see it immediately."

Pilate scowled and snatched the parchment. He unrolled it and read: "Have nothing to do with that righteous Man; for last night I suffered greatly in a dream because of Him."

Pilate handed the scroll back to the page and excused him. *Who is this man? What am I to do with him?*

The main doors to the Praetorium swung open, and the detail of soldiers marched out. At the rear of the two columns, two soldiers held Jesus up with His arms draped over their shoulders. The soldiers partially dragged Him—His legs unable to hold His weight or keep up their pace. The soldiers positioned Him on the porch, lifted His arms from around their shoulders, and braced Him for several moments until He could stand on His own. They took two steps back and stood at attention in the trail of blood on the marble tile.

Pilate looked at the battered prisoner. He wore nothing but the purple robe Herod had sent Him back in. The robe hid the raw flesh of His back, but the amount of blood pooling at His feet left little to imagine. On His head, the soldiers had driven a crown of thorns into His scalp. The blood and swelling forced one eye completely shut and left the other barely open. With the open cuts and bruises and swelling, His face hardly looked human. Blood matted all over His beard, His mustache, His hair.

Pilate looked away. He had seen plenty of blood and torture over the years, but this made even his stomach turn. He stood up to address the crowd. Pilate said to them, "Behold, the man!"

Surely this will be sufficient to appease the crowd.

The chief priests and officers cried out, "Crucify, Crucify!"

Pilate gazed over the unrest throughout the crowd. *What is going on here today? Never have I seen so many come forward over a single man. Their discontent is without rational cause.* He called out to the Jewish leaders, "Take him yourselves and crucify Him, for I find no guilt in Him."

One of the chief priests called back, "We have a law, and by that law He ought to die because He made himself out to be the Son of God."

The Son of God? A shudder of terror shot through his body. *Who is this man?*

Pilate turned and marched off toward the Praetorium. He passed Jesus and said to the soldiers, "Bring Him."

Inside the judgment hall, Pilate waited for the soldiers to prop Jesus up in front of the judgment seat. He tried to look Jesus in the eyes, but when he saw the thorns jabbing through His eyebrow and into the swollen mass around His eye, he looked away. He cleared his throat and said to Jesus, "Where are you from?"

Jesus gave him no answer.

Pilate said, "You do not speak to me? Do you not know that I have authority to release you, and I have authority to crucify you?"

Jesus answered, "You would have no authority over Me, unless it had been given you from above; for this reason he who delivered Me to you has the greater sin."

Beads of sweat rolled down Pilate's forehead. He dabbed it with a silk handkerchief. He looked Jesus in the face but turned away again. He stood, turned to the side, and exited the judgment hall into his back room.

Alone in the room, he wrestled with his thoughts. In his heart, he knew this man had no guilt. In his heart, he knew he should release him, regardless of the demands of the people. But thoughts kept bubbling up from somewhere and invading his mind.

Maybe He is guilty. He certainly brings much unrest among the people. There is only one way to deal with insurrectionists.

He dabbed his forehead again.

No! Not only is He innocent, but there is something about this man. I am going to release Him.

He moved toward the door but stopped. An icy chill bristled the hairs on the back of his neck.

But what about the people? They will probably riot. They are near that now. Then Rome will require it of me.

He dropped into his chair and buried his face into his hands.

There is still a way stay innocent of his blood. Remember Barabbas. Make the people choose. If they choose to release Barabbas, Jesus' blood will be on their heads.

He wiped away his sweat again.

It is the only way.

He took a deep breath, rose, and trudged to the door. Opening it a crack, he called for the squad leader. "Go to the prison," Pilate said to the soldier. "Bring me Barabbas. Quickly!"

Fifteen minutes later, the guard shoved Barabbas through the prisoner door of the Praetorium with wild hair, an unkempt beard, and bare, grimy feet. Pilate looked at him with contempt and shook his head.

To the soldier, Pilate said, "I shall make another plea to the people. If I do not prevail, bring both these prisoners out to the judgment seat on the porch."

Pilate stepped back outside and took his position on the judgment seat. The crowd became quiet. He pronounced, "After further examination, I still find no fault in this man. Behold, he has been punished. Now I will release Jesus of Nazareth to your hands."

"No! No!" the crowd cried out. "If you release this Man, you are no friend of Caesar; everyone who makes himself out to be a king opposes Caesar."

These words cannot be told in Rome. Look at them, they are ready to riot.

He motioned to the guards, and they brought the two prisoners out, facing the crowd.

Pointing toward Jesus, Pilate shouted, "Behold, your King!"

So they cried out, "Away with Him, away with Him, crucify Him!"

Pilate said to them, "Shall I crucify your King?"

The chief priests answered, "We have no king but Caesar."

Pilate shook his head and wiped his forehead with his handkerchief. He gritted his teeth. He called out, "Behold, Barabbas, a convicted murderer and enemy of the state. And Jesus, a man in whom I find no fault." He paused and took a breath. "Which of the two do you want me to release for you?"

And they said, "Barabbas."

Pilate said to them, "Then what shall I do with Jesus who is called Christ?"

They all said, "Crucify Him!"

And he said, "Why, what evil has He done?"

But they kept shouting all the more, saying, "Crucify Him!"

I am accomplishing nothing here. These people are sure to riot. I have no choice.

He stood and stepped over to a table with a large bronze bowl filled with water. He dipped his hands into the water, rubbed them together as though washing off blood, and dried them with a towel. He turned to the people and said, "I am innocent of this Man's blood; see to that yourselves."

And all the people said, "His blood shall be on us and on our children!"

"Release Barabbas," Pilate said to the guards. "Take Jesus and crucify Him."

* * *

The victory march from the Praetorium to Golgotha began. Satan sat on a dark throne resting on a large platform, carried by a dozen of his choice generals. The generals lifted the platform high with their arms extended straight above their heads. Black smoke emanating from the base of the throne spilled over the platform edges and into the generals' faces, who stretched to lift the platform higher so they could see as they walked. Satan held his scepter up, and bolts of lightning flashed from the glowing skull at the scepter crown. Deep thunder rolled like a perpetual wave of unstoppable energy.

Behind the throne marched all the enemy generals—all the great princes over every region of the earth. Marr led the procession of generals, carried on the shoulders of Asherah, Molech, and Yarikh. He held his sword high and waved to all the beaelzurim lining the route.

Demons from everywhere piled in along the parade route. They extended from the ground up to the layer of darkness—a solid mass of evil faces screeching, yelling, and shouting victory chants. Smaller demons swarmed through the air over the parade like erratic bats.

Behind the generals, the Roman execution squads pressed the human prisoners forward. Three men were to be crucified this day, and each had to carry his own cross. The soldiers cleared a path through the streets, now filled with people in town for Passover, with extended spears and impatient demands. The labored steps of the prisoners under the load of the heavy wood timbers made the march slow, and the soldiers around the prisoners held the people along the sides back as they passed by.

Behind the prisoners, the whole crowd that had packed the Pavement court followed, shaking their fists and clubs and swords in the air and cheering at full volume.

At the very rear of the parade, Elric and his team stood on the vanquished platform and listened to the jeers from the beaelzurim spectators as they passed by on the shoulders of the demon captains. Their taunts cut Elric deeper than before. Not for his own sake, but for the thought of all the King had just been through and for the defeat He now carried. *I wonder if the Son of Man can see all the mayhem and mocking in the Middle Realm. I hope not.*

The marching stopped, and Elric strained past the crowd of people to see why. From his position in the back, he couldn't tell for sure, but it looked like Jesus had collapsed from the loss of blood, and the soldiers were forcing some passerby to carry His cross. Two soldiers propped Jesus up with His arms around their shoulders, and the march resumed.

How can this be? The One with the power to speak everything into existence—doesn't have the strength to walk? The last flicker of hope stretched thin and vanished. *This is really going to happen. The enemy is really going to kill Him. He is not going to stop it.*

He looked up at the layer of darkness above them through a pool of tears. All the sicknesses of the world still swirled through the darkness, and he wondered again what it meant. The enemy host seemed oblivious to it. They were too drunk on pride and the excitement of their moment to notice.

The march stopped again, and Elric turned his attention back to the Physical Realm. They had crossed outside the city wall and come to a stop at the hill called Golgotha, the Place of the Skull. The air reeked of death, and thousands of spiritual stones from the blood of men lay in heaps on the ground in the Middle Realm. The incessant sound of buzzing flies filled the air.

This is it. The demon captains lowered the vanquished platform down in a place with a good view. *This is really going to happen.*

47

SACRIFICIAL LAMB

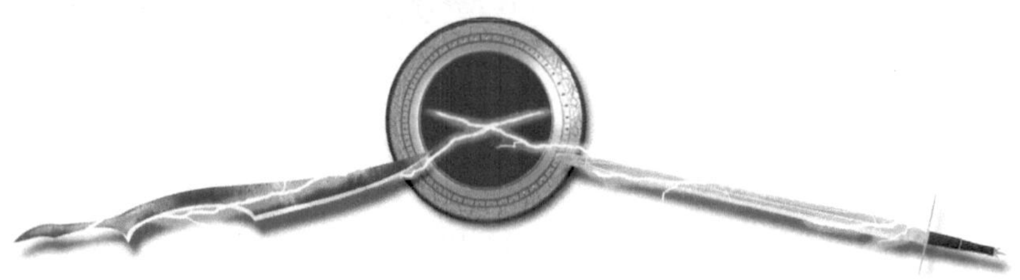

Battle: 9:00 a.m.

The Roman execution teams prepared the prisoners for crucifixion under a cloudless morning sky with quiet, rough efficiency. Elric closed his eyes, forcing his mind back to a happier place and time. Back to the time when the King walked with him in that unknown, secret meadow. Back when the King first told him about His plan to enter the world and commissioned him to keep Him safe. A time filled with excitement and joy. Oh, the peace and love that permeated every living thing in that meadow. The sweet fragrance of the presence of the Spirit. The anticipation of the day when the King would defeat His enemies and set everything in the Kingdom right again. The depths of the wisdom in the King's eyes. The joy of overflowing life in the waves of the river as it—

Clang! A metal hammer struck an iron spike and echoed through Elric's collapsing world.

Jesus cried out.

Timrok struggled so hard against his bindings, he fell off the platform.

Elric heard Jesus say as He gritted His teeth through the pain, "Father, forgive them; for they do not know what they are doing."

Elric flinched and closed his eyes each time the hammer rang out. *Enough! Enough already!* The hammering stopped—finally, but Elric's eyes stayed closed until he heard the unmistakable thud of the cross dropping into its footing. The beaelzurim horde went wild. Elric opened his eyes to the mass hysteria of celebration in the Middle Realm.

That's it. They did it. They've won.

The Roman soldiers divided up Jesus' clothes they had stripped off His bloody body. They all touched his tunic and felt the material, admiring the remarkable smooth texture. Elric remembered when he first received this material from the King to use as a covering to hide His divine Spirit from the enemy. The day he first used it to cover Mary when she was pregnant seemed like a lifetime ago. The memory of the day he left it in the stable for Mary to wrap the baby in floated away like a vapor. And all the times the young boy played hide and seek under it were nothing but distant nostalgias. Now, these boorish brutes gambled for it like some festival prize.

These men have no idea what they are doing. They are not worthy to handle this—

Elric felt a bump from behind. He turned. Lacidar motioned upward with his eyes. Elric turned his gaze toward the layer of darkness. Something new stirred within it. Into the bath of sickness and disease, the sins of mankind began to pour. Pride, selfishness, hatred, jealously, and strife gushed into the mixture of darkness like a flood. Murder, lying, idolatry, and adultery streamed in.

Elric looked at his lieutenants, who all appeared as baffled as he was.

What is this? Is this the enemy's doing?

He scanned the enemy's reaction—they seemed oblivious to it. They continued their celebration with dancing and victory chants. The people, of course, didn't notice. They continued with their mocking and insults.

While the men and the enemy reveled in their victory, Elric watched the container in the sky fill with sin. Now, not just the sins, but the curses that those sins invoke poured into the mixture. The layer of darkness became thicker and thicker as it filled with every sin known by man.

Elric watched and wondered about the mysterious spectacle in the sky for three hours. By noon, every sin of every man across all time—past, present, and future—had been poured into the giant bath of darkness. Every curse of sin had been poured in. Every sickness and disease had been poured in. Everything from the beginning of time that brought enmity between the King and mankind filled the layer of darkness until it seemed like it would burst from the pressure.

Then, the real darkness set in.

* * *

Battle: 12:00 p.m.

A new darkness dropped over the earth. A darkness so deep fell that all light from the heavens vanished, even within the Physical Realm. No sun, no moon, no stars—only darkness.

Elric squinted into the pitch black. *Something just happened. I know what this is. When that layer of darkness first rolled in after the battle in the garden, I sensed nothing about it other than an emptiness that left us feeling cut off from the King's Realm. I actually wondered if the omniscient King could see beyond it. Now, three hours after the enemy nailed the Son of Man to the cross, the cloud of darkness contains all the sin and sickness of all mankind. Everything is prepared.* He gazed upward at the darkness. *The King has just turned His face away from His Son.*

The men on the ground gawked at the sky and scrambled around lighting torches.

The beaelzurim all stopped their celebration and became silent. For several minutes, a tense hush gripped the Middle Realm, with every spirit looking toward the sky.

A small strand of darkness descended from the cloud and landed on Jesus. The instant it touched His spirit, it absorbed into His body. The thin filament of darkness grew until it became a small vortex. The contents of the layer of darkness swirled down the vortex into Jesus. The vortex grew. More of the darkness drained downward. The vortex increased still more. The vortex became a monstrous tornado of sin, disease, and curses spiraling downward into Jesus' body.

"What is this?" Marr shouted over the howling wind from the tornado.

Satan stood speechless with his mouth hanging open for a full minute. Then, a flash of understanding hit Satan's eyes.

"No, no, no!" Satan roared.

"What?" Marr shouted. "What is happening?"

With exasperated gestures, Satan shouted, "The King is placing all the sin of man on His Son! He is making Him into His sacrificial lamb! He is pouring out His wrath on Him!"

"No!" Marr screamed. "That means if He dies, the payment for man's sin will be paid."

"This was His intent from the beginning," Satan groaned.

Marr paced and wrung his hands. "He is purchasing back the fallen race of man!"

"It is worse than that," Satan said. "Since He has accomplished this *as* a man, He will reclaim the authority given me by Adam. This was always His intent."

"No!" Marr screamed. "We must stop this! We cannot let Him die! We have to get Him down from that cross!" Marr grabbed a commander standing beside him by the arm. "You, go bring Him down!"

The commander pulled his arm away. "You bring Him down. I am not touching Him."

"Somebody do something!" Marr shouted. "Somebody get Him off that cross or we are all defeated!"

Many of the smaller demons scrambled away like frightened rabbits. Most of the demon host looked confused and continued gawking at the spiritual whirlwind. A small group of commanders and captains apprehensively approached the cross with the tornado raging just above their heads.

"Get in there!" Marr commanded. "Do it!"

Two desperate commanders reached out toward Jesus. The instant they contacted His body, they vanished in a cloud of sulfurous smoke. All the others backed away in horror. Dozens more of the demon spectators fled.

Marr launched a barrage of fireballs at Jesus, "Come down off that cross!" "The Father has deserted you!" "Save Yourself!"

None of his words entered Jesus' spirit. Every one bounced off Him like exploding glass. Some of the shards hit the men on the ground, and the men called out to Jesus, "Ha! You who are going to destroy the temple and rebuild it in three days, save yourself, and come down from the cross!" The soldiers also shouted, "If you are the King of the Jews, save yourself!"

Jesus didn't answer them, and the darkness continued to spin downward.

One of the criminals on a cross next to Jesus echoed the same message. "Are you not the Christ? Save yourself and us!"

The other criminal, a man named Dismas, rebuked him and said, "Do you not even fear God, since you are under the same sentence of condemnation? And we indeed are suffering justly, for we are receiving what we deserve for our deeds; but this man has done nothing wrong." Turning to Jesus, Dismas said, "Jesus, remember me when You come in Your kingdom!"

Jesus answered him, "Truly I say to you, today you shall be with Me in Paradise."

Elric gazed at the King through tear-filled eyes. *While taking on all the sin of the world, He still takes thought of this one man.*

The realization of the meaning of the tornado spread throughout the beaelzurim ranks, and they shuddered and cowered. Dozens of demons fled. It became more and more clear that the King's intent could not be stopped, and they escaped by the hundreds. Then by thousands. With shrieks of shock and panic, they flew away in all directions.

Within an hour, Elric found himself and his team alone in the Middle Realm.

Only Satan remained. The dark cherub stood, shaking his head and watching the vortex. Defeat draped over him like a heavy blanket. In an uncontrolled outburst of rage, Satan enlarged to a monstrous size—towering a hundred feet above the landscape. He roared, "If You are going to die, then it will be by *my* hand!"

He opened his mouth and held his hands outward toward the cross and spewed a torrent of molten fire down on the Son of Man. Giant bolts of crimson lightning shot from his fingertips. Elric had never seen this much raw power unleashed by Satan, not even during the Rebellion. Thick clouds of black smoke rose from the ground at Satan's feet, billowed upward, and sank back to the ground from its own weight. The heat felt like the surface of the sun, and the rumbling, crackling, sizzling shock waves of sound pounded against Elric's chest. The expanse of the fiery barrage was large enough to swallow all of Golgotha and more.

Elric turned his face away from the heat and looked toward the cross. None of Satan's onslaught came close to men on the ground. All of it—the fire, the bolts of lightning, the smoke—bent inward toward the swirling vortex of sin and curses, became entrapped in the circulation of the vortex, and then flung outward like mud from a spinning wheel. The deluge of flames became tiny sparks ejected from the vortex. They spiraled outward with a brief lingering glow and evaporated into nothing without even a trace of smoke.

The ineffectiveness of his attack enraged Satan even more, and he increased the intensity when Elric thought it couldn't be any stronger.

No effect. Nothing touched the Son of Man. Nothing touched any of the men on the ground.

After another hour, Satan finally quit his storm of rage. He looked at the Son of Man, still alive and still taking on all the sin and disease of the world. He watched a while longer. Then he turned and flew off over the horizon.

Alone, but still bound, Elric could to nothing but watch the darkness drain down into Jesus' body.

* * *

For three hours, darkness gripped the earth. Elric watched the last of the contents of the container of sin and death empty into Jesus' body, and he could see the despair from the separation from the Father overwhelm the Son. Jesus pushed against the nail in His feet, gasped for air, and cried out, "Eloi, Eloi, lema sabachthani?"

The people around the cross said to themselves, "Listen, he's calling Elijah." Elric shook his head. *These people don't understand the language.* He understood the desperate words—"My God, my God, why have you forsaken me?"—and he understood the depth of the pain behind them.

One of the men ran, filled a sponge with wine vinegar, put it on a staff, and offered it to Jesus to drink. "Now leave him alone. Let us see if Elijah comes to take him down," he said. Those standing around watched by torch light to see if anything would happen.

Elric took a deep breath. *With all the sin of mankind laid upon the Lamb, only one thing remains.*

Jesus pushed up against the nail for another breath and called out, "Father, into your hands I commit my spirit."

Here it comes.

Jesus pushed up again, took His last breath, and pronounced, "It is finished."

He bowed His head and released His Spirit. The moment He stepped out of His body, a brilliant flash blinded Elric, a giant earthquake rocked the ground, and the sun returned to its afternoon radiance.

* * *

The two temple guards outside the temple door—one on the left and one on the right—staggered from the earthquake. The shaking stopped. They regained their composure.

Suddenly, a deafening tearing sound shredded the quiet of the inner temple and rattled the massive doors.

"What was that?" one of the guards said, turning toward the doors.

"I don't know. Should we check?"

"I'm not going into the Holy Place! Go get a priest."

The guard scrambled down the steps and into the Court of the Priests. He grabbed the first priest he could find and dragged him back up the steps.

"We heard something inside the temple," the guard said.

"That's right," the other guard said. "A great tearing. Something calamitous has happened in there."

"What do you want me to do?" the priest said.

"Go see what happened!" a guard said. "You're a priest."

"But I'm not anointed to enter the Holy Place," the priest said. "I cannot go in."

"Then just *look* in," a guard said. "Someone has to check. We will hold the door."

The priest inched forward to the center of the double doors. He muttered under his breath, "Oh God, have mercy and do not kill me." He closed his eyes and said, "Open the doors. Just a little."

The guards cracked open the left and right doors while standing behind them, away from the view of the inside.

The priest peeked through squinted eyes into the temple. He screamed, "Shut the doors! Shut the doors! Oh God, don't kill me. Don't kill me."

He sprinted down the steps.

"What is it? What happened?" a guard yelled.

The priest hollered over his shoulder as he ran, "The veil has been rent top to bottom. I saw into the Holy of Holies! Let no one in! I have to get Caiaphas!"

* * *

Elric blinked, regaining his eyes, and he didn't see Jesus' Spirit anywhere. He scanned all around the Middle Realm and saw nothing—no Jesus, no enemy, no layer of darkness. Only he and his team remained. The spiritual air had become absolutely silent.

The universe still holds together. Though I don't understand how.

Warmth of the light from the Throne surrounded him.

The Father remains enthroned in the King's Realm.

He turned his attention to the Physical Realm. Only a handful of people remained. They wandered off, dazed and disturbed by all the amazing events. The disciple, John, and a few women, including Mary, stood at a distance, weeping and clinging to each other. The centurion and his men looked unsettled by the darkness, the earthquake, the reappearance of the sun after Jesus death.

Even they can tell this was no ordinary death.

A runner in a Roman uniform appeared at the site and approached the centurion. "Sir," the runner said between breaths, "the governor has issued orders that these men's legs be broken."

"For what purpose?"

"Today is the Jewish preparation day for Passover. The chief priests of their temple desire these men's death quickly so they can be brought down before sundown."

The centurion gave a "humph" and shook his head. "These Jews and their laws," he muttered to himself. "You," he called out to one of his men, "go break their legs."

Elric's eyes brightened. *The Passover. Of course, this very hour the Passover lamb was slaughtered at the temple. The Passover lamb—this has always been His intent.*

The rod of the Roman soldier snapped the legs of the first criminal on the cross. The man screamed and groaned.

With the realization of the King's true intent, a rush of words from the King's prophets over the centuries flooded through Elric's mind. *"Like a lamb that is led to slaughter, and like a sheep that is silent before its shearers, so He did not open His mouth." "They pierced my hands and my feet. I can count all my bones. They look, they stare at me; they divide my garments among them, and for my clothing they cast lots." "He poured out Himself to death, and was numbered with the transgressors; yet He Himself bore the sin of many." "He would render Himself as a guilt offering."* Elric shook his head. *How did we miss this? This has always been His great plan.*

The second criminal on the cross cried out.

The soldier approach Jesus' cross. "This one is already dead," the soldier called back to the centurion. "Do I also break His legs?"

The centurion marched over and inspected Jesus' body, paying no attention to the waning gasps for breath from the other two crosses. "Hand me your spear," he said to one of the other soldiers. With the detached proficiency of a hardened warrior, he thrust the iron point of the spear into the side of Jesus' body. He scrutinized the lack of reaction and the wound with clinical authority. He handed the spear back to the soldier and said, "This one is dead. There is no need to break His legs."

"They will look on Me whom they have pierced."

Elric turned his head and looked at his team. They all had the same look of dawning realization. Yet, they all remained bound and gagged. Timrok still lay on the ground, flat on his back, with tears streaming down the sides of his face. Jenli gave Elric a look as if to say, "What now?"

Elric shook his head and shrugged his shoulders. *What now?*

48

SHEOL

Burial minus 1 hour

The Roman soldiers lowered the crosses and removed the dead bodies. Elric and his team could do nothing but watch in silence. Still bound with cords of darkness, they stood on the vanquished platform, alone in the Middle Realm with no help in sight. The soldiers worked with emotionless efficiency, speaking little, grunting from the weight of the timbers and the bodies.

Elric spotted a tiny light in the sky, high and distant. It approached as fast as a comet, and within a second, Elric could see the form of the incoming angel. *Gabriel!*

Gabriel landed in front of Elric's team. His wings disappeared into his back. Gabriel paused a moment, and his eyes met Elric's, the bright silver in his eyes glinting in the afternoon sun. Without a word he turned and walked over to the platform that held the pile of weapons and shields from Elric's team. He found Elric's sword, lifted it, examined the engraving of the morning star at the base of its hilt, felt its weight and balance, and nodded. He walked back to the vanquished platform and stood in front of Elric. Pulling a sleek dagger from inside his cloak, with one careful flick of the dagger he nipped off the bindings over Elric's mouth.

"He will justify the many, as He will bear their iniquities." Elric blurted out.

With a sly smile, Gabriel sliced through the remaining bindings, beginning at Elric's ankles all the way up to his neck. The black cords fell away, and Elric stretched his arms. Gabriel handed Elric his sword and smiled. "Who has believed our message? And to whom has the arm of the Lord been revealed?" Gabriel said.

Elric jumped down off the platform. "This mystery was certainly not revealed to us until now." He stepped over to Timrok on the ground and released him from his bindings with a single slice of his sword.

Timrok popped up and headed straight to the pile of weapons.

Gabriel loosed Jenli, then Lacidar. Their bindings fell away, and Timrok tossed each their sword. They each snatched their weapon out of the air by the handle. The three lieutenants released the rest of their teams, and the whole troop gathered around Gabriel in a semicircle while strapping on their weapons and shields.

"Why was this held from us?" Jenli asked. "Why were we left to—"

Elric put his hand on Jenli's shoulder. "Jenli . . . don't," he said with a hushed tone.

Gabriel smiled and said, "Let him be, Captain. We all long to look into this mystery. Since before the foundations of the world, the King has desired to reveal it." He lowered his voice to just above a whisper. "And there is still more to be revealed." He raised his chin and folded his hands behind his back. With a full voice he said, "To your question . . . it was important that the enemy believe he was in control. He needed to believe he had defeated the King's defenses, or he might have suspected the King's true intent. For this purpose, the King needed you to make every true effort to protect Him."

"We are ever in His service," Timrok said, his hands resting on his sword hilts.

Gabriel smiled. "Servants of the Most High King—your valor, your faithfulness, your sacrifice honors the King, and He is well pleased. Your deeds here this day have enabled the King's will on earth."

Elric's team all smiled at each other with sparkling eyes.

"But," Gabriel continued, "your work is not yet complete. Three days and nights remain before the King rises with His resurrected body. The enemy may try to steal the Lord's body from the tomb to create doubt among the people. You must secure His body until then. Also, His disciples face great danger from the Jewish leaders. You must protect them."

"Master Gabriel," Elric said. "Where is the Spirit of Jesus now, and where will He be until the third day? I looked, but I did not see where He went."

Gabriel took a deep breath. His gaze fell to the ground. "He was the Son of Man. He has gone the way of all men."

Timrok shook his head. "The King—in Sheol? Descended into the lowermost parts of the earth? May it never be!"

Gabriel answered, "This, too, was foretold: "For You will not abandon my soul to Sheol; Nor will You allow Your Holy One to undergo decay."

"But," Elric said, "where in Sheol? Hades or Paradise?"

"I think you know," Gabriel said. His voice became low and solemn. "There is a reason the smell of the burnt sin offering is a soothing aroma to the Lord."

"Every day," Elric said, "He amazes me anew."

"See now," Gabriel said with a quick, bright tone, "the man named Joseph, a member of the council, a righteous man from Arimathea, has received permission to remove Jesus' body and place it in his tomb nearby."

Everyone's attention turned to the Physical Realm. The rabbi Joseph spoke with the Roman centurion, who read a parchment and nodded his head.

Jenli leaned into Elric and said, "Joseph of Arimathea! He was my last assignment before this, remember? That was when he purchased this tomb."

Elric nodded and smiled. "He was with a rich man in His death."

"Your work continues now," Gabriel said.

"In His service," Elric announced with a crisp voice. He looked at Timrok and pointed toward Jesus' body, which was already being carried off on a stretcher by two soldiers with Joseph of Arimathea and the women following. Timrok nodded, and without a word, he and his team deployed.

Gabriel extended his wings and smiled at Elric. "I will see you in two days," he said. Like a shooting star, he disappeared into the sky.

* * *

A sea of faces in Sheol turned upward and watched with intense anticipation during the moments before the Son of Man breathed His last. All the spirits of the righteous dead gathered at the very edge of Paradise to witness the outcome of this amazing event. Among them stood Amichai of Beersheba, and beside him stood the spirit of his earthly wife, Hannah. Amichai stared across the expanse in front of them, where nothing but utter darkness prevailed. In that part of Sheol, the spirits of the unrighteous suffered in fiery agony, but as hard as he tried, he could not see them. He could not hear them. He saw only empty blackness.

He looked back over the crowd around him. Thousands upon thousands—thousands of thousands—waited in silence. Behind them the pleasant green backdrop of Paradise looked peaceful and clean. Above them the glowing orange canopy served as a reminder that, even though the King provided a place of rest for them in Sheol, Satan still owned legal rights over them according to the King's own law. Amichai turned back toward the black chasm and waited.

"Look!" someone shouted. "That must be Him!"

A single light, like a falling star, descended through the canopy on the far horizon and landed in the middle of the darkness. The light disappeared, swallowed up by darkness. The crowd gasped.

"What is happening?" Amichai said to those around him. He turned to Hannah. Her eyes looked as perplexed as everyone else's. A tense murmur swept across the multitude, and everyone strained to see a glimmer of light, a spark of hope, from across the chasm. Several minutes passed with no sign of anything. The crowd became restless.

Amid the tension, an escort angel alighted next to Amichai and Hannah with the spirit of a man just deceased. The angel bowed his head, smiled at the man, and launched upward, disappearing through the canopy and leaving the man behind.

"Dismas," Amichai said to the man, "welcome. You arrive at a most critical time."

Dismas looked around at the crowd and said, "I . . . was just crucified. I . . . died . . . beside a man named Jesus of Nazareth. Now I am—"

"In paradise. I am Amichai. This is—"

"Hannah," Dismas said. "How do I know you?"

Amichai and Hannah smiled. Amichai said, "We are all known as we were known. You know everyone here. Look, over there, that's Abraham. There's Jeremiah, Isaiah, David, Judah . . . "

Dismas continued. "Zadok, Nathan, Asa, Rebekah . . . I know all these people!"

"And they know you," Amichai said.

"How long have you been here?" Dismas asked.

"Almost thirty-five years," Amichai answered. "But it seems like a single day."

"What is happening? Why is everyone gathered here like this?"

Amichai gazed back across the chasm into the darkness. "As you know, the King has just laid down His life. To our surprise, His spirit descended into the place of punishment. His light disappeared. And now, we're waiting to see what will happen."

"It isn't possible that He could be trapped there, is it?" Dismas asked.

A voice from behind them said, "Shall I ransom them from the power of Sheol? Shall I redeem them from death?"

Amichai turned around to see who was speaking.

"It's the prophet, Hosea!" Dismas shouted, bouncing on his toes.

"You saw this long ago," Amichai said to Hosea, "didn't you?"

Hosea gave a halfhearted grin. "Only in part. I never saw the fulfillment of the King's words in my day, though I longed for it. All His prophets—we only received a little here, a little there, line upon line. And then we all came here never having seen the fulfillment of—"

A massive explosion rocked the spiritual ground of all Sheol. The multitude in Paradise braced themselves with hands on the shoulders of each other. At the center of the explosion flashed a light, brighter than ten suns, and a horizontal ring of light expanded outward in a radial slice. The ring's intensity matched the brightness of the explosion, and within a second it crossed the chasm and streaked over the crowd watching from Paradise. The flash blinded all the onlookers, who covered their eyes a second too late. A blast of wind stronger than a hurricane traveled with the ring of light and tossed everyone to the ground. The wind lasted only a moment, and the multitude fumbled back to their feet, rubbing their eyes.

Amichai started to regain his sight, and he said, "What was that—"

"Look," Hannah said.

Amichai looked behind them. There, in the spiritual air above Paradise, just high enough for the entire multitude to see, hovered the spirit of a Man. His whole being radiated the purest, whitest light Amichai had ever seen, and it lit all of Paradise with its brilliance. Amichai squinted into the light.

A voice called out, "It's the Lord! The Lord is here!"

Amichai turned toward the voice. *John the Baptist. Of course.*

Amichai dropped down with his face to the ground. Everyone else around him responded the same way.

Beside him he heard the trembling voice of Hosea. "O Death, where are your thorns? O Sheol, where is your sting?"

The air became absolutely still. The multitude remained absolutely still.

A voice—low as rolling thunder and strong as a crashing ocean wave, yet warm, round, and peaceful—said, "My beloved, stand and behold your salvation."

Amichai rose to his feet along with the multitude. Every face turned toward Jesus. Amichai started to squint from the intensity of the light emanating from Him but realized he could peer into the fullness of the light with no harm. He could see the Lord's eyes.

He is looking directly at me! The multitude still surrounded him, but he felt as though he alone had made a deep connection with the Lord. Without another word spoken, peace and joy overwhelmed him—stronger than he had ever known, more even than all his time in Paradise until now. The power of the presence of the King consumed him. In that moment, he knew nothing but the King's presence— inviting, full of love, full of purpose. Everything else faded away.

"You are here because of your faith," Jesus said.

Amichai's eyes stayed locked with the Lord's. *He's talking directly to me!*

"Your faith," Jesus continued, "in the mercies the great I Am. You could only look forward and trust the words of my prophets. You did not know my name. But now, behold, I Am the One in whom you trusted. Though you were considered righteous for your faith, you have had to wait until this day. I Am the righteous judge. And I will judge in righteousness and true justice. Since I am eternally bound by my word, the law of sin and death must be satisfied—the law that every man since Adam has transgressed. Today, this debt has been paid in my own blood. I now have full legal rights to declare you righteous and truly holy. Hear the good news I preach to you this day: you are the very righteousness of God, accepted by the Father, and forever a son in my kingdom."

"Worthy is the Lamb!" someone shouted.

Amichai turned. A multitude of people still surrounded him. He smiled. *That's right, there are others here.*

Someone else shouted, "Worthy is the Lamb who was slain!"

The overwhelming joy exploded from within, and Amichai leapt into the air. He joined the shouts with his arms raised high. "Worthy is the Lamb who was slain!"

The entire multitude shouted in unison. "Worthy is the Lamb who was slain!" Over and over they shouted. They jumped up and down like excited children and waved their arms and shouted. For hours, the celebration filled the spiritual air of Paradise. Jesus received the praise with a warm smile—not as a vain king, but as a father receiving the love of his children. Through it all Amichai felt as though Jesus connected with only him, and all the others provided background support.

The shouts of joy continued without waning, and eventually Jesus raised His hands to motion for quiet. The crowd responded in an instant, and a hush of anticipation fell over Paradise.

"My work is not yet complete," Jesus said. "I have the authority to lay down my life, and I have the authority to pick it back up again. My earthly temple has been destroyed, but in three days, I will raise it back up again. I will be first to receive my resurrection body, and when I do, I will lead you out of this place with your glorified body and bring you into the King's Realm."

"Worthy is the Lamb!" Amichai shouted—along with the multitude.

Jesus motioned again for quiet. "Until then," He said, "come. I've been longing to meet with you." He descended to the ground in Paradise in the middle of the crowd.

Amichai's joy exploded again, and he pressed forward to the place where Jesus landed. Millions of people surrounded Him. *How will I ever reach Him? It's impossible for Jesus to meet with every person in just three days. But I must try.*

To his utter amazement, Jesus stood right before him. The sparkle in His eyes and the smile on His face caused everything else to melt away.

Breathless, Amichai searched for something to say. Before he could utter a word, Jesus jumped forward and wrapped His arms around him and embraced him for a long time. The love saturated Amichai's being until he thought he would burst. Jesus pulled back, keeping His hands on Amichai's shoulders, and looked deep into his eyes. The life and power and wisdom within Jesus' eyes filled Amichai with awe.

"Amichai," Jesus said, "my beloved. *You* are *my* great joy. How I have longed for this moment."

"Thank you, Lord," Amichai said. "Thank you. I love you."

Jesus smiled and embraced Amichai again. He lingered—in no hurry.

Amichai wondered for a fleeting moment how Jesus could spend this much time with just him. It didn't matter. Only Jesus mattered. Perhaps, somehow, He was meeting with everyone else the same way.

49

SEALED

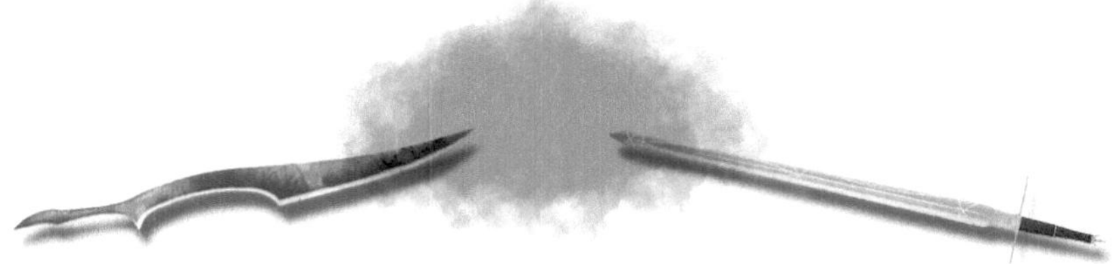

Burial plus 6 hours

The night held a strange stillness for Elric. With the Son of Man dead and His body lying alone in the tomb just feet away, the bittersweet victory still tasted more bitter than sweet. The unspeakable brutality of the physical torture was bad enough, but the vision of all the sin, disease, and curses pouring into the Son of Man carved a valley of pain through his heart like he had never known. And then, the darkness when the Father looked away—Elric grimaced. And now, during this strange interlude, with the pain behind and the final victory still ahead—his heart felt numb, torn by pain and anticipation.

He started to replay the scene at Golgotha again in his mind but stopped and shook his head. He took in a deep breath and let it out slowly. He turned his attention to his team. Timrok, on the ground in front of the tomb, stood with both swords drawn and a stern face. A large, chiseled stone, like a giant wheel four feet high and a hand-width thick, covered the entrance of the tomb, which had been cut into the limestone face of the hillside. From his post on the hill opposite the tomb, Elric spotted Timrok's team at regular intervals down the path leading to the tomb. Lacidar and his team held positions on the high ground above the tomb.

Through the hollow silence, muffled voices of men drifted over the hillside from around the corner of the pathway. Their tones were boisterous and jovial, and after a few seconds, Elric could make out some of their conversation.

"A ring!" one of the voices said. "One meager ring."

"What did you expect? These aren't Egyptian pharaohs."

Another voice piped in. This one had a different characteristic—weightier, more substantial in the Middle Realm. "You should hit another one. Check around this corner."

Elric palmed his sword handle.

"Let's find another one," a man's voice lilted.

"Why not?" another voice answered. "It's a high Sabbath. Everyone is shut up in their houses. We're all alone out here."

Riotous laughter echoed over the hill.

The group appeared from around the corner on a main path and stopped at the branch that led back toward Joseph of Arimathea's tomb. Four young men. And a beaelzur lieutenant with two of his warriors. One of the men held a large wineskin up to his mouth and took a long drink. He wiped his mouth with his sleeve and handed the skin to one of the other men, who laughed and did the same.

"Look!" one of the men called out. "Another tomb."

"Look at that stone! It's nothing like the little square mushroom plugs we've seen so far."

"You know what that means?"

"It will be easier to get into?" The man's words came out in a drunken slur.

One of the other men gave him a playful shove. "No, fool. It means this is the tomb of a rich man!"

All four laughed and took another round of drinks from the skin.

"We should find valuable things here."

"But what if there's nothing in there but old bones?"

The demon lieutenant extended his wings, overshadowing the whole group. "Take the body. Hold it for ransom." His words bounced off his cupped wings, focused inward, and shot into the men's spirits with ease.

"We could take the body," one of the men slurred.

"What? That is disgusting! What would we get out of that?"

"Money! A lot of it! Imagine this—we take the body, leave a note, and say they can have the body back for a price."

Another man laughed. "Ha ha! I like it. A family rich enough to have a tomb like this would pay anything to get their lost loved one back."

"It could be months before anyone even notices the body is gone."

"So? It will be worth it."

The four laughed again and took another round of drinks.

"Let's do it!"

The men stumbled forward. The demons led the way.

Flash! Flash! Flash! Lacidar and his team hit the ground like bolts of lightning just in front of the demon warriors.

Lacidar and Stephanus engaged the lieutenant. Lacidar and the demon lieutenant's blades collided, sending sparks sizzling through the spiritual air. Lacidar spun to the left with an upward swing. *Crash!* The demon met his steel with a downward parry. More sparks. Lacidar spun to the right with a mid-chest horizontal slice. *Crash!* The demon deflected it away. The demon leapt forward and brought his blade downward toward Lacidar in a high arc. *Crash!* Their blades locked and crackled inches above Lacidar's head. Stephanus bounded over both in a tight flip and swung his blade on the way down. He clipped the back of the demon's thigh, and yellow sulfur exploded from the gash. The demon screeched and reached for his leg. Lacidar twisted his blade around and flung the demon's sword off to the side. And in one continuous motion, he thrust his sword through the lieutenant's chest. In a cloud of yellow smoke, the demon fell backward, and Lacidar followed him down with his foot planted on the demon's neck. Stephanus bound him with cords of pulsing white light, and Lacidar pulled his sword out and stood back.

Jaeden and Ry took on one of the other warriors. Ry landed in front of the demon and leveled his sword. Jaeden shot down from behind and planted his feet in the middle of the demon's back. The force of Jaeden's kick sent the demon flailing forward into Ry's blade, which penetrated the front of his belly and came out through his back amid a cloud of sulfur.

Kelsof and BaeLee went after the third demon. Kelsof attacked from the left, and BaeLee attacked from the right. The demon warrior spun in frantic circles, deflecting their blows for the first few spins.

He could not match the speed of angels' blades, and Kelsof slashed a gaping, sulfur-spewing gash across the demon's back. The demon screamed, arched his back, and tumbled forward. BaeLee bound him chest to foot before he hit the ground.

The entire battle lasted only a heartbeat. Three beaelzurim lay bound and immobilized. Elric motioned to Lacidar with his hand. Lacidar nodded and pointed to Jaeden, Ry, and BaeLee, who each grabbed one of the demons by the back of the bindings and flew off over the horizon.

The men continued down the path to the tomb, but Timrok's team converged in front of them.

"Leave this tomb alone," each of Timrok's team said to the men.

Their words shot like arrows of glimmering light toward the men, but most of their energy deflected off the men's hard, dark spiritual armor.

Prestus reached with his hand into the Physical Realm and tripped one of the men. The man stumbled forward, bounced off one of the other men, and flopped onto the dirt. The other three laughed and continued forward.

"Get up, you drunken little girl," one of the men called back. "We're going to need your help moving this stone."

The man hobbled back to his feet and said, "Maybe we should leave this tomb alone. I have a bad feeling about it."

"You just can't handle your wine. Go throw up in the bushes and you'll feel fine. Then get over here."

The angels continued to speak to the men, but the men could not hear. The first three men passed through Timrok and reached the tomb. Timrok held his position with his swords sheathed and his arms crossed, looking unconcerned. He pointed to Micah and motioned with his head toward the tomb. Micah stepped forward and put one hand on the left side of the giant wheel-shaped stone.

The stone was designed to roll inside a channel cut into the level ground at the base of the tomb entrance. And though its size was too much for a single man to move it, several men could roll it along its track once it started moving.

The three men gathered on the right side of the stone and prepared to roll it away. One went low and braced his shoulder against the stone. The other two reached above him with both hands on the right edge of the stone.

"Ready," one of the men said. "Go!"

All three pushed with all their might, but the stone didn't move.

"Again . . . go!"

Micah kept his hand on the left side of the stone and smiled at Timrok.

"Get over here and help," one of the three men shouted to the fourth.

"I still don't think—"

"Get over here!"

All four got into position for a more concentrated attempt—one down low with his back against the stone, one above him with his shoulder against the stone, and the other two above leaning in with both hands.

"Ready . . . go!"

Grunts and strained groans. No motion.

"Again . . . go!"

Nothing.

"Again!"

Prestus stepped up and slid his hand between the stone and one of the standing men's hand. The man's hand slipped off the stone, and he fell headlong into the dirt in front of the tomb.

All four men burst out in drunken laughter.

Timrok, with his arms still folded, said, "You will never get in. You should just go home."

The man on the ground said, "I don't think we're getting into this one."

"I don't understand it," one said. "It shouldn't be this hard."

The fourth man said, "I've had enough for tonight. I'm ready to go home."

Another said, "I agree. I don't feel well. Let's go."

Micah took his hand off the stone and stepped aside as the four men stumbled back toward the main path. Their boisterous banter faded into the darkness, and Timrok and Lacidar's teams resumed their posts.

Elric unfurled his wings and glided down toward the tomb. He landed beside Timrok.

Timrok smiled and said, "Not a problem."

Elric shook his head. "It was a feeble attempt. It seemed more like a glory-hungry underling seeking a chance opportunity. This was not a planned mission by the ruling powers."

"Do you expect a more coordinated attack?"

"I am not sure. It does not really make sense for them to steal His body. That would create the appearance that He rose from the dead as He predicted. What they need to do is prevent Him from rising from the dead and have His body still lying here in this tomb after the third day."

Timrok scowled. "Still, we *are* going to guard His body. I would not have some traitorous beast come and dishonor—"

"Yes, yes," Elric said. "But it does make me think . . . "

"What?"

"We need to seal up this tomb in the Physical Realm. We need there to be incontrovertible evidence that His body remained in this tomb until the third day. Evidence that the chief priests will not be able to refute."

"How?"

Elric paused. He smiled. "The Roman army."

"Sir?"

"I have an idea. Maintain your posts. I will return in the morning."

* * *

Burial plus 15 hours

Early the next morning, before Caiaphas and the chief priests and elders had entered the temple complex, Elric translated in the Physical Realm as a small gray lizard. Scrambling along wall edges of the temple grounds, he crept inward toward the main chambers of the high priest. Across courtyards, around stately columns, through open window casements, under thick wooden doors, he crawled. He chuckled to himself at the words of the psalmist, "The lizard you may grasp with the hands, yet it is in kings' palaces."

Small on the earth, but exceedingly wise. We shall see. I'll get into his chambers unnoticed, but will I be able to reach any of the chief priests with the message I need them to hear?

All throughout the courtyards and inner rooms, the spiritual air had the same unsettled stillness he experienced in the garden at the tomb. Quiet, yet tense and unresolved. Very few beaelzurim seemed to be in the temple grounds. And those that were skittered from shadow to shadow with uneasy haste. The elzurim present worked with solemn deliberation. Elric didn't see a single skirmish.

It is a very strange day, indeed.

The few people who had come to the temple early didn't seem to notice the uneasiness in the Middle Realm. The first day of Passover—so much to do, so many errands of life, so many traditions to keep.

Elric slinked in under the door of Caiaphas's chamber unsure of what enemy presence he might find. There would certainly be no men here this early, but what would the enemy be doing? He stopped with only two tiny lizard eyes beyond the threshold and surveyed the room.

No one is here. Where are they all?

Marr's throne sat empty behind Caiaphas's chair. No demon captains. No Asherah. Or Molech or Yarikh.

He continued in and crawled up the wall to an inset alcove where he settled in under a stack of parchment rolls. He had a good view of the whole room and a good place to stay hidden.

Now, I wait.

Within an hour, the first of the elders arrived. They greeted each other with "shalom" and pious head nods but spoke very little. They each wore smug smiles which they tried to hide with pursed lips. And while their eyes sparkled with arrogant satisfaction over the unspoken deed of yesterday, Elric could sense apprehension in their spirits.

Apprehension for the future, but no guilt. These men have no idea what they have done.

More priests arrived, but still no beaelzurim.

This may be easier than I thought. I can speak to them directly without any enemy interference.

With a dozen chief priests and elders gathered, a light rain of light began to fall on each of them in the Middle Realm. Elric jumped, and the scroll just above him crinkled. He ducked low and concentrated on the words of light.

It's the King! He is speaking directly to these men the very word I came to deliver! "Seal the tomb. Ask for a Roman guard. Do not let anyone disturb the body." But will they hear the word?

The words did not deflect off the men's dark spiritual armor. Instead, they smeared across it and made it look wet. Little by little, it soaked in.

The word is entering their spirits. Of course, this word is neither good nor evil, so if it fits within the stronghold of their spirit, their mind can find a place for it.

He smiled, but then felt silly because lizards can't really smile.

The King is always speaking, and He can reach even the darkest of souls.

Caiaphas entered the room. All the men stepped aside and bowed their heads as he passed on his way to his seat.

Still no Marr.

Caiaphas cleared his throat and announced, "It is done. We have silenced the troubler of Israel and we did so without a riot from the people. With Yahweh's help, perhaps now we can return to a state of peace and normalcy. The people are still a danger. Many were deceived by his teachings, and we must be careful not to stoke any residual flames of support for him. Instruct the priests, rabbis, scribes, and lawyers to speak no more of this man. The people will most surely have heard of his fate and will have questions. He was tried, convicted, and legally executed according to our laws. Do not permit any talk beyond this."

One of the priests asked, "What of his disciples?"

Caiaphas thought for a moment, then answered, "Bring them in. We shall question them. If they hold to their allegiance to the Nazarene, we will charge them with crimes against the state and press for . . . appropriate punitive actions."

Another priest said, "Master, you may recall that when that deceiver was still alive, he said, 'After three days I am rising.' I recommend we petition Pilate for a Roman guard to seal the tomb and make it secure until the third day. Otherwise, his disciples may come and steal him, and say to the people, 'He has risen from the dead,' and the last deception will be worse than the first."

Perfect, Elric thought.

The other chief priests all nodded their heads and stroked their beards.

"This is wise counsel," Caiaphas said. "Take a delegation to Pilate immediately."

A group of chief priests shuffled out the door. A few others lingered.

Elric scampered down the wall and out into the open courtyard.

* * *

Burial plus 18 hours

"Here they come," Elric said to Timrok. "That was fast."

Elric and Timrok watched from the hill opposite the tomb as the Roman guard tromped in step down the main path, led by a dozen chief priests from the temple.

"Down here," one of the priests called out. "This way."

The priests turned down the pathway to the tomb where Jesus lay. The Roman guard, a squad of sixteen soldiers, plus their captain followed, with their spears bobbing up and down with the cadence of their steps. They all came to a halt in front of the tomb.

"Open the tomb," the eldest chief priest said to the Roman captain.

Timrok reached for his swords, but Elric put his hand on top of Timrok's hand and shook his head.

The Roman captain motioned to three of the soldiers, who jumped out of ranks and braced themselves against the right side of the stone.

"Push!" the captain commanded.

The stone rolled to the left, just a little, then rotated back. The soldiers pushed again, and it rotated a little farther. After it rolled back, they pushed again in phase with its oscillation, and it broke free. They used its building momentum to roll it the full length of its track. Small stones lying loose in the track crunched as the weight of the large stone crushed them into dust.

The rectangular opening in the rock face lay bare before the men. Inside revealed only darkness.

"Bring a torch," the Roman captain commanded.

A soldier with a prepared torch—a stout stick with oil-soaked linen wrappings on the end—stepped out of the ranks and used a flint stone to light the torch. He handed it to the captain.

The captain ducked through the low opening into the tomb with the torch. Once inside he called out to the priests, "Come and see. Inspect the tomb."

One by one, each of the priests entered the tomb and came out nodding with satisfaction.

The captain came back out and said, "You have each seen with your own eyes and can attest to the fact the body of Jesus of Nazareth, and *only* his body, is currently lying in this tomb."

The priests all nodded. The eldest said, "We attest."

The captain motioned for the three soldiers who rolled the stone away to roll it back. The stone lodged into its closed position, and the captain called out, "Seal the tomb."

The soldiers all broke ranks and went to work. They drove large iron spikes with iron rings on the ends into the stone wall on each side of the rolling stone. Then they secured a thick rope through each of the rings and pulled the rope tight across the face of the stone. Then they affixed a large glob of wet clay to the stone over the rope in two places—on the left and the right side of the stone.

The captain took a metal stamp, the size of a small plate, and pressed it into the clay. He pulled it away, revealing a Roman eagle crest signet. He stamped the second clay seal. He stepped aside and said, "This clay will dry, and the official seal of Rome will be set. No one can enter this tomb without breaking these seals. Do you attest that we have sealed the tomb to your satisfaction?"

"We attest," the chief elder said.

The captain ordered, "Form the guard."

The sixteen soldiers split into four squads of four.

The captain spoke to the priests. "Each shift consists of four sentries. Each squad serves a four-hour shift. Squad one starts their shift now. Squad two will relieve them in four hours; Squad three in eight hours; Squad four in twelve hours. Shifts will continue to rotate until the conclusion of this detail. Pilate has authorized this guard duty for three days. If anything happens to this tomb during this time, the entire guard unit is punishable by death. Do you attest that we have secured the tomb to your satisfaction?"

"We attest."

"Guard, take your posts," the captain called out.

Four soldiers moved to the front of the tomb and stood at attention. The other twelve reformed ranks and marched toward the main path. The captain stepped in behind them.

The priests milled about for a few minutes and sauntered away.

"The tomb is sealed," Timrok said.

Elric smiled. "For now."

50

REGROUP

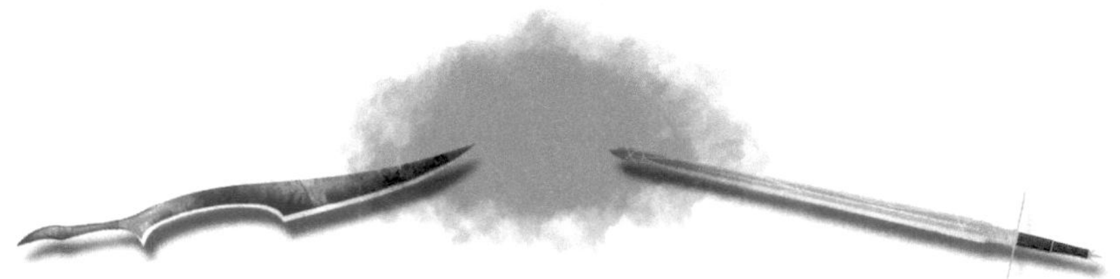

Burial plus 20 hours

Marr landed on the ledge of a rock-faced mountain thousands of miles from any civilization. He eyed the small entrance of the cave and shook his head.

I hate this place. Whenever he wants to lord his preeminence over us, he calls us here. The big cave with the outer court and the inner court. Marr snorted a puff of yellow smoke. *It doesn't make him the true king.*

The last time Marr was here, he had a full entourage. Today, with everything in disarray, he arrived alone. His wings folded away, and he stepped forward. The cave opening reached no higher than his knees, but he proceeded through the stone wall into the immense cavern.

Inside, as expected, thousands of demons crammed into the outer court cavern amid the toothy stalactites and stalagmites. Musty yellow smoke gathered near the ceiling in the Middle Realm, and a thick crust of bat guano carpeted the ground in the Physical Realm. Usually, fights and jostling for position filled this outer court, but not today. The mass of evil spirits pressed shoulder to shoulder, chest to back without moving. No shoving, no elbowing, no intimidating. Silent shock hung heavy on every shoulder, and all eyes stayed fixed on the entrance to the inner chamber.

Across the room, the stalactite fangs hung down at the entrance to the inner court, marking the special place for only the most powerful and privileged. The inner court glowed red, and black smoke belched out and rolled along the floor. A low, continuous tremor pulsed through the walls.

"Hmph," Marr snorted to himself. "I hate this place."

He pushed his way through the horde toward the inner court. No one resisted, but the solid mass had little room to give. Undeterred, he used his sheer might to carve a path through the mass at the expense of the lesser beasts.

He reached the two guards at the entrance. He sneered and wondered if they would give him the appropriate level of honor. Last time they only nodded, and he had to teach them a painful lesson. He waited.

The guards nodded once and motioned for him to enter.

Rage exploded within, and his clenched hands shot straight for their throats.

He stopped halfway. He let his arms drop. *What's the use?* He let out a long stream of yellow smoke through his nostrils.

He stepped into the inner court.

All the usual powers had gathered—generals from all over the world, mighty princes over vast areas. All the commanders. Marr spotted Asherah, Molech, and Yarikh. The air in the inner court had the same blanket of subdued dread that the outer court had, but hushed discussions smoldered throughout the room.

In an instant, the room became silent as death. Every eye turned toward Marr. Hateful grimaces contorted every face.

They blame me. How was I to know it was the King's intent to provide the sacrificial Lamb? Was it not always our goal to destroy Him?

Normally, Marr would force his way to the front to a place of honor near the throne. Instead, he slid in and stiffened his back against the back wall. He lifted his chin, gritted his teeth, and stared at the black throne elevated at the front of the court. The spiritual air may have felt devoid of power and purpose, but the throne still radiated with energy, glowing red with bolts of fiery lightning flashing. More generals and commanders arrived, and Marr could still feel the burning eyes of everyone locked onto him. He focused on the throne without blinking.

Hurry up. Let us be done with this.

He didn't have to wait long. A massive explosion rocked the court. Smoke obscured the throne. It lingered a moment, then sank to the ground and revealed Satan sitting on the throne—slouched back with his arms draped over the armrests. The smoke finally cleared away, and Satan sat up. The room became heavy with anticipation.

"As you know," Satan began, "the flesh of the Son of Man has been killed." His voice rumbled low like the reverberations of a seething volcano. "And it is true that the King placed upon Him the curse of the law and made Him to be His sacrificial Lamb. His sacrifice satisfies the justice of the King and provides an agency for men to obtain right standing before Him. It is also true that, since the Lamb is of the seed of Adam, He has taken back the authority to rule on earth, which was given me by Adam."

The weight of his words settled on the already somber gathering and smothered everyone with despair.

"However," he continued, "*I* still have power over death and the grave. *And* the spirit of the Son of Man is presently in Sheol. In order for Him to take possession of His inheritance, He must break free of Sheol and resurrect His body—which He has foretold He would do on the third day."

The assembly fidgeted in place and shot terrified glances to each other.

Satan stood. His voice changed from low and solemn to forceful and commanding. "Which we are going to spoil. We need only to prevent His resurrection, and the kingdom will be ours. His sacrifice will have been for nothing. Our victory will nullify His rights as redeemer. And, with part of the Godhead trapped in Sheol, I will be able to overthrow the Throne and ascend the mount of assembly in the recesses of the north."

The gathering took in a collective breath of hope.

"I call every beaelzur warrior to this cause. Gather every warrior from the ends of the earth, from the greatest to the least. We shall stack up in layers around Sheol and create an impenetrable barrier. If He is to escape the bonds of death, He will have to come through *all* of us. I will personally guard His body and make sure He is not able to take it up again. He may think He has won a significant victory, but the battle is not done. We still have the power to reign victorious."

The assembly let out a collective breath of resolve.

"But be sure of this—if you fail, all our destinies are forever sealed."

The assembly couldn't breathe.

"Go now. We have two days to get into position."

* * *

Burial plus 24 hours

The day after the unspeakable turn of events, the disciple Matthew came around the corner and scurried up the street past the plaster-covered faces of the buildings lining the street in Jerusalem. He stayed on the west side of the street where the buildings and the occasional awning cast a long shadow from the waning evening sun. Careful not to disrupt the other foot traffic, he weaved his way through while shooting uneasy glances over his shoulder.

He reached a single-story home with a white painted wooden door. The window shudders had all been bolted shut. He rapped on the door with an impatient beat and stared back toward the end of the street. The door cracked open. Matthew spoke to someone inside, never taking his eyes off the street. The door opened more, and he slipped in.

A moment later, a squad of four Roman soldiers marched around the corner and headed up the street. One of the soldiers pointed toward the first building on the left, and the squad approached its front entrance. The soldier pounded on the door. As soon as the door opened, the soldier barged in sword first, followed by the other three brutes. Minutes later, all four reemerged and moved to the next building.

One by one, the squad worked their way up the street, forcing their way through every door and disregarding angry protests from the occupants. Each stop lasted only a few minutes, and soon they had covered half the street. The soldiers turned their backs to the irate woman shouting curses through the doorway of their last stop, and they proceeded on to their left. The next stop—a single-story building with a white painted door on the west side of the street. With professional military efficiency, they moved toward—

Crash!

Across the street, from a side alley, a man came flailing out backward, landing on top of a stack of empty wooden bird cages. His fall busted the cages into splinters and sent dust and broken slats of wood flying into the street. An instant later, a second man emerged from the alley with another wooden cage raised high above his head. He leapt forward and brought the cage crashing down on the first man. The two wrestled in the dirt, writhing and rolling, shouting, and kicking up a large cloud of dust.

The head soldier shook his head and pointed his sword at the two combatants. "Go break it up."

The squad ran across the street. Two soldiers pulled one of the men off the other and stood him up with his arms pinned behind his back. The third soldier pulled the second man up and had to wrap his arm around the man's neck in a chokehold to keep him from attacking the other.

The senior soldier stood between the two with his sword drawn. "What is going on here?" he demanded.

Neither man said a word.

"Will you not answer?" the soldier growled. He lifted his sword toward the first man. "I can be very persuasive." He edged his blade closer to the man's neck.

"He started it!" the man blurted out.

The other man shouted back, "No, he started it! He was the one—"

"Stop!" the soldier shouted. "I do not care about your petty squabble. We have work to do. But if you continue to disturb the peace, I will have to arrest you and bring you to the jail. Is this what you wish?"

"No," one man answered in a sheepish voice.

"No," said the second man.

"My men are going to release you now, and you will not start fighting again, right?"

"Right."

"Right."

The ranking soldier motioned to the others, and they let the men loose.

"What are your names?" the soldier asked.

"I am Jessik," the first man answered, wiping blood from his lip.

"Kaylar," the second man said.

"Jessik and Kaylar, you are fortunate that you are getting only a warning today. If we did not have other pressing matters, you would surely spend the night in jail."

Jessik and Kaylar nodded.

"You are not from Galilee, are you?" the soldier asked.

"No."

"Do you know any men from Galilee who were followers of Jesus of Nazareth?"

"Who?"

"Surely you have heard of him."

"We are not from around here."

"Very well, go about your business. No more disturbing the peace."

The soldiers turned back to the west side of the street. "Which house was next?" the lead soldier asked.

"I'm not sure," a soldier answered. "They all look the same."

"Sir!" one of the soldiers said. "Look! Where did Jessik and Kaylar go? They were just here."

He looked back toward the alley and then up and down the street. "I don't know. It does not matter. We have work to do. Did we check this house with the white door?"

"I think so."

"I don't know for certain, but something inside says 'yes.'"

"It feels like we did."

The lead soldier took a decisive step forward. "Then we move to the next. Let's go, it is already getting dark."

51

FORTIFIED

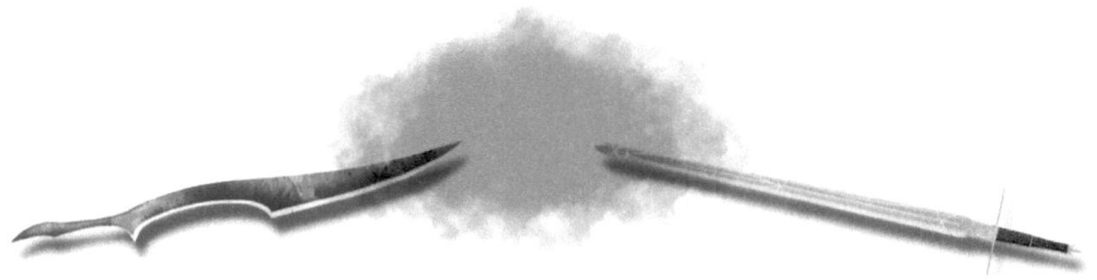

Burial plus 2 days

Saturday morning, in the Middle Realm, a thin, black mist rolled in across Elric's feet.

Timrok, who stood next to Elric in front of the sealed tomb, swished his foot through the mist. "It appears the enemy is coming with a large army."

Elric nodded. "It is not surprising." He lifted his wings and leapt to the top of the hill opposite the tomb. Timrok followed. The eerie black mist covered the ground for as far as he could see, and it all crept inward toward the tomb.

"If this mist is any indication," Elric said, "it will be the largest contingent we have ever seen."

Timrok rested his hands on his sword handles. "Are we going to fight?"

Elric looked at Timrok with raised eyebrows. "Do I hear apprehension in your voice?"

"No!" Timrok cleared his throat. "No, never. I would stand against ten thousand to protect the King and His honor. But . . . " he glanced down toward the tomb. "With the King's flesh lying dead in the tomb and His Spirit in Sheol, I must admit that our chances of victory are . . . "

Elric put his hand on Timrok's shoulder. "I know." He looked toward the sky. "I have received no direction. Until we do, we follow our last orders—protect the tomb."

Timrok nodded.

They watched the mist roll in. Silent and sinister, thick and threatening.

"Sir!" Timrok said, pointing toward the horizon.

"I see them." Elric scanned all the way around. "They approach from every direction."

Thousands. Ten thousands of thousands. Marching hordes of demons too numerous to count.

"And they are moving fast," Timrok said. "We do not have long."

Elric pulled his sword and gripped it hard. Already, the sound of tromping feet began to rise in the Middle Realm.

"There are more," Elric said pointing toward the sky.

A boiling cloud of blackness filled the sky just above the horizon.

"They are moving even faster," Timrok said. His two swords came out of their sheaths.

"Those are the chief powers," Elric said. "I suspect Satan is among them."

The rumble of the advancing horde vibrated up through the spiritual ground. The roar of countless wings shook the air like a hurricane gale.

"Have you ever seen so many?" Timrok shouted.

"Not since the Rebellion."

"Surely the King is sending reinforcements. We will not stand long before such an army."

"I don't—" Elric stopped. He pointed upward. "Look!"

A blazing white light came shooting straight down like a fiery meteor. In an instant, it reached Elric and Timrok, and it exploded in a brilliant flash.

Elric blinked hard and then squinted through the receding glare. "Master Gabriel!" he shouted. "Do you bring reinforcements?"

Even with his booming voice, Gabriel had to shout over the rising tumult. "On the contrary. I am here to see that you and your team get out. Come quickly!"

Elric flashed a signal with his sword and sounded a desperate blast on his war trumpet.

A canopy of darkness overshadowed them as they took to the sky. Lacidar and his team, Timrok and his team, and Elric all followed Gabriel as fast as their frantic wings would carry them.

Gabriel called back, "Head to the temple! Stay low!" With his massive blade, he decimated a dozen beaelzur captains who had descended low enough to block their path. Several demon commanders suffered the same fate.

Below, on the ground, the demon horde seemed too intent on their destination to care about the escaping band of angels.

It felt to Elric like an eternity as they squeezed between the layers of enemy ranks and blazed through the hole burrowed in the sky by Gabriel, but in reality it took only a few heartbeats to travel less than a mile to the temple complex. They reached the outer wall, flew into the inner court, and landed on the steps leading into the main temple.

The horde of demons on the ground diverted around the temple complex, but the canopy of darkness continued to boil overhead.

"We will be safe here," Gabriel said. "They are not interested in the temple today."

Elric and the team watched with mouths hanging open. It reminded Elric of the time the sea of enemy forces washed over them on their way back from Egypt—a glowing red wave amid black clouds with crimson lightning and fire, with thousands of contorted faces and raging eyes, caught up in the furious flurry.

The influx of enemy warriors lasted several minutes, and then the sky above the temple became clear.

"Come," Gabriel said. "Let us witness this."

The team, lead by Gabriel, flew to the top of the outer court wall on the western side. They spread out in a single line along the outer edge and looked out beyond the city walls toward the tomb. There a writhing mass of darkness, like an enraged mound of ants, overwhelmed the area on the ground. Above, a giant tornado of evil swirled.

"There are so many," Elric said.

"It is every fallen one who is not currently in the abyss," Gabriel said. "Satan has summoned them all."

"The King's body!" Timrok moaned.

Gabriel smiled. "Fear not. They cannot touch Him. Even if they wanted to—which they do not. It is not their intent to spoil His body."

"They need His body to be there after three days," Elric said.

"True," Gabriel said. "They are here to try to keep Him trapped in Sheol and prevent His resurrection."

"Surely, that is not possible," Lacidar said.

"No, of course not," Gabriel answered. "He is the ever-living self-existent One. No created thing could ever take life from the eternal One who created it."

"And yet, they try," Elric said. "From the day of the Rebellion, I have never understood this."

Gabriel shook his head. "Pride creates a blindness that we cannot comprehend."

"Look," Timrok said. "Something is happening."

The mound of darkness began sinking into the ground.

"They are descending into the lower parts of the earth," Gabriel said. "There they plan to surround Sheol and create an impassable barrier."

The dark mass on the ground disappeared. Then the mighty ones swirling in the air came down and descended through the ground. Soon every beaelzurim had vanished below the surface.

Then, from the center of the confluence, directly above the tomb, Satan arose. Initially no more than twenty feet high, he expanded his frame until he towered two hundred feet above the ground. He extended all four cherub wings as his frame increased. Then he released a deafening, spine-chilling screech, followed by an earth-rattling low roar. Lightning and fire shot out from all over his body, and thick black smoke settled around his feet.

"Very impressive," Gabriel said. "But pride comes before the fall. Tomorrow the King shall put all these under His feet. I recommend we all stay right here and witness it."

Lacidar said, "Sir, Jenli, his team, and Zaben's team are out with the disciples. Permit me to retrieve them also."

"Yes, of course," Gabriel said. "The disciples are safe for the night."

"Thank you," Elric said to Lacidar.

52

MY PEOPLE

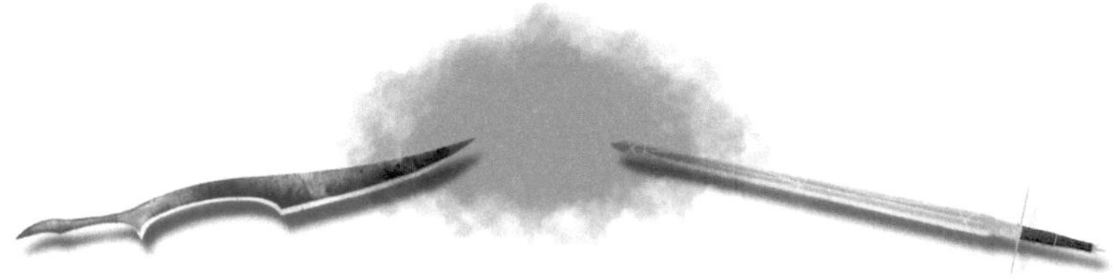

Burial plus 2 days

Saturday afternoon, Daniel approached a small house on the outskirts of Nazareth—close enough to town to be considered Nazareth, but far enough out to have easy access to pasture lands for sheep.

I think this is the place. It's been so long. The house looks smaller than I remember.

He didn't see any activity around the house—no workers, no Jesse. A large pen to the left of the house held two dozen sheep.

I don't remember this pen. Maybe this isn't the right house.

Something in his gut prodded him forward. This was the right house. He knew it was. *And there's the big olive tree in the back yard, gnarled and full of memories. I know that tree.*

He took a step forward, then stopped. The last words of his father plowed through his mind, *"From this day forward, you are no longer my son. You are dead to me."* The words echoed again, *"You are dead to me. You are dead to me."* Every word had been branded onto his heart and rehearsed a thousand times. Fear paralyzed him.

Maybe this isn't a good idea.

Again, something deep inside wouldn't let him walk away. The fear weakened, and a glimmer of peace took its place.

I have to do this. Jesus told me to go home to my people. These are my people. If Father rejects me, he rejects me. But at least I will have tried.

"Here we go," he spoke aloud. He stepped up to the door, paused another moment, then knocked.

An old woman, small and frail, opened the door.

Daniel squinted as he examined her, looking for familiar features.

It kind of looks like her, but it's been so long, and she's changed so much.

"Ruth?" Daniel said. "Ima?"

The old lady squinted back. "Daniel?"

Daniel nodded.

"Daniel? Is it really you?" She held her hand over her heart and heaved deep breaths. "Good heavens, it is you!" She broke down into uncontrollable sobbing and launched herself toward him. She wrapped her arms around him so tightly he could hardly breathe.

How does one so small have such strength?

She didn't let go and kept muttering between sobs, "I can't believe it's you. It's a miracle. It's a miracle. My Daniel is alive. You're really here."

After an eternity of clutching and blubbering, Ruth composed herself and wiped her eyes. "Come in! Come in!"

The place seemed foreign, yet somehow familiar—like the memory of a dream too distant to recall, yet too real to forget.

An entire lifetime happened here without me.

The large dinner table looked familiar. And the fireplace.

"Where is Father?" Daniel asked. "Is he still alive?"

Ruth cleared her throat. "Yes, yes. But he is not as strong as he used to be. He is in bed in the back room. He is . . . full of years."

"Can I see him? I mean, will he be willing to see me?"

"I am sure he will receive you, but he may not *see* you very well. His eyes are dim."

The front door latch rattled, and the door swung open. A rugged, weathered-looking man in his early fifties stepped in. He closed the door and stood at the threshold, staring at Daniel.

"Oh good," Ruth said, "it's Jesse. Jesse comes by every Sabbath after synagogue. He and his wife have a nice place in town. They have four children—well, they're not really children anymore. He has been running the family business for many years now. Jesse, it's Daniel. You remember Daniel?"

"Daniel," Jesse said.

"Jesse," Daniel answered.

This was not a good idea. I should go.

"Come, dear," Ruth said. "Let's go see your father."

Ruth led the way to the back room with spry shuffling steps. Daniel followed close. Jesse came along a step behind.

At the doorway, Jesse whispered to Daniel, "Why are you here?"

Daniel dropped his gaze to the floor, then over at the bed. Without answering, he moved toward the bed.

"Who is it?" Jeremiah asked in a raspy voice. "I thought I heard a voice out there I don't recognize."

Ruth moved a chair next to the bed. Daniel sat down.

"It's Daniel," Ruth said. "Daniel has come home."

"Daniel?" Jeremiah said. "Is it true?"

Daniel took Jeremiah's hand into his and said, "It is true, Father. It's me, Daniel."

"My son, I thought I would never see you again."

"It has been a long time," Daniel said. "At least twenty years."

Jeremiah lifted his chin. "Twenty-four years, seven months."

Jesse, from the corner of the room with his arms crossed, said, "Why are you here?"

"Jesse!" Ruth scolded.

Jesse pressed. "Have you come to bring more shame to your father? Have you not caused enough pain?"

"Jesse!"

"It's all right, Ima," Daniel said. "Jesse is right. I have come to seek forgiveness. Forgiveness from you, Father." He turned back toward Jesse. "And forgiveness from you."

Jesse still held his arms crossed.

"I have come to tell you all about the great things God has done for me. If you will hear me."

Jeremiah propped himself up in the bed to a sitting position and said, "Tell us. We want to hear your story."

"It all started after Levi was killed," Daniel began.

Jeremiah's face twisted with pain. "That was a hard day for all of us."

"Something happened to me. It was probably my own fault because I was seeking something I didn't understand. But I became possessed by an evil spirit."

"An evil spirit?" Jesse said. "A demon?"

"I didn't know what it was. At first, I thought it was the spirit of Levi. He would talk to me and tell me things. I entered a very dark time. My mind was filled with hate and guilt and murder. And there were times when it took control, and I did things without knowing I was doing them. Bad things. I would wake up covered in blood."

Heavy silence filled the room.

"You were right, Father, for putting me out. If I had stayed, I might have done terrible things . . .to you." His gaze dropped to the floor. "To all of you."

"Where did you go? How did you live?" Ruth asked.

"I went to the Sea of Galilee. I mostly stole what I needed. And I was always getting into fights. Eventually, I did get a job as a fisherman. But I would still wake up with blood all over me."

"Have you killed a man?" Jeremiah asked.

"I don't know—I never did while I was aware. I would wake up and see the blood and I would run. I had to keep moving around. I could never stay in one place very long. I ended up on the other side of the lake and even tended swine for a while."

Jesse covered his mouth and shook his head.

"But then, one day in Capernaum, I was mostly passed out from wine. I drank a lot of wine to try to drown all my pain and loneliness. And Jesus, from Nazareth, was in town. With a single word, He commanded the demon to come out of me, and it did! For the first time in as long as I can remember, I was free from all the dark and evil that was tormenting me."

"Jesus, Joseph and Mary's son?" Jesse said. "We heard that he had developed a following and was teaching and doing miracles. He came here to Nazareth, but we didn't see anything miraculous."

"All I know is that whatever had a hold of me was gone," Daniel said. "And Jesus was the one who set me free. I continued fishing on the other side of the lake, and I was doing really well. Then, one day, the demon returned and brought a thousand more with it. I don't remember much after that. The next thing I knew, I was living amongst the tombs outside Gergesa without any clothes and eating raw pig flesh."

Ruth gasped.

"I did unspeakable things—to others and to myself. Look." He pulled back his sleeves to reveal horrible, raised scars all over his forearms.

"Oh, dear Lord," Ruth panted. She looked away.

Jeremiah felt Daniel's arm with his fingers and grimaced.

"And see my back," Daniel said. He raised his tunic. Ten nasty triangular-shaped scars covered his back. "These are from Roman spears. Apparently, I broke metal chains to escape that time. The demons are very powerful."

Jesse said, "But you obviously got free from them?"

"One day, Jesus showed up on the shore. I don't know for sure, but I think He came just for me. He commanded all the demons to come out and to leave me alone. They did. I have been free ever since."

"That's amazing," Jesse said.

"And there is more," Daniel said. "He healed my ear. I can hear out of my right ear! You know that I was deaf. He healed me. He made me whole."

Jeremiah put his hands on his cheeks and shook his head. "He delivers the oppressed and gives hearing to the deaf. Could Jesus actually be—"

"The Messiah!" Daniel blurted out. "I think He is. He has also given sight to the blind and raised people from the dead. I believe He is the Promised One."

"The Messiah," Jesse said.

"I wanted to join Him, to become one of His followers. Levi and I always talked about joining the Messiah's army and fighting with Him to deliver Israel. But He said it was not my time. He told me to go home to my people and tell them all the great things God has done for me. I went all over the Decapolis and told my story. But eventually I realized that I needed to come *home*. I needed to tell you that I am a different person and that I hope you can forgive me for all the pain I caused you."

"My son, my son," Jeremiah said. "You *are* forgiven. And you have brought peace and joy to this old gray head. I can rest with my fathers in peace now. My son has come home."

"Jesse?" Daniel said, looking back to his brother.

"Yes, my brother. Welcome home. I think *I* would like to see this Jesus and hear His teachings."

Ruth had no words. Only quiet sobbing and joy-filled tears.

A commotion outside interrupted the happy moment—horse hooves and people's voices.

"What is going on out there?" Jeremiah asked.

Jesse led the way out. Daniel followed. They both went outside while Ruth stood at the threshold. A small crowd had gathered outside the city gate, and a single rider maneuvered a strutting stallion.

"It looks like a messenger," Jesse said. "It must be important news. Come on."

Jesse and Daniel ran out to the crowd. The rider galloped off to another destination.

"What is it?" Jesse said as they approached. "What word does he bring?"

The group looked shocked. No one could answer.

"Tell us!" Jesse said.

"Jesus has been killed," one of the townspeople said. "He was crucified two days ago by the Romans in Jerusalem."

"No!" Daniel cried out. He fell to his knees. "No, this can't be true! This isn't supposed to happen!"

Back in the house, they gathered again in the room with Jeremiah. Daniel sat in the chair bent over with his face buried in his hands. Ruth stroked his back.

"I can't believe this is happening," Daniel cried. "He was supposed to be the Messiah. I was going to join Him."

"Maybe the Romans feared an insurrection," Jesse said. "They are always quick to put down uprisings."

"But He wasn't even raising an army yet. It doesn't make sense."

In a motherly tone, Ruth said, "It's probably good that you *weren't* with him. You could have been crucified too. Remember, they crucified two thousand men when they defeated the insurrection at Sepphoris."

"Were any others executed?" Jeremiah asked.

Jesse shrugged. "I don't think so. The rider only mentioned Jesus."

Daniel stood up and paced. "I have to go to Jerusalem. I have to find out what happened. None of this makes sense. I know the power of God was working in Him. I know what He did for me. He has to be the Messiah. And the Messiah will deliver Israel. I have to go."

"There is nothing you can do," Jesse said.

"I don't care. I have to go."

"Dear," Ruth said, "it is already getting late. Have supper with us and spend the night. It will be better if you start the trip in the morning. We'll help you with provisions."

Daniel wiped his eyes. "Yes, Ima. But tomorrow I need to go find answers."

53

RESURRECTION

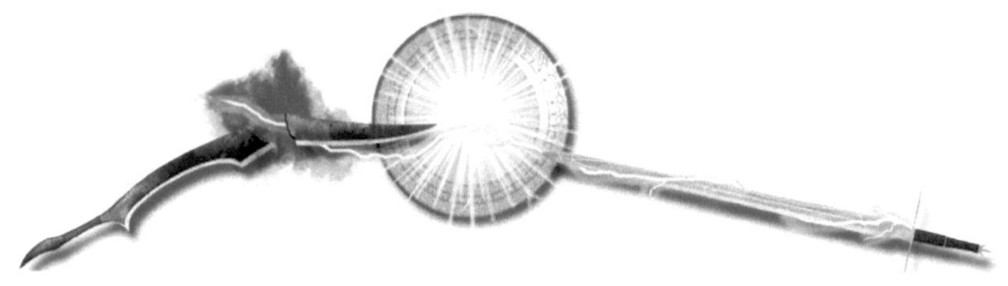

Burial plus 3 days

The moon, only three days waning from its fullness at Passover, lit up the city of Jerusalem and the countryside outside the city walls. Elric stood next to Gabriel on the outer temple court wall and smiled at the midnight blue landscape. Beside him, his faithful lieutenants and their brave teams formed a crisp line along the stone balustrade. The moonglow shown on their cheeks, and their eyes all had their own glow of wonder and excitement. All the way down the line, every familiar face brought a memory of valor, honor, and service.

Yes, the night is strangely quiet. And yes, the King's body lay alone in a tomb. And yes, every vile demon on the planet has the King's spirit surrounded in Sheol. But none of these valiant warriors doubt the outcome of the coming battle. It has been an honor to have served with them.

And then another memory drifted through his mind. *Zaben.*

Tears welled up in his eyes. He wiped his eyes with his sleeves. *Zaben, how could you—*

"Master Gabriel," Jenli said, breaking the silence. "We saw all the sin and curses of the law of every man from all time enter the Son of Man. Does that mean every man's sin is atoned for once for all?"

"It does," Gabriel answered.

"So then," Jenli said, "every man will be saved?"

"The gift is available. But not every man will receive it. Remember when Moses lifted the bronze serpent on the pole in the wilderness—those bitten by the vipers who believed and looked upon the bronze serpent lived. But there were those who chose not to believe and perished."

Lacidar said, "Surely all men will want to receive forgiveness."

Gabriel shook his head. "Many perished from the serpents' venom."

Silence fell over the group again, and they gazed back out over the moonlit landscape.

"Master Gabriel," Elric said, "There was a time, early in His ministry, when the Lord had curious words for the rabbi Nicodemus. We have pondered them and have yet to come to a full understanding."

Jenli, Timrok, and Lacidar turned their attention away from the tomb in the distance and looked at Gabriel.

Elric continued. "The Lord said, 'You must be born again.' Clearly, He spoke of a rebirth of the spirit. But we have not seen this. Not even the closest disciples have reborn spirits. How can a man bring to life that which is dead?"

Gabriel laughed. "The revelation of the mystery is not yet complete. His birth, His ministry, His death—these were all just the beginning. The mystery yet to be revealed is so beyond comprehension that you could not believe it if it were told you."

Jenli muttered under his breath, "I could believe."

Gabriel laughed. "You will see very soon."

Silence returned. The line of warriors on the outer court wall stood and waited for hours.

Four hours before sunrise, the skies in the Middle Realm began to stir. Tiny lights appeared. Some descended to the ground. Some remained hovering in mid-heaven. All approached Jerusalem and surrounded the tomb. Shining elzurim landed on the outer temple court wall behind Elric's team. More landed behind them on the inner court walls. Within an hour, the tops of the temple walls were packed with elzurim ten deep. Angelic warriors covered the blue-shadowed land around the tomb for as far as Elric could see. And a complete canopy of shimmering white wings filled the sky. All silent, all tense with anticipation. The angels had gathered.

At the center, on the ground above the tomb, Satan continued to seethe and roar and spew fire and shoot red lightning bolts in every direction.

"Master Gabriel," Timrok said, "what is our signal to begin the battle?"

Gabriel laughed. "There is no battle. Simply watch our victorious King."

* * *

Two hours before dawn.

The spiritual ground trembled. All around the tomb glowed with a faint blue light. Tiny shafts of light sprouted and rose ten feet into the air.

"Here He comes," Gabriel said.

Satan, still towering two hundred feet over the tomb, extended all four wings, braced his feet, and raised his monstrous sword.

A moment of tense silence gripped the Middle Realm.

Shhh-boom! An explosion like Elric had never seen shook the spiritual world.

A fireball of light brighter than a thousand suns blinded everything.

A shockwave slammed into Elric's face, nearly knocking him over backward.

An earthquake shook the Physical Realm.

Elric peeked through the slits between his fingers covering his eyes. Still too bright to see. He peeked to the side. Even Gabriel had his eyes covered. He glanced between his fingers again. The light receded enough to squint into the blaze.

Shhooop!

The fireball imploded down to the size of man, centered at the tomb, shining only as bright as ten suns. Proceeding out of the ball of light—millions of individual shafts of light, like straight, thin filaments of hair extended a hundred feet into the air in all directions. And at the end of each filament—Elric squinted and focused hard— tiny blobs of darkness skewered by the shafts of light.

Are those? Yes! They are!

Every evil spirit, no bigger than a large cockroach, hung suspended in the air at the end of each shaft of light.

Elric looked for Satan. *There! Just above the tomb.*

Another dark blob at the end of a skewer, no larger than a rat—immobilized and insignificant.

And then—motion. From everywhere around the tomb, more lights emerged from the ground. Their brightness paled next the King. Elric looked close.

"Those are people!" he said out loud.

Gabriel said, "Released captives from Sheol. The righteous with new bodies. The first fruits ready for entrance into the King's Realm."

The mass of resurrected people fanned out and formed a ring around Jerusalem. In the Middle Realm, the ring stretched for hundreds of miles. In the Physical Realm, it equated to the perimeter of the wall around Jerusalem. The ring parted, forming a corridor in the middle, with a hundred people deep on each side. The corridor started at the tomb, wrapped around the city, passed through the eastern gate, and ended at the temple.

From over the horizon, another display of lights approached. Elric squinted at the incoming mass. *It looks like . . . a large squadron of elzurim.* Thousands, flying low and fast and headed toward the temple. The group arrived over Jerusalem in just a few moments and then passed over the outer court walls. One of them broke away and landed next to Elric.

"Lorr! You're free!" Elric shouted.

"Captain! It is so—"

Elric threw his arms around Lorr, lifted him off the ground, and spun in circles. The two laughed while all those around them patted Lorr's back in turn as they spun. Elric set Lorr back on the ground and held his shoulders while he looked into his eyes. Both had tears streaming down their faces.

Two more angels landed on the wall nearby and Elric heard Jenli shout, "Deenr! Luxor!"

Elric laughed again and turned to Gabriel. "The King has freed *all* the captives!"

Kaablamm!

Elric jumped and turned toward the noise from the tomb. All the demons who were suspended in air now formed a long line on the ground. A single shaft of light, attached to shackles of light bound around their wrists, still tethered each of them to the ball of light at the tomb. They stood on their feet, but all their sizes remained tiny and trivial. Satan sulked at the head of the line. The remainder crowded shoulder to shoulder fifty demons wide and a mile long.

Gabriel smiled and said, "Come. The assembly is formed, and it is time to move the stone."

With Gabriel leading, Elric and the whole team glided over Jerusalem toward the tomb.

54

VICTORY

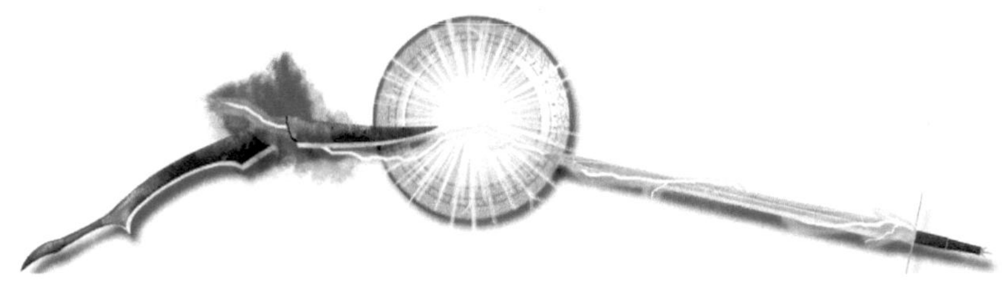

Resurrection: 4:00 a.m.

Gabriel and Elric landed in front of the tomb. The lieutenants formed a line one step behind them, and the team assembled in formation one step behind the lieutenants. Light blazed from within the tomb as though no stone separated them from the risen King within.

In the Physical Realm, four Roman soldiers stood guard with their spears resting against their shoulders. They appeared edgy to Elric. *They felt the earthquake. And though their eyes cannot see, they surely can sense something happening in the Middle Realm.*

Gabriel turned to Elric and smiled. He wrapped his wings around his body and translated into the Physical Realm. He took the form of a man, twelve feet tall. His appearance was like lightning, and his clothing as white as snow. The guards shook from fear of him.

They leveled their spears toward him but backed away, trembling and looking for somewhere to run.

Gabriel turned toward the tomb and stepped up to the great round stone at the entrance. With one hand on the top edge of the stone, he rolled it away with ease. The clay seals broke away, and the rope snapped like brittle twine. Gabriel translated back into the Middle Realm.

Light blasted out of the tomb entrance in the Physical Realm, and the instant it hit the Roman soldiers, they fell backward and became like dead men.

And then, from the middle of all the light, Jesus appeared through the entrance and stepped into the open air.

Gabriel, Elric, and all of the team fell prostrate with their faces to the ground.

"Rise," Jesus said, "my good and faithful servants."

Elric stood. His team behind him did also, but all Elric's attention focused on the King. He had the form of a man. Flesh, yet spirit. Physical, yet eternal. The firstborn of humanity to put on immortality.

He is amazing.

Jesus announced in a loud voice, "*This* is the day which the Lord has made."

Elric and the team shouted back in unison, "Let us rejoice and be glad in it!"

"Come," Jesus said. "Follow me." He walked away from the tomb and headed toward the corridor of people leading around Jerusalem. Gabriel marched behind Him. Elric marched behind Gabriel. The lieutenants and warriors marched in step behind him.

Still emanating from the light shining from the King, millions of thin filaments of light trailed behind. The filaments passed through Elric as though he wasn't there. He followed the lines back with his eyes. Just behind his team's formation, a tight line pulled on the shackles around Satan's wrists, and he trudged forward.

This is a victory march!

The entire mass of defeated demons plodded forward. Still no larger than bugs, they looked pathetic and powerless.

These are the ones who have troubled the earth?

Elric smiled and looked forward. All the people forming the corridor for as far as he could see lifted hands into the air and cheered a continuous roar of joy and praise. Behind the wall of people, angels on the ground tilted their trumpets upward and blasted a triumphant fanfare. The canopy of angels in the sky shouted and sang. The deafening roar of it all thumped against Elric's chest.

The King advanced through the lane, and the people on both sides fell to their faces as He passed. After He passed, the people leapt back up and continued to cheer. The defeated enemy had to pass through the lane, but the people wasted no energy jeering or mocking them. They only shouted praises to the King and rejoiced for their freedom.

For two hours the procession made its way around Jerusalem.

Finally, the King entered the city through the eastern gate, and the sound of the cheering doubled. All the elzurim on the temple court walls shouted and shook their swords in the air. The voices of the giant senturim stationed around the temple rolled like thunder and shook the spiritual ground.

The King entered the temple gate. All the angels in and around the temple complex fell to their faces in silence. The senturim lay prostrate.

Jesus climbed the steps to the main temple. He turned around with His back to the temple entrance. The entire Middle Realm fell silent. The Physical Realm faded away before Elric's eyes, and all he could see was the King standing before a great temple of light. All the defeated enemy crammed together in front of Him at the bottom of the shining steps. Around them, the freed captives. Around them, myriads of angels stacked from the ground to the overarching canopy above. No one moved or made a sound.

Jesus pinched one filament of light between His fingers and pulled on it. Satan stumbled forward. Jesus drew Satan all the way up the steps until he stood trembling before Him. Jesus put His foot on Satan like a man might step on a rat. He pressed down just hard enough to drive Satan to the ground.

"Today," Jesus announced, "all authority has been given me in heaven and on earth." His booming voice shook the spiritual ground. "The price for sin has been paid in my blood, and I have purchased legal rights for the sons of Adam. The authority to rule and reign on the earth, which Adam forfeited to Satan, has been redeemed. The enemy is defeated, and his fate is forever sealed."

The whole Middle Realm erupted in cheers and shouts of joy.

Jesus raised His hand, and everyone became quiet.

"But today is not the end of days. That day is still reserved in the deep counsel of the Father. Instead, today is the beginning of days. Today I give my authority to men—to those who call upon my name. Just as the enemy is now below my feet, so the enemy is below the feet of my people. I will write my word upon their hearts as foretold by my prophets, and they will know me. Just as the Father and I are one, so I and my people will be one. Together we will establish the Father's kingdom on earth."

Jesus motioned with His hand, and all the shafts of light binding the enemy disappeared. He lifted His foot off Satan's head. "Go!" He shouted. "Be gone from my presence. But know this—your power is broken, and your judgment is sure."

Like a swarm of wild locusts, the demons took off and disappeared over the horizon.

"Victory!" Jesus shouted. "Victory!"

All the angels in the canopy overhead shouted, "Victory! Victory!" and shot across the sky in every direction in a breathtaking light spectacle that left Elric shaking his head.

To the angels on the ground, Jesus commanded, "Take these first fruits to the house of my Father."

One by one, pairs of angels and resurrected people shot up into the sky and disappeared. As they went, Jesus shouted, "Enter into the joy of the Lord." After several minutes, Elric realized that he and his team were the last ones left, along with Gabriel, before the King.

Jesus came down the steps and stopped in front of Gabriel and Elric. He looked past Elric and said to the lieutenants, "Your work is not yet complete. My brothers and sisters, the disciples, are still in danger. The enemy will be back and will seek to destroy them. These men and women do not yet understand all that has been accomplished and who they are in me. Until they do and are endued with the power of the Spirit, they are vulnerable. Go and protect them. Escape to Galilee. It will be safer for them there during these next days. We will bring them back to Jerusalem before Pentecost in fifty days."

Timrok, Jenli, and Lacidar did a brisk about face. They nodded to their teams and raised their wings. In an instant, the whole team disappeared over the temple wall.

Jesus looked to the east. The sun had not yet risen, but the morning light would be turning the horizon red soon. He looked back to Gabriel and Elric and said, "Meet me at the tomb in the garden. I have an appointment there and work for you to do."

Jesus disappeared.

Elric raised his eyebrows. "This new body can translate across space."

Gabriel laughed and unfurled his wings. "I enjoy the flight."

55

THE GARDEN TOMB

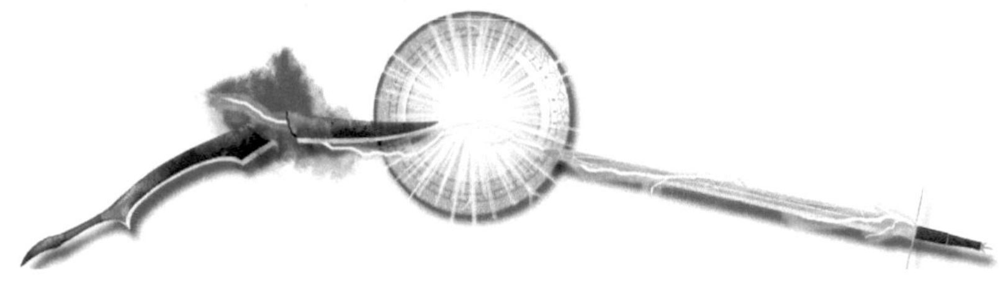

Resurrection: 6:00 a.m.

Elric and Gabriel glided to a landing in front of the tomb. Their feet touched down, and their wings folded away. Jesus was already there in the Middle Realm, standing beside three of the Roman soldiers.

The fourth soldier emerged from the tomb with a torch. Shaking his head he said, "It's empty. Nothing but linen wrappings, folded and sitting where the body should be. And the facecloth folded up in a place by itself."

"What are we going to do?" one of the soldiers said with a crackling voice.

"We have to go tell the captain of the guard."

"We'll be executed! We and the other twelve in the guard."

"We have no choice. First of all, it is our duty. And if we don't, where can we go where they cannot find us?"

"What will we tell him?"

"The truth. That is all we can do."

"I'm not sure *I* know what happened. If I didn't know better, it almost seemed like he rose from the dead like he said he would."

"None of that kind of talk. Just say what you saw."

The four trudged down the pathway away from the tomb, dragging their feet and carrying the weight of a death sentence on their shoulders.

"How long were we unconscious?" one of them said.

"I don't know. I don't remember a thing after the light from the tomb hit us. It seems like only a moment, but it could have been hours."

"I always thought I would die in battle."

Their voices faded in the distance.

"Will they be executed?" Elric asked Jesus.

"No," He answered. "Their testimony is too dangerous. The enemy will bribe them to lie and say the disciples stole my body in the night. If they comply, the temple officials will promise to keep them safe." He paused. Then He smiled. "Look. Mary Magdalene approaches."

Mary came around the corner holding a small wooden box of spices. She took one step up the path and stopped cold. She dropped the box and covered her mouth with her hands. She sprinted toward the tomb. Running her hand along the stone as she passed it in its open position, she ducked her head just inside the entrance. She spun around and leaned her back against the stone with her hands covering her mouth. She paused just long enough for her eyes to fill with tears. Then she ran back down the path and turned left on the main path toward town.

Jesus gave a sad smile. "She thinks someone has taken my body."

After only a minute, voices on the main path from the right wafted around the corner. Women's voices.

"Who will roll away the stone from the entrance of the tomb for us?"

"I don't know. I hadn't thought about that. We can't anoint His body with these spices if . . . "

Mary, the mother of James, and Salome came around the corner.

"Look! What is that?" Mary said.

"It looks like a box of spices spilled on the ground. That's strange," Salome said. "Where is Mary Magdalene? She said she would come down early."

Mary squealed, "Oh! Look!"

Both women gawked at the open tomb. Stepping over the box of spices on the ground, they approached with tentative steps.

Jesus said to Gabriel, "Appear to the women. Tell them the good news and tell them I am going ahead of them to Galilee. They will see me there." To Elric He said, "Show yourself to them inside the tomb."

Gabriel and Elric wrapped their wings around their bodies and translated into the Physical Realm. Gabriel appeared seated on top of the stone, glowing with a brilliant white robe.

Mary and Salome screamed and jumped back.

Gabriel said, "Do not be afraid; for I know that you are looking for Jesus who has been crucified. He is not here, for He has risen, just as He said. Come, see the place where He was lying."

The women ducked into the tomb. Elric sat at the right wearing a white robe. They looked at him with wide eyes and open mouths.

Elric said, "Do not be amazed; you are looking for Jesus the Nazarene, who has been crucified. He has risen; He is not here; see, here is the place where they laid Him."

Mary and Salome stepped out of the tomb with shock etched across their faces.

"Go quickly and tell His disciples that He has risen from the dead," Gabriel said. "And behold, He is going ahead of you to Galilee. There you will see Him; behold, I have told you."

They bolted down the path without speaking a word and disappeared on the main path to the left.

Gabriel and Elric translated back into the Middle Realm.

Jesus smiled and said, "I will show myself to them along the way. But first I must appear to Mary Magdalene and Peter."

The sun had just peeked over the horizon when more women's voices came from around the corner to the right.

"Where is Mary Magdalene and the other Mary? And Salome? They said they would meet us here."

"I don't know. With everyone in hiding in different places in the city, it is hard to coordinate meetings."

Joanna and three more women appeared around the corner. They all stopped. Joanna pointed at the box of spices on the ground. One of the other women pointed at the tomb.

"What is going on?" one said as they approached the stone.

Jesus nodded to Gabriel and Elric and said, "Now."

Gabriel and Elric translated into the Physical Realm and appeared in a flash before the women. Their white robes gleamed, and a bright blue glow surrounded them. The women dropped with their faces to the ground, terrified and shaking.

"Stand up!" Elric commanded. "We are merely servants of the King."

The women clambered to their feet but didn't lift their eyes above the ground.

Gabriel said to them, "Why are you seeking the living One among the dead? He is not here, but He has risen. Remember how He spoke to you while He was still in Galilee, saying that the Son of Man must be handed over to sinful men, and be crucified, and on the third day rise from the dead."

Elric said, "But go, tell His disciples and Peter, 'He is going ahead of you to Galilee; there you will see Him, just as He told you.'"

The women ran off, and Gabriel and Elric translated back the Middle Realm.

Minutes later, the disciple John came running around the corner and went straight to the tomb. He stooped and looked in. Then he stepped to the side and leaned one hand against the stone, breathing hard from the run.

Peter arrived, panting. He slowed down just enough to duck and enter the tomb. A minute later, he came out, still trying to catch his breath. "He is gone. Just as Mary said." He bent over with his hands on his knees.

John moved to the entrance and ducked.

"Nothing but linen wrappings," Peter wheezed.

John went in.

He came back out. He ran his fingers through his hair and shook his head. "Where is He? What does this mean?"

Elric said to Jesus, "Shall we appear to these also?"

"No," Jesus answered. "I will reveal myself to them later."

Peter and John sauntered away with aimless strides. Mary Magdalene came around the corner out of breath, just as Peter and John reached the main path.

"Did you see anything?" Mary asked.

"Nothing," Peter answered. "He is gone. John, you go on ahead. I am going to stay here in the garden for a while."

John took the main path to the left. Peter meandered off to the right. Mary came back to the tomb. She stood outside and wept.

Jesus walked over to her and put His hand on her back. His eyes filled with tears. "It grieves me to see her in so much pain. If they only had faith to believe—this pain should be joy." He turned to Gabriel and Elric and said, "Meet her inside the tomb."

They translated into the Physical Realm inside the tomb—Gabriel sat at the head and Elric at the feet, where the body of Jesus had been lying. They waited several minutes and listened to Mary sobbing outside.

Then, Mary stooped down and looked in. She jumped, and her mouth dropped open. She wiped her eyes and squinted into the shadows.

Gabriel said, "Woman, why are you weeping?"

She said to them, "Because they have taken away my Lord, and I do not know where they put Him."

When she had said this, she turned around and stood up.

Gabriel whispered to Elric "The King is going to reveal Himself to Mary! Quickly, let's go see this!"

Gabriel and Elric translated back to the Middle Realm outside the tomb.

Jesus had entered the Physical Realm and was standing near Mary.

He said, "Woman, why are you weeping? Whom are you seeking?"

Mary gazed back toward the tomb and answered, "Sir, if you have carried Him away, tell me where you put Him, and I will take Him away."

Jesus said to her, "Mary!"

She turned and shouted, "Rabboni!" She leapt forward and wrapped her arms around Him and wouldn't let go.

Jesus said to her, "Stop clinging to Me, for I have not yet ascended to the Father; but go to My brothers and say to them, 'I am ascending to My Father and your Father, and My God and your God.'"

Mary nodded.

Jesus brushed her hair back from her face with His finger. "This is a time of rejoicing. Do not fear. Only believe."

In an instant, He disappeared from the Physical Realm and appeared with Gabriel and Elric. He smiled.

Mary shuffled down the path and picked up the spilled box of spices.

Jesus said, "I must go now and show myself to Peter and the other women. Then I will walk with two of the disciples to Emmaus. Later tonight, I will show myself to some of the others. Captain Elric, see that the disciples are safe and bring them together for tonight."

56

A NEW CREATION

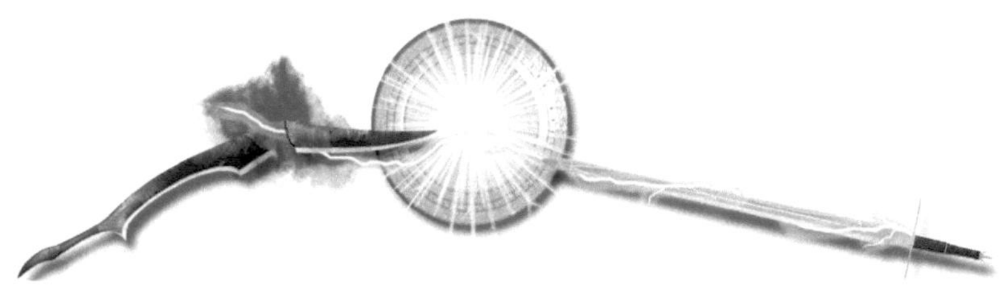

Resurrection: 7:00 p.m.

"Thomas will not be here tonight," Jenli said to Elric. "His position is surrounded by too many patrols, and we cannot get him here safely."

Elric took stock of the room. Ten of the disciples had gathered in an inner room of an inconspicuous home in the lower city near the Water Gate. The room had no windows and one door, which had been bolted shut from the inside. Timrok guarded the door, filling the full width and height of the entrance with his giant frame. The austere walls glowed yellow from the single oil lamp on the wooden table in the middle of the room. Baskets of bread, plates of fish and fruit, and drinking cups littered the table. Matthew, John, Andrew, Philip, Bartholomew, and James the son of Alphaeus fidgeted in chairs around the table. Jude and Simon the Zealot brooded near a corner of the room. James stood behind John. Peter paced along the length of one wall. Elric, Lacidar, and Jenli had positions on the wall opposite Peter.

"Very well," Elric said to Jenli. "It is better to keep Thomas safe." He turned to Lacidar. "And the women who were at the tomb?"

Lacidar replied, "They are with other disciples in three groups hidden at different locations throughout the city. They are safe."

"There are hundreds of other followers beyond this inner circle," Elric said. "What is their condition?"

Timrok answered from his position at the door. "Many have fled the city. The rest are in hiding. Most have not received word of the resurrection yet."

Elric nodded and crossed his arms. He turned his attention to the Physical Realm. "*These* men are struggling to believe."

"Why do you not believe me?" Peter said. "John and I both saw the empty tomb. And then, while I tarried in the garden, Jesus appeared to me."

"How do you know it was Him?" the Zealot asked.

"It was Him. I know it."

"But why would He appear to you and Mary and the other women and not to us?" Andrew said.

"The story of the women seems like nonsense to me," Jude said. Most of the others nodded.

"Is my word nonsense also?" Peter grumbled.

"I heard Pilate ordered a Roman guard to keep the tomb secure," Matthew said. "Did you see them? What did they have to say?"

John answered, "We did not see them. There was no one there."

"What are we supposed to do now?" Philip said.

"It is too dangerous to stay here in the city," James the son of Alphaeus said.

James, standing behind John, said with a contemplative tone, "He did say He would rise again on the third day. What if—"

A muffled rapping at the door echoed through the tense room.

Timrok pressed his face through the door and pulled it back. He gave a single nod of approval to Elric.

Peter unbolted the door and cracked it open just enough to look out. He paused a moment and then drew two men in with urgent gestures. The bolt clanged shut and Peter announced, "It's Cleopas and Matthias."

Cleopas blurted out, "We have seen the Lord!"

The disciples at the table looked at each other with incredulous eyes.

"It's true," Matthias said.

Peter smiled. "Tell us."

Cleopas said, "We were walking to Emmaus and a man joined with us."

"It was the Lord," Matthias said.

"But we didn't know it at the time," Cleopas said. "We didn't recognize Him. He talked the whole way about all the things written about Messiah in the Scriptures, beginning with Moses and all the Prophets—about how it was necessary for the Christ to suffer these things and to come into His glory."

"And then," Matthias picked up, "He reclined at the table to eat with us, and He took the bread and blessed it, and He broke it and began giving it to us. Immediately, we recognized Him."

Cleopas said, "And then, He disappeared."

The room sat in silence.

Simon the Zealot said, "Again, how do you know it was Him?"

"Where is He?" Andrew asked. "Why does He not show Himself to all of us?"

In a blink, without a sound and without a flash of light, Jesus appeared in the Physical Realm.

Peter, Cleopas, and Matthias jumped. "Aughh!"

Everyone at the table leapt to their feet. Chairs toppled over. All twelve backed away.

"Peace be to you," Jesus said. "Behold, it is I."

His words entered the Middle Realm like a calming mist. It filled the room. The shock in the disciples' eyes dimmed, but their eyes stayed wide and fixed on Jesus.

"Why are you frightened, and why are doubts arising in your hearts? See My hands and My feet, that it is I Myself; touch Me and see, because a spirit does not have flesh and bones as you plainly see that I have."

He held His hands out, palms up.

The disciples inched forward and gawked at the nail prints.

"See my side." Jesus lifted His tunic to reveal the wound from the soldier's spear.

Some stared; some looked away; some covered their mouths; some shook their heads.

Jesus said, "Have you anything here to eat?"

Andrew handed Him a piece of broiled fish; and He took it and ate it in front of them.

John said, "Lord, it really is you!"

"Did I not tell you I would rise on the third day?"

The disciples broke into nervous laughter. They looked at each other with wonder.

"It's the Lord."

"He rose from the dead!"

"It's really true!"

They erupted into joyous laughter.

Elric just watched and smiled.

"Peace," Jesus said.

They quieted down.

"Peace be to you," Jesus repeated. "These are My words which I spoke to you while I was still with you, that all the things that are written about Me in the Law of Moses and the Prophets and the Psalms must be fulfilled. So it is written, that the Christ would suffer and rise from the dead on the third day, and that repentance for forgiveness of sins would be proclaimed in His name to all the nations, beginning from Jerusalem. You are witnesses of these things. Just as the Father has sent Me, I also send you."

Jesus' eyes sparkled with excitement and anticipation. He paused, as though savoring the moment.

Elric furrowed his brows. *What is He going to do?*

Jesus breathed on them and said, "Receive the Holy Spirit."

The words drew light from Jesus' chest and rushed into the Middle Realm like a hurricane, swirling around the men. The light whirred around the room a dozen times and then spun outward through the walls.

The instant the words touched the disciples' spirits, an explosion happened within each man, and their spirits came to life—glowing with a radiance as strong as—

"That's the Spirit of the King!" Elric shouted. "His Spirit united with their spirits!"

The fragrance of the inner court of the King's Realm overwhelmed Elric's senses. By instinct he started to kneel, but then stood up straight. *No, these are mere men. But the Holy Spirit . . .*

"Captain," Timrok called out, "what do we do?"

"I . . . I . . . don't . . . "

Jesus translated to the Middle Realm. Elric, Jenli, Timrok, and Lacidar fell to their faces before Him. In the Physical Realm, movement and muffled voices continued under a veil of shadow— "Where did He go?" "He just disappeared."

"Rise, my faithful warriors," Jesus said to Elric and the lieutenants. "I proclaim to you new things from this time, hidden things which you have not known. They are created now and not long ago; and before today you have not heard them. I make my dwelling in the hearts of men. Living temples, a royal priesthood, a new creation which has not been seen before."

He smiled. He disappeared.

Kelsof burst through the ceiling and landed in front of Elric. "Captain! Something has happened! The women who saw the Lord— their spirits just . . . " He stopped and looked around at the men in the room with his mouth hanging open.

Chase shot in through a side wall. "Captain! You must come and see this . . . " He glanced around the room.

Ry blasted through the ceiling. "Captain! Captain!" He froze.

Elric laughed.

The regional captain Byroth appeared. His wings folded away as he assessed the room. "Captain Elric," he said, "I am not surprised to see . . . " He glanced around the room again and motioned with his hand. "This. Although, I do not know what has happened or what it means."

"We are still trying to fully understand it ourselves," Elric said.

Byroth nodded. "You should know—as we were examining the war map, dozens of bright lights appeared throughout Jerusalem. They are all from the King's followers. However, it did not happen to all His followers."

Kelsof said, "That's right. Where I was, it was only the women."

Flash! The room exploded with light.

When the light receded, Elric smiled at the enormous figure who appeared. Gabriel—brilliant white. His silver eyes shined with power and wisdom. "Master Gabriel," Elric said, "it is good to see you."

"This day has been long-awaited by the King," Gabriel said.

Elric asked, "Is it true that the Holy Spirit is now abiding *within* these men?"

Gabriel smiled. "It is. Not only has their spirit been reborn, but they are now temples of the Holy Spirit."

"It appears," Elric said, "that all of His followers did *not* receive this rebirth."

Gabriel nodded. "Only those who believe. They must receive it by faith."

Timrok said, "If they have the Holy Spirit, they carry His authority?"

"Yes."

"And power?"

Gabriel's eyes sparkled. "Yes, but there is still even more mystery yet to be revealed. You shall see *power* on the day of Pentecost."

Timrok bounced on his toes and gripped his sword handles. "The Lord said, 'This is the beginning of days.' I am excited to see it. Imagine an army of men filled with the Spirit of the King. The enemy will never be able to stand against it."

Gabriel raised his chin and folded his hands behind his back. "What you say is true, but it is not the King's intent to wage physical war. He did not come to raise an army. He came to create a family. All these are now sons and daughters of the King. Co-heirs of Jesus in the inheritance of the Kingdom. There *will* come a time, at the end of the age, when He will return to earth and vanquish His foes as you desire, but now—we are in the age of grace."

"Every day," Elric said, "He amazes me anew."

Gabriel smiled. "An infinite King with unlimited depths." He looked around the room at the men. "Now, help these and the other disciples escape Jerusalem tonight. Use the cover of darkness while the patrols are few."

"Master Gabriel," Lacidar said, "if the men have the Holy Spirit, do they not have the very mind of the King? Why would they need prompting from us?"

Gabriel laughed and nodded his head. "Yes, you are correct. They have direct access to the Throne—through their spirits. But remember, man is a three-part being—body, soul, and spirit. Their spirit may be alive now, but their mind does not yet know how to connect to it. They will need additional help."

"We will leave Jerusalem tonight," Elric said.

Gabriel gave Elric an affirming head nod, wrapped his wings around his body, and disappeared in a blinding flash of light.

Byroth said, "I will bring this word back to the regional warriors. Galilee is their destination?"

"Yes."

Kelsof, Ry, and Chase unfurled their wings. Kelsof said, "By your leave, Captain."

Elric nodded. The three disappeared.

Lacidar said, "I should also . . . "

"Go."

"And I—" Jenli started.

"Go."

Elric looked at Timrok and smiled. He turned his attention to the men in the room for the first time in several minutes. "Do you think they can tell? Do they know what just happened to them?"

"How can they not? The presence of the Spirit is so strong."

Those who had been sitting at the table had returned to their seats. Peter no longer paced but had squeezed in beside Andrew, leaning forward with his hands on the table.

"But it has to mean something," Peter said. "Or the Lord would not have said it."

"*What* does it mean?" Andrew said. "I didn't see anything."

"Of course you didn't," John said, "The Holy Spirit is a spirit. You can't see Him."

"Did anyone *feel* anything?" Peter asked.

"Not really," Jude said from the corner.

Several others shook their heads and shrugged their shoulders.

Matthew said, "I feel . . . clean, new."

Several others nodded their heads.

Timrok cocked his head and said, "It appears the connection to their spirits is weaker than I thought."

Elric rubbed his chin and nodded. "It is time to get them moving." He took a step forward and said in a loud voice, "You must escape Jerusalem tonight. It is not safe for you to stay here. Go quickly to Galilee. The Lord will meet you there."

His words shot like arrows into each of the men.

"Regardless of what the Lord meant," James the son of Alphaeus said, "I still say it's too dangerous to stay here in the city. I think we should leave quickly."

"I agree," Andrew said. "We can't stay in hiding like this."

"Where do we go?" Simon the Zealot asked.

"Galilee," James said. "That's where the Lord told us to go. And He said He would meet us there."

The others nodded.

"It is settled," Peter said. "We escape Jerusalem tonight. Immediately. We should travel in pairs. Go first to the others in hiding and tell them. Split up and take different routes. Some will go through Jericho to the east. Some by way of Lydda to the west. We will meet in Capernaum in five days."

"Very good," Elric said to Timrok. "I am going to the roof."

Elric lifted his wings and popped through ceiling to the roof. The night was quiet, and the moon still gave a calm blue luster to the city. Around the outskirts of the city, the tent villages of the travelers in town for Passover looked asleep. Day three of the festival—plenty of distractions for those hoping to remain unnoticed.

No enemy warriors visible anywhere. *Probably still regrouping from this morning.*

No Roman patrols in view. *There will be fewer in the middle of the night, but I know some are out there.*

James and John slipped out the front door with traveling packs slung over their shoulders. They paused, then slunk off to the left. Christov, who had been hidden, leapt from the rooftop across the street to the next rooftop on the left. Carothim, with sword unsheathed, walked with the men.

Five minutes later, Matthew and Bartholomew came out the front door and headed right. Kaylar and Jerem appeared and provided escort.

Elric crossed his arms and nodded his head. *Their spirits are bright as beacons in the Middle Realm, but the enemy is too preoccupied right now to notice. We will surely reach Galilee with no difficulty.*

57

APPEARANCES

Resurrection plus 4 days

Théodor walked with Daniel into the temple on the last day of the Passover festival. He looked at all the people bustling around like a colony of ants.

These people carry on with their rituals and lives as though nothing has happened. How can they not see? How can they not understand?

The familiar smell of burning animal flesh from the altar permeated the atmosphere, both in the Physical and Middle Realms. Théodor shook his head.

Daniel stopped a passerby. "Excuse me. Shalom. Do you know where I can find Jesus? Jesus of Nazareth?"

"Who?"

"Never mind. Thank you."

Daniel approached a young family—a man, his wife, and two small children. "Shalom. I am looking for a man named Jesus. From Nazareth. Do you know where He is staying?"

The wife shot a wary glance to her husband.

The man said, "I heard that he was crucified by the Romans a week ago."

"Really? So, it is true?" Daniel sighed. "Do you know what happened?"

"No. I only heard people talking about it."

"Thank you."

Théodor spotted Nicodemus under the portico, praying by himself. Théodor said to Daniel, "Look, see that priest over there. He is sure to know what happened. Look to your left." He waited while his words filtered into Daniel's spirit.

Daniel gazed with glassy eyes at the thousands of people stirring about the outer court. He looked lost, bereft of focus.

"Look to your left," Théodor repeated.

Daniel's gaze meandered left.

"Talk to that priest."

Daniel took a deep breath and moved toward the portico.

Théodor put his hand on Daniel's back and spoke strength into his flesh. "Good," he said. "Do not fear. Speak to the priest."

Daniel approached Nicodemus, an elderly statesman with priest's robes and a distinguished gray beard. "Excuse me, rabbi," Daniel said with a crackling voice.

Nicodemus raised his head from praying and looked at Daniel.

"Shalom," Daniel said.

"Shalom."

"I am sorry to bother you, but I was hoping that you might be able to tell me what happened to Jesus of Nazareth."

Nicodemus shot nervous glances left and right and over Daniel's shoulder. "He . . . was crucified. Legally charged, tried, and convicted. According to the law. There is no more to say."

"I don't understand," Daniel said. "What did He do?"

"Why? Why do you ask me these questions?"

"I just arrived in Jerusalem. I wanted to join his disciples and follow Him."

"Shhh!" Nicodemus said. "Do not speak these words in the open."

Nicodemus pulled Daniel away from the people to a shadowed corner under the portico.

"It is dangerous to be a follower of Jesus right now," Nicodemus whispered. "Temple officials have issued orders to arrest anyone who calls on His name."

"Why? What did He do?"

"Nothing. Other than speak truth—and bring life and healing. The chief priests and elders were jealous and afraid of His growing influence. They brought false charges against Him and compelled Pilate to crucify Him."

Daniel's eyes filled with tears. "I don't understand. He delivered me from a legion of demons and healed my deaf ear. I thought He was going to be the Messiah."

Nicodemus did another nervous survey of the area. He whispered, "He may still be."

"What? What do you mean?"

"There is word that He has risen from the dead."

"What?"

"Shhh! Before He died, He said He would rise again in three days. The tomb is empty. I have confirmed this. And there is rumor that some of His disciples have seen Him."

Daniel's mouth hung open. "Then where are His disciples? I should speak with them."

Nicodemus checked left and right again. "They have left Jerusalem. I believe they went to Galilee. Go to Galilee. Search for them there. But do not speak of Jesus here in Jerusalem. I must go."

"Thank you."

Nicodemus gave a melancholy smile, spun around, and shuffled away.

"Back to Galilee," Daniel muttered to himself. "But where do I look?"

Théodor said, "Capernaum. We should start in Capernaum."

* * *

Resurrection plus 8 days

Eight days after the resurrection, the eleven disciples and the women gathered at Peter's home in Capernaum. The doors to the meeting room off the inner courtyard were shut and locked.

Elric said to Timrok, Jenli, and Lacidar, "Let's go inside. The Lord is going to reveal Himself to these again today."

They stepped through the wall into a sizable room, well suited for large gatherings. Storage crates sat stacked against one wall. Thirty empty chairs had been pushed together against another wall. A table large enough for twenty near the middle of the room had been set for a meal. All the disciples sat around the table.

Elric crossed his arms and said, "It has been a while since we have been here."

Jenli nodded. "Remember all the times this place was packed while Jesus taught the people? Sometimes it was overflowing into the courtyard."

Timrok pointed to the ceiling. "You can still see the patch to the roof where they lowered a man in for healing."

"It feels like a lifetime ago," Elric said. "So much has happened."

The disciples' conversation caught their attention.

"What are we supposed to do now?" Philip asked.

Simon the Zealot said, "I really thought that, by now, we would be in the King's army fighting for deliverance from Roman oppression. Is that not what Messiah was supposed to do?"

"We should have known," John said. "All His teachings were about truth and life and Kingdom principles. He never began preparing us for an insurrection. He only sought to reveal the true nature of the Father."

"It is clear that we are not going to topple Rome," Philip said. "So, what do we do now?"

Andrew said, "I suppose we go back to our lives."

James added, "Knowing that we are forgiven and that He is risen."

Thomas gave a "humph" and shook his head.

"You still do not believe our report?" Peter said. "We all saw Him."

"It is too much," Thomas said. "Unless I see in His hands the imprint of the nails, and put my finger into the place of the nails, and put my hand into His side, I will not believe."

"But Thomas," Matthew said, "There have been multiple—"

Jesus appeared in a blink without a sound and stood in their midst.

Everyone at the table gasped and jumped up.

"Peace be to you," Jesus said. He walked straight over to Thomas, who stood shaking and gasping for air. He said to Thomas, "Place your finger here, and see My hands; and take your hand and put it into My side; and do not continue in disbelief, but be a believer."

Thomas dropped to the floor with his face to the ground. With a trembling voice he said, "My Lord and my God!"

In the Middle Realm, a torrent of light blasted through the ceiling with a loud rush of wind and enveloped Thomas. A detonation within Thomas sent shafts of light shooting outward like an exploding star. Elric squinted through the flash. And then, the sweet fragrance of the Spirit from the Throne room. Thomas's spirit was alive. And the Holy Spirit had taken up residence.

Elric shouted, "Yes!"

Elric grabbed Timrok's arm, they locked elbows, and they danced around the room with high steps, energetic spins, and shouts of joy. Jenli and Lacidar spun in the air shouting and singing. The celebration lasted only a few seconds because Jesus began to speak again.

Jesus said to Thomas, "Stand up." He took Thomas by the hand and lifted him up. Still holding his hand, He looked Thomas in the eyes and said, "Because you have seen Me, have you now believed? Blessed are they who did not see, and yet believed."

Jesus disappeared from the Physical Realm and appeared in front of Elric and the lieutenants. Without hesitation, the four angels broke into singing and shouting and dancing circles around Jesus. Jesus stood in the middle of them smiling. He remained for a minute, but then disappeared.

The dance continued.

* * *

Resurrection plus 11 days

Daniel sat under the old, gnarled olive tree in the back of his parent's yard in Nazareth. It had been seven days since he spoke with the priest in the temple, two days since he had reached home. The tree provided pleasant shade, and a light breeze carried the sweet bouquet of springtime wildflowers.

Théodor stood in the sun with his arms crossed. *Two days now I have been prompting him to go on to Capernaum. He either isn't hearing me, or he is too full of disappointment and fear. He needs to find the disciples.*

"Oh God," Daniel said aloud. "What is going on?"

Good. At least he is praying.

Daniel rested his head between his knees. "You delivered me. And you healed me. I know it was You. But now, how can You leave me alone? You said the Father in heaven sees me and knows my pain. But do you see me now? Do you see my pain now? I am so lost and confused. I don't know what to think. I don't know what to do."

Jesus appeared in the Middle Realm next to Théodor.

Théodor dropped. "My King," he said, face to the ground.

"Rise, Théodor. Today salvation comes to Daniel. And his house."

Théodor stood but kept his head bowed. Jesus put His hand on Théodor's shoulder and smiled. Jesus translated into the Physical Realm.

"Daniel," Jesus said, approaching the tree.

Daniel looked up with tears in his eyes.

"Daniel, it is I."

Daniel leapt up and ran forward. "Jesus?"

"Look. See the nail prints in my hands and feet."

"It is true. You were crucified. But now . . . You are alive?"

"I Am that I Am. I have the authority to lay down my life and to pick it up again."

"But why, Lord?" Daniel said. "What does this all mean?"

Jesus smiled. "Do you remember when you were a little boy, and you visited the temple? Remember how you thought God was unapproachable and purposely tried to create barriers to keep men from drawing close?"

"You saw me? You knew me then?"

"Sin is the thing that separates man from God. The outer court, the inner court, the temple with the Holy of Holies—this was all meant to help man see their need for the remission of sin."

"And all the sacrifices?"

"A legal means by which the remission of sin can be accomplished. The wages of sin is death. And by trusting in the substitutionary death of another, a man can receive forgiveness."

"But Lord, what does that have to do with You being executed by the Romans?"

"They did not kill Me. I laid my life down. I took on all the sin of the world and nailed it to the cross."

"You became the sacrificial lamb!"

Jesus smiled. "And the barrier between man and the Father has been removed. The veil in the Holy of Holies—has been rent in two, top to bottom, by the Father Himself. You can go boldly before the Thone of God."

Daniel stood with his mouth open and blinked. "But how? What do I do?"

"Only believe. Believe that I paid the price for your sin and that I rose again to give eternal life to everyone who calls on My name."

"I do believe! I believe you are the promised Messiah!"

Whoosh! In the Middle Realm, a torrent of light rained down from heaven with a loud rush of wind and enveloped Daniel. An explosion within Daniel sent shafts of light shooting outward in all directions. Théodor squinted. The sweet fragrance of the Spirit from the Throne room filled the back yard.

"Look at that!" Théodor shouted. He shot straight up in a tight corkscrew shouting and laughing. He landed and danced in circles.

Daniel still had questions. "But Lord, I am still confused. Isn't the Messiah supposed to deliver Israel? I always dreamed of serving in Your army and defeating Rome."

"You seek a political revolution. Nations rise and fall. But the kingdom of God is forever. It is spiritual. I came to establish my kingdom on earth and to call many sons and daughters into that kingdom."

"What is Your will for me?"

"Go to Capernaum. Find my disciples there. Learn My ways. The Holy Spirit will guide you."

"Yes, Lord." Daniel bowed his head.

He lifted his head, and Jesus was gone.

Théodor continued to dance in the backyard while Daniel rushed back to the house.

Daniel's words rang across the field before the door closed. "Ima! Father! Jesse! I just saw the Lord!"

Ten minutes later, three rushing torrents of light fell down through the roof of the house.

Théodor kept laughing and dancing and beating the air with imaginary drumsticks to accompany the triumphant beat in his heart.

* * *

Resurrection plus 13 days

From his position atop the hill overlooking the Sea of Galilee, Elric watched Jesus in the Physical Realm kindle a campfire beside the shore in the predawn light. Behind Elric and to the east, the town of Capernaum still slept. Out on the water, almost a hundred yards from shore, seven of the disciples had been fishing all night.

He is amazing. The King of the universe, who could set this entire city ablaze with the breath of his nostrils, rubs sticks together to make a fire to cook breakfast for a few men.

Elric shook his head.

He surveyed the area. Some of the team stood at posts around the disciples in the boat. Jenli was on the boat. Timrok and his team had the beach surrounded.

Elric laughed. *Timrok cannot let an opportunity to guard the King go by. Even though the King obviously does not require it. Sometimes I think that Jesus lets him do that because He knows how important it is to Timrok.*

He paused. Then he laughed again—this time at the irony of his thoughts and his own role in everything.

It is always about relationship with the King. He . . . wait . . . what's happening now?

Jesus stood at the water's edge and yelled to the men in the boat. *Can't hear what He is saying.*

The men threw their nets into the water on one side of the boat. A few seconds later, they all struggled to pull in a large catch. Then, one of the men jumped out of the boat and swam toward the shore. *Peter.*

The Lord met Peter knee-deep in the water with hugs while the other men struggled to get the catch aboard and row back to shore. They couldn't get the net into the boat, so they dragged it all the way. When they got close enough, Peter went out and helped them pull it ashore.

Then they all sat around the campfire and had broiled fish and bread for breakfast, laughing and talking as if Jesus was one of them.

It is strange to see them all together like this. Before, the King's spirit was the only one that shined like the sun. Now, at least from here, they all look the same in the Middle Realm. It is still hard to grasp.

Movement along the shore from the right—Elric strained to see who it could be.

An elzur warrior. And another believer? His spirit is bright. It is definitely a believer.

The angel walking by the shore took off and flew toward Elric. Two wing beats and he arrived. He landed in front of Elric, and his wings folded away.

"Théodor!" Elric said. Elric spoke the word "faithfulness" into his hand, and a large plasma ball formed.

Théodor spoke "joy unspeakable" and formed his own plasma ball. They smashed the energy together, and faithfulness with joy unspeakable showered over them.

"That must be your charge, Daniel, down there," Elric said.

"It is!"

"And I see that he has been born again."

"Yes! It has been a long journey from the tombs in the Gerasenes. But the Lord appeared to him two days ago in Nazareth. Daniel has come to seek out the disciples. The Lord told him to join them and learn His ways."

"Excellent," Elric said. "If he stays on this path, he will meet them in a few minutes. Some of the disciples are right down there on the shore. They are just finishing breakfast. The Lord has been talking with them and . . . oh . . . He just disappeared."

Elric and Théodor laughed.

Théodor said, "It will be good for Daniel to be surrounded by other believers."

Elric nodded. "They are still trying to understand their place in the Kingdom, but I believe the Lord has prepared them well. They can all grow together."

* * *

Resurrection plus 20 days

Just outside Capernaum on a large outcropping of boulders between a hill and the approach to the shoreline, Elric, Jenli, Lacidar, and Théodor formed a line at the bottom and watched the meeting up on the hillside. At the top of the hill overlooking the Sea of Galilee, Jesus sat and spoke with His followers just as He had done so many times before.

The stands of trees along the sides and around the back, which formed a natural boundary and typically hid the hungry red eyes of the enemy, looked noticeably empty.

"We have not had to contend with enemy forces when the King is present," Jenli said.

Elric scanned the tree line. He gave sly smirk. "They were afraid of the Son of Man. They are terrified of the risen Lord."

Timrok and his team, with the full extent of their frames expanded in the Middle Realm, stood in a straight line behind the King with their weapons drawn.

Elric smiled and crossed his arms.

Jenli flipped through his ledger. "Over five hundred here today, sir."

Elric nodded. "And every one born again from what I can see. This hillside looks much different from the last time we were here."

"Have you noticed," Lacidar said, "the King is only revealing Himself to those who were His followers."

"Heh," Jenli said. "If it were me, I would have gone straight to Pilate."

"Or Caiaphas," Lacidar said.

Elric shook his head. "That is not His way."

Théodor said, "I am still trying to understand this new race of man. They have the Holy Spirit living within, but they still seem to struggle with things they should have victory over. I have seen more than a few believers who are sick. How is that possible?"

"Their spirit is new," Elric said with a grimace, "but their bodies are mortal, and their souls are carnal. They have spent their whole lives controlled by their soul, and now they must learn to be controlled by the spirit. It appears that the more they can renew their minds, the more they can walk in the spirit and access all the life, power, and authority that is there."

Elric pointed toward the crowd. "Just look at all of them. See how many still carry dangerous strongholds? These strongholds did not break at the new birth. It will take work for the believers to take thoughts captive to the obedience of the Spirit."

"At first," Jenli said, "I thought we were looking at an army of people who would be exactly like the Son of Man."

Elric cocked his head. "That is because you see them in the spiritual realm. Here, they *are* just like the Son of Man. They have the King's power and authority in earthen shells. They just do not know it or know how to walk in it. I believe that, with time, they can learn."

"In the meantime," Lacidar said, "we still have much work to do."

"Gabriel said something else after the resurrection," Elric said. "He mentioned something about Pentecost. He said there was still more mystery to be revealed. Something related to power. I am anxious to see what new thing the King will do."

They all nodded and gazed up the hill. At the top of the hill, Jesus stood up, paused, and disappeared.

The people stood. Most dispersed in different directions. Some milled around, talking.

Timrok glided to the bottom of the hill, skimming just over the people's heads. He landed in front of Elric.

"Any new direction from the King?" Elric asked.

"Yes, sir. He told the people to be in Bethany on the fortieth day. He will lead them to a place where He will ascend back the King's Realm, and they will not see Him anymore. Then they are to tarry in the city until Pentecost."

"Twenty days," Elric said. "Our time is short."

58

ASCENSION

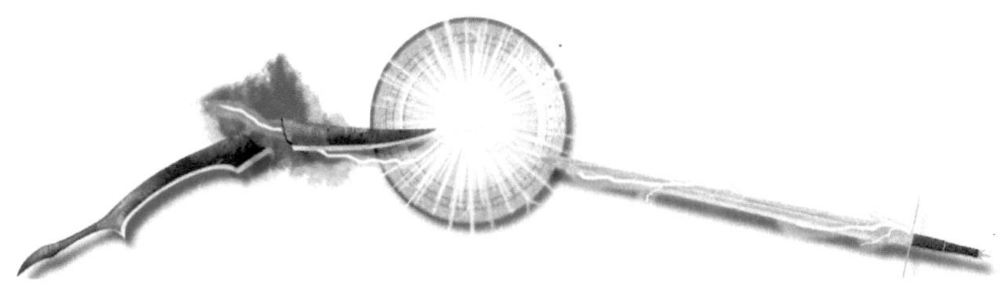

Resurrection plus 40 days

On the fortieth day, in the morning, Elric and his team assembled outside Bethany. Billowy white clouds filled the sky, but the air felt still and peaceful.

"Form a single column on each side of the road," Elric said to the team. "The people will gather here. Then the King will lead them up to the top of the Mount of Olives, and we will march in columns along with them."

Smart columns, perfectly spaced, formed on each side of the road. The warriors stood at attention and waited.

Mary, Martha, and Lazarus of Bethany arrived first. Then the eleven disciples: Peter and Andrew; James and John; Philip; Thomas; Bartholomew; Matthew; James the son of Alphaeus; Simon the Zealot; and Jude. And the devoted women: Mary Magdalene; Salome, the mother of James and John; Mary, widow of Alphaeus and mother of James and Joses; Joanna; and six other women.

People trickled in from all around.

Daniel and his brother Jesse arrived, accompanied by Théodor. Elric motioned to Théodor, who nodded and joined a column of warriors.

A flash of light erupted in front of Elric. Elric blinked hard and opened his eyes.

"Master Gabriel," Elric said.

"The march that marks the end of one age and the beginning of a new one," Gabriel said. "It is a good day."

More people arrived. Some came with additional elzurim, who joined the formations at the ends of the columns. The mood among the people seemed solemn. Talking remained sparse and subdued. The angelic warriors maintained strict discipline in their columns.

"Look," Gabriel said to Elric. "Here comes Mary."

Elric looked left and nodded. "And all her children."

Mary, the mother of Jesus, along with James, Joseph, Elizabeth, Simon, Jude, and Rachael approached the crowd.

"And look who is escorting them!" Elric said.

"Raziel! Excellent." Gabriel said.

More came. Matthias and Barsabbas, Cleopas, and Joses, the brother of James.

"Very good," Gabriel said as he pointed at two more approaching from the direction of Jerusalem. "It was my hope that they would come."

"Nicodemus," Elric said, "and Joseph of Arimathea. It is a difficult thing for them. It took great courage for them to be here."

The influx dwindled. Finally, one more approached from the south.

"Is that?" Elric started. "It is! That is Caleb, the eldest son of Hannah and Amichai all the way from Beersheba. It does not surprise me."

Without warning or a sound, Jesus appeared at the head of the gathering.

Gabriel and Elric and both columns of angels fell to their faces.

"My brothers and my sisters," Jesus said. "Today I am ascending to My Father and your Father, and My God and your God."

Elric looked over to Gabriel. It seemed clear that they would not receive direct orders from the King. Gabriel nodded, and he and Elric stood. Both columns of warriors stood and maintained their positions at attention.

Jesus continued. "And I tell you the truth, that it is better for you that I go. For the Holy Spirit is with you now. He will guide you into all the truth; for He will not speak on His own, but whatever He hears, He will speak; and He will disclose to you what is to come. He will glorify Me, for He will take from Mine and will disclose it to you. And I say to you, if you ask the Father for anything in My name, He will give it to you. Until now you have asked for nothing in My name. Ask and you will receive, so that your joy may be made full."

He paused and folded His hands behind His back.

"After I depart, you are to go to Jerusalem and tarry there. Do not leave Jerusalem, but wait for what the Father has promised, which you heard of from Me; for John baptized with water, but you will be baptized with the Holy Spirit not many days from now."

He turned on the path in the direction of the Mount of Olives and called out, "Come. Follow Me."

The two columns of warriors made sharp facing maneuvers in unison and marched in step along the King's path. Gabriel and Elric moved in behind Jesus.

The crowd, nearly a hundred, shuffled ahead between the two columns of angels.

Within ten paces, legions of angels suddenly appeared on each side of the path. Ten rows of trumpeters per side with long silver trumpets pointed their horns inward and upward in unison. They blew a triumphant fanfare that melted Elric's heart. The tone and precision of the melodies was so pure, Elric felt as though he was walking through a dream. Behind the trumpeters, rows of angels shouted praises to the King.

Elric looked at the Jesus. The King's stride looked regal, and He gave satisfied grins and an occasional head nod to the musicians as He passed. *He sees! With His glorified body, He is not restricted to the Physical Realm.*

Elric looked back at the people. They lumbered ahead in silence. *How can they not see any of this? Surely with the Holy Spirit within, they should be able to sense it.*

The climb up the mountain became slower and more laborious for the people as the grade became steeper, but the angelic fanfare continued the entire trip.

Finally, they reached the top. Jesus stopped and turned back toward the people.

The trumpeters halted in an instant and snapped their instruments down to a rest position. All the Middle Realm became silent.

Peter stepped forward and asked, "Lord, is it at this time that You are restoring the kingdom to Israel?"

Jesus gave him an understanding smile and said, "It is not for you to know periods of time or appointed times which the Father has set by His own authority." He paused and continued with a resolute voice, "But you will receive power when the Holy Spirit has come upon you; and you shall be My witnesses both in Jerusalem and in all Judea, and Samaria, and as far as the remotest part of the earth."

Then He lifted His arms into the air and said, "Father, I am no longer going to be in the world; and yet they themselves are in the world, and I am coming to You. Holy Father, keep them in Your name, the name which You have given Me, so that they may be one just as We are."

The trumpeters snapped their horns back to the ready position and waited.

Sharp rays of light beamed down between the clouds—dazzling light visible even in the Physical Realm. One giant shaft centered on Jesus, and a shimmering glow radiated from His whole body. He lifted off the ground like an ember floating on a rising current of air.

The trumpeters launched into a new fanfare—high and exultant.

The crowd of people all gasped. Speechless, they gawked into the sky.

Jesus continued to ascend, reaching as high as the clouds. Finally, He disappeared into the cloud, and the rays of light dissipated.

The trumpeters blew a glorious finale and blasted into the heavens like shooting stars. With a roar that rattled the Middle Realm, the rest of the legions streaked across the sky and disappeared.

Elric and Gabriel stood alone with the two columns of warriors and a crowd of people.

Gabriel laughed and said to Elric. "Come, let us speak to the people."

Gabriel and Elric wrapped their wings around themselves and translated into the Physical Realm. Gleaming white and radiating with power, the two stood before them. Most of the people didn't notice them because they still had their attention focused into the clouds.

Gabriel called out in a loud voice, "Men of Galilee, why do you stand looking into the sky? This Jesus, who has been taken up from you into heaven, will come in the same way as you have watched Him go into heaven. Go now and do as the Lord commanded."

The two translated back to the Middle Realm and watched the people meander away.

Gabriel turned to Elric and said, "Captain, I believe you and your team are in need of new assignments now. Report immediately to Commander Kai."

"In His service." Elric answered.

59

A NEW DAY

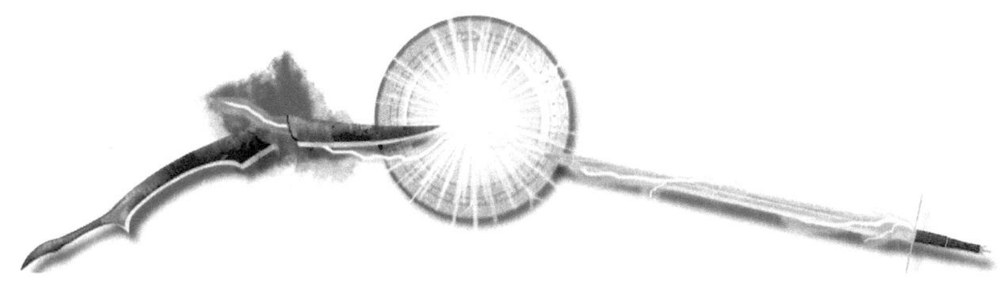

Resurrection plus 40 days

Elric always felt small when standing in Commander Kai's headquarters. The vast open room with pulsing white columns and glowing white walls, the crystal floor with the warm blue glow, the massive war map that dwarfed the ones he used for regional work—it all surged with energy and wisdom.

Behind Elric, in a tight line, stood Jenli, Lacidar, and Timrok. Behind them, in a formation of four columns and five rows stood Brondor, Jennidab, Jerem, Jessik, and Kaylar; BaeLee, Stephanus, Kelsof, Jaeden, and Ry; Prestus, Chase, Nalyd, Kylek, and Micah; Emms, Lorr, Xarjim, Christov, and Carothim.

All the warriors still wore their Middle Realm battle gear and carried their swords and shields. The earthiness of their appearance made Elric feel even more out of place in the pristine command center.

Commander Kai motioned with his hand, and the war map faded away. He stepped forward toward Elric. "Captain Elric," Kai said. His deep voice echoed in the large room. "First of all, let me commend you and your team for your—"

A voice from the doorway announced, "Presenting the King of Kings!"

Every angel in the room fell prostrate to the ground.

Footsteps vibrated across the floor and rumbled through Elric's chest.

"Rise, my warriors." Jesus said as He approached the formation. "Stand at ease."

The team jumped to their feet but stayed at strict attention.

Jesus stood in front of Elric and spoke loud enough for the whole team to hear. "The task that was set before you was a challenging one. It is always difficult to battle the enemy, but you had to proceed without direction from the Throne. I know the mystery of the mission placed you in perilous positions, but your dedication to Me and your faith in My intent has been proven pure and true. Thank you for your service."

He pulled out a large pouch with shiny gold material and a golden tie string.

"All of My elzurim serve an essential role in the Kingdom. But this group will always be known as the one who served the Son of Man on the earth. It is a special honor, and it is My joy to present to you today an eternal token of honor."

He pulled something out of the pouch. A diamond, as large as a large grape—tear shaped with perfect facets to reflect every ray of light. Its sparkling red color magnified the light and brought the core to life like a flame. It was attached to a rugged leather band, long enough to go over someone's head.

"For each of you," Jesus said. "It is red to commemorate the blood of the Lamb. And every one has a name engraved that only you and I will know. The leather band will supplement your battle uniform as you return to the Middle Realm. One day, at the end of the age, I will replace this leather with gold."

Jesus checked the engraving of the diamond in His hand. He smiled and stepped up to Elric. He placed the band over Elric's head and said, "Well done, My good and faithful servant."

Next, He pulled another out, checked its engraving and stood before Timrok. He placed the band over Timrok's head and said, "Well done, My good and faithful servant." Each lieutenant received a red diamond with a secret name.

Then, the King stepped through the ranks and gave every warrior the same commendation. Every one an individual name. Every one a personal connection.

The King walked toward the door, and they all bowed low again. The footsteps stopped.

Jesus' voice rang out from across the room. "Your weapons—the special swords and shields fashioned by the great artisan Timrok— these are singular works of art and unique to the mission you just completed."

Elric's heart sank into his belly. *No, please don't—*

"I want you to keep them. You will find none better."

Yes!

The footsteps continued. The door closed.

Command Kai said, "Please stand."

The team stood, and Elric's anticipation for what might come next stuck like a lump in his throat.

"You all need new assignments," Kai announced. "I have some prepared."

He pulled out a silver parchment and unrolled it.

"Lieutenant Timrok," he said.

Timrok took one step forward with his eyes drilled forward.

"You are assigned to Ephesus. The Lord plans to bring about a great revival in this city in the near future. You are to go and prepare the way for the men the Lord will send there. As you know, this is a very dark place. Worship of the goddess Artemis of the Ephesians is widespread. The enemy has many very powerful strongholds. You will be greatly outnumbered."

Timrok smiled and palmed his sword handles.

"Do you have any questions?" Kai asked.

"Master Kai, after the King, my team is my great honor. With your permission, I request they come with me."

"As you wish. Lieutenant Timrok and his team are assigned to Ephesus."

Timrok continued grinning and stepped back.

"Lieutenant Jenli," Kai said.

Jenli stepped forward.

"As a recorder in the King's court, you are overdue for your rotation in the King's Realm due to this last unique assignment. You are therefore released to return to the King's Realm and—"

"Master Kai," Jenli interrupted. "If possible, I would like to request the opportunity to stay on earth. I am currently assigned to the disciple Peter, and I am eager to be a part of this new day."

"I see."

"And, if I may—all the warriors assigned to the disciples, both my team and Zaben's, have expressed a desire to remain with their charges."

"I see."

"It is an exciting time, sir."

"Very well," Kai announced. "Lieutenant Jenli and all those currently assigned to the disciples will remain with their charges. Lorr, the disciple Matthias will replace Judas. He will be your charge. I will find someone to take Simon the Zealot."

"Sir, may I request Luxor?" Jenli said.

"Very well," Kai answered.

Jenli smiled, looked back into the ranks, nodded, and took one step back.

"Lieutenant Lacidar."

Lacidar took a step forward.

"I suppose you want to keep your team intact as well?"

"They are skilled and faithful warriors, sir."

Kai nodded and looked down at the scroll. "I know you prefer long-term assignments of encouragement and strength. I will have something for you in Rome with some chief architects there in time. But for now, I have a shorter-term mission. Benjamin and Rachael—in Egypt. They were valuable servants of the King at a time when we needed them. The Lord desires that they be reached with the good news of the gospel. You cannot bring this news yourself because it must be delivered by the mouths of men, so your mission is to bring believers to them that they may believe and be saved."

Lacidar smiled and said, "Excellent, master. I have often thought about them." He took a step back.

"Captain Elric."

Elric stepped forward.

"I give you a choice. You may return to your regional position that you held before this mission, or . . . " Kai paused and checked the parchment. "There is a man named Saul. From Tarsus. He is a devout young Pharisee, a student of Gamaliel. He is zealous for the Mosaic law and will become an extreme danger to the believers. The Lord desires to see him turn and to call upon His name. If he does, he can become an effective weapon to advance the Kingdom. His journey will require the services of a captain."

Elric didn't hesitate. "Master Kai, I will take Saul of Tarsus. As Jenli said, these are exciting times." He stepped back and gripped the red diamond hanging around his neck. His eyes sparkled and he couldn't help from grinning.

"It is settled," Kai said. "You all have your assignments. Go forth in the power of the King for His honor and for His glory."

In unison, the whole troop answered back, "In His service."

APPENDIX

References to quoted passages.

Chapter 1

Matthew 4:3 (NASB): "If You are the Son of God, command that these stones become bread."

Matthew 4:4 (NASB): But He answered and said, "It is written: 'MAN SHALL NOT LIVE ON BREAD ALONE, BUT ON EVERY WORD THAT COMES OUT OF THE MOUTH OF GOD.'"

Chapter 5

John_2:1–10 (NASB): On the third day there was a wedding in Cana of Galilee, and the mother of Jesus was there; and both Jesus and His disciples were invited to the wedding. When the wine ran out, the mother of Jesus said to Him, "They have no wine." And Jesus said to her, "What business do you have with Me, woman? My hour has not yet come." His mother said to the servants, "Whatever He tells you, do it." Now there were six stone waterpots standing there for the Jewish custom of purification, containing two or three measures each. Jesus said to them, "Fill the waterpots with water." So they filled them up to the brim. And He said to them, "Draw some out now and take it to the headwaiter." And they took it to him. Now when the headwaiter tasted the water which had become wine, and did not know where it came from (but the servants who had drawn the water knew), the headwaiter called the groom, and said to him, "Every man serves the good wine first, and when the guests are drunk, then he serves the poorer wine; but you have kept the good wine until now."

Deuteronomy 11:13–15 (NASB): "And it shall come about, if you listen obediently to my commandments which I am commanding you today, to love the Lord your God and to serve Him with all your heart and all your soul, that He will provide rain for your land in its season, the early and late rain, so that you may gather your grain, your new wine, and your oil. He will also provide grass in your field for your cattle, and you will eat and be satisfied.

Proverbs 3:9–10 (NASB):

Honor the LORD from your wealth,
And from the first of all your produce;
Then your barns will be filled with plenty,
And your vats will overflow with new wine.

Psalm 103:2–3 (NASB):

Bless the LORD, my soul,
And do not forget any of His benefits;
Who pardons all your guilt,
Who heals all your diseases.

Chapter 6

John 2:13–17 (NASB): The Passover of the Jews was near, and Jesus went up to Jerusalem. And within the temple grounds He found those who were selling oxen, sheep, and doves, and the money changers seated at their tables. And He made a whip of cords, and drove them all out of the temple area, with the sheep and the oxen; and He poured out the coins of the money changers and overturned their tables; and to those who were selling the doves He said, "Take these things away from here; stop making My Father's house a place of business!" His disciples remembered that it was written: "ZEAL FOR YOUR HOUSE WILL CONSUME ME."

Psalm 30:2 (NASB): LORD my God, I cried to You for help, and You healed me.

Chapter 7

John 3:1–10 (NASB): Now there was a man of the Pharisees, named Nicodemus, a ruler of the Jews; this man came to Jesus at night and said to Him, "Rabbi, we know that You have come from God as a teacher; for no one can do these signs that You do unless God is with him." Jesus responded and said to him, "Truly, truly, I say to you, unless someone is born again he cannot see the kingdom of God."

Nicodemus said to Him, "How can a person be born when he is old? He cannot enter his mother's womb a second time and be born, can he?" Jesus answered, "Truly, truly, I say to you, unless someone is born of water and the Spirit, he cannot enter the kingdom of God. That which has been born of the flesh is flesh, and that which has been born of the Spirit is spirit. Do not be amazed that I said to you, 'You must be born again.' The wind blows where it wishes, and you hear the sound of it, but you do not know where it is coming from and where it is going; so is everyone who has been born of the Spirit."

Nicodemus responded and said to Him, "How can these things be?" Jesus answered and said to him, "You are the teacher of Israel, and yet you do not understand these things?"

John 3:16–18 (NASB): "For God so loved the world, that He gave His only Son, so that everyone who believes in Him will not perish, but have eternal life. For God did not send the Son into the world to judge the world, but so that the world might be saved through Him. The one who believes in Him is not judged; the one who does not believe has been judged already, because he has not believed in the name of the only Son of God."

Chapter 8

John 3:26–36 (NASB): And they came to John and said to him, "Rabbi, He who was with you beyond the Jordan, to whom you have testified— behold, He is baptizing and all the people are coming to Him." John replied, "A person can receive not even one thing unless it has been given to him from heaven. You yourselves are my witnesses that I said, 'I am not the Christ,' but, 'I have been sent ahead of Him.' He who has the bride is the groom; but the friend of the groom, who stands and listens to him, rejoices greatly because of the groom's voice. So this joy of mine has been made full. He must increase, but I must decrease.

"He who comes from above is above all; the one who is only from the earth is of the earth and speaks of the earth. He who comes from heaven is above all. What He has seen and heard, of this He testifies; and no one accepts His testimony. The one who has accepted His testimony has certified that God is true. For He whom God sent speaks the words of God; for He does not give the Spirit sparingly. The Father loves the Son and has entrusted all things to His hand. The one who believes in the Son has eternal life; but the one who does not obey the Son will not see life, but the wrath of God remains on him."

John 4:13–14 (NASB): Jesus answered and said to her, "Everyone who drinks of this water will be thirsty again; but whoever drinks of the water that I will give him shall never be thirsty; but the water that I will give him will become in him a fountain of water springing up to eternal life."

Chapter 9

Luke 4:16–21 (NASB): And He came to Nazareth, where He had been brought up; and as was His custom, He entered the synagogue on the Sabbath, and stood up to read. And the scroll of Isaiah the prophet was handed to Him. And He unrolled the scroll and found the place where it was written:

"THE SPIRIT OF THE LORD IS UPON ME,
BECAUSE HE ANOINTED ME TO BRING GOOD NEWS TO THE POOR.
HE HAS SENT ME TO PROCLAIM RELEASE TO CAPTIVES,
AND RECOVERY OF SIGHT TO THE BLIND,
TO SET FREE THOSE WHO ARE OPPRESSED,
TO PROCLAIM THE FAVORABLE YEAR OF THE LORD."

And He rolled up the scroll, gave it back to the attendant, and sat down; and the eyes of all the people in the synagogue were intently directed at Him. Now He began to say to them, "Today this Scripture has been fulfilled in your hearing."

Luke 4:24–27 (NASB): But He said, "Truly I say to you, no prophet is welcome in his hometown. But I say to you in truth, there were many widows in Israel in the days of Elijah, when the sky was shut up for three years and six months, when a severe famine came over all the land; and yet Elijah was sent to none of them, but only to Zarephath, in the land of Sidon, to a woman who was a widow. And there were many with leprosy in Israel in the time of Elisha the prophet; and none of them was cleansed, but only Naaman the Syrian."

Chapter 10

Deuteronomy 28:8 (NASB): The LORD will command the blessing for you in your barns and in everything that you put your hand to, and He will bless you in the land that the Lord your God is giving you.

Luke 5:4–10 (NASB): Now when He had finished speaking, He said to Simon, "Put out into the deep water and let down your nets for a catch." Simon responded and said, "Master, we worked hard all night and caught nothing, but I will do as You say and let down the nets." And when they had done this, they caught a great quantity of fish, and their nets began to tear; so they signaled to their partners in the other boat to come and help them. And they came and filled both of the boats, to the point that they were sinking. But when Simon Peter saw this, he fell down at Jesus' knees, saying, "Go away from me, Lord, for I am a sinful man!" For amazement had seized him and all his companions because of the catch of fish which they had taken; and likewise also were James and John, sons of Zebedee, who were partners with Simon. And Jesus said to Simon, "Do not fear; from now on you will be catching people."

Hebrews 11:1 (NASB): Now faith is the certainty of things hoped for, a proof of things not seen.

Deuteronomy 28:11 (NASB): And the LORD will give you more than enough prosperity.

Chapter 11

Luke 4:33–35 (NASB): In the synagogue there was a man possessed by the spirit of an unclean demon, and he cried out with a loud voice, "Leave us alone! What business do You have with us, Jesus of Nazareth? Have You come to destroy us? I know who You are—the Holy One of God!" But Jesus rebuked him, saying, "Be quiet and come out of him!"

Chapter 12

Isaiah 9:1–2 (NASB): But there will be no *more* gloom for her who was in anguish. In earlier times He treated the land of Zebulun and the land of Naphtali with contempt, but later on He will make *it* glorious, by the way of the sea, on the other side of the Jordan, Galilee of the Gentiles.

> The people who walk in darkness
> Will see a great light;
> Those who live in a dark land,
> The light will shine on them.

Matthew 8:1–4 (NASB): When Jesus came down from the mountain, large crowds followed Him. And a man with leprosy came to Him and bowed down before Him, and said, "Lord, if You are willing, You can make me clean." Jesus reached out with His hand and touched him, saying, "I am willing; be cleansed." And immediately his leprosy was cleansed. And Jesus said to him, "See that you tell no one; but go, show yourself to the priest and present the offering that Moses commanded, as a testimony to them."

Chapter 15

John 7:31 (NASB): But many of the crowd believed in Him; and they were saying, "When the Christ comes, He will not perform more signs than those which this man has done, will He?"

Chapter 18

Matthew 5:43–45 (NASB): "You have heard that it was said, 'YOU SHALL LOVE YOUR NEIGHBOR and hate your enemy.' But I say to you, love your enemies and pray for those who persecute you, so that you may prove yourselves to be sons of your Father who is in heaven; for He causes His sun to rise on the evil and the good, and sends rain on the righteous and the unrighteous."

Chapter 20

Luke 7:13–16 (NASB): When the Lord saw her, He felt compassion for her and said to her, "Do not go on weeping." And He came up and touched the coffin; and the bearers came to a halt. And He said, "Young man, I say to you, arise!" And the dead man sat up and began to speak. And Jesus gave him back to his mother. Fear gripped them all, and they began glorifying God, saying, "A great prophet has appeared among us!" and, "God has visited His people!"

Psalm 30:11 (NASB): You have turned my mourning into dancing for me; You have untied my sackcloth and encircled me with joy.

Chapter 20

Luke 7:18–19 (NASB): The disciples of John also reported to him about all these things. And after summoning two of his disciples, John sent them to the Lord, saying, "Are You the Coming One, or are we to look for another?"

Chapter 22

Matthew 11:4–15 (NASB): Jesus answered and said to them, "Go and report to John what you hear and see: those who are BLIND RECEIVE SIGHT and those who limp walk, those with leprosy are cleansed and those who are deaf hear, the dead are raised, and the POOR HAVE THE GOSPEL PREACHED TO THEM. And blessed is any person who does not take offense at Me."

As these disciples of John were going away, Jesus began speaking to the crowds about John: "What did you go out into the wilderness to see? A reed shaken by the wind? But what did you go out to see? A man dressed in soft clothing? Those who wear soft clothing are in kings' palaces! But what did you go out to see? A prophet? Yes, I tell you, and one who is more than a prophet. This is the one about whom it is written:

'BEHOLD, I AM SENDING MY MESSENGER AHEAD OF YOU,
WHO WILL PREPARE YOUR WAY BEFORE YOU.'

Truly I say to you, among those born of women there has not arisen anyone greater than John the Baptist! Yet the one who is least in the kingdom of heaven is greater than he. And from the days of John the Baptist until now the kingdom of heaven has been treated violently, and violent men take it by force. For all the Prophets and the Law prophesied until John. And if you are willing to accept it, John himself is Elijah who was to come. The one who has ears to hear, let him hear.

Chapter 23

Matthew 8:5–13 (NASB): And when Jesus entered Capernaum, a centurion came to Him, begging Him, and saying, "Lord, my servant is lying paralyzed at home, terribly tormented." Jesus said to him, "I will come and heal him." But the centurion replied, "Lord, I am not worthy for You to come under my roof, but just say the word, and my servant will be healed. For I also am a man under authority, with soldiers under me; and I say to this one, 'Go!' and he goes, and to another, 'Come!' and he comes, and to my slave, 'Do this!' and he does it." Now when Jesus heard this, He was amazed and said to those who were following, "Truly I say to you, I have not found such great faith with anyone in Israel. And I say to you that many will come from east and west, and recline at the table with Abraham, Isaac, and Jacob in the kingdom of heaven; but the sons of the kingdom will be thrown out into the outer darkness; in that place there will be weeping and gnashing of teeth." And Jesus said to the centurion, "Go; it shall be done for you as you have believed." And the servant was healed at that very moment.

Chapter 24

Mark 4:38–41 (NASB): And yet Jesus Himself was in the stern, asleep on the cushion; and they woke Him and said to Him, "Teacher, do You not care that we are perishing?" And He got up and rebuked the wind and said to the sea, "Hush, be still." And the wind died down and it became perfectly calm. And He said to them, "Why are you afraid? Do you still have no faith?" They became very much afraid and said to one another, "Who, then, is this, that even the wind and the sea obey Him?"

Chapter 25

Matthew 8:29–32 (NASB): And they cried out, saying, "What business do You have with us, Son of God? Have You come here to torment us before the time?" Now there was a herd of many pigs feeding at a distance from them. And the demons begged Him, saying, "If You are going to cast us out, send us into the herd of pigs." And He said to them, "Go!" And they came out and went into the pigs; and behold, the whole herd rushed down the steep bank into the sea and drowned in the waters.

Mark 5:8–9 (NASB): For He had already been saying to him, "Come out of the man, you unclean spirit!" And He was asking him, "What is your name?" And he said to Him, "My name is Legion, for we are many."

Mark 5:18–19 (NASB): And as He was getting into the boat, the man who had been demon-possessed was begging Him that he might accompany Him. And He did not let him, but He said to him, "Go home to your people and report to them what great things the Lord has done for you, and how He had mercy on you."

John 10:10 (NASB): The thief comes only to steal and kill and destroy; I came so that they would have life, and have it abundantly.

Chapter 26

Mark 5:22–23 (NASB): And one of the synagogue officials, named Jairus, came, and upon seeing Him, fell at His feet and pleaded with Him earnestly, saying, "My little daughter is at the point of death; please come and lay Your hands on her, so that she will get well and live."

Mark 5:25–34 (NASB): A woman who had had a hemorrhage for twelve years, and had endured much at the hands of many physicians, and had spent all that she had and was not helped at all, but instead had become worse— after hearing about Jesus, she came up in the crowd behind Him and touched His cloak. For she had been saying to herself, "If I just touch His garments, I will get well." And immediately the flow of her blood was dried up; and she felt in her body that she was healed of her disease. And immediately Jesus, perceiving in Himself that power from Him had gone out, turned around in the crowd and said, "Who touched My garments?" And His disciples said to Him, "You see the crowd pressing in on You, and You say, 'Who touched Me?'" And He looked around to see the woman who had done this. But the woman, fearing and trembling, aware of what had happened to her, came and fell down before Him and told Him the whole truth. And He said to her, "Daughter, your faith has made you well; go in peace and be cured of your disease."

Luke 8:43–50 (NASB): And a woman who had suffered a chronic flow of blood for twelve years, and could not be healed by anyone, came up behind Him and touched the fringe of His cloak, and immediately her bleeding stopped. And Jesus said, "Who is the one who touched Me?" And while they were all denying it, Peter said, "Master, the people are crowding and pressing in on You." But Jesus said, "Someone did touch Me, for I was aware that power had left Me." Now when the woman saw that she had not escaped notice, she came trembling and fell down before Him, and admitted in the presence of all the people the reason why she had touched Him, and how she had been immediately healed. And He said to her, "Daughter, your faith has made you well; go in peace."

While He was still speaking, someone came from the house of the synagogue official, saying, "Your daughter has died; do not trouble the Teacher anymore." But when Jesus heard this, He responded to him, "Do not be afraid any longer; only believe, and she will be made well."

Proverbs 18:21 (NASB): Death and life are in the power of the tongue.

Proverbs 16:15 (NASB): In the light of a king's face is life.

Chapter 27

Mark 6:22–25 (NASB): And when the daughter of Herodias herself came in and danced, she pleased Herod and his dinner guests; and the king said to the girl, "Ask me for whatever you want, and I will give it to you." And he swore to her, "Whatever you ask of me, I will give it to you, up to half of my kingdom." And she went out and said to her mother, "What shall I ask for?" And she said, "The head of John the Baptist." Immediately she came in a hurry to the king and asked, saying, "I want you to give me at once the head of John the Baptist on a platter."

Chapter 28

Mark 6:30–38 (NASB): The apostles gathered together with Jesus; and they reported to Him all that they had done and taught. And He said to them, "Come away by yourselves to a secluded place and rest a little while." (For there were many people coming and going, and they did not even have time to eat.) And they went away in the boat to a secluded place by themselves.

The people saw them going, and many recognized them and ran there together on foot from all the cities, and got there ahead of them. When Jesus went ashore, He saw a large crowd, and He felt compassion for them because they were like sheep without a shepherd; and He began to teach them many things. And when it was already late, His disciples came up to Him and said, "This place is secluded and it is already late; send them away so that they may go into the surrounding countryside and villages and buy themselves something to eat." But He answered them, "You give them something to eat!" And they said to Him, "Shall we go and spend two hundred denarii on bread, and give it to them to eat?" But He said to them, "How many loaves do you have? Go look!" And when they found out, they said, "Five, and two fish."

John 6:5–10 (NASB): So Jesus, after raising His eyes and seeing that a large crowd was coming to Him, said to Philip, "Where are we to buy bread so that these people may eat?" But He was saying this only to test him, for He Himself knew what He intended to do. Philip answered Him, "Two hundred denarii worth of bread is not enough for them, for each to receive just a little!" One of His disciples, Andrew, Simon Peter's brother, said to Him, "There is a boy here who has five barley loaves and two fish; but what are these for so many people?" Jesus said, "Have the people recline to eat."

John 6:12 (NASB): And when they had eaten their fill, He said to His disciples, "Gather up the leftover pieces so that nothing will be lost."

John 6:14 (NASB): Therefore when the people saw the sign which He had performed, they said, "This is truly the Prophet who is to come into the world."

Chapter 29

Matthew 14:26–31 (NASB): When the disciples saw Him walking on the sea, they were terrified, and said, "It is a ghost!" And they cried out in fear. But immediately Jesus spoke to them, saying, "Take courage, it is I; do not be afraid."

Peter responded and said to Him, "Lord, if it is You, command me to come to You on the water." And He said, "Come!" And Peter got out of the boat and walked on the water, and came toward Jesus. But seeing the wind, he became frightened, and when he began to sink, he cried out, saying, "Lord, save me!" Immediately Jesus reached out with His hand and took hold of him, and said to him, "You of little faith, why did you doubt?"

Chapter 30

John 6:60 (NASB): So then many of His disciples, when they heard this, said, "This statement is very unpleasant; who can listen to it?"

Chapter 31

Luke 9:35 (NASB): And then a voice came from the cloud, saying, "This is My Son, My Chosen One; listen to Him!"

John 11:43–44 (NASB1995): When He had said these things, He cried out with a loud voice, "Lazarus, come forth." The man who had died came forth, bound hand and foot with wrappings, and his face was wrapped around with a cloth. Jesus said to them, "Unbind him, and let him go."

John 11:47–57 (NASB1995): Therefore the chief priests and the Pharisees convened a council, and were saying, "What are we doing? For this man is performing many signs. If we let Him go on like this, all men will believe in Him, and the Romans will come and take away both our place and our nation." But one of them, Caiaphas, who was high priest that year, said to them, "You know nothing at all, nor do you take into account that it is expedient for you that one man die for the people, and that the whole nation not perish" . . . So from that day on they planned together to kill Him . . . Now the chief priests and the Pharisees had given orders that if anyone knew where He was, he was to report it, so that they might seize Him.

Chapter 33

Mark 11:9–10 (NASB):

> And those who went in front and those who followed were shouting:
> "Hosanna!
> Blessed is He who comes in the name of the Lord;
> Blessed is the coming kingdom of our father David;
> Hosanna in the highest!"

Luke 19:39–40 (NASB): And yet some of the Pharisees in the crowd said to Him, "Teacher, rebuke Your disciples!" Jesus replied, "I tell you, if these stop speaking, the stones will cry out!"

Chapter 35

Matthew 21:23–27 (NASB): When He entered the temple area, the chief priests and the elders of the people came to Him while He was teaching, and said, "By what authority are You doing these things, and who gave You this authority?" But Jesus responded and said to them, "I will also ask you one question, which, if you tell Me, I will also tell you by what authority I do these things. The baptism of John was from what source: from heaven or from men?" And they began considering the implications among themselves, saying, "If we say, 'From heaven,' He will say to us, 'Then why did you not believe him?' But if we say, 'From men,' we fear the people; for they all regard John as a prophet." And answering Jesus, they said, "We do not know." He also said to them, "Neither am I telling you by what authority I do these things.

Matthew 21:28–32 (NASB): "But what do you think? A man had two sons, and he came to the first and said, 'Son, go work today in the vineyard.' But he replied, 'I do not want to.' Yet afterward he regretted it and went. And the man came to his second son and said the same thing; and he replied, 'I will, sir'; and yet he did not go. Which of the two did the will of his father?" They said, "The first." Jesus said to them, "Truly I say to you that the tax collectors and prostitutes will get into the kingdom of God before you. For John came to you in the way of righteousness and you did not believe him; but the tax collectors and prostitutes did believe him; and you, seeing this, did not even have second thoughts afterward so as to believe him.

Matthew 22:16–21 (NASB): And they sent their disciples to Him, along with the Herodians, saying, "Teacher, we know that You are truthful and teach the way of God in truth, and do not care what anyone thinks; for You are not partial to anyone. Tell us then, what do You think? Is it permissible to pay a poll-tax to Caesar, or not?" But Jesus perceived their malice, and said, "Why are you testing Me, you hypocrites? Show Me the coin used for the poll-tax." And they brought Him a denarius. And He said to them, "Whose image and inscription is this?" They said to Him, "Caesar's." Then He said to them, "Then pay to Caesar the things that are Caesar's; and to God the things that are God's."

Matthew 21:33–44 (NIV): "Listen to another parable: There was a landowner who planted a vineyard. He put a wall around it, dug a winepress in it and built a watchtower. Then he rented the vineyard to some farmers and moved to another place. When the harvest time approached, he sent his servants to the tenants to collect his fruit.

"The tenants seized his servants; they beat one, killed another, and stoned a third. Then he sent other servants to them, more than the first time, and the tenants treated them the same way. Last of all, he sent his son to them. 'They will respect my son,' he said.

"But when the tenants saw the son, they said to each other, 'This is the heir. Come, let's kill him and take his inheritance.' So they took him and threw him out of the vineyard and killed him.

"Therefore, when the owner of the vineyard comes, what will he do to those tenants?"

"He will bring those wretches to a wretched end," they replied, "and he will rent the vineyard to other tenants, who will give him his share of the crop at harvest time."

Jesus said to them, "Have you never read in the Scriptures:

"'The stone the builders rejected
    has become the cornerstone;
the Lord has done this,
    and it is marvelous in our eyes'?

"Therefore I tell you that the kingdom of God will be taken away from you and given to a people who will produce its fruit. Anyone who falls on this stone will be broken to pieces; anyone on whom it falls will be crushed."

Matthew 22:35–40 (NASB): And one of them, a lawyer, asked Him a question, testing Him: "Teacher, which is the great commandment in the Law?" And He said to him, "'YOU SHALL LOVE THE LORD YOUR

GOD WITH ALL YOUR HEART, AND WITH ALL YOUR SOUL, AND WITH ALL YOUR MIND.' This is the great and foremost commandment. The second is like it, 'YOU SHALL LOVE YOUR NEIGHBOR AS YOURSELF.' Upon these two commandments hang the whole Law and the Prophets."

Matthew 23:13 (NASB): "But woe to you, scribes and Pharisees, hypocrites, because you shut the kingdom of heaven in front of people; for you do not enter it yourselves, nor do you allow those who are entering to go in.

Matthew 23:15–39 (NASB):

"Woe to you, scribes and Pharisees, hypocrites, because you travel around on sea and land to make one proselyte; and when he becomes one, you make him twice as much a son of hell as yourselves.

"Woe to you, blind guides, who say, 'Whoever swears by the temple, that is nothing; but whoever swears by the gold of the temple is obligated.' You fools and blind men! Which is more important, the gold or the temple that sanctified the gold? And you say, 'Whoever swears by the altar, that is nothing; but whoever swears by the offering that is on it is obligated.' You blind men, which is more important, the offering or the altar that sanctifies the offering? Therefore, the one who swears by the altar, swears both by the altar and by everything on it. And the one who swears by the temple, swears both by the temple and by Him who dwells in it. And the one who swears by heaven, swears both by the throne of God and by Him who sits upon it.

"Woe to you, scribes and Pharisees, hypocrites! For you tithe mint and dill and cumin, and have neglected the weightier provisions of the Law: justice and mercy and faithfulness; but these are the things you should have done without neglecting the others. You blind guides, who strain out a gnat and swallow a camel!

"Woe to you, scribes and Pharisees, hypocrites! For you clean the outside of the cup and of the dish, but inside they are full of robbery and self-indulgence. You blind Pharisee, first clean the inside of the cup and of the dish, so that the outside of it may also become clean.

"Woe to you, scribes and Pharisees, hypocrites! For you are like whitewashed tombs which on the outside appear beautiful, but inside they are full of dead men's bones and all uncleanness. So you too, outwardly appear righteous to people, but inwardly you are full of hypocrisy and lawlessness.

"Woe to you, scribes and Pharisees, hypocrites! For you build the tombs for the prophets and decorate the monuments of the righteous, and you say, 'If we had been living in the days of our fathers, we would not have been partners with them in shedding the blood of the prophets.' So you testify against yourselves, that you are sons of those who murdered the prophets. Fill up, then, the measure of the guilt of your fathers. You snakes, you offspring of vipers, how will you escape the sentence of hell?

"Therefore, behold, I am sending you prophets and wise men and scribes; some of them you will kill and crucify, and some of them you will flog in your synagogues, and persecute from city to city, so that upon you will fall the guilt of all the righteous blood shed on earth, from the blood of righteous Abel to the blood of Zechariah, the son of Berechiah, whom you murdered between the temple and the altar. Truly I say to you, all these things will come upon this generation.

"Jerusalem, Jerusalem, who kills the prophets and stones those who have been sent to her! How often I wanted to gather your children together, the way a hen gathers her chicks under her wings, and you were unwilling. Behold, your house is being left to you desolate! For I say to you, from now on you will not see Me until you say, 'Blessed is the One who comes in the name of the Lord!'"

Chapter 36

John 13:21 (NASB): "Truly, truly I say to you that one of you will betray Me."

John 13:27 (NASB): "What you are doing, do it quickly."

Chapter 42

John 18:20–23 (NASB): Jesus answered him, "I have spoken openly to the world; I always taught in synagogues and in the temple area, where all the Jews congregate; and I said nothing in secret. Why are you asking Me? Ask those who have heard what I spoke to them. Look: these people know what I said." But when He said this, one of the officers, who was standing nearby, struck Jesus, saying, "Is that the way You answer the high priest?" Jesus answered him, "If I have spoken wrongly, testify of the wrong; but if rightly, why do you strike Me?"

Chapter 43

Matthew 26:61 (NASB): "This man stated, 'I am able to destroy the temple of God and to rebuild it in three days.'"

Mark 14:58 (NASB): "We heard Him say, 'I will destroy this temple that was made by hands, and in three days I will build another, made without hands.'"

Matthew 26:62 (NASB): "Do You offer no answer for what these men are testifying against You?"

Matthew 26:63 (NASB): "I place You under oath by the living God, to tell us whether You are the Christ, the Son of God."

Luke 22:67–68 (NASB): "If I tell you, you will not believe; and if I ask a question, you will not answer."

Mark 14:62 (NASB): "I am; and you shall see the Son of Man sitting at the right hand of power, and coming with the clouds of heaven."

Mark 14:63–64 (NASB): "What further need do we have of witnesses? You have heard the blasphemy; how does it seem to you?"

Chapter 44

John 18:29–31 (NASB): Therefore Pilate came out to them and said, "What accusation are you bringing against this Man?" They answered and said to him, "If this Man were not a criminal, we would not have handed Him over to you." So Pilate said to them, "Take Him yourselves, and judge Him according to your law." The Jews said to him, "We are not permitted to put anyone to death."

Luke 23:2 (NASB): And they began to bring charges against Him, saying, "We found this man misleading our nation and forbidding us to pay taxes to Caesar, and saying that He Himself is Christ, a King."

Luke 23:4 (NASB): But Pilate said to the chief priests and the crowds, "I find no grounds for charges in the case of this man."

Luke 23:5 (NASB): But they kept on insisting, saying, "He is stirring up the people, teaching all over Judea, starting from Galilee, as far as this place!"

Luke 23:13–15 (NASB): Now Pilate summoned to himself the chief priests, the rulers, and the people, and he said to them, "You brought this man to me on the ground that he is inciting the people to revolt; and behold, after examining Him before you, I have found no basis at all in the case of this man for the charges which you are bringing against Him. No, nor has Herod, for he sent Him back to us; and behold, nothing deserving death has been done by Him.

Luke 23:18 (NASB): But they cried out all together, saying, "Away with this man, and release to us Barabbas!"

Matthew 27:17 (NASB): So when the people gathered together, Pilate said to them, "Whom do you want me to release for you: Barabbas, or Jesus who is called Christ?"

Luke 23:22 (NASB): And he said to them a third time, "Why, what has this man done wrong? I have found in His case no grounds for a sentence of death; therefore I will punish Him and release Him."

Chapter 46

John 19:4 (NASB): And then Pilate came out again and said to them, "See, I am bringing Him out to you so that you will know that I find no grounds at all for charges in His case."

Matthew 27:19 (NASB): And while he was sitting on the judgment seat, his wife sent him a message, saying, "See that you have nothing to do with that righteous Man; for last night I suffered greatly in a dream because of Him."

John 19:5–7 (NASB): Jesus then came out, wearing the crown of thorns and the purple robe. And Pilate said to them, "Behold, the Man!" So when the chief priests and the officers saw Him, they shouted, saying, "Crucify, crucify!" Pilate said to them, "Take Him yourselves and crucify Him; for I find no grounds for charges in His case!" The Jews answered him, "We have a law, and by that law He ought to die, because He made Himself out to be the Son of God!"

John 19:9–12 (NASB): And he entered the Praetorium again and said to Jesus, "Where are You from?" But Jesus gave him no answer. So Pilate said to Him, "Are you not speaking to me? Do You not know that I have authority to release You, and I have authority to crucify You?" Jesus answered him, "You would have no authority over Me at all, if it had not been given to you from above; for this reason the one who handed Me over to you has the greater sin." As a result of this, Pilate made efforts to release Him; but the Jews shouted, saying, "If you release this Man, you are not a friend of Caesar; everyone who makes himself out to be a king opposes Caesar!"

John 19:14–15 (NASB): Now it was the day of preparation for the Passover; it was about the sixth hour. And he said to the Jews, "Look, your King!" So they shouted, "Away with Him, away with Him, crucify Him!" Pilate said to them, "Shall I crucify your King?" The chief priests answered, "We have no king except Caesar."

Matthew 27:21–23 (NASB): And the governor said to them, "Which of the two do you want me to release for you?" And they said, "Barabbas." Pilate said to them, "Then what shall I do with Jesus who is called Christ?" They all said, "Crucify Him!" But he said, "Why, what evil has He done?" Yet they kept shouting all the more, saying, "Crucify Him!"

Matthew 27:24–25 (NASB): Now when Pilate saw that he was accomplishing nothing, but rather that a riot was starting, he took water and washed his hands in front of the crowd, saying, "I am innocent of this Man's blood; you yourselves shall see." And all the people replied, "His blood shall be on us and on our children!"

Chapter 47

Luke 23:34 (NASB) [But Jesus was saying, "Father, forgive them; for they do not know what they are doing."] And they cast lots, dividing His garments among themselves.

Mark 15:29–30 (NASB): Those passing by were hurling abuse at Him, shaking their heads and saying, "Ha! You who are going to destroy the temple and rebuild it in three days, save Yourself by coming down from the cross!"

Luke 23:37 (NASB): And saying, "If You are the King of the Jews, save Yourself!"

Luke 23:39–43 (NASB): One of the criminals who were hanged there was hurling abuse at Him, saying, "Are You not the Christ? Save Yourself and us!" But the other responded, and rebuking him, said, "Do you not even fear God, since you are under the same sentence of condemnation? And we indeed are suffering justly, for we are receiving what we deserve for our crimes; but this man has done nothing wrong." And he was saying, "Jesus, remember me when You come into Your kingdom!" And He said to him, "Truly I say to you, today you will be with Me in Paradise."

Mark 15:34–35 (NASB): At the ninth hour Jesus cried out with a loud voice, "ELOI, ELOI, LEMA SABAKTANEI?" which is translated, "MY GOD, MY GOD, WHY HAVE YOU FORSAKEN ME?" And when some of the bystanders heard Him, they began saying, "Look! He is calling for Elijah!"

Mark 15:36 (NASB): And someone ran and filled a sponge with sour wine, put it on a reed, and gave Him a drink, saying, "Let us see if Elijah comes to take Him down."

Luke 23:46 (NASB): And Jesus, crying out with a loud voice, said, "Father, INTO YOUR HANDS I ENTRUST MY SPIRIT." And having said this, He died.

John 19:30 (NASB): Therefore when Jesus had received the sour wine, He said, "It is finished!" And He bowed His head and gave up His spirit.

Isaiah 53:7 (NASB): Like a lamb that is led to slaughter, and like a sheep that is silent before its shearers, so He did not open His mouth.

Psalm 22:16–18 (NASB): For dogs have surrounded me; a band of evildoers has encompassed me; they pierced my hands and my feet. I can count all my bones. They look, they stare at me; they divide my garments among them, and they cast lots for my clothing.

Isaiah 53:12 (NASB): Therefore, I will allot Him a portion with the great, and He will divide the plunder with the strong, because He poured out His life unto death, and was counted with wrongdoers; yet He Himself bore the sin of many, and interceded for the wrongdoers.

Isaiah 53:10 (NASB): But the LORD desired to crush Him, causing Him grief; if He renders Himself as a guilt offering.

Zechariah 12:10 (NASB): "And I will pour out on the house of David and on the inhabitants of Jerusalem the Spirit of grace and of pleading, so that they will look at Me whom they pierced; and they will mourn for Him, like one mourning for an only son, and they will weep bitterly over Him like the bitter weeping over a firstborn."

Chapter 48

Isaiah 53:11 (NASB): My Servant, will justify the many, for He will bear their wrongdoings.

Isaiah 53:1 (NASB): Who has believed our report? And to whom has the arm of the LORD been revealed?

Psalm 16:10 (NASB): For You will not abandon my soul to Sheol; You will not allow Your Holy One to undergo decay.

Isaiah 53:9 (NASB): His grave was assigned with wicked men, yet He was with a rich man in His death.

Hosea 13:14 (NASB): Shall I ransom them from the power of Sheol? Shall I redeem them from death? Death, where are your thorns? Sheol, where is your sting?

Chapter 49

Proverbs 30:28 (NASB): The lizard you may grasp with the hands, yet it is in kings' palaces.

Matthew 27:63–64 (NASB): And they said, "Sir, we remember that when that deceiver was still alive, He said, 'After three days I am rising.' Therefore, give orders for the tomb to be made secure until the third day; otherwise, His disciples may come and steal Him, and say to the people, 'He has risen from the dead,' and the last deception will be worse than the first."

Chapter 54

Psalm 118:24 (NASB): This is the day which the LORD has made; let's rejoice and be glad in it.

Chapter 55

Matthew 28:5–7 (NASB): And the angel said to the women, "Do not be afraid; for I know that you are looking for Jesus who has been crucified. He is not here, for He has risen, just as He said. Come, see the place where He was lying. And go quickly and tell His disciples that He has risen from the dead; and behold, He is going ahead of you to Galilee. There you will see Him; behold, I have told you."

Matthew 28:8–10 (NASB): And they left the tomb quickly with fear and great joy, and ran to report to His disciples. And behold, Jesus met them and said, "Rejoice!" And they came up and took hold of His feet, and worshiped Him. Then Jesus said to them, "Do not be afraid; go, bring word to My brothers to leave for Galilee, and there they will see Me."

Mark 16:3–7 (NASB): They were saying to one another, "Who will roll away the stone from the entrance of the tomb for us?" And looking up, they noticed that the stone had been rolled away; for it was extremely large. And entering the tomb, they saw a young man sitting at the right, wearing a white robe; and they were amazed. But he said to them, "Do not be amazed; you are looking for Jesus the Nazarene, who has been crucified. He has risen; He is not here; see, here is the place where they laid Him. But go, tell His disciples and Peter, 'He is going ahead of you to Galilee; there you will see Him, just as He told you.'"

Luke 24:4–7 (NASB): While they were perplexed about this, behold, two men suddenly stood near them in gleaming clothing; and as the women were terrified and bowed their faces to the ground, the men said to them, "Why are you seeking the living One among the dead? He is not here, but He has risen. Remember how He spoke to you while He was still in Galilee, saying that the Son of Man must be handed over to sinful men, and be crucified, and on the third day rise from the dead."

John 20:11–17 (NASB): But Mary was standing outside the tomb, weeping; so as she wept, she stooped to look into the tomb; and she saw two angels in white sitting, one at the head and one at the feet, where the body of Jesus had been lying. And they said to her, "Woman, why are you weeping?" She said to them, "Because they have taken away my Lord, and I do not know where they put Him." When she had said this, she turned around and saw Jesus standing there, and yet she did not know that it was Jesus. Jesus said to her, "Woman, why are you weeping? Whom are you seeking?" Thinking that He was the gardener, she said to Him, "Sir, if you have carried Him away, tell me where you put Him, and I will take Him away." Jesus said to her, "Mary!" She turned and said to Him in Hebrew, "Rabboni!" (which means, Teacher). Jesus said to her, "Stop clinging to Me, for I have not yet ascended to the Father; but go to My brothers and say to them, 'I am ascending to My Father and your Father, and My God and your God.'"

Chapter 56

John 20:19–22 (NASB): Now when it was evening on that day, the first day of the week, and when the doors were shut where the disciples were together due to fear of the Jews, Jesus came and stood in their midst, and said to them, "Peace be to you." And when He had said this, He showed them both His hands and His side. The disciples then rejoiced when they saw the Lord. So Jesus said to them again, "Peace be to you; just as the Father has sent Me, I also send you." And when He had said this, He breathed on them and said to them, "Receive the Holy Spirit."

Luke 24:26–27 (NASB): "Was it not necessary for the Christ to suffer these things and to come into His glory?" Then beginning with Moses and with all the prophets, He explained to them the things written about Himself in all the Scriptures.

Luke 24:30–31 (NASB): And it came about, when He had reclined at the table with them, that He took the bread and blessed it, and He broke it and began giving it to them. And then their eyes were opened and they recognized Him; and He vanished from their sight.

Luke 24:36–41 (NASB): Now while they were telling these things, Jesus Himself suddenly stood in their midst and said to them, "Peace be to you." But they were startled and frightened, and thought that they were looking at a spirit. And He said to them, "Why are you frightened, and why are doubts arising in your hearts? See My hands and My feet, that it is I Myself; touch Me and see, because a spirit does not have flesh and bones as you plainly see that I have." And when He had said this, He showed them His hands and His feet. While they still could not believe it because of their joy and astonishment, He said to them, "Have you anything here to eat?"

Luke 24:44–48 (NASB): Now He said to them, "These are My words which I spoke to you while I was still with you, that all the things that are written about Me in the Law of Moses and the Prophets and the Psalms must be fulfilled." Then He opened their minds to understand the Scriptures, and He said to them, "So it is written, that the Christ would suffer and rise from the dead on the third day, and that repentance for forgiveness of sins would be proclaimed in His name to all the nations, beginning from Jerusalem. You are witnesses of these things.

Isaiah 48:6–7 (NASB): I proclaim to you new things from this time, hidden things which you have not known. They are created now and not long ago; and before today you have not heard them.

Chapter 57

John 20:25–29 (NASB): So the other disciples were saying to him, "We have seen the Lord!" But he said to them, "Unless I see in His hands the imprint of the nails, and put my finger into the place of the nails, and put my hand into His side, I will not believe."

Eight days later His disciples were again inside, and Thomas was with them. Jesus came, the doors having been shut, and stood in their midst and said, "Peace be to you." Then He said to Thomas, "Place your finger here, and see My hands; and take your hand and put it into My side; and do not continue in disbelief, but be a believer." Thomas answered and said to Him, "My Lord and my God!" Jesus said to him, "Because you have seen Me, have you now believed? Blessed are they who did not see, and yet believed."

Chapter 58

John 16:7 (NASB): But I tell you the truth: it is to your advantage that I am leaving; for if I do not leave, the Helper will not come to you; but if I go, I will send Him to you.

John 16:13–14 (NASB): But when He, the Spirit of truth, comes, He will guide you into all the truth; for He will not speak on His own, but whatever He hears, He will speak; and He will disclose to you what is to come. He will glorify Me, for He will take from Mine and will disclose it to you.

John 16:23–24 (NASB): And on that day you will not question Me about anything. Truly, truly I say to you, if you ask the Father for anything in My name, He will give it to you. Until now you have asked for nothing in My name; ask and you will receive, so that your joy may be made full.

Acts 1:4–8 (NASB): Gathering them together, He commanded them not to leave Jerusalem, but to wait for what the Father had promised, "Which," He said, "you heard of from Me; for John baptized with water, but you will be baptized with the Holy Spirit not many days from now."

So, when they had come together, they began asking Him, saying, "Lord, is it at this time that You are restoring the kingdom to Israel?" But He said to them, "It is not for you to know periods of time or appointed times which the Father has set by His own authority; but you will receive power when the Holy Spirit has come upon you; and you shall be My witnesses both in Jerusalem and in all Judea, and Samaria, and as far as the remotest part of the earth."

John 17:11 (NASB): I am no longer going to be in the world; and yet they themselves are in the world, and I am coming to You. Holy Father, keep them in Your name, the name which You have given Me, so that they may be one just as We are.

Acts 1:10–11 (NASB): And as they were gazing intently into the sky while He was going, then behold, two men in white clothing stood beside them, and they said, "Men of Galilee, why do you stand looking into the sky? This Jesus, who has been taken up from you into heaven, will come in the same way as you have watched Him go into heaven."

NOW WHAT?

The primary angelic characters in this story are fictional, and the specific actions they carry out are the simple musings of a single man. However, the underlying battle for the throne of the universe and the individual souls of mankind is real. Whether we know it or even believe it, we are embroiled in a perilous struggle that stretches from ancient times to the present day. All around us spiritual forces struggle for the hearts of men. The good news is that the King is and always has been working His plan for the redemption of man. This is the amazing story found throughout the Scriptures.

Because of sin, man is separated from God and enslaved to spiritual forces of darkness. The only payment for sin that will satisfy the righteousness of God is death. This is the primary issue facing every person who has ever lived—how can we ever hope to stand before a holy Creator with any, even one, sin on the ledger of our life? If we were left on our own, our situation would be desperately hopeless indeed.

But God did not leave us in our impossible condition. According to His plan, He Himself entered the world, lived as a man, and lived a sinless life as only He could. Then, He took all the sins of all mankind upon Himself and paid the price to satisfy the law of sin and death. The spiritual forces of darkness did not win a victory by killing Him—rather it was always His intent to take our place in death so He could offer us life while still satisfying His holiness. This is the greatest story of good news imaginable. Instead of facing the eternal wrath of God, He has provided a way for us to be set free from the bondage of sin, enter His Kingdom as beloved children, and live with Him in glory forever.

So how do we step from darkness into light? The scriptures make it clear that there is no work we can do to earn His righteousness. Only His perfect blood can cleanse us. All we need to do is simply believe with our heart that Jesus' death and resurrection provide the way to God and confess with our mouth that Jesus is Lord, and we will be saved. When we put our faith in Him, our spirits that were dead because of sin become alive to God, His very Spirit takes up residence within our mortal bodies, and He transfers us into the Kingdom of light.

If you're not sure what you believe about Jesus, I challenge you seek the truth. Get a Bible and read it for yourself. Start with the Gospel of John and ask the King of Heaven to reveal Himself to you.

Angels are fun to think about, and hopefully my story provides a different view of Jesus' life and work on earth, but do not focus on the angels themselves. The real story is about how God Himself came to make a way for us to reach Him. He accomplished His intent. Now you need to decide what you are going to do about the cross.

ABOUT THE AUTHOR

Scott Wells's journey in His service began with missionary aviation—a private pilot license and some Bible college. It continued with an Air Force career, spanning twenty-one years, during which he earned a Masters and PhD in aeronautical engineering, specializing in feedback control theory. He taught aero engineering at the Air Force Academy, where he reached the academic rank of Associate Professor and served as an adjunct instructor at the Air Force Test Pilot School. In 2008, he retired as a Lieutenant Colonel and took a senior engineering position serving an aerospace company. His analytical and military background, combined with his lifelong studies of the scriptures, form a unique canvas for his speculative world of multidimensional realms and angel physics.

Dr. Wells lives in Arizona where he designs flight control systems and writes. He married his high-school sweetheart in 1983 and has three children. He enjoys playing saxophone on the worship team at church.